THE SHADOW CARTEL

PRAISE FOR THE DOMINIC GREY SERIES

"Relentless." —*Publishers Weekly*

"One of the top ten books of the year." —*BloodWrites Mystery Blog*, on *The Summoner*

"Layton Green is a master of intellectual suspense." —JT Ellison, *New York Times* bestselling author of *EDGE OF BLACK*

"*The Summoner* is one of those books that make you want to turn on all the lights in your house and lock the doors . . . [t]he settings are authentic and you can feel and smell the countryside . . . [t]his is a wonderful read for those who enjoy both suspense and action stories" —*Seattle Post-Intelligencer*

On *The Egyptian*: "Stirring and imaginative, with an engaging premise that is briskly paced. Both the characters in the story and the reader are in for a wild ride." —Steve Berry, *New York Times* bestselling author of *The King's Deception*

"I do believe Layton Green has moved into my top 5 author category - not an easy feat to attain!" —*A Novel Source*

"The confines of a page are not enough for Layton Green's writing. His work begs to be translated into 100-foot high IMAX images, rendered in 3D, and given a score by Hanz Zimmer" —*Biblioteca*

On *The Diabolist*: "A well-crafted and exciting thriller with a pair of interesting protagonists . . . and a charismatic villain who makes our skin crawl." —*Booklist*

"This is what you get when you combine Indiana Jones with Ludlum's Jason Bourne . . . A must read for all you lovers of conspiracy theories, thrillers and mysteries alike!" —*Baffled Books*

"Layton Green is an absolutely brilliant writer." —*Everything to Do With Books*

"Green's debut *The Summoner* was such a great read, I was hoping that he'd duplicate his literary excellence. In his second book, *The Egyptian*, Green exceeded my expectations." —*BookPleasures.com*

"Favorite book of the year so far." —*A Novel Source*

"A blend of action, history, anthropology, thrills, and chills, all delivered with a mature, polished voice. I am eager for more from this author." —Scott Nicholson, bestselling author

"Layton Green has written a tale with supernatural and political undertones that unravels with ever increasing suspense . . . The book is plain terrific." —Richard Marek, former president and publisher of E.P. Dutton

"An awesome read . . . . The writing is polished and evocative, the subject matter fascinating, the characters intriguing, and the pace non-stop. Spooky and occasionally metaphysical, *The Summoner* harkens back to *The Serpent and the Rainbow* in its ability to convincingly portray seemingly paranormal events in a realistic (and therefore even creepier) manner." —*BloodWrites*, Mystery Pick of the Week

"[T]his book is above and beyond in its narrative, its cohesiveness, the depth of its characters and the quality of the writing. This is one of the best books I've ever read for Odyssey Reviews." —*Odyssey Reviews*

"Green writes like a dream." —Melody Moezzi, award-winning author, *Haldol and Hyacinths*

"[C]alls to mind such series as Jason Bourne and Indiana Jones, with supernatural/religious overtones thrown in. I recommend *The Summoner* to anyone looking for a suspense-filled journey into a unique—and at times, terrifying—culture that'll keep you guessing." —*Bookhound's Den*

"Yes, I did put TWO Five Stars up there . . . giving Green's *The Summoner* Five stars and Five stars alone downplays how I felt about this book." —*1000+ Books to Read*

"Dan Brown is pretty good at what he does and I don't begrudge him his success, but when it comes to interesting characters embarking on a thrilling exploration into the dark world of cults, religions and magic Layton Green does it SO much better." —*Nylon Admiral Reviews*

"Layton Green kicks things up a notch and delivers a novel that should, if there's any justice to be found upon the shelves, make him a household name. *The Diabolist* is a dark, intelligent, spellbinding novel . . . I cannot recommend this one highly enough." —*Beauty in Ruins Reviews*

"Green's *The Summoner* proved his great talent. *The Diabolist* ensures his place at the top of crime fiction: his number 1 place. Unbelievably good, unbelievably intricate, unbelievably Green." —*The Review Broads*

On *The Diabolist*: "[A] story that will move you to the edge of your seat." —*Seattle Post-Intelligencer*

To Dad,
the father Dominic Grey
wishes he could have

Published by Sixth Street Press

Book cover design by Jeroen ten Berge (jeroentenberge.com)
Author Photo by Robin Shetler Photography
Interior by JW Manus

THE SHADOW CARTEL

LAYTON GREEN

"I can believe anything, Corporal. Life has made me the most believing man in the world."

—*Death in the Andes,* Mario Vargas Llosa

PEOPLES TEMPLE AGRICULTURAL PROJECT, NORTHWEST GUYANA NOVEMBER 18, 1978

The man known as John Wolverton cocked his head at the sound, a faint *thwap* that echoed through the vines and trees. He reasoned the shot had come from a poacher's rifle.

Surely it hadn't come from the Port Kaituma airstrip. From Congressman Ryan's delegation, sent to investigate the conditions of Reverend Jones's utopian cult that had set up shop in the middle of the Guyanese jungle. Reverend Jones was a sociopath, but he wasn't suicidal, and the doctors agreed the two were mutually exclusive.

All of the doctors, that was, except the forensic behavioral psychologist who speculated that in extreme cases, a sociopath who knew his joy ride was finished might use suicide as a tool. A final act of defiance against the societal forces that dared inhibit his desires.

John Wolverton picked up his pace. This was not a fairy tale jungle, inviting and familiar. Instead it was dank, stale, mottled. Forbidding. A place where all things foreign were sucked inside, leeched of life, and left to decompose.

Thwap thwap thwap thwap thwap.

Gunfire, staccato and rapid.

John Wolverton ran.

The gunfire continued for minutes that seemed like days, then ended as abruptly as it had begun. The jungle was quiet once again, entropy alive and heaving.

John Wolverton ran faster.

He smelled it first, the acrid tang of gunpowder simmering in the air. Sight followed: bodies, including Congressman Ryan's, spilled like fallen dominoes in the clearing around the two planes.

Oh God.

He was still seven miles from Jonestown, deep in the jungle, light years from help. Adrenaline whipped through him like a flailing live wire as he ran down the path beside the road, his thoughts ping-ponging inside his head. The Reverend had ordered him to walk to Port Kaituma that afternoon on one of his "character building" errands. Somehow, he must have found out who he really was. Had the Reverend sent him to bear witness to his madness?

And Tashmeni, where was she? He prayed she was safe in the cottage with the baby, smart enough to stay out of sight. Even better if she had fled into the jungle.

Or maybe she didn't know. Maybe none of them did. The Reverend would realize there was no turning back—a United States congressman was dead—so now what would he do? Leave his people to their fate, flee to the capital and seek asylum with the Russians?

John Wolverton concentrated on the path, pushing his pace to the limit. As he neared Jonestown, he kept waiting for the town's loudspeaker to interrupt the silence of his run, for the Reverend's narcotic voice to start pumping propaganda into the air. Yet he heard nothing except a series of screams, arcing out of the jungle like streaking missiles.

The screaming had ceased by the time he crossed the perimeter of the settlement, the outskirts eerily quiet, a hot wind stirring up dust like the breath of an evil spirit.

Where were the guards? The children playing in the road?

He approached on silent feet from the north, stalking past the clinic and the dining hall, knowing something was terribly wrong, knowing the camp smelled of death. When he reached the center, the sight slammed into him with the power of a gale-force wind.

Bodies draped the floor of the meeting pavilion and the ground outside, hundreds of them, men and women, children, babies. Lying senseless and haphazard like some photo of a concentration camp.

He stumbled towards the cottages, almost tripping over Tashmeni's body. The baby was close against her, tucked into her chest. He checked for a pulse on both, and then a half-formed heave escaped his throat from someplace primal, taking part of his soul as it released into the air. He collapsed on Tashmeni's corpse, retching and weeping until he had nothing left to give.

When he could stand, he forced himself to step across the sea of bodies into the open-air pavilion. Reverend Jones was lying on the ground, head slumped on a pillow, a bullet wound cratering his temple.

John Wolverton's eyes swept the pavilion. He saw the vat of juice that, judging by the cups strewn next to the bodies, was a poisonous concoction that the members of The Peoples Temple had willingly consumed. He shivered at the terrifying power of the dead cult leader.

His eyes caught something else: a cassette recorder on the table next to the Reverend's body.

He leaned down, eyes widening.

It was still recording.

His mind numbed by grief, hands jittery from shock, he carried the tape recorder outside, sat next to Tashmeni's corpse, and entwined his fingers in her hand.

Then he pressed "Rewind."

1

NEW YORK CITY
PRESENT DAY

Dominic Grey carved the streets of the Bronx on his Kawasaki, racing towards a block of abandoned warehouses. Fear had scooped out a rough-hewn pit in his stomach.

Not fear for himself, but for Charlie, one of the teenage students in Grey's jujitsu class at the Washington Heights homeless shelter. Though Grey strove not to have favorites, Charlie possessed the combination of talent, heart, and drive that could one day lead to a black belt in authentic Japanese jujitsu.

A day that was a very long time away.

He knew he'd found the place when he saw tricked-out cars and crotch rockets sprawled in front of a warehouse, the gritty urban isolation, the energy crackling in the air. He knew it all too well.

As he jumped off his bike and raced inside, the murmur of the crowd increased to a roar. He let the two hulking doormen frisk him because he didn't have time for a scene. Though Grey was much smaller, six foot one and lean as a distance runner, the doormen caught his hard stare and hurried through their job. Then Grey was wading through the crowd, the crater in his stomach deepening with every moment.

Past the betting pit, through the makeshift stands filled with leering faces, towards the blood-spattered ring that brought it all crashing back: Grey himself a scrawny sixteen-year-old in Tokyo, pushed by his father into the ring for the first time, already a black belt but not prepared for *this*, feeling his skin crawl as a grown man twice his age and size strutted across the ring like a peacock, fists waving yen all around, the smell of sweat and blood and curdled humanity.

He saw Charlie approaching the ring, a tall and wiry black girl who could pass for a young man in dim lighting, dreadlocked hair tied in a bun. The same age Grey had once been, the same gut-turning fear bulging out behind the compressed mouth and eyes.

She was by herself in her too-clean *gi*, a child with the eyes of a war veteran, a little girl who had learned the game of life on the cracked and unforgiving asphalt of Washington Heights. When she saw Grey, her jaw slackened and her eyes slid away.

He took her gently by the elbow. "Let's go, Charlie."

"How'd you know?"

"You never miss class."

"Who narc'd?"

"Someone who cares about you," he said.

"I want to fight."

"No, you don't."

"I need the money."

"I'll give you the money."

The energy of the crowd sputtered, jeers and catcalls replaced the excited shouts. Grey saw her opponent enter the ring, a muscled Latino with wrists thicker than Charlie's arms. Judging by his smashed face and the way he loosened his muscles, Grey pegged him for a lifelong boxer with a few years of mixed martial arts training.

It would be a bloodbath.

He had another flash of remembrance, to the darkness he had summoned to win that first fight. To the door it had opened, the thrill of violence and domination he'd been fighting ever since.

"You told them you had a black belt, didn't you?"

"I can take him," she muttered.

"Look at your opponent, Charlie. Look at these people. Is this what you want from life?"

"Life don't want nuthin' from me. Never did."

"I do. I want you as my student. And as your teacher, I'm giving you a choice. You can do this, or you can stay with me. Not both."

"You wouldn't—"

"I am."

She balled her fists and stepped away, facing the now-hostile crowd. Grey couldn't see her eyes, and it was one of the longest moments he had ever endured, a bubble of compressed time filled with a lifetime of self-doubt and insecurities, asking him how he could hope to teach others, children, after the life he had led.

Oh, he could teach them how to fight. How to kill. But could he teach them how to live?

He had never wanted so much for someone to make a simple choice. Every week fresh students slipped away from class like a school of troubled minnows, and every time he lost a little more hope.

As if moving underwater, she turned away from the table. A flash of white teeth appeared. "Can I drive the bike?"

A rush of emotion filled him, and he led her away by the arm. "No."

"How I'm gonna get some of this honor you always talking about?"

Grey forced himself to keep a straight face. "By not fighting."

"Say what? You watch the new *Karate Kid* this morning or sumthin'?"

"We'll talk later."

The boos increased in volume, and Grey walked faster. Halfway to the door an enormous man in a double-breasted suit and a shaved head stepped in front of them. His accent was Russian. "He can't leave."

Grey moved Charlie behind him. "It's a she, not a he. An underage she."

The man grinned through crooked teeth. "Bets are placed."

"So un-place them."

"You don't know how it works."

"I know *exactly* how it works."

He pointed at Grey. "Then you fight, instead of the monkey."

Every muscle in Grey's body tightened. "Get out of my way."

"The money's swung. Someone has to fight."

"Find someone else."

He thrust a finger towards Grey's chest. "I have."

Grey snatched the digit out of the air before it reached him, then switched his grip to manipulate the two joints. Moving only his hand, he increased the pressure until the Russian bellowed and sank to his knees. Grey made him stand again, nodded for Charlie to follow, and walked towards the door, leading the man like a circus pet.

Grey looked down at the Russian, corkscrewed with pain and scrambling to keep up. "Now who's the monkey?"

Every time the Russian tried to escape the grip, Grey reversed the pressure with a flick of his wrist, walking calmly towards the exit while the man jerked and twitched like a marionette. The crowd silenced to watch the spectacle. When Grey reached the exit he made a motion with his forearm like casting a fishing line, and the Russian somersaulted into the two doormen. Grey led Charlie outside as the men scrambled on the floor.

No one followed.

———•———

Charlie shouted into the wind as they sped away. "Where'd you find this bike, the nursing home?"

"The word is vintage," Grey said.

"I thought you said not to fight."

"I said you should never fight to gain honor."

"But you don't let no one lay their hands on you."

"That's right," he said.

"I seen that Russian dude before, he tore up some Brazilian with mad skills. I thought he was some kinda badass Mongol warrior, but yo, yo, he just a gang-banger compared to you. You an *artist*."

———•———

Grey dropped her off at the shelter just before curfew. He tried not to think about the abomination of a homeless child, about the perspective on life forming in Charlie's young mind.

An abomination and a perspective he knew firsthand.

He entered his brick studio loft in Hudson Heights, tossed his keys and saw a message on his cell that he must have missed while riding. The number was unlisted. He put the phone on speaker while he reached for a beer.

He hoped it was Professor Viktor Radek—his employer—requesting Grey's presence on an investigation in some far-flung locale. Viktor was an expert on religions and cults, and Grey helped him conduct investigations around the world for both private individuals and police agencies. Grey loved his students, but he went stir-crazy if too much time passed between assignments.

The message began, but instead of Viktor's Slavic baritone he heard a rich English accent, a sultry female voice possessed of impeccable diction and brimming with intelligence.

Not English, he corrected. African.

Zimbabwean.

A voice he hadn't heard for more than a year. A voice he had never expected to hear again.

Nya's voice.

Grey . . . I know it's been some time, but I need to talk to you. I'm in Miami, hey? Can you please give me a ring?

The message ended, the echo of her voice faded, and Grey stood with his hand poised in midair, clutching his beer.

He couldn't seem to find enough air.

2

NORTH MIAMI

DEA agent Federico "Fred" Hernandez cruised through downtown Miami, weaving among the glass behemoths and concrete eyesores. He took in the ramshackle eateries from the forgotten corners of Latin America, the homeless shuffling in the heat, the maddening carelessness of the drivers. Steam rose on the asphalt from a morning shower, residual moisture dripping from every building, street sign, and overhead wire.

Fred draped a hairy, muscled forearm on the console. He could feel sweat trickling down his thighs under his jeans, but he refused to wear the shorts or, God forbid, linen pants the local agents wore. "Miami sucks," he said.

Rookie agent Anthony Miller, Fred's driver, nodded in agreement. "You think this is bad, wait till you see where we're going."

Fred knew Anthony was nervous about working with him. Fred did nothing to dispel the sentiment. "Drug deal hit in the ghetto? Can't wait."

"Don't forget the crackhead witness and the bag of human bones," Anthony said.

"This city is a *Lord of the Flies* waiting to happen."

Anthony laughed in that hollow way that meant he didn't get the reference. Fred cranked the air conditioning to the limit. "How'd you stand growing up here?"

"I'm from Fort Lauderdale," Anthony said.

"Yeah, right up the coast."

"Fort Lauderdale's in South Florida. Miami's in Latin America."

They turned north on Biscayne Boulevard, paralleling the ocean. The seventies eyesores faded into the background, and they passed the coconut palms and flame trees sprinkling the verdant sprawl of Bayfront Park. The egret-white sands of Miami Beach waited just across the causeway.

White sands, white sailboats, white high-rises, white boutique shops, the white Adrienne Arsht Center, even a gleaming white Publix grocery store. Fred had to shield his eyes from all the bling. The entire north end of downtown looked dressed for a South Beach nightclub.

"You may not like Miami," Anthony said, "but you gotta admit she's hot shit."

Fred waved a hand. "She's shallow hot, like a one-night stand with a model. Overtown's on the other side of those buildings."

"Since when do you complain about one-night stands?"

Fred rubbed at his wedding ring, out of habit. "I may hit it, but I'd never see a girl twice who can't speak English or follow a single damn law."

"You're the most racist Latino I've ever known."

"The term would be self-loathing, which I'm not. Why do you think half the product in the country flows through this city? Because everyone turns up a palm and looks the other way. You want to talk racist, talk to the Cubans. Being Mexican in this town is like being a third-class citizen. Anyway, look at these rundown strip malls and barefoot mothers. Miami's like any banana republic, a pair of perky silicone titties surrounded by a cancer-ridden body."

Fred chewed on a toothpick and kept marveling at the dichotomies of wealth. Seven- and eight-figure mansions on the right overlooking the water, cheap pastel motels on the left, flat sprawling ghettos extending to the horizon behind them.

They passed Little Haiti, which Fred considered to be the eighth circle of Hell. A few minutes later they turned onto an unmarked side street with low-hanging wires, entering a no-man's-land between Little Haiti and El Portal. They cruised by a trailer park that looked more like an internment camp, dozens of dilapidated single-wides arranged in a tight square and enclosed within a chain-link fence, hard-eyed shirtless men sitting on stoops, trash littering the grounds, naked children dashing between the trailers, the sun wringing every last drop of life out of the shadeless compound.

Fred grimaced. *A few more months*, he told himself, *and my dues are paid. Maybe I will think twice before I shoot another playground-stalking meth dealer in the head.*

Nah, probably not.

A few blocks later they reached their destination, an empty field comprised of weeds and gravel. A few emaciated palms and banyans dotted the periphery. Officers and lab techs were gathered in the center of the field, hovering over the crime scene.

They parked next to the squad cars. When Fred opened the door, the humidity whisked his breath away. He swatted at the mosquitoes and gnats and tramped across the field, already catching a whiff of decomposition. The sun pulsated overhead, sapping his energy, the morning shower a distant memory.

If I wanted to tramp through a goddamn rain forest, I'd go live in Borneo.

It was a bloodbath. Four bodies were sprawled a few feet apart, but blood had spattered in a much wider swath, coagulating out to a thirty-foot radius. Even stranger, there was some sort of pot in the center of the bodies, a round iron container with splayed legs.

One of the cops, a tall and bronzed Cuban, turned to Fred. "DEA?"

"Yeah. What is this, a cooking show gone bad? What the hell's that iron pot doing here?"

The cop didn't smile. "Look inside."

Fred stepped to the container. The rest of the entourage stopped talking and watched him. He peered inside, then had to force himself not to jerk away. "Jesus Christ," he muttered, crossing himself.

The pot was full of dirt, sticks, leaves, a few unidentifiable objects, and bones. Lots of bones. They poked out of the debris at all angles, a dozen or more, one of them a half-buried human skull.

Fred turned to Anthony, who was peering over his shoulder. "You said a bag of bones. I was picturing a Ziploc from forensics, not a . . . *cauldron.*"

"I might have mistranslated," Anthony muttered.

"What's with all this blood?" Fred asked, to no one in particular.

One of the forensics approached, a petite blond woman with alabaster skin. Fred got an immediate vibe of competency from her. "Most of the blood on the ground is avian."

"What, like animal sacrifices? Classy." Fred stood and folded his arms, sweeping his gaze across the small gathering. "So who wants to tell me what the hell's going on here? Some kind of gang initiation? Is Lord Voldemort dealing drugs now? What kind of ice we talking? Whose territory is this?"

The tall cop, whose badge read Jimenez, answered. "It's a bit of a free-for-all up here. Maybe Cuban, Haitian, Jamaican. The vic closest to the, um, cauldron is Frankie García, a known dealer. And not an insignificant one."

"He is now."

"Is he Cuban?" Anthony asked.

"His name's García, in Miami," Fred snapped. "Send what you've got on him to my office. We have any idea what happened?"

Jimenez gazed over the crime scene. "Not yet. Someone called it in at first light. It looked like this when we arrived."

"And the witness?"

The cop gave a bitter laugh. "If you want to call her that. Dumb *puta* wandered over here, high as a kite, wanted a hundred bucks to talk. Probably didn't see a thing."

"Nah," Fred said, "she saw something, or she wouldn't risk talking to us. I'll talk to her." He turned to the blond forensics woman. "Looks like Frankie got his throat slit, what's the cause of death on the others? I don't see any gunshot wounds. Surely these guys were packing?"

She flicked a bead of sweat off the pointed tip of her nose, then walked him to a foldout evidence table near the vans. Four guns in baggies lay on top of the table.

"Two of them were fired, two weren't," she said. "We haven't found the bullets yet."

Fred took a closer look at the bodies, noticing each had blood-caked indentations on the sides or backs of their heads. "What're those?"

"Those," the woman said, holding up a plastic bag filled with three spherical stones about an inch in diameter, "were made by these."

Fred said nothing, looking from the stones back to the woman. She looked him in the eye. "My best guess is a slingshot."

Fred laughed. "You don't need DEA, you need Steven Spielberg. Lady, I've seen trunks full of severed heads, cocaine stuffed inside frozen shark carcasses, underground drug tunnels with escalators and air conditioning, and more insane, depressing shit than Mother Teresa could imagine. But I gotta say, I've never seen a drug dealer's crew killed by a slingshot next to a bucket full of bones." He waved a hand. "Let me know what the autopsy shows, who wanted this guy rubbed. Only rival cartels hit drug dealers."

Fred opened a bottle of water and took a sip. His powerful wrestler's body was layered by a slab of middle-aged fat, now dripping sweat. His hometown of Lawrenceville, Georgia wasn't exactly the French Riviera, but it was nothing like this. "Anything else?" he asked.

No one answered.

"Then let's see this witness."

———•———

A short, middle-aged Latina with rheumy eyes waited in the back of one of the cop cars. Her pockmarked skin and hollowed-out cheekbones betrayed her hobby of choice.

Fred slid into one side of the back seat, Anthony the other. Fred sighed in pleasure from the air conditioning. "Where're you from?"

The witness couldn't keep her hands still, and her head kept jerking forward, like a human penguin. "*Nicaragua. Ya les dijo que—*"

"Speak English."

She looked Fred over, confused. "Why?"

"Because my gringo partner speaks cocktail Spanish he learned in community college, not Nica crack-whore ghetto Spanish, and he won't understand a word you're saying. So where're your kids?"

"What?"

Fred talked slowly so the woman could understand him. "People cross the border at your age for their kids. Let me guess, you went through hell and back to get across the border, then found yourself in a safe house in some no-name town, got raped and hooked on drugs, you couldn't get a job, and now you can't think about anything but that high, including your kids. I was just curious if they're still in Mexico or in the States, whether I should call them for you."

She licked her lips and looked as if she might vomit, and then her whole body started trembling violently. "What you want?"

"Just what happened here."

Her mouth started moving back and forth, as if she were chewing with her mouth closed. "What you got for me? Like I told them, I got some information for sale."

Fred brayed and slapped his knee. "I know you're desperate, but you haven't been to prison yet, have you? If you had, you'd never have risked sticking around to talk to us. You know how it feels as if there's insects crawling under your skin when you don't have a hit? Probably like it is right now? And how it gets worse, until your skin's on fire and your brain feels like it's gonna pop right out of your skull? Imagine that times one thousand, in a jail cell, with no hope of relief. You'll suffer like the saints never did. What I have for you is that I'll open this door and let you out of this car so you can go back to your whoring and panhandling until you get enough money to see your dealer. If I'm in a good mood, maybe a pair of doubles."

Fred saw Anthony's eyes slide away. "Now," Fred said, "what'd you see last night?"

She started plucking at her forearms, her movements exaggerated. "I no afford the bus *anoche* and I find this field. I sleeping under the big *palma* when I hear people. I see'a four men carry in that big pot and *dos* chickens, and I know is *brujería*—"

"Witchcraft," Fred said to Anthony. "The Cubans are into all kinds of crazy shit. Do you know what it was?" he said to the woman. "Santeria?"

"I no mess with that, you know? I Catholic."

"Yeah, I can tell. So what happened? They killed the chickens, did some chanting and dancing?"

"I no see much, they kill the chickens and stand next to the pot and put things in it. Then three of them, they die."

"Come again?"

"I hear something like'a . . ." She looked at a loss for words, then brought her hands together in a sharp clap. Anthony jumped.

The witness grinned, showcasing rotting teeth. "One man falls over, he no scream or nothing. The other three no move for a *momentico* and then they have their guns. Then another," she clapped again, "and another dead man." Again she struck her hands together, grinning, enjoying the game.

"Three men down, just like that?"

"*Sí.*"

"Then what?"

She leaned her head back against the seat and started cackling. "Then I went loco."

Fred snapped his fingers in her face. "Stay with me."

"The last man, he walk around that pot and I hear him saying words very fast, like he praying. I no understand the words, it was no Spanish. He has a gun and he wave it in the dark. There is one more"—she clapped a fourth time—"and he make a yell and drop the gun like something hit him in the hand. Then there is a blue woman right next to him and he looks at her and scream and says '*Los muertos!*'"

"As in, *the dead*?" Fred asked. "What are you talking about?"

"I tell you I crazy."

"A blue woman?" Fred pressed. "I thought you said it was dark."

"The last man, he have a light. He point it at her."

"And all you know is that she was blue. Oh, and dead."

"She look alive to me, he say she dead."

"Was she a gringa, a Latina, a Russian?"

"*Indígena.*"

"An Indian? A blue Indian."

She cackled. "*Sí.*"

Anthony laughed, and Fred grimaced. He didn't think she was lying. He just thought she had been bombed out of her mind and didn't know a blue Indian from Bill Clinton.

"And this blue Indian," Fred said, "what'd she do?"

She grinned a final time, tracing a finger across the base of her neck. "She kill him with her knife."

3

MIAMI BEACH

The door opened and Nya stood in front of him, her caramel skin glowing in the afternoon light streaming in from the balcony. Her hair was scattered and lovely, her lithe body thinner than when Grey had last seen her.

She hesitated for a moment, cool and reserved as ever, then came to him and buried her face in his shoulder. He felt her sobs but never heard them, and when she lifted her head the only evidence of her grief was the redness of her mascara-free eyes.

She held him at arm's length. "Thank you for coming. Do you mind to wait on the balcony? I've a call to make, and then I'll join you. There's tea by the counter and beer in the fridge."

He took the beer and moved to the balcony, a rectangle of white with a view of Miami Beach. A steady ocean breeze ruffled his dark hair and popped the sleeves of his black linen shirt.

At least she had touched him. When he'd last seen her, standing in her garden in Harare and unable to deal with the demons inside him, she couldn't even hug him good-bye.

They had met when Grey was a diplomatic security officer posted in Harare, on a case involving the disappearance of an American diplomat. Grey was the lead investigator, Viktor the expert on African religion, and Nya was their local liaison, an agent with the Zimbabwean Ministry of Defense. However controlled, Grey's capacity for violence had become for Nya a reminder of her torture at the hands of the sadistic priest they had faced. She had been scarred beyond imagining, inside and out.

She knew who Grey was—it had brought them together, the anger and darkness inside them both and their struggle against it— but in the end it pulled them apart.

He understood.

He abhorred it himself.

It was his price to pay. He had taken too many lives and so the violence had taken what he loved, a quietly confident girl from a forgotten country, achingly beautiful and sincere.

He squinted in the light and watched her pace as she talked, head bowed. All he knew was that her deceased father's eighteen-year-old goddaughter, Sekai, who was like a little sister to Nya, had died from a hit of Ecstasy in a South Beach nightclub, along with five other exchange students. It had been all over the papers. Not an overdose, but a bad batch. Sekai's family didn't have any money, so Nya had come to Miami to repatriate the body.

She came outside and set her tea on the table, her smile soft and sad. "Everything's prepared. I fly back with her tomorrow."

Grey picked at the label on his beer as he stared off the balcony. "I'm glad you didn't have any trouble."

She took his chin in her hand and turned his head to face her. "I'm sorry I can't stay longer."

"I understand."

They held each other's gaze as the breeze picked up and then settled.

"How's Zim?" he asked.

"As always, hey? The Chinese steal our resources, and the boss men let them. The power cuts have stabilized to once a day in the northern suburbs. Worse, of course, in other places." She looked away, bitter. "What is there to say?"

"The dogs?" Grey asked. He wanted to ask if she had recovered enough to go back to work, but he didn't.

Her smile brightened. "Mischievous as ever. And you? Still working with Viktor? How's it?"

"I can't complain. Viktor is never dull, and I'm teaching . . ." He trailed off, hesitant to bring up jujitsu.

She laid a hand on his arm. "It's okay."

He took a swallow of beer. "It wasn't before."

"I wanted you to know," she said, lifting the tea to her lips, "that I'm doing a little better."

"That's great," he said carefully. "I'm happy to hear that."

She set the tea down. Her eyes found his. "Perhaps we could talk again. I understand . . . if you prefer not to, and I know I've no right to ask. You've probably moved on."

Grey studied the bottle, telling himself that he should think long and hard about what he said next, telling himself some doors were better left closed, telling himself she lived two continents away and hadn't said anything except they should talk.

But all he could feel was shivery with hope.

"I'd like that," he said.

She smiled and placed a hand over his. A tingle arced through him, a not-so-dormant reaction to the touch of the one girl he had truly loved.

"There's something else," she said, "and I hate to ask. But I can't stay, and I can no longer . . ."

He finished the beer and rolled the bottle between his palms, knowing what she would ask and already knowing his response.

"Sekai was here as an exchange student," she continued. "The first person in her family to travel abroad. She"—Nya took a moment to regain control of her expression—"she was a good girl, Grey, and she was family. I promised I'd look after her. I know she did a reckless thing, but she shouldn't have died because of it."

"Of course not."

Then she stared at him, really stared at him, and he saw a flash of the old Nya, a storm cloud of strength and determination sweeping across her visage.

"The police said the tablets were laced with a cheap contaminant," she said. "This drug dealer, this *animal*, who did this to her . . . he took her life to save a few extra dollars. What kind of world is this?"

"I don't know. I never have."

She opened her mouth to speak, but the cloud passed and the new Nya returned, the one tortured to the edge of her sanity, her father murdered, her beloved country ruined, struggling to deal with the senseless violence and evil that had settled over her life like a toxic cloud.

When she looked away he took her hands in his own. She squeezed them as if she were falling off a building and his hands were the edge of the roof.

"I'll stay," Grey said, "and do my best to find who did this."

"Thank you," she whispered. "And Grey?"

"Yeah?"

"What I said earlier, about talking again? This has nothing to do with that."

"I know it doesn't."

4

CANCUN, MEXICO

The men—and the lone female, an über-madame with a stake in every pleasure palace from Cancun to Tijuana—clustered around the marble conference table like eagles perched on a hummingbird feeder. Incongruent. Unstable. A simmering teapot of violence.

It was an extremely rare gathering of representatives from some of Mexico's largest crime syndicates—mainly drug cartels, but also arms dealers, migrant smugglers, and a few outlying specialties. No one present knew why each particular faction was represented, except their leaders were beholden in some manner—and terrified of disobeying—someone named *El General*. That moniker was rarely used, and he was also known simply as *El Jefe*.

The Boss.

Felix Gutierrez, the short but compact spokesman for Mexico's oldest surviving drug cartel, spoke first. *"Buenas Señor Guiñol, ha sido mucho tiempo. Como está El Jefe?"* It's been a long time, Mr. Guiñol. How's the Boss?

The twinge of nervousness in Felix's voice made everyone more on edge than they already were. Felix was a hard man, feared across the country for his dispassionate brutality.

His question had been addressed to a man with thinning hair and a double chin at the head of the table, a man whose intelligent but paunchy face and wire-framed glasses evoked a dissolute urbanity. The madame found her pheromones repulsed by this man.

Though wearing a suit, Guiñol looked as if he would be more comfortable slouched over a computer in a food-stained shirt, stalking an Internet chat room. He was the representative of El Jefe and the only participant allowed the presence of bodyguards—four heavily armed men standing in the corners, each a mercenary from a different South American country.

Instead of answering, Guiñol stood and stepped to the wall of windows showcasing the dreamy slice of the Caribbean separating the Yucatan Peninsula from Cuba.

"*El Jefe es El Jefe*," Guiñol said. *The Boss is the Boss*, uttered in a tone that implied that El Jefe was as unchanging as God, and the question needn't ever be asked again. He stood over his seat, placed his palms on the table, and spoke with a Colombian accent. "You know why I've come."

A goateed man seated near the door gave a nervous tug on his chin. His name was Ricardo "Ricky" Orizaga, and he was high in the food chain of the Alianza Cartel, which controlled a sizeable portion of the South Florida drug trade. He was in charge of the Alianza's Miami subsidiary, and was ultimately responsible for the Ecstasy overdoses at the nightclub in Brickell.

Guiñol leveled his gaze on Ricky. "I'll attend to you in a moment," he said, causing another grab at the goatee. Ricky also felt an odd lightness, as if he had taken a hit off a joint, as well as a tingling in his jaw that seemed to be spreading downward. He chalked it up to stress.

"The deaths in Miami—the third such incident in a year—are endemic of a larger carelessness," Guiñol said. "The cardinal sin in El Jefe's organization is public exposure. Do you think that you are untouchable, or that the society in which you live is so easily cowed? Do you think that a few well-placed bribes of local politicians and law enforcement officials allow you to operate with the relative impunity in which you work? Especially those of you with a foothold in the United States?" Guiñol wagged a finger, only the hum of the air conditioner breaking the silence. "No, no no no no."

Ricky's weightless feeling had spread, and he was having trouble concentrating on Guiñol's words. Somewhere deep inside, in the mysterious core of the subconscious, he felt a shiver of fear.

"El Jefe has much larger concerns," Guiñol continued. "The ICE, NAFTA, MERCOSUR, federal judges, presidents, dictators. People who can legalize drugs and shut down borders and seize your banks. People who can put all of you out of business." A snap of his fingers crackled through the room. "Like that."

Guiñol walked slowly around the table until he was standing behind Ricky, whose entire body had numbed. "Do you know what happens," Guiñol asked, his voice now low and insidious, "when the will of the people is pushed too far? They say *no more* and press the government to become involved. The elected officials forget our bribes and a revolution results—against us. Look at Colombia: a shell of its former self. If the internal war does not calm, Mexico will suffer the same fate."

A smirk lifted Guiñol's face, a heavy violence brightening his eyes. He slipped on a pair of gloves, placed one hand on Ricky's shoulder, and a scalpel appeared in his other hand. "We allow you many things, but we will not tolerate a risk to our principal market. We are powerful, but only in the shadows, outside of the public eye. We must—we *must*—avoid the publicity that the incident in Miami has caused. Do you not agree, Ricardo?"

"Yes," Ricky said, though his brain seemed lost in the grayest of fogs. He couldn't seem to form his own opinion on what had been asked.

"So your cartel will punish those responsible?"

"*Sí.*"

"And be careful whom you employ from now on, never letting such a careless act happen again?"

"Of course," Ricky said.

"Excellent. Now put your hand on the table, so that I can remove one of your fingers as punishment, as a lesson to all present."

Ricky did as he asked, in complete agreement with everything Señor Guiñol had proposed.

Hardened criminals all, not a single person at the table uttered a sound as Guiñol leaned down and sliced off Ricky's index finger with the scalpel, spraying blood across the room.

What shocked them was not the act itself, which most of them considered a rather routine response to failure, but Ricky's chilling complicity.

The real lesson.

"Pick up your finger," Guiñol said.

Ricky obeyed. He felt no pain, and had the overwhelming urge to do whatever Señor Guiñol asked. The same submerged part of Ricky's subconscious that had shivered in fear was now screaming, buried alive and clawing through the dirt, but the barest whisper of that scream, a flicker of synapse, reached Ricky's conscious mind.

Guiñol's eyes swept the room, to ensure he had made his point. "Show your punishment to your cartel," he said to Ricky, "and see that this mistake is properly handled."

"*Sí, Señor Guiñol.*"

5

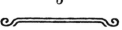

MIAMI

Grey sweltered in jeans and a black T-shirt on the patio of a nightclub in Brickell, Miami's swanky business district. A row of banana trees at his back provided some relief from the declining sun, and he had a view of the entire establishment, from the sofa patio seating to the stainless steel bar to the living room-size dance floor, thrumming with frenetic Latin techno.

Salsa, in his opinion, was not something that needed a faster beat.

It was Friday night and sleek Miami patrons were spilling in, thinly clad women with skin tones all over the map, groomed and handsome men in designer slacks and open-collared shirts.

This was the club where Sekai and the others had died. Grey had used Viktor's Interpol connections to check on the status of Sekai's case, and so far no progress had been made. The girls who had died were black, African, and had been using drugs. Probably not a priority for Miami PD.

Grey had been in place for an hour, watching the scene unfold, eyes in perpetual motion for underground activity. He concentrated his attention on a young and tanned white guy with cropped blond hair and an untucked teal shirt. He was sitting at a corner booth with a much larger dark-haired man. More than a few patrons had slid in beside the blond guy, exchanged greetings, and traded hand movements under the table.

Grey had also been watching a swarthy guy on the other side of the room, dressed more akin to Grey than to the socialites, trying to blend in but not doing a great job. The police presence, Grey assumed, keeping an eye on the place after the recent tragedy. The blond guy was not in the cop's line of sight.

Something else of interest: two of the managers dropped by on occasion to trade grins with the blond guy, but the third manager, a ferret-faced man with a businesslike manner, avoided both the blond guy and the cop.

Grey maintained his vigil, but his mind kept wandering back to Nya. It didn't seem to want to travel anywhere else since they had dined at a hole-in-the-wall Argentinean steakhouse on South Beach, talked the night away as only they could, and taken a cab to the airport the next morning. He held her while she cried over Sekai, and after that she had hugged him tightly, brushed her hand through the cowlicks in his hair, given him a lingering kiss on the mouth, and entered the line for airport security.

Then she was gone.

He stood in the airport for a long time after she left, engulfed by a wave of regret. Miami lost its luster, and he was left with the familiar stab of loneliness that came from being in a beautiful place and not belonging.

Maybe he had built Nya up too much, let the memory overcome the reality, but he didn't think so. He had never met anyone with her combination of gentleness and strength, beauty and character. She had plenty of rough edges, but Grey understood why. Nya didn't know how to deal with the state of her world and those who had ruined it, so she chose not to trust, and made you prove otherwise.

Enough. He would fill the hole inside him by fulfilling his promise to her, and deal with the rest later. If she really wanted to give their relationship another chance, he had some decisions to make.

After waiting until the blond guy was alone with his bodyguard, Grey sauntered to their booth. "Mind if I join you?"

The blond guy looked him up and down, eyes shrewd. "Do I know you?"

"No, but I hear you're the guy to talk to."

"Yeah? About what?"

"About a good time."

The blond guy cocked his head, indicating for Grey to sit. Grey slid in beside him. The dark-haired muscle watched Grey like a bird of prey.

"So? What kind of girl you like? Cindy, Hannah, Xena, Isabella? I got some painted ladies also."

"Xena," Grey said.

The blond guy clicked his tongue. "Single, twins, triplets?"

"Single. But hey," Grey leaned in closer, "I heard about what happened in here. She'll be clean, right?"

His face tightened. "Listen, asshole. I wasn't even here that night. You want something or not?"

Grey put his hands up. "Easy. After something like that, I gotta ask. You know how it is, some people sell the good stuff, some don't. Who was the guy, anyway? I'd like to know who to avoid."

The dealer's white teeth flashed like a tiger's. "You just stick with me, you'll be fine."

"Sure. Never hurts to know, though."

"You want the girl or not?"

Grey rose. "I'll come back another night," he said, moving his arm away, "when it's calmer."

"How about you go someplace else from now on."

The bodyguard rose, and Grey took a step back. He put his hands up in mock submission, lowering his eyes as if cowed by the presence of the larger man. Backing away, he noticed the heft of a handgun under the bodyguard's shirt.

He left the club hoping the goon would follow, but he never did. After taking a walk around Brickell, Grey stopped for a late-night snack at a dive bar called Tobacco Road. By the time he returned to the nightclub, the place was winding down, and both the dealer and the cop were gone.

Grey stood by one of the banana trees and nursed another beer. When the music cut off and the lights came on, Grey approached the third manager, the one who had avoided the dealer.

"Mind if I ask you something?" Grey said.

The manager kept straightening tables. "Sure."

"Not too fond of that blond drug dealer, are you?"

The manager stilled. "Are you a cop?"

"No, but I know you're also not very fond of the one on the take who was here. Jeans and tight-fitting T-shirt at the corner table."

He grimaced. "Look, man. I don't know who you are or what you want. If it were up to me, things would be different around here, but they aren't."

"I'm looking for the guy who sold the stuff that killed those girls."

"You know one of the girls?"

"Something like that."

He nodded in understanding, eyes sparking. "I'll tell you what I already told the *cops*. That cocky piece of shit Frankie García was dealing that night. Everyone knows, but doing something about it is a different story."

"No one's willing to come forward?"

"You don't mess with the Cubans in this town. Frankie wasn't a kingpin, but the people he works for are."

"Any idea where I can find him?" Grey asked. "Wait—did you say *wasn't*?"

"Yeah, you can find him at the morgue. Police found his body a few days ago in a field in North Miami. His supplier probably whacked him in retaliation. Don't you read the *Herald*?"

"I don't suppose you know the supplier?" Grey asked, knowing he probably wouldn't.

"Do I look like DEA? I don't *want* to know. I know his partner, though. Manny Lopez. No big secret on the club scene. Manny cut pills for Frankie, and they ran the UM beat out of Manny's house. My sister used to buy from him."

UM = University of Miami, Grey guessed.

"I know because she called me to pick her up once," he continued, "bombed out of her mind. Dumpy purple and white bungalow a few blocks behind UM, just off Sixty-Second Terrace. Though if he cut up that X for those girls, he might have skated."

"I appreciate the info," Grey said. If Manny Lopez was still around, he and Grey were going to have a little chat.

"I got no love for dealers, man, especially ones who sell to my sister. But take my advice and let it go. Manny's a nasty piece of work."

6

DER HEILIGKEIT DES LUFT SANATORIUM, SWITZERLAND

Cappuccino in hand, Viktor Radek leaned on the windowsill and indulged his eyes on one of the most beautiful vistas on earth: the jagged, snow-capped peaks of the Swiss Alps sweeping across the horizon.

Renowned professor of religious phenomenology at Charles University in Prague, perhaps the world's foremost expert on cults, descendant of Czech nobility, Viktor had found the process of admitting himself into the sanatorium most humiliating.

His last investigation had led him someplace dark and terrifying, a prison of the mind that was the one place he had proven unable to escape on his own: the cobwebbed corners of his past. To cope, he had embraced his longtime companion, his emerald absinthe muse, a bit too fiercely.

Six weeks since his last drop. Four more to go.

It wasn't the wormwood that had gotten the better of him, Viktor knew, but the accumulation of horrors he had witnessed over the years. The psychotics and madmen, demagogues and megalomaniacs: it was a bitter tea in which his life's work was steeped. Adding the memory of his beloved fiancée to the mix had tipped the scales too far.

Yet he accepted his past, and was eager to resume his investigations—and not just because he enjoyed apprehending some of the world's most devious criminal minds. Viktor's true work, what he risked his life to unearth in the shadowy world of religious phenomenology, was knowledge. Probing the minds of believers, observing their rituals, unlocking their secrets.

Viktor was currently ruminating on the voicemail Grey had left, as well as the police report Grey had emailed concerning the drug murders in Miami. Too proud to discuss his admittance into the sanatorium, yet unwilling to lie to Grey, Viktor had to decide how to respond.

Because there was information Grey needed to know. There wasn't much to go on, but if Viktor's instincts were right, he knew what religion was involved, and it was a particularly bizarre one. Bizarre and dangerous.

Steepling his fingers, he sighed as he contemplated the grandeur of the mountain peaks. He would have to conduct some research and ponder the wisdom of pursuing the case, but knowing Grey's sense of justice and his feelings for Nya, he doubted anything he said would matter. Dominic Grey was Viktor's employee in name, but if anyone marched to the beat of his own drummer, it was he. Grey had marched all the way out of the parade.

As Viktor pushed away from the window, preparing to dress for dinner, his mind lingered on the part about the blue Indian woman. Viktor agreed with Grey's assessment: Why concoct such an unusual element to the story? Most likely the witness had been hallucinating and *thought* she was telling the truth.

The thing was, the coroner's report had confirmed that a slingshot, or something like it, had caused the death of three of the men.

A blue Indian woman with a ritual knife and a slingshot, murdering four drug dealers and then disappearing into the night.

Now *that* intrigued him.

7

DEA OFFICE, MIAMI

Fred drummed his fingers next to the keyboard, eyeballing the report before he made it official. He almost deleted the portion about the slingshot and the Blue Lady of Death, but decided to keep it. It made for a good laugh, and God knew this world needed one.

Especially his world. The drug scene seemed to worsen every year. If it wasn't the Colombians, it was the Haitians or the Jamaicans or the Venezuelans, and the current Mexican turf battles were as vicious as any war ever waged by man. If the average citizen knew of the atrocities he had seen, knew how much violence spilled across the border, knew how infested with dealers and cartel loyalists and crooked cops every city in America with more than a single stoplight was, then the next round of immigration reform would make Arizona look like an enclave of free-loving hippies.

And anyone who thought America was the innocent victim needed to look at the user statistics. Which country's insatiable drug appetite did they think fueled the industry?

The current buzz was Krokodil, a homemade heroin concoction that literally ate people's flesh from the inside out. Big in Russia, created by mixing codeine with gasoline or oil, it was a matter of *when*, not *if*, the drug hit the United States.

It was all so hilarious. A creepy iron cauldron? Of course there was a cult involved! No one selling crank to kids bothered with a nice little religion like Buddhism. Narcos liked skulls and animal sacrifices and voodoo dolls and stupid colored beads. Drugs and cults had gone hand in hand in Latin America since the beginning of the drug wars.

Anyway, the DEA did not investigate cult behavior, they investigated drugs and related crimes. And unless there was an angle, the DEA did not investigate the murder of a drug dealer by other drug dealers.

Which was how Fred saw this case.

The word on Frankie was that he had been a mid-level player at best, a pawn for one of the stateside cartel distributors who pushed their product to a bevy of South Florida dealers, an army of cockroaches carrying lice across the Southeast.

The problem was, squashing Frankie was just like squashing a cockroach. He was filthy, dead, and very, very replaceable. It was not a DEA-caliber murder. If Miami PD wanted to investigate, that was up to them, but Fred knew they wouldn't.

Fred hit "Send" and pushed away from the desk. Though frustrated by his job, Fred believed deeply in what he did. He had three kids, a teenage son from his first marriage and two girls in elementary school. He chose not to think about the methadone clinic in which his teenager was currently enrolled, and he shuddered at the dangers awaiting his younger two as they grew up.

After leaving the office, he skirted downtown and took Coral Way home. Even Fred had to admit it was a nice street, shaded by mature banyans and lined with sidewalk cafés and restaurants from over two dozen countries.

He took Douglas and crossed over U.S. 1, debating hitting a strip club but deciding he would rather go home, crack a beer, and call his kids before bed. Hearing their voices put him in a different universe, washed away the grime.

He pulled into Coconut Grove, a neighborhood nurtured by bohemian artists in the fifties and sixties, now filled with renovated bungalows and Spanish-style mansions hidden inside a tropical paradise.

Good job, hippies. You did something right.

Fred, however, lived on the edge of what was called the Black Grove: a dense collection of shanties next door to the mansions, filled not with lush vegetation but with broken sidewalks and dilapidated houses whose roofs curled from the heat. It was called the Black Grove because only black people lived there. Not white people, not Latinos, just black people.

And it was avoided like a quarantine zone.

Fred lived in a modest rental with an insipid square of a backyard. The location was great, close to everything, and Fred felt a kinship with the residents of the Black Grove, who were as invisible in Miami as he was.

He cracked a Miller Lite and rang his former house in the suburbs of Birmingham, his home before his wife kicked him out.

No answer. He tried her cell, then tried both the home phone and her cell three more times.

Damn her. It wasn't that late.

He tried to enjoy the evening, but he missed his kids, and dusk had brought out The Enemy. While his neighbors in the fashionable part of Coconut Grove enjoyed the protection of lanais, Fred sat under a sterile lime tree, tortured to the edge of sanity by battalions of mosquitoes. After ten minutes he was sweating from the humidity, scratching his mosquito bites, casting wary glances at the incontinent parrots flying overhead, listening to the bass from some inane rap song rattling half the Black Grove, and cackling insanely as a pair of tiny lizards started humping right beside his feet.

He gave up, stomping inside after kicking his lawn chair across the yard. Shotgunned another beer to relieve the itching. Cranked Springsteen to drown the rap.

Fred was glad he had shot that meth dealer. He was just sad he had done it in front of an undercover cop. If he hadn't, then Fred might be sitting in his trimmed green lawn in Vestavia Hills, looking at magnolia trees and tidy shrubs instead of man-size weeds and vines that could crack a foundation. There would be stars glittering in a svelte Alabama night, neighbors waving goodnight, Southern belles in tight shorts casting suggestive looks at the edgy DEA agent who kept their neighborhood safe from outsiders and drug dealers.

That was where he would be, all right. Smack in the middle of the goddamn United States of America.

His cell rang, and he glanced down. HQ in Arlington.

Odd. Very odd.

He put the phone on speaker. "Agent Hernandez."

"HQ dispatch here. Apologies for the late call. I understand from your supervisor you're working the Frankie García murder?"

"I was. Not much to work."

"We need you to attend a meeting concerning this matter, tomorrow morning at seven a.m. Details are in your inbox. I assume you can make it?"

Fred frowned at his cell. He had only released his report a few hours ago. "Sure. Who's the meeting with?"

"The CIA."

8

SOUTH MIAMI

Grey was hunched in his rental Civic a few blocks from the purple and white bungalow, secure in the parking lot of a clapboard Baptist church. With a six-pack of water and two Publix sandwiches to see him through, Grey had arrived at six a.m. to start his stakeout of Manny Lopez, Frankie García's partner.

The neighborhood surprised him. Located just a few blocks behind the University of Miami's posh Coral Gables campus, Manny's bungalow was in a dilapidated pocket of South Miami with dealers on the corners and low-slung sedans cruising the streets.

Set at the end of a cul-de-sac, most of the bungalow was obscured by foliage. Iron bars guarded the windows and a high stone wall shielded the rear of the property. A Hummer occupied the driveway, arriving earlier with four men carrying takeout and clutching firearms. The house had the feel of a rebel camp under siege.

Eyes trained for signs of movement, binoculars at the ready, Grey took another swig of water as sweat trickled off his body. He felt as if he were back in the jungle, scoping a target for Marine Recon.

Dusk arrived and Grey grew restless. His plan was to scope out the scene, then go to the police and offer to wear a wire. He wasn't sure how far he was prepared to go after that. He just knew Nya needed his help and she was going to get it.

It wasn't just about Nya. If Grey didn't investigate this matter, no one else would, and Sekai's death would be another ripple in an ocean of unheard voices.

The sounds of laughter and men speaking Spanish spilled into the night. Grey wasn't sure, but he thought they had come from behind the purple bungalow. After a moment of waffling, he grabbed his binoculars, stepped out of the car, and slipped into the shadows. The sickly sweet smell of rotting mangoes drifted on the breeze.

He confirmed that the voices were coming from behind the rear wall of Manny's place. Approaching any closer was risky, and he debated calling it a night. Then the cacophony ceased, and Grey heard a single voice intoning a mantra in an unfamiliar tongue. A bongo drum accompanied the voice. It reminded him of chanting he had once heard at a Juju ceremony in Zimbabwe, and the thought chilled him.

The other houses looked abandoned, and Grey wondered if Manny owned the whole block. That or the neighbors were too scared to attract attention.

The chanting took on a more singsongy tone. It was an African language, Grey was sure of it. Feeling exposed, he scanned the street and then shimmied up the rope-like aerial root of a banyan tree, taking cover under the heavy foliage.

He focused the lenses on the rear wall, swept his gaze to the middle of Manny's yard, and gripped his binoculars at what he saw.

Vines, wild bougainvillea, and shaggy palmettos had overtaken the property. Tiki torches illuminated a patio, where a bevy of tense Latino men clutched handguns to their sides. But what harpooned Grey's attention was the shirtless, barefoot man in the middle of the property, singing as he tossed a handful of dirt into a knee-high iron pot with sticks poking out of it. White crosses had been painted on the man's cheeks and forehead and chest, and a jumble of necklaces swayed downward as he bent over the pot. Next to the priest, another man sat on the ground, hands banging a steady rhythm on a leather drum.

Near the top of the cauldron, Grey noticed a blackened human skull. The priest stirred the pot with one of the sticks, and the skull rotated, exposing the empty eye and nose sockets. He stopped singing and grabbed a plastic bottle off a table next to the pot, took a swig, and sprayed the contents into the cauldron.

Focusing on the table, Grey saw an array of items: chalk; a bottle of cheap rum; a cigar; a lit candle sitting in a teacup inside a glass jar; a bag of desiccated lizards; an assortment of herbs and mushrooms; and a bundle wrapped in black cloth, about half the size of a meatloaf.

A chill tiptoed down Grey's spine, and he wished Viktor were there to observe.

The priest grabbed a handful of dirt out of a sack and sprinkled it into the pot. Next he lit the cigar, puffing and ashing on the dirt, and then he grabbed the chalk and made a series of markings on the ground. As he worked, he continued to puff on the cigar and spray rum into the cauldron.

After finishing with the chalk, the priest sliced his palm with a razor blade, then held his hand over the black-cloth bundle, saturating it with blood. He stirred the cauldron again, forearms twisting with the effort, and the skull rotated through the dirt in a macabre dance, uncovering other bones in its path.

One of the armed men disappeared into the house, then returned holding a black cat by its neck. The cat jerked and thrashed, its screams escalating until they sounded like the cry of a child, but just before the priest swiped the razor blade, everyone stilled and was looking towards the house.

Grey whipped the binoculars around and saw two college kids— a slender girl in a miniskirt and a long-haired guy with a backpack— at the door of the purple bungalow. They must have rung the doorbell, customers from UM looking for a good time.

Tension radiated outward from the backyard, and Grey didn't like the feel of the situation. These people would not appreciate being disturbed.

The meowing stopped. The hum of insects replaced the low beat of the drums.

The girl in the miniskirt reached for the doorbell again, and Grey tensed. He refocused the binoculars on the backyard. It had emptied.

Leave, you stupid kids. Get your fix somewhere else tonight.

Instead of leaving, the girl pressed the doorbell two, three, and then four times. Finally the door opened. Grey strained but couldn't see inside.

The college kids disappeared into the house. Grey guessed they were infrequent customers who didn't have their ear to the ground. He prayed the dealers would make a quick sale and let them go.

Just in case they didn't, Grey grabbed his cell and dialed.

"Emergency 911."

"I'm a private investigator," Grey said, "and I need to report—"

A burst of gunfire erupted into the night.

"Sir—was that *gunfire?*"

Grey cursed and gave them the address, then scampered down the tree and sprinted towards the house. He had no weapon and knew he was heading into a maelstrom, but he had no choice. He couldn't leave those two coeds to their fate.

The shots ceased. Nurturing a foolish hope that the gunfire had been a nervous reaction, he veered left, deciding to scale the rear wall. As he flung a leg over, the gunfire picked up again, this time longer and accompanied by screams.

Grey's adrenaline spiked. He had to get to those kids. He flattened on the wall, seeing nothing out of place except for the bulk of the iron cauldron, looming in the grass like something out of a Brothers Grimm story.

The gunfire ceased again, and Grey slipped off the wall and against the rear of the house. He crept forward and pulled one of the long tiki torches out of the ground.

As he edged along the patio, two Latino men burst out of a screen door right in front of him, waving firearms. Grey jabbed the torch into the stomach of the lead man, causing him to drop the gun. The torch thudded into his gut, spilling oil, and his linen shirt burst into flames.

Neither Grey nor the second man had time to use their weapons before engaging, but Grey embraced that fact and his opponent didn't. Grey dropped his torch and leapt onto the second man, grabbing the barrel of his gun with both hands. As his opponent struggled to free the weapon, Grey head-butted him in the face, then swept the back of his opponent's legs out. Grey ended up standing over him with the man's arm straightened, both of Grey's hands torquing the wrist with the gun.

The man managed to fire off a useless round before Grey slammed his knee into the distended elbow, shattering the joint. Grey yanked the gun away and stomped on his opponent's temple to finish the job. The other man was still rolling around trying to extinguish the flames, and Grey pistol-whipped him unconscious.

Grey couldn't afford to wait; the kids might still be alive. He had seen nine men and only accounted for two. *Where were those cops?*

At least now he was armed. He held the gun in his left hand, crouching as he eased the screen door open.

It was a bloodbath.

A lava lamp in the corner cast the room in an eerie red glow, and Grey counted six bodies on the floor, all pockmarked by bullets. Blood spattered the walls. The stench of gunfire filled the air.

No sign of the kids. *What had happened in here?*

A scream and then two more shots, this time the muted *thwaps* of silencers, coming from a hallway to Grey's left. He crouched almost to a squat and swung the gun into the corridor. Unwilling to risk exposure, he hung back, training his weapon on whoever emerged.

Seconds later, the girl in the miniskirt stepped into the hallway, the long-haired guy right behind her. Instead of innocent college students, Grey saw two experienced killers, their steady movements and the flatness of their eyes giving them away. Both had semi-automatics. Both saw Grey. Both opened fire.

Grey scrambled to the side, his gun leveled at the entrance to the hallway. The gunfire ceased, and there was a prolonged silence. Grey knew trained assassins wouldn't risk coming down that hallway, and he wasn't about to walk into their line of fire. He debated slipping into the backyard but decided to hold his position. Climbing that wall would be too risky.

He firmed his grip and hoped the sirens came soon.

PEOPLES TEMPLE AGRICULTURAL PROJECT, NORTHWEST GUYANA NOVEMBER 18, 1978

After listening to the tape of the mass suicide, John Wolverton felt as if the world had flipped on its axis, gravity had reversed, and he was floating away.

The majority of Reverend Jones's flock had killed themselves at his command, after injecting their own children with cyanide. Offering their lives to him as if disrobing for a lover.

How could a human being possess that kind of control over another? Over so many? It was a power that seemed almost . . . supernatural.

Near the end of the tape, Jones's bodyguards had killed each other, until only Jones and one other remained. The final guard had shot Jones and then himself. Or at least that was John Wolverton's presumption, since the final two shots were the last recorded man-made sounds.

He saw a flicker of movement in the trees, and he stilled. Men in black fatigues creeping forward. Firearms raised. White skin glowing.

The cleanup crew.

After what he had heard at the beginning of the tape, Reverend Jones's tell-all and the part that had caused John Wolverton to feel outside of his body, he wasn't surprised by the men in the trees—just enraged.

He should have known about the cleanup crew. The fact that he didn't meant that he wasn't part of their plans.

He was part of the cleanup.

His mind worked fast, and he spotted a pen and a piece of scrap paper on a table. The men in the trees were fanning out, a pattern of engagement he knew all too well. Creating a perimeter around the danger zone.

Spotting an opening to the south, he planned his escape route. He knew he could disappear in the jungle, since he had roamed it for months.

So he fled.

And he took the tape with him.

And he left them a note.

———•———

As he slipped into the trees, following a path to the creek, his mind spun on what he had learned.

They had left him to die. Worse: they had sent their own people to kill him. *His* people. Why?

According to the Reverend's confession, John Wolverton's handler had told Reverend Jones that the CIA couldn't stop Congressman Ryan from coming, their partnership was over, and the Reverend would have to disappear to Russia.

Then it clicked in his mind. The CIA hated Congressman Ryan and the emasculating Hughes-Ryan Act—they *knew* Jones would kill him. They also knew, from the reports John Wolverton had written, that the Reverend's pride would not let him admit defeat, would never allow him to give up his flock.

They had just solved both the congressman problem and the Jonestown problem.

He looked to the sky. Soon the sweepers would disappear in their helicopters, and the official investigation would begin. He guessed the Guyanese were an hour or two behind the troops.

But what about him? Granted, they had known about Tashmeni and the baby. A serious mistake on his part, but it had happened. He had loved them.

The knowledge surprised him. He had not known he was capable of such love, of any love other than self-love. The personality tests, his own experience, suggested otherwise. But she had captured him in her own quiet way, the beautiful village girl who was kinder and funnier and more clever than anyone he had ever known. A world-class talent born into the most obscure circumstances imaginable.

His relationship with Tashmeni had surprised his superiors as well, and they knew he was compromised. He forced away the lump in his throat and returned to piecing together the puzzle. He had warned them this could happen, the mass suicides. Hell, Jones had made his people *rehearse* it.

John Wolverton had told his handler they had gone too far. The experiment was over, they couldn't risk this much blood on their hands.

He laughed to himself. How naïve he had been. What was the blood of hundreds to people willing to sacrifice whole nations for their cause?

In the end, it was simple. Loose ends had been tied. He knew too much, he was compromised. He had delivered his last report two days ago, so they knew everything he knew.

Or at least they thought they did, he thought with a smile as cold as the last touch of Tashmeni's fingers.

———◆———

He knew he had to get to Georgetown, the impoverished capital of Guyana. There he could blend in and disappear. After days in the jungle and many a brush with death, he stumbled gibbering out of the vines and onto the highway. Emaciated and half-mad, he hitchhiked to Georgetown, scraped in garbage cans for food, slept in alleys.

After regaining his strength, he put his skills to good use. Training for a clandestine officer could have doubled for training as a world-class thief. Over the next few months, he clawed his way out of the gutter by stealing and conning and bribing his way to a respectable position in the criminal underworld. Specializing at first in petty theft and break-ins, moving to more complex robberies and cons, he learned he had even more of a talent for crime than for espionage.

And it paid far, far better.

After accumulating enough funds to rent a fortified house in one of the suburbs, he contemplated his next steps. He knew he could never go back to his old life, nor did he want to. Not only was he a target, but a normal life had never been his goal. It was why he had chosen the CIA in the first place.

He was young, and Jonestown had been his first overseas posting. Guyana, with its tropical languor and miles of lawless streets, was like the Wild West set in the Garden of Eden. It suited him well. But he yearned to explore the rest of the continent, the stories of which had always fascinated him. The lost cities in the jungle, unearthly beaches, Nazi hideaways, cloud forests and deserts and jungles, rumors of mystics and shamans, the Latina beauties who could steal your soul with a shake of their hips and a twirl of their lustrous black hair.

There were a few things to do before he embarked on his journey. The first was to fake his own death, so he could officially disappear. After paying the right people a handsome sum of money, he had a reporter take pictures of him coated in pig's blood and lying in an alley, and then in the morgue at the police station.

There was an official press report and a death certificate. Though the corpse was under an alias, he made sure the report made it to the right media outlets. The people he was trying to reach would see it, he was certain.

Now he had two life insurance policies.

His petty scams and robberies were adequate, but he was ready for something more lucrative, and that traveled better. A few weeks later, he was approached at a nightclub by a deputy of Rabbi Washington, the leader of a religious community in Guyana that was eerily similar to Jonestown. Rabbi Washington was a fugitive from Cleveland who had managed to convince thousands of Guyanese and American blacks they were part of the Lost Tribe of Israel, and he had wormed his way into a thuggish sort of political power in Guyana.

Truly, John Wolverton thought, *one couldn't make these things up.*

A few months before, he had purchased and refurbished a few dilapidated warehouses on the wharf. As it was off the grid, shockingly poor, and chaotic, Georgetown was a smuggling hotspot, and the warehouses had already turned a nice profit.

Rabbi Washington's chief deputy got word of him and wanted to know if he was interested in using his warehouses in a more profitable industry. This industry, the deputy said, had become a burgeoning one in the capital, especially since Georgetown was less regulated than some of the region's other ports—which was saying something.

John Wolverton had put his elbows on the table and asked, "What industry are we talking about?"

"Drugs," answered the deputy, who John Wolverton knew was a convicted murderer from Harlem who had skipped the country on parole.

"Coming from where? Bolivia?"

"That's right."

"Who's buying?"

"Ah, that's the kicker, man. You're gonna like this one. They're using a front, of course, but you know who the brothers are driving this thing? I almost fell out of my chair when the Rabbi told me."

John Wolverton knew, but he asked anyway. "Who?"

"The Company, man. The CIA. You believe that smack?"

John Wolverton just smiled.

9

SOUTH MIAMI
PRESENT DAY

Grey was crouched in the hallway in a state of hyperawareness, pores flooded with adrenaline. He had *felt* the *chi* of the two assassins in the hallway, not just thugs with guns and an order to kill, but two people to whom violence came naturally, a second skin that fit snug and warm.

If the assassins decided to come down the hallway or double back through the front or rear entrances, there would be a swift and violent clash, and someone would die.

But Grey liked his position. He had a clear view in all directions, and felt secure he could take out at least one of them. And high-priced, basilisk-eyed killers like those did not step lightly into the great beyond. They did not deal in fifty-fifty odds.

That said, Grey had seen their faces, and they wouldn't like that. They might decide the risk of exposure was too great.

Still no sounds from the hallway. Were they creeping towards him, perhaps slipping onto the patio? He kept his fingers tight against the trigger, eyes on constant patrol.

Finally the sirens came, and Grey heard the sound of shattered glass. As the uniforms burst through the door, Grey's adrenaline faded, and he finally took in the contents of the room: a flat-screen TV and a brown sectional sofa, bags of coke and drug paraphernalia on a table, a slew of incense candles, a vintage poster of Varadero Beach, an array of potted herbs, two crossed scythes on a wall, and a long cane with a serpent's head leaning against the couch.

An open shopping bag rested on the floor inches from Grey. Inside were more candles, chalk, and what looked like a replica bull horn with a mirror attached to the base. Printed on the side of the bag was the name *Botánica Caldez*.

The cops approached him warily, guns trained on his chest. The lead one asked, "Who the hell are you?"

"I called 911. Check my cell, it's in my pocket. My ID's there, too. I'm a private investigator."

One of the cops checked Grey's cell for the 911 call, then flipped open his wallet. His eyebrows lifted. "Interpol?"

"We consult for them sometimes," Grey said.

"You'll need to come with us when we're done."

"I'd expect nothing less."

Fred entered the conference room talking loudly on his cell, discussing the Braves game with a buddy from Atlanta. The CIA agent sitting at the table in the snappy dark gray pantsuit, one Lana Valenciano according to the email, shot him a disdainful look that said *get off that phone, you uncouth ape.*

Exactly the effect he was going for.

Fred ended the call, took a seat across the table, and tipped his head. "Agent Valenciano."

A smirk of acknowledgment creased her lips, and he sized her up. Light brown hair, patrician Spanish face, athletic, nose too large and wrists too thick to be beautiful, driven enough to resent the fact that she was merely very pretty.

When Nixon declared war on drugs in 1971 in response to the growing heroin problem among servicemen in Vietnam, the conflict had begun with the Bureau of Narcotics and Dangerous Drugs, forerunner of the DEA. At last count, more than fifty government entities were engaged in the drug conflict in some manner.

Of those agencies, Fred liked the CIA the least.

"We need your assistance," Lana said.

He leaned back and folded his arms. "So I was told."

Fred's email had contained no information other than the time, place, participants, and general purpose of the meeting, which was that it involved the Frankie García murder.

"I assume you've put everything you know about the García murder in the report," she said.

She spoke English with the slight lilt distinctive to Miami-born Cubans, and her voice was no-nonsense and high class, as if she had ordered maids around as a child.

"You assume correctly."

"If there was anything you held back that you thought unimportant or didn't, for whatever reason, see fit to include, I need to know. Rest assured I'm not concerned in the least with protocol."

Fred rose and walked to the coffee pot in the corner. "Maybe you need to tell me what this is about. Or, let me guess: you can't tell me what I don't need to know, and what I need to know is jack."

"Fair enough," she said. To her credit, she didn't bother trying to massage the nature of their relationship. He supposed those days were over.

"I'll tell you what I can," she continued. "You might want to sit down."

He stirred in cream. "Really? You know I'm DEA, right? Not much I haven't seen."

"Have you heard of El General?"

Fred blinked, recalling a conversation with an informant a lifetime ago, in a rum bar in Key West. He had also heard the rumor tossed about once or twice at the DEA watercooler. "Surely you don't mean *the* General? The mythical crime lord who flits around South America like a ghost, pulling the strings on half the cartels, unable to pose for a single photo over the last few decades?"

"He's not a myth."

Fred laughed, but his laughter died as Lana continued looking him in the eye.

"We don't know his identity or the extent of his activities," she said, "but we're certain he exists and is an active player."

Fred sat, coffee unsipped. Lana did not look like a woman who was joking. Or who had ever joked.

"Whoa," he said. "There's a major power broker in play in the Southern Cone whose name we don't even know? How do *you* know he exists?"

"As you know, our monitoring abilities have increased dramatically since 9/11. The chatter is unequivocal. We're no longer in doubt that El General is an actual person."

"There's got to be more than just chatter. Chatter doesn't warrant an in-person visit from the CIA."

She gave a slow nod to acknowledge the point. "Two things. The first I'm not at liberty to discuss at the moment."

Fred snorted. The games had begun.

"The second," she continued, crossing her legs and draping one forearm on the table, the other resting in the contours of her lap, "is why I'm here. In the three and a half decades since El General has been on our radar—an extraordinarily long period for a criminal— there's been one common thread."

Fred thought about the García crime scene. "The cauldron?"

"No."

"Must be the slingshot, then," he said, though he couldn't fathom why it might be important.

"More importantly, the wielder."

"The blue Indian?" Fred laughed again, running a hand across a hairline that looked more like twigs in winter than a spring thicket. "Jesus, you're still not joking. He's used her before?"

"Three times that we know of. About once a decade, someone with the description of a 'blue Indian' has murdered a drug dealer, either with a slingshot, a knife, or an atlatl."

"A what?"

"It's an ancient throwing spear, used by various indigenous Indian communities."

"Oh, those old things. I keep one around the house."

Lana didn't smile, instead rising for a cup of coffee. Fred stared at her ass as she walked across the room, admiring its buoyant dimensions. He imagined his hands cupping it.

She turned, and he let her catch him staring. She smirked again. "You wouldn't know this, because there was no official report, but last month a similar murder occurred in Ciudad Juarez."

His eyes widened. "A blue Indian?

"It was an apparent response to the incidental murder of two American tourists who were boating on a lake just across the border."

"So let me get this straight: this General guy—I'll assume his existence for the sake of conversation—has twice, in the last month, murdered drug dealers who were responsible for the accidental deaths of U.S. citizens?"

"Two U.S. citizens and six exchange students on U.S. soil," Lana corrected.

"Whatever—shouldn't we be giving this guy a medal?"

"We think the reasons for the retaliations are more nefarious. The past appearances of this . . . assassin . . . have involved similar circumstances. Mistakes by criminals—almost always drug dealers— involving American or Western European casualties, which had the potential to lead to uncomfortable scrutiny by the press. Our guess is that the Mexicans have gotten out of control—"

"No shit," Fred interrupted.

"—and that he's tightening the reins."

"Okay, that's chilling, if true. So who's this blue Indian lady?"

"We've no idea."

"I suppose it could be *the General* himself," Fred mused, "or I suppose herself—nah, that's ridiculous. This is South America we're talking about."

Lana bristled. "The chatter points to El General being a male, and Griselda Blanco wasn't a man. Neither was Sonia Atala."

Fred inclined his head towards the ceiling camera in mock surprise. "Wow, I'm surprised they let you say her name. You know, that whole deal about the CIA propping up the Cocaine Coup?"

"Drugs are a small piece of the political puzzle," she said evenly.

Fred chortled. "It takes a big person to see the big picture, eh? Someone able to ignore the collateral damage, all those innocent people tortured and murdered and hooked on crack? How do you all justify it over there at Langley, anyway?"

"The same way you justified shooting a drug dealer in the face?"

"That's different," he muttered. "Look, what do you need me for, anyway? Everything I know is in the report."

"Spotty as your ethical record may be, you're the most experienced field agent down here right now." Lana's tone had softened ever so slightly, letting Fred know they were both on the same side. Fred didn't trust the switch in the slightest.

She continued, "An appearance of the General's favored assassin on U.S.

soil—this is the best lead we've had on this mark, ever. You're DEA, you know this world, the mules and informants. I need you to be my eyes and ears on the ground. Langley wants a lead."

"I've only been here a year. Why not someone local?"

"Like I said, we need someone who understands the bigger picture," she said. "And I need someone I can trust."

He guffawed. God, the venom these people spewed.

"If there's one thing you proved in Atlanta, it's that you're not on the take. You're a true believer, Fred. And *that* makes me trust you. I've already requisitioned you for the next week."

Whatever. Even if there wasn't any truth to this—and he had serious doubts—it would be better than cruising up and down Biscayne Boulevard.

He finished his Danish, took a long sip of coffee, and extracted a toothpick from the case he kept in the pocket of his short-sleeved, white dress shirt. "Million dollar question," he said, inserting the toothpick between his front teeth. "Why the hell does the CIA care about this? Drugs are passé politically, except to a few Arizona senators and lifers like me. Or let me guess: too many white kids are dying from meth, and the government has finally decided to get serious?"

She ignored the wisecrack and cupped her mug in her hands. "What's the number one concern of our government today, besides the economy?"

"The Canadian military threat?"

Still no laugh. *Damn, she's tough.*

"Terrorism," he said.

"And what are top priorities when it comes to terrorism and national security?"

"Borders and nukes."

"That's right," she said, watching him with shrewd blue eyes, waiting for him to piece it together.

"The General has nukes?"

"Not that we know of. But he dabbles in far more than drugs— human trafficking, arms manufacturing and smuggling, all the high-dollar operations. Someone like him has access to nukes, bio, and chem weapons."

Fred drummed his fingers on the table. "South American cartels and Islamic terrorists don't mix much, despite what you hear. Hell, the cartels *need* the U.S. But someone like El General . . . he could destabilize the border. And he's open to the highest bidder."

"He's become a threat that needs to be eliminated," she said.

"So fractious drug cartels decapitating Mexicans by the busload and poisoning our kids are tolerable to the CIA, as long as they don't open any mosques in Tijuana."

"Like it or not," Lana said coldly, "there *is* a bigger picture. Hard decisions have to be made by someone."

Fred matched her stare. "Then I guess in this case, our interests coincide."

"They better, since it's your job."

Fred snorted and looked away. He had long ago made his peace with how the U.S. government operated, but that didn't mean he had to like it. In his mind, he worked for the American people, suits and politicians and duplicitous CIA operatives be damned. Fred's belief system was his children and their future. "So what do we know about him?"

"Not much. We have no idea where he operates from except that it's within the Southern Cone. According to the chatter, he's got a hand in half the major cartels, and we suspect he played a part in enabling the power shift from Colombia to Mexico. Also, the cartels over which he holds sway appear terrified of him."

"That's not very comforting," Fred said.

"No."

"How?" Fred asked.

"Excuse me?"

"What kind of hold does he have?"

Lana took another sip of coffee. "Fear or protection, I assume. Probably both."

"Protection as in connections?"

"A man like this, the only way he could have existed is with help from above."

"Maybe he's above your pay grade, if you know what I mean," Fred said.

Instead of the retort he expected, she said, "That would put him in a very small club. And I doubt I'd be here right now."

Thoughtful, Fred extracted the toothpick and twirled it in his fingers. She continued, "This is our first and only lead on U.S. soil. We might not get another chance."

"Then I suppose I'll get started. Anything else?"

"I assume you're aware of the Manny Lopez hit last night?"

"I glanced at the briefing before we met. Manny supplied Frankie, so it's obviously part of the same message. I'll start tracing it back."

"Read the whole thing. There was a witness who got a look at the assassins. His name's Dominic Grey, an ex-diplomatic security guy. I want to have a chat with him."

The next morning Grey took a coffee on his hotel patio, which fronted Lummus Park on Ocean Drive. Nya's absence felt like a port without ships. He took a jog along the beach to dull the pain of their parting, remembering their long runs together in the cool Harare mornings, dodging potholes and fallen mangoes.

The police had looked a little incredulous at his story, but his connection to Nya and Sekai checked out and, combined with his Interpol liaison badge garnered due to Viktor's consulting gigs with the organization, secured his release.

Grey had also provided a composite sketch of the assassins, to no avail. He doubted they were in the system, or at least this system.

Miami PD confirmed that Manny Lopez had been one of the slain drug dealers. Grey decided he would call Nya later that day and let her know the principal two figures involved in Sekai's death had been killed, probably by an unhappy employer. Hell of a way to have your pay docked.

Blinded by the morning sun glinting off the patio, he thought of the darkness he had seen the night before. Working for Viktor had been an eyelid-peeling parachute jump into a strange and mysterious world. Grey himself did not possess religious beliefs, especially since witnessing his mother's death when he was fifteen, after her protracted bout with stomach cancer. A devout woman, she had put her faith in divine intervention rather than modern medicine, and Grey watched as she prayed every second of every sleep-deprived day, right until her pain-wracked death.

Grey knew that hatred of God did not equate to disbelief, and over time his anger had softened into numb agnosticism. If God existed, then He had created a beautiful world and left it, like a used target at a shooting range, riddled with degradation and despair. Perhaps one day Grey would feel differently.

But not that day.

What he had seen the night before had felt different, off the grid. It left him unsettled, as if he had dipped a toe into the abyss and it had come back dripping with a slimy, stygian residue.

Viktor was the expert, but judging by the armed guards and the feel of the ceremony, Grey guessed those men had been beseeching their god to protect them from the threat they knew was coming.

Two people passed by on their way to the lobby: a swarthy, capable-looking man with hairy arms sticking out of a coffee-stained guayabera, and a woman in sunglasses and a sharp business suit walking a step ahead of the man. Both looked Latino, though the woman had pale skin and more Anglicized features. They eyed Grey as they passed, and the woman stopped and turned just before she reached the hotel entrance.

"Dominic Grey?" she asked.

Grey stiffened. Though both possessed the guarded mannerisms of law enforcement, the woman looked like a government agent, the guy more like a cop.

Before Grey could answer, the man produced identification. Agent Federico Hernandez, Miami DEA. Grey eyed the woman, and she eyed him back.

Grey took a sip of coffee. "Can I help you?"

"Sorry to interrupt your morning," the man said, gruff but respectful, "but we need you to come with us for a bit. It concerns the two sketches you helped Miami PD draw up."

"We can't talk here?" Grey said, sweeping a hand around the empty patio. At eight in the morning, he had South Beach to himself.

"Our sketch artists are better. I wish I could say the same," the man said, cracking an easy grin, "about the coffee."

The ride was short, across MacArthur Causeway and four blocks into downtown, to one of South Florida's numerous DEA offices. After Lana introduced herself, no one spoke on the drive. Though Grey was highly curious about the CIA's interest in the case, he had worked in government long enough to know that questions at this stage were pointless.

They filed into a bland conference room. Grey and Fred prepared coffees while Lana texted on her smartphone.

"The sketch artist is on his way," Fred said.

Grey sat. "No interest in letting me know what's going on?"

Lana turned to him and crossed her legs. "As Agent Hernandez intimated, we've reviewed the police report and the interview transcript, and we'd like you to provide another sketch of the two assassins. As you probably know from your time with Diplomatic Security, our computer banks are much more internationally focused."

"Yeah, I gathered all of that. Why is this a CIA matter?"

"That's not the concern of this meeting," Lana said.

Grey chuckled. "I'll be happy to provide a sketch. But I've found that understanding all angles of a crime can be crucial to an investigation. It might help me know what to focus on." He looked Lana in the eye. "Jog my memory."

Lana met his gaze. "You realize, of course, that it's a crime to withhold information."

"I told the police everything I remember. Like I said, memory's a funny thing, and sometimes it depends on perspective."

Lana kept staring at him and drumming her fingers on a folder, which Grey assumed contained his file. "You've got an impressive background," she said, "at least until you were discharged from Diplomatic Security for insubordination."

Grey didn't bother blocking the jab. The choice had been between keeping his job or trying to save Nya's life. Nor was it the first black mark on his CV.

"You were almost one of us," Lana continued. "Lived abroad most of your life, fluent in three languages, no relevant family ties, high I.Q. tests, hand-to-hand combat instructor for Marine Recon. The last is particularly impressive."

"Keep reading. I'm sure there's something in there about my poor social skills and refusal to toe the line. All true, you know." He glanced at Fred and then back at Lana. "I suck at joining."

Fred crossed his arms and grinned.

Lana was good at concealing her expression, Grey gave her that. He wondered again at her involvement, and didn't miss the bureaucracy and hidden agenda of government work in the slightest.

"Does this particular cartel have CIA ties?" Grey wondered out loud. "Someone who needs protecting? Sensitive diplomatic issues at stake?"

Lana dismissed his speculations by returning to her smartphone. Moments later there was a knock at the door, and the sketch artist entered. Fred and Lana left the room.

After Grey finished profiling, Fred popped back in and asked him to wait a bit longer, offering pastries and more coffee. An hour later Fred and Lana both returned. Lana set an open laptop on the table in front of Grey. She stood behind him and he could smell the subtle spice of her perfume.

Staring at him from the left half of the screen was the woman he had seen in the hallway of Manny Lopez's bungalow. The photo looked shot in a chaotic Latin American market, and she looked different: shoulder-length black hair as opposed to blond, more mature clothing, less makeup. But it was the same trim athletic body and youthful face, and the eyes gave her away: boring through the camera, sharper than the scenery around her yet at the same time as lifeless and indifferent as two brown pebbles in a dried-up riverbed.

To her right was a man who looked more similar to the woman than Grey had realized in the hallway. Caught sipping a beverage on the columned balcony of a crumbling villa, he was taller and thicker but had the same smooth skin and dead eyes. Grey nodded in recognition. "That's them. God, how old are they?"

Lana closed the laptop and sat beside Grey. "We call them the Alianza twins, Lucho and Angel. Orphans raised in a slum of Mexico City, approximately twenty-five years old, drug mules for the Alianza Cartel since they could walk and *sicarios*—cartel assassins—since they were thirteen. Over a hundred reported hits between the two of them."

Grey tipped his head down and shook it. There wasn't much to say.

Lucho's heavy brow and downturned mouth lingered in Grey's vision, a fellow orphan who had fallen into the black hole of violence and never escaped its pull.

"Don't let their youth and good looks fool you," Fred said. "They're two of the most feared enforcers in Mexico. A particular specialty of theirs is seducing Mexican cops, handcuffing them to the bed, and burning them alive."

"I've seen their handiwork firsthand," Grey said. "They're good."

Fred grunted. "We've already got APBs out on them."

"You don't think they're gone by now?"

"Probably." Fred leaned forward on his elbows. "Look, we appreciate you coming down here, and while it's likely these two wastes of sperm fled back to Mexico, you should know they aren't the types inclined to leave witnesses alive."

Grey took a sip of coffee.

"You want some protection for a few days?"

"I fly back to New York tomorrow. I'll watch myself."

Fred reached for a toothpick and gave a slow nod. "I thought you might say that."

Lana rose. "Gentlemen, if you'll excuse me." She reached for Grey's hand. "We appreciate your assistance in this matter."

Grey shook her hand, which felt cool and firm and callused, like her personality. He couldn't stand when government agents used "we" instead of "I," as if they were trained to disavow all personal responsibility for their actions.

"I'll give you a ride," Fred said.

As they rolled through downtown, Fred said, "Your file says you're an expert in cults, or something like that?"

"That's my employer, Viktor Radek. He's a professor of religious phenomenology. I help on the investigations."

Fred clamped down on his toothpick. "What do you make of that stuff you saw last night? It's gotta be Santeria, but . . . you think it's strange that both the García and Lopez hits happened during a ceremony?"

"I think common sense tells us it's strange."

"Hey, what do you think about looking into the cult angle? I can probably get authorization for a couple of days' work, but don't go crazy or anything. I just want to know what we're dealing with. It'd help me out. If you have time?"

"I can spare a day or two. Want to tell me why everyone cares so much who murdered a bunch of drug dealers?"

Fred chewed harder on the toothpick. "You don't look like the kind of guy who deals in bullshit, so I won't bullshit you. Is the fact that we're looking for a bigger and badder player good enough for you?"

Grey was quiet for a moment. He had the impression he and Fred spoke the same language. "For now."

Fred's sedan crested the lime-green waters of the Intracoastal Waterway, swept onto Miami Beach, and took the off-ramp onto Fifth. When they reached the hotel and Grey stepped out of the car, Fred put his arm across the passenger headrest. "I assume you got hold of the police report?"

"I did."

"Any idea if that blue lady thing means anything? You know, cult-wise?"

"No idea," Grey said, "but I'll look into it."

Fred nodded, flipped the toothpick onto the sidewalk, and drove off.

11

After Fred dropped him off, Grey felt the need to cleanse. Hyper-aware of his surroundings as always, he took a long run on the crowded boardwalk, then relaxed in the ocean until his body cooled. Floating on his back, he admired the South Beach skyline hovering above the palms.

While the gritty energy of New York was more his style, the beauty of Miami helped relax his mind. It was harder to dwell on a troubled past and the injustices of the world when surrounded by a sleek metropolis with a gorgeous Caribbean backdrop.

In a haze of sunshine, Grey changed into jeans and a loose-fitting green T-shirt and walked to a sushi bar on Collins. Fresh fish and a bottle of crisp *sake* was the perfect digestif to an afternoon in the sun.

He wondered why Viktor hadn't called him back, and shrugged it off. It had only been a day, and Viktor always had a lot on his plate.

As he walked back to the hotel, Grey thought about the two cartel assassins, the sicarios. They had only gotten a quick look at him, and good luck finding out who he was—he lived as under the radar as anyone.

If the Alianza twins did happen to ID him and wanted to make a run at him, well, this wasn't Mexico, and they wouldn't find a passive target.

Grey made the call from his balcony, bottle of water in hand, the pinkening hues of dusk merging with the neon lights of the art deco district. Viktor answered on the fourth ring.

"Good evening, Grey. I apologize for not calling."

"Are you in Prague?"

There was a prolonged silence. "I'm in Switzerland. At a sanatorium."

"New case?"

"Not exactly," Viktor said, and Grey heard a note of uncertainty he had never heard in his friend's voice. As if he couldn't bring himself to say what he wanted.

Then it clicked, and Grey understood why Viktor had been so hard to reach the last few weeks. "The absinthe," he said, his voice quiet.

Viktor's voice was just above a whisper, as proud as a thousand-year-old glacier. "Yes."

"You checked yourself in?"

"At the urging of my niece."

"I didn't know you had a niece."

"My brother's daughter," Viktor said. "We've stayed close."

"After what you went through," Grey said softly, "I think you're doing great. No one should have to relive the past like that."

"I confess that greatness is not my current state of mind."

Grey chuckled. "Give it time, you'll return to form. I'm guessing it's a little bit better? Day by day?"

"Yes," Viktor said, though every word sounded forced. Grey could have eased the conversation away, or feigned ignorance in the first place, but in his opinion it was better to confront one's demons. A confronted demon is one with less power to subvert and consume.

The one thing Grey had truly desired during his years of aimless wandering, simmering in loneliness and shame and self-loathing, fighting a constant war against the rage and violence within, was someone in whom to confide. Not just anyone, but someone who could understand. Commiserate.

It had taken awhile, but for him, that someone had been Nya. Grey had never lacked confidence with women, but he saw the reflection of his soul as a cracked fun house mirror. Nya had started to correct the distortion, heal the broken edges.

Grey didn't know if he was that person for Viktor, but he would offer himself up, no matter how clumsy the attempt.

"I'm not very good at this sort of thing," Grey said, "but I'm always here if you need me. The way I see it, a struggle with the past is a struggle with the soul. Which means you have a good one."

"Not everyone turns to addiction to cope. It's a sign of weakness."

"It's a sign of empathy with the world. Who's able to cope with everything life can throw at them? Anyone who claims otherwise needs to go live in the

Horn of Africa during a drought. You've seen more tragedy than most, and yeah, sometimes we turn to other things and sometimes we need help. The best thing you can do is try to understand yourself so you can manage it better. Locking it away doesn't help. Trust me."

"Thank you, my friend. Sincerely."

Grey heard Viktor exhale, as if talking had exorcised some of his pent-up fears and worries.

"Let's discuss the matter at hand," Viktor said, "though I won't be discharged for a few more weeks, and my research capabilities are limited."

"Miami DEA wants us to look into the cult angle," Grey said. "I assume that's okay, at our usual rate?"

"Of course. How did that come about?"

Grey caught Viktor up on the events of the last twenty-four hours. After Viktor absorbed the information, Grey said, "What do you think? How are the Santeria ceremonies connected to the murders?"

"It wasn't Santeria. The ritual belonged to Palo Mayombe, a derivative of a Congolese religion known in the Americas as simply Palo."

"That's a new one on me. Is it anything like Juju?" Grey asked, feeling uneasy at the mere mention of the Yoruban religion. Though the cult in Zimbabwe had been a derivation of traditional Juju, some of what they had witnessed had forever altered Grey's view of reality. The *N'anga*, the Juju priest who had kidnapped Nya, had made Grey see things that weren't real, feel things that weren't there.

"Palo is completely distinct. In fact, it's one of the more complex and intriguing religions I've ever encountered, though the theology is quite . . . alien . . . to a Westerner."

"So far," Grey said, "this alien theology has produced a pair of black cauldrons filled with sticks and dirt and human bones."

"Santeria and Palo are the two predominant surviving African religions in Cuba," Viktor said, as if he hadn't heard Grey's comment, "though Santeria is far more prevalent. Few outsiders have heard of Palo Mayombe, and those in the know hesitate to speak of it."

Grey rubbed at his four-day stubble as he leaned against the balcony door. "That's never a good thing."

"I'm aware of the presence of Palo in Miami—this is not the first time the South Florida police have found human bones inside a *prenda*, or cauldron."

"I hate to ask," Grey said, "but why do people hesitate to talk about it?"

"Palo's belief system has lent it a rather . . . unwholesome . . . reputation. It's difficult to summarize, but at its core, a practitioner of Palo Mayombe works with the dead in order to affect the living."

"Come again?"

"Palo practitioners believe that a vast sea of dead spirits—known as *Kalunga*—surrounds us. Imagine the living as the fish in the ocean, and the dead as the water. To a believer of Palo Mayombe, we are quite literally swimming through a sea of the dead."

"I fully agree with you," Grey said. "That is, without a doubt, an alien worldview that lends itself to an unwholesome reputation. And the cauldrons?"

"In Palo, it's believed the most effective way to influence human affairs is to beseech Kalunga. The cauldron contains everyday items believed to hold the residue of the dead. Each prenda also contains the bones of a *nfumbe*, a deceased human being whose spirit, with the proper supplication and nourishment, will do the bidding of the Palo priest, or *palero*."

Grey held the phone away and frowned at it. "I gotta say, I don't like the sound of this religion."

"Palo Mayombe is viewed as a haven of sorcery and black magic. But like Juju, it's not an evil religion—just ancient and foreign."

Grey leaned an arm on the balcony railing. "How do you think the rituals are connected to the murders?"

"Beyond the obvious, that both took place during Palo ceremonies, I'm unsure."

"I found a shopping bag full of religious trinkets at the Lopez house: candles, chalk, beads and necklaces, some sort of bull's horn with a mirror on it."

"Vintage Palo material. The mirror allows the nfumbe, or resident spirit, to see the reflection of its soul."

"Yeah, well, speaking to *this* world, there was a receipt in the bag with the name Botánica Caldez. I looked it up; a botánica is an herb shop, though apparently in Miami they double as supply shops for Santeria."

"That's right," Viktor said. "Checking it out would be wise. Be discreet, but look for evidence that the shop supports Palo Mayombe."

Viktor sometimes forgot that Grey did not have a PhD and had not witnessed thousands of religious ceremonies. "Like black cauldrons full of skulls?"

"You'll know if the botánica is involved with Palo," Viktor said. "It will have a different feel."

"We'll see how it goes."

"Not to be dramatic, but Palo Mayombe is a secretive religion whose worshippers do not generally approve of outsiders probing their affairs. Add murderers and drug dealers to the mix and, well, I think you understand."

"I understand perfectly. That's why you hired me, remember? Hey, what about the blue lady in the witness report? Any idea what that's about?"

"It's an angle I'm still researching. I hope to have a better answer next time we speak."

"Fair enough. Take care of yourself, Viktor. Enjoy the clean air."

———————

Grey finished the night with a cold beer on the balcony. Though the details of the investigation disturbed him, especially the bizarre religion and the involvement of the CIA, he was happy to be working.

He also didn't deny that a part of him longed to please Nya with news of more arrests, higher up the poisoned food chain. He knew he still loved her, and felt his wall of carefully constructed denial starting to crumble.

As the night deepened, the lights of the art deco district illuminated the swirl of people on the street below, South Beach fashionistas striving for the most addictive drug of all, the elusive crown of social majesty. The fancy cars, yachts, clothes, people: he felt like the city was full of human squirrels scurrying around to collect as many shiny nuts as possible.

Where did it all get us? Grey wondered. When we left the jungle and washed and clothed ourselves, trimmed our hair and nails? Did it bring us closer to a creator, fulfill another step in evolution? Would we all be shiny hairless gods one day, smooth and golden and clothed in the universe's finest?

He took a swallow of beer. He didn't know.

He just knew he was fine right where he was.

12

After dropping Grey off, Fred headed to the office to fill out some paperwork. He cranked the A/C and pondered the case as he drove.

A South American crime lord with some kind of weird hold on the cartels? A blue Indian offing drug dealers at cult ceremonies? Cult *investigators*?

He still didn't get the CIA angle. Lana's explanation of the issues was reasonable, but why not involve Homeland Security? ATF? Border Patrol? All he knew was that if the CIA was in the game, there were reasons involved beyond what Lana was telling him. Reasons he probably wouldn't like.

He also wasn't sure what to make of Dominic Grey. Grey's government record was spottier than chicken pox on a leopard, and that professor he worked for sounded like a kook. Fred couldn't deny, though, that Grey was one cool customer. According to the police report, he'd taken out two of the dealers himself before facing down the sicarios in the hallway.

Fred was a fifteen-year veteran of hard-core sting operations, and he could take one look at someone and know if he could handle himself on the street. When he had first laid eyes on Dominic Grey, watching Fred and Lana coolly from in front of the hotel, danger vibes had radiated off of him like steam off a glacier.

Besides, Fred's record wasn't any better than Grey's, nor his career on any sort of upward trajectory—that ship had sailed. That ship was at the bottom of a whirlpool in the Pacific Ocean.

He was in a slump, the office shrink had told him.

Slump? He was participating in a personal cataclysm.

Fred hated the Suits in DEA headquarters who had steamrolled his career and who chose politics over what was right, and he got the feeling Dominic Grey felt the same. Idealistic and jaded, street smart and burned by the government, independent to a fault—maybe the two of them weren't so different after all.

After finishing his paperwork, Fred found an empty witness room and placed a call to Jimmy Nichols. Jimmy and Fred had been stationed in Tijuana together back in the nineties. *Now that,* Fred thought with a smile, *had been some crazy shit.* Busting up celebrity coke parties every week, riding motorcycles through underground drug tunnels, Wild West shoot-outs up and down the Baja.

Jimmy was a Suit now, but one of the rare ones who fought the good fight. Or at least tried to. With three kids in college and retirement looming, Jimmy had moved to the upper floors for the money and the pension, and Fred didn't blame him.

Jimmy's voice was an odd combination of a copacetic surfer and a smoker's growl. "Freddie, man! How's Northern South America treating you?"

"I can't stop sweating here. It's like someone left the oven on, all the time."

Jimmy chuckled. "You're the only Latino I know who doesn't like hot weather or soccer. I know you're loving that sweet eye candy, though."

"Yeah, sure, go to Lincoln Road any given night and you'll see twenty girls who make Jennifer Lopez look frumpy. It's not like they want my hairy paws groping them."

"If I know you, you're doing all right for yourself."

"To be honest," Fred said, "most nights I sit at home and wish I was with my kids."

"Hey, I hear you, man. You and Linda still separated?"

"Yeah."

"Sorry to hear that."

"I'm a real sob story these days," Fred said. "Listen, lemme run something by you, since you're the only Suit I trust."

"Shoot."

"You ever hear of a legendary dealer called El General?" Fred asked. "The General?"

"Course I have. I've heard of Batman and the chupacabra, too."

Fred bit down on his toothpick. "Yeah, that was my impression. You think it's possible there's any truth to it? Ever heard any of the other Suits talking about it?"

Jimmy took a moment to respond. "Here's the thing that makes me pause—

over the years there's been a lot of chatter about this guy, enough that we've got a file on him. But it doesn't make me pause long. One person couldn't possibly have the reach attributed to this guy, everything from Miami to Santiago. What would be the yoke? And the rumors have been around since the early eighties, maybe earlier—who do you know's been around that long?"

"No one," Fred said.

"That's right. And like I said, there's a lot of chatter on the chupacabra, too. Doesn't make it real, though *campesinos* from Puerto Rico to Texas will swear otherwise."

"So what is it, then?" Fred said. "How does a rumor like that even get started?"

"Headquarters thinks it's some sort of bogeyman for drug dealers. Someone they can blame when they don't want to take the heat, or maybe someone to keep the troops in line."

"When have cartels ever had a problem keeping troops in line? And what's this blue Indian lady all about? She's been seen before."

"The one who shows up once a decade to murder wayward drug dealers? C'mon, Freddie. You know how reliable eyewitness reports are. Someone way back in the day probably saw a Panamanian sicario in a blue poncho, and the legend grew from there. Hell, maybe someone's *impersonating* a blue Indian now, just to rile up the masses. What's this all about, anyway?"

"There was a hit a few nights ago in North Miami. We've got a crack whore said she saw a blue Indian take out a crew of dealers. I interviewed her myself, made the report. The next day a spook came to Miami talking about investigating El General."

Jimmy laughed.

"That's the reaction I thought you'd have," Fred said.

"They've got balls, don't they? The CIA would spread disinformation about Santa Claus if it served their purpose."

Fred chatted a while longer and then closed his cell. He sat at the conference table, legs crossed, toothpick in his mouth, unable to shake the sight of that cracked-out witness in the back of the police car, the pot of bones sitting in the field outside, and the four dead bodies rotting in the sun.

Just after noon Fred drove over to Flanigan's, a neighborhood bar in Coconut Grove festooned with fisherman's kitsch. The place did a brisk lunch hour, and Fred walked past tables of boisterous patrons feasting on fried shrimp platters and blackened snapper sandwiches.

At the rear of the joint, he slid into a booth across from Ernesto Reinas, an accountant with a nasty coke habit who had spent the last three years on the DEA payroll. Caught with an eight ball of coke during a traffic stop, fearing the loss of his cushy lifestyle in paradise, Ernesto had told the police he had two minor drug dealers as clients and would give them up in exchange for amnesty.

Amnesty had been given, but at a much higher price: the DEA had insisted that Ernesto grow his client base and work as a narc. With the DEA's help, the poor accountant's reputation within the drug world had exploded, as had his stress level and coke habit. He now advised a bevy of mid-level players on how to launder their money, while the DEA kept promising to release him once he handed over a few big fish. Fred knew Ernesto would be their pawn until the day he offed himself in his garage.

Ernesto was hunched in the back of the booth, underneath a fishing net nailed to the wall. The metrosexual type, he had manicured nails and a curling feminine mouth. On weekends Fred imagined he drove around in a golf cart all day, then sipped fruity martinis poolside at his country club.

"I don't have anything new," Ernesto said, his voice low and defeated. He snuffled, and Fred noticed the redness lining his nostrils.

Fred gave him a broad grin, then ordered a plate of ribs and a Budweiser. Once the waiter left, Fred said, "I'm not here to bust your balls today."

Ernesto took a nervous sip of iced tea, pushing his half-finished salad to the side. "Yeah."

"How's the family?" Fred asked.

"Fine," he muttered.

"The business?"

"Good."

"Great. You're a busy guy, I won't waste your time. I just need a bit of info."

Fred chomped down on a succulent bit of pork fat. Flanigan's had the best ribs in town. "I know this is a little off the wall, but you ever heard of someone called El General?"

"There're plenty of generals on the cartel payrolls. You know that."

"I mean *El* General."

"What? No."

"Take a moment to think about it," Fred said, chewing as he watched Ernesto, who exhibited no signs of deception. After a few more bites Fred asked, "Aren't you curious who he is?"

"Not really."

"It's a name we've been hearing. Someone high-level, maybe very high-level, who has a hand in the cookie jar. Maybe a few of them."

"I'll check the books if you want," Ernesto said, his voice devoid of emotion.

"Do that, though I'm sure the payments are off the books or under a series of fronts."

"That's what I meant."

"Look for a string of payments by various cartels to one source," Fred said.

"I would have noticed that."

"Probably, but check again. Be clever, think of an angle. You're much smarter than they are."

Ernesto didn't respond to the flattery, merely took another sip of tea and slumped farther in his seat.

"Start with the Alianza Cartel. You have a couple of clients there, right?"

"Oh God," Ernesto muttered, mashing his hands together in front of his glass. "I don't even like thinking about them."

"Sorry pal, you know the deal. I'll check in again on Friday. That should be enough time, right?"

This time Fred couldn't even hear Ernesto's response, just saw his lips move in affirmation.

Later that afternoon Fred took to the street, trolling the fringes of Overtown looking for Freckles, an informant whose light African-American skin was dotted by so many pepper-colored marks that his face looked like a Pointillist painting.

Freckles had been a cocaine dealer for most of his life before succumbing to the lure of his own product. Though not as useful as he used to be, Freckles had his ear to the ground and was a wealth of information on the old guard.

Fred rolled through the treeless, sunbaked streets, flat and narrow as tapeworms, possessed of an eerie calm that he knew was due to the residents' fear of venturing outside. Overtown was one of the oldest neighborhoods in Miami, developed to house the railroad construction workers—ex-slaves—who had helped carve Miami out of the swamp. The construction of I-95 and the Dolphin Expressway had gutted the historic neighborhood.

After a few hours of rolling through the ghettos and trash-filled streets, he gave up and moved a few blocks north to Liberty City, an even worse neighborhood, its street corners marked by toys that served as memorials to slain children.

He found Freckles lounging on a cardboard box underneath I-95. Somewhere around forty-five years old, he looked seventy.

"Let's take a ride," Fred said.

Freckles didn't even argue, just got in the car with his hand out, his movements quivery. Fred kept a hand on his gun, wary that Freckles might be part of the "bath salts" epidemic plaguing the homeless population. "Ivory wave," "zoom," and "cloud nine" were a hodgepodge of cheap synthetic chemicals that poured dopamine into the brain and led to violent hallucinations. The drug had resulted in a rash of gruesome crimes, including a homeless man in Miami who had eaten the face off another man in broad daylight.

Fred slipped him a twenty, checking Freckles's eyes for signs of dilation or disassociation. "There's two more of those at the end of the ride."

"What'cha need, my man? You know I ain't know much no more. Gonna change, though. Gonna change."

For some reason, Fred had a tiny soft spot for Freckles. Maybe it was because no matter how bad things got, Freckles remained an optimist, at least on the surface. In a country full of depressed middle- and upper-class citizens with full bellies and two-car garages and 401(k)s, Fred found that refreshing.

"You hang in there, Freckles. Want me to drop you at the treatment center when we're done?"

"Nah, you just drop me right where you got me. Now what's it be?"

"You know about the recent murders? Frankie Garcìa and Manny Lopez?"

"Everybody heard."

"What's the word on the street? Seemed a bit excessive, even for the Alianza. And I'm told Manny was on the fast track."

"Well, that don't matter none, these days there's a kid on every corner waitin' to take his place. Twenty of 'em. But those there murders, make no mistake about it. They was a message."

"A message from the Alianza?" Fred asked.

"Well, that's the thing don't make no sense, cuz them cats ain't known for caring who get hurt. Ain't like the old days. We had codes and shit, you know what I'm sayin'?" His fingers slipped as he tried to crack a knuckle. "But that done changed."

"Think you can make some inquiries, maybe get me a name? It might be something we're interested in, if you know what I mean."

Fred saw a greedy light in the corner of the informant's drug-addled eyes. "Yeah, sure, I'll ask around."

"I want to know who put the order in. Those were professional hits on American soil. Extradition fodder."

"Like I said, I ain't got no pull like I used to, but I'll see what I can do."

"Good man," Fred said, then decided to go out on a limb. "Back in the day when you were dealing, you ever hear about someone named the General? Some high-level player down South who pulls strings?"

"Freddie, you finally been dippin' into that DEA stockpile?"

Freckles cackled, and Fred caught a whiff of breath that smelled like a dead squirrel decomposing in a garbage can. Funnily, he also thought he heard a nervous edge underlying the laughter. He'd known Freckles to be many things, but never nervous.

They rolled to a stoplight, and Fred tightened his grip on his weapon as a group of teenagers approached his car with rags and a bottle of Windex. He waved them off. "Nah, I'm serious. What if someone like that ordered those hits? Like you said, making a statement."

Freckles tried to grin, but it turned into a spasm and contorted his face. "Hey man, I need me some crib. What say you take me back?"

Fred did a U-turn at the light and wound back through Liberty City. As they reached the underpass where he had found Freckles, Fred took a hundred-dollar bill out of his wallet and placed it on his thigh. The informant's eyes were twin lasers focused on the bill.

"What do you know about this guy, Freckles? A rumor's fine. Does it have anything to do with the recent hit, the blue lady?"

"Creepy blue Indians killin' folk with slingshots and knives? You know we a superstitious race. I don't want no part of that."

"We kept the slingshot out of the police report."

Freckles swallowed as his eyes slipped downward. Fred handed him the bill, retaining his grip as his informant reached for it.

Freckles sat back. "Okay, yeah, back in the day rumor was there was someone bad out there. *Real* bad. Someone even the high-level cats were scared of. And they don't scare."

"Who is this guy?"

"I got no idea, man. I always figured it was bullshit. Hey, we dealers got urban legends just like the straight folk do. All I know is there's supposed to be somebody down in South America who pulls strings like you said, and can hit you anytime, anywhere. That blue Indian, he uses her to get under people's skin. S'posed to be some spirit he calls up for vengeance on dealers who step outta line."

Fred would have laughed if Freckles didn't look so serious. "Why don't you see if the rumor's still around?" He released his grip on the hundred-dollar bill. "There's more of these if you dig something up, on this or who ordered the Lopez hit."

Freckles snatched the bill, then pointed a crooked finger at Fred. The tip of the digit couldn't stay still, like a fishing bob with something nibbling on the line. "I'll ask around 'bout Manny, but you leave that other thing be. Ain't no one gonna help stir that pot. Even the DEA got limits."

13

Lana woke bleary-eyed, having spent most of the night poring over CIA records. She was looking for a connection, a ghost in the machine, that ephemeral association among seemingly unrelated parts that would lead her to her quarry.

Unfortunately, she had come up short. And that did not sit well with Lana Valenciano. Trained to look for patterns in both people and databases, she had been one of the Company's best analysts before switching gears to become one of their most driven field operatives.

After reviewing the painfully thin CIA file on the General for the umpteenth time, she had pored over the records of agents who had gone missing in action south of the border over the last four decades. Not an easy task. Eventually she might have to broaden her search; she supposed the General could have dropped off the radar somewhere else and made his way to Latin America. It made less sense, but at this point, she was willing to try anything.

She prepared a *cafecito* and stepped onto the balcony of the Brickell condo at which she was staying, one of the CIA's safe houses. Brickell was Miami's new business district, full of lush foliage and chic restaurants and sleek glass buildings. It had exploded since Lana had left Miami after high school.

As she turned to go inside, she saw her reflection in the window, the hardened limbs and stress-filled eyes. The city wasn't the only thing that had changed since graduation.

Needing a break from the data, she pondered her options as she showered. The analysts would monitor the chatter. Fred would work the street for her. What she needed was a different sort of information, something beyond the scope of the DEA.

Something that shouldn't exist.

Or someone, rather. Colonel Ganso was a distasteful resource, and consulting him required authorization from the highest levels.

Luckily for Lana, she had such authorization. And she had something even better: she had grown up next door to him.

———•———

After a power breakfast of oatmeal and a fruit smoothie, Lana took her customary morning jog, followed by taekwondo and self-defense routines. She scanned the news outlets and her inbox, then headed out in her company sedan.

Memories of her childhood in Miami overcame her as she left Brickell via the corridor of flame trees on South Miami Avenue. She loved this city, with its sensual humid nights, afternoon showers, and endless sunny mornings that could scatter the worst of memories into tiny motes of light.

And Miami, for Lana, possessed the worst of memories.

She could still draw a map of the Fairchild Botanical Gardens, picture the evening light sinking into No Name Harbor, and tell friends visiting the city where to find the best ceviche, the most authentic sangria, the perfect little wine shop hidden in the maze of Cuban bakeries on Coral Way. She loved the smell of roasting coffee, the sexy fashion boutiques, the day trips to the Everglades and the weekend trips to the Keys, the serendipity of a peacock sighting on the way to the grocery store, the delight of biting into one of the mangoes weighing down the limbs of neighborhood trees in summer.

She knew that for most people, Miami was not a shade-filled paradise with maids and lanai-covered pools. Yet she also knew, all too well, that money did not buy happiness. Though her mother still owned the house in Coral Gables, Lana almost never visited. She loved her mother, but had never forgiven her for not standing up to her father. A prominent importer who spent most of his time in Europe, her father had kept his wife resigned to the life of a show poodle and held Lana, whose will he could never quite overcome, at arm's length.

Lana rolled down Miracle Mile, though the only miracle about this stretch of Coral Gables, littered with bridal boutiques and surgically enhanced telenovela wannabes, was that it had not dropped into a sinkhole under the weight of its own pretension. Shaking her head, she turned her attention to Colonel Ganso.

Since the Freedom of Information Act reared its ugly head, it was known that in the early 1980s, in order to oust the socialist-minded Bolivian government, the CIA had supported a group of cocaine overlords and neo-fascist mercenaries who took over the country, resulting in a violent dictatorship known for torturing its citizenry. Dubbed the "Cocaine Coup," Colonel Ganso had been a key player in the new government. Trained in the art of torture by the Argentine secret police during the Dirty Wars, who were in turn trained by the CIA, Colonel Ganso had gone on a rampage to oust "leftists" from Bolivia. They called him the Butcher of Santa Cruz.

The CIA had turned a blind eye because, at the time, it was the expedient thing to do. Colonel Ganso was an unfortunate by-product, a known torturer and murderer who, along with countless other Latin American strongmen stashing drug money and damning information on the United States offshore, had been given asylum and new identities when their brutal regimes were overthrown.

And where did a disproportionate amount of those former torturers and dictators call home?

Miami.

If the residents of Coral Gables and Pinecrest knew just how many of their neighbors were in fact war criminals given a free pass by the U.S. government, they might have relocated to Alaska.

Lana knew, and she could feel the sticky sins of the past crawling up the vines of the banyans and worming through the eaves of the ivy-covered mansions. Even growing up, before she had access to CIA files, Lana had felt the Colonel's reptilian gaze when she was in her swimming pool, had felt his eyes stripping not just her clothes, but her essence, her dignity. It was what he was trained to do: use torture to reduce another human being to such a state that his or her identity was lost, subsumed in pain and fear.

And Lana had felt it from across the lawn.

Passing by the majestic Biltmore Hotel, she delved deep into the heart of her old neighborhood. Chock full of Mediterranean architecture and enveloped in mature hardwoods and fruit trees, Coral Gables screamed wealth and power.

She passed by the house where the Bad Thing had happened, the one that had changed the course of her identity, and a few houses later she was pulling into the driveway of her childhood home, a double-story villa with a terracotta roof and a walkway lined with royal palms.

Her mother was visiting relatives in Tampa, and Lana didn't bother going inside. Instead she smoothed her pants and walked next door to Colonel Ganso's flat-roofed stucco house, painted a soothing soft orange and shrouded by a forest of bamboo.

Lana had negotiated with dictators and arms dealers, CEOs and heads of state, but none affected her as this man had, which she attributed to the impressionability of childhood.

She pressed the doorbell and forced herself to remember who she was and where she had been. The Colonel himself answered. Still a handsome man, tall and trim, he looked remarkably like her own father, something she had always held against them both.

But it was the secrets hidden behind the Colonel's green eyes that always spooked her. A gaze that contained the knowledge of souls stripped bare, bodies wracked by torture.

"Lana! *Que sorpresa.*" *What a pleasant surprise.*

Lana switched to English, where she had the advantage. "Do you have a moment? I know this is an unofficial visit, but there's something on which I'd like your opinion."

"Of course, of course," he said, unfailingly polite as always. "Would you care for coffee?"

"Please," she said.

He led her down a garden path on the side of the property adjoining Lana's house, to a sitting area that overlooked Lana's mother's pool. A maid brought two cups and a *moka* pot of coffee.

After the maid retreated, the Colonel asked, "And to what may I attribute the pleasure of such a rare treat? Are you visiting your mother?"

"I'm in Miami on business."

His forehead lifted. "Business that involves me?"

She nodded slowly. They each knew who the other was; Colonel Ganso was a high-level informant for the CIA, and Lana had interviewed him on occasion. Though the first time interviewing her neighbor had been awkward, Lana had requested the assignment. She was a woman who confronted her demons.

Nor was she worried about her identity. Except for the blackest of operatives, complete anonymity was a Hollywood myth, and the Colonel had no idea what she did at the CIA. Also, like other war criminals with asylum in the States, the Colonel's life depended on the discretion of the U.S. government.

And somehow, Lana knew he would never put her in harm's way—unless that harm involved the Colonel himself.

"Just a few questions about the past," she said.

He grinned. "Isn't that what it always is? I have no present or future. How's your father, Lana?"

Lana stiffened. "The same as always, I assume. I wouldn't know."

"Yes, yes. And your mother?"

"Even more static. And your family, how are they?"

It was a jab. The Colonel's wife and daughter had been slain by hit men from a rival cartel days before the CIA had brought him to the States.

"Tsk tsk," the Colonel said. "I was being polite."

"No, you weren't. You know how I feel about my father."

"I was hoping things had changed."

"Were you? I think you were trying to get under my skin, as you always have."

The smile broadened even farther. "So wrong, Lana, so wrong. I've always cared for you."

The way he said the words *cared for you* sent a shiver down her spine. When the Bad Thing happened in the house down the street, a group of Cuban street thugs had stumbled on the scene, presumably when trying to break in. The thugs had freed Lana and disappeared, along with the serial rapist. A week later, her attacker had been found in a dumpster, shot and tortured almost beyond recognition.

The authorities assumed it had been the vigilante work of one of the victims' fathers, but Lana knew better. She knew the Colonel had somehow found the man and defended her honor and lost virginity.

She should have been relieved, but it only made her feel more uneasy around him. As if something of his had been taken, and he had rectified it.

The incident had changed her forever, morphing her from an easy-going cheerleader destined for a U of F sorority into a laser-focused overachiever with a death wish, destined for the highest levels of the CIA.

"Let's dispense with the small talk," Lana said. "I need your input on something. I'm looking for a man, a criminal, known as El General. Not *un* general, but *El* General. Do you know of whom I speak?"

Colonel Ganso unfurled his left palm, revealing a stack of dominoes. As was his habit, he began to stand the dominoes on the table and let them fall into his palm. "You know, Lana, I remember what your dream job used to be. You used to aspire to open your own wedding boutique."

Lana gave a harsh laugh. "The inventor of the AK-47 wanted to be a poet. What's your point?"

"That is my point. We often get the opposite of what we want in life, find ourselves in the most absurd situations. But we accept them. Sometimes the choice is to accept them or die."

"Thus your shadow existence in this prison of a house."

He tipped his head downward, acknowledging the point. "But there is often a turning point. A fateful moment when we still have the opportunity to follow our dreams, no matter the consequences—or bow in resignation and accept our fate. It may be a choice of career or love or family, or something else entirely. You might think that your turning point has already passed. In my humble opinion, you would be wrong."

"Are you trying to tell me that pursuing this man is my turning point?"

The dominoes stacked and fell on the table, stacked and fell. "I am simply saying," he said softly, "that you might wish to consider carefully such an inquiry. I would not wish to see your future choice taken from you."

"I believe I can take care of myself."

His eyes found hers as he continued to sort the dominoes, and she knew what he was thinking. *Like I took care of myself when I was raped?*

Lana checked her watch, though she didn't have an appointment. "Don't forget at whose mercy you exist," she said coldly. "I'd prefer to keep this visit cordial. All I'm asking for is information. What do you know about this man?"

"A former colleague of mine dealt once with his associate, Señor Guiñol. Are you aware of him? I believe he's known in Colombia as *el doctor de zombi*."

"Doctor Zombie. We're aware. He went underground years ago."

"This man arrived one night at a meeting between my colleague and one of our Colombian partners," Colonel Ganso said. "I was out of the country on business. At the meeting, we learned that our Colombian partner had failed to pay Señor Guiñol's superior the proper allotment for his services."

"What kind of services?"

"Bribery of a customs official."

Lana leaned forward. "What happened?"

"Our associate left the meeting under the care of Señor Guiñol. Voluntarily. He was never seen again."

Lana interlaced her fingers. "What else do you know?"

He clacked the dominoes together. "Only that he was a man to whom we could always turn for help, and who even the *Colombianos* would not cross."

"Help?"

He waved a hand. "Extra product. Government relations. Bribes."

"But who is he? Where is he based, where does he keep his money?"

"Simple questions all, yet I do not have the answers."

"His nationality?"

Colonel Ganso shook his head.

"Do you know of anyone who has met him in person?"

"No."

"Physical appearance, even the rumor thereof?"

"He was a man without a face."

Lana sat back, frustrated. "This is absurd."

"Have you ever considered, Lana, where a man who protects himself so extraordinarily well might have learned his craft?"

She looked at him sharply, but his eyes betrayed nothing. "I need you to think long and hard about our conversation," she said, "and whether there's anything in your past that might help. I'll check back in a few days."

His cultured voice was a purr that sent a shiver down her spine. "I look forward to it."

14

The next morning Grey followed his Google directions through downtown and onto Eighth Avenue, known as *Calle Ocho* in Miami, delving into the heart of Little Havana.

It was another world. Grey had been posted in Bogotá and had traveled in other Latin American nations, and he could not tell the difference. The signs in Little Havana were in Spanish, pedestrians and stray dogs crowded the streets, sketchy health clinics and panhandlers and iron-barred grocery stores selling strange fruits and vegetables lined the sidewalks.

But it was also a world of banyan-shaded patios, street art and tiled murals, cozy cigar lounges, Cuban diners, parks filled with wizened old men in guayaberas pushing squadrons of clacking dominoes across a table, aromas of garlic and rum and dried tobacco. Every block full of life, throbbing to the unique cacophony of Miami: techno and merengue blasting above vendors shouting in Spanglish, the rattle of low-riding hoopties competing with the roar of exotic sports cars, the melodic chatter of tropical birds a calming backdrop to it all.

Grey parked a few blocks from the botánica and grabbed a *cortadito*, a sugary Cuban espresso, from one of the coffee windows fronting the street. By ten a.m. the humidity took his breath away. He thought about his game plan and then strolled to Botánica Caldez, the name on the bag of paraphernalia he had spotted at Manny Lopez's bungalow.

There were no windows, and a bell tinkled as he stepped inside. A sign just inside the door read SI LO ROMPES, TE VAMOS HACER UNA BRUJERIA. *If you break it, we curse you.*

A strong whiff of incense hit him as he strolled around the shop. Metal shelves lined the walls, stuffed with the tools of the trade: candles, oils, plastic and ceramic statues of saints, feathers, cowrie shells, beads. Grey browsed a bookshelf along the rear wall, rubbing shoulders with two other patrons.

As far as Grey could tell, none of the literature involved Palo. He circled the shop and returned to the side of the counter nearest the exit.

The sallow-skinned Latino man behind the counter eyed Grey with a neutral expression. He was medium height and dumpy, with a round face and oily hair. Grey noticed faint chalk marks on his fingertips. "Can I help you?" the man said, in heavily accented English.

"I think so." Grey tried to reduce his predatory vibe and sound like a curious patron. Though uncomfortable in social situations, for some reason Grey had no problem playacting. He supposed it was because he had to reveal nothing of his true self. "This is my first time to a botánica."

"And you're looking for . . . ?"

Grey put a hand on the counter and gave a hesitant grin. "Religious material."

The man swept an arm outward, palm up. "There is something particular I can help with?"

Grey eyed the rack of books. "I noticed you have lots of material on Santeria."

"*Sí, señor*. This is a botánica."

"Yeah, I was actually looking for something different. You don't carry anything on Palo Mayombe, do you?"

The man's demeanor changed in an instant. His eyes narrowed and he folded his arms into a wary defensive stance. Grey also sensed a level of competence, a shrewdness, he hadn't noticed before. Out of the corner of his eye, he saw the other two patrons stop moving.

"Who tell you this?" the man behind the counter said.

Grey put his hands up. "Hey man, just a friend who's into it. I can't seem to find anyplace that carries supplies."

The man eyed him for a long moment. "Maybe your friend, he is misinformed," he said. "We no carry Palo here."

"No? That's too bad. Any idea where else I might look?"

"No, *señor*."

Grey shrugged. "Thanks anyway. I'll try another botánica."

As Grey turned to leave, another customer stepped through a swinging door behind the counter, carrying a bundle of sticks. Grey got a glimpse of a small back room filled with more stick bundles, unmarked glass bottles, animal skulls, colored candles, and a row of black cauldrons squatting on the floor.

The man at the counter caught Grey's glimpse. His eyes followed Grey out the door.

The sun made Grey squint as he stepped outside, and the sensory overload of Calle Ocho returned in a rush. He took out his cell and called the number Fred had given him.

"Agent Hernandez."

"It's Grey. I need you to look something up for me. Names and addresses for the owner and employees of Botánica Caldez on Eighth Street."

"Sure. What gives?"

"I saw a bag of goodies from this place at the Lopez house. I checked it out and I think there's a connection. I'll explain more when we meet."

"Which is when?"

"Depends on how fast you get me those names."

"I'll get back to you this afternoon."

On his way back to his car, Grey saw a giant *jaguey* tree providing shade for a sliver of green space, its latticework of roots jutting three feet off the ground. As a pair of roosters scrambled through the park, Grey noticed an odd-looking bundle embedded in the roots.

He stepped closer, and saw it was similar to the bundle he had seen in Manny Lopez's house: a small packet wrapped in black cloth and sealed with wax. Next to the bundle was a bull horn topped with a dirty mirror, warping Grey's visage as he peered into it.

After leaving Little Havana, Grey swung into a coffee shop in Coconut Grove on his way back to the hotel. He checked his email on his cell—no messages—and did a spot of research on Palo Mayombe. Reading through websites of dubious scholarship echoed what Viktor had told him, with more inflamed rhetoric. Palo was indeed a bizarre religion, though to Grey it possessed a strange sort of logic, if one believed in spirits. Dead souls in history outnumbered the living by a vast majority, and if consciousness was not destroyed but stuck around in another form of energy, then yeah, everyone could be swimming in a sea of ghosts. It fit with the laws of science concerning conservation of matter—weird science, that was.

Like most obscure religions, it was hard to go past the surface on the Internet, which was why Viktor's firsthand knowledge was often so crucial to law enforcement. The only thing Grey learned was that Palo Mayombe involved a lot of blood and bones and was shrouded in secrecy, and everyone seemed terrified of it.

He also found a few Miami news articles from recent years describing gruesome crime scenes with suspected connections to Palo, including a pile of decapitated goats discovered near Biscayne Bay, human fetuses found inside jars at the Miami airport, and a ring of grave robbers charged with stealing bones from local cemeteries.

He logged off and walked through the Grove's touristy center to find some lunch. As he passed a series of charming cafés with chalkboard menus and ivy-covered patios, he wished he and Nya were sitting at a table together, fingers intertwined, speaking with eyes instead of words.

Miami could be a good place for them. Nya said the city's foliage and smells reminded her of Harare, and Miami felt like nowhere else to Grey, a limbo in time and place, an edgy paradise poised somewhere between the slick commerce of North America and the seedy languor of a banana republic. A place to drift and dream and disappear. The perfect haven for two lost souls.

His cell rang at the same time he decided on Peruvian take-out. The call was from Fred.

"What'cha got?" Grey asked.

"There's only one owner and one employee at Botánica Caldez, and they're one and the same. Name's Hector Fortuna."

"Criminal record?"

"Not yet. He's legal, too. Born in Cuba, came to the States on lottery. Passport records show he spent six months in Mexico a few years back, and hasn't left Miami since. Shall we set up a little chat with him?"

"Yeah, but I'd like to see who shows up for dinner first," Grey said. "Can that be arranged?"

"You bet."

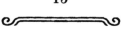

15

Later that evening, Grey found himself kneeling next to Fred on the roof of an apartment complex on U.S. 1, also known as South Dixie Highway, the main artery through South Miami. With the aid of high-powered binoculars, the rooftop provided a convenient view of Hector Fortuna's front door.

The stretch of U.S. 1 below them separated the affluent neighborhood of Pinecrest from Kendall, a sprawling suburb that was the epicenter of the Cuban-American middle class. Hector's property was on the Kendall side, bordered by a canal and a scruffy park. Fred and Grey had been camped out since four p.m., an hour before Hector's botánica had closed. So far, no one besides Hector had appeared.

Fred handed Grey the binoculars. "Keep an eye out for a minute? I need a soda. You want one?"

"No thanks."

Fred wiped his forehead and guzzled half a can of Coca-Cola. "I've never looked so forward to sunset. Maybe if I was as thin as you I'd stay cooler. You on the South Beach diet or something?"

Grey chuckled. "I run."

"You look pretty athletic, ever tried your hand at a proper sport?"

"My father taught me to fight from the age of five. I was never allowed to do anything else."

"Military?"

"Yeah. Marines."

"He must've been a proud papa when you made Recon."

Grey didn't answer.

"I'm sorry," Fred said. "He passed?"

"No idea. I left home at sixteen, haven't seen him since."

Fred returned to the binoculars. "So how about those Yankees?"

Grey had always been insanely jealous of the other kids who played sports, especially those he saw tossing a baseball with their dads. Grey's shining moment with his father had occurred after a fight at school when he was nine, just before moving to Japan. In the principal's office, the principal had told Grey's father that although Grey hadn't started the fight, he had refused to quit when the teachers broke it up.

On the car ride home, Grey's father asked him if he had won. Grey said yes.

The pat on the knee that followed was the only praise he had ever received from his father.

"Tell me about the Alianza Cartel," Grey said.

"They're one of the older ones, more Mafia-like, not as high profile as the Zetas or the Knights. But they're no less deadly."

"Where's the power base?"

"The Yucatan Peninsula. Cancun."

Grey flicked his eyes Fred's way, surprised. "I didn't realize there was a cartel in Cancun."

Fred laughed. "There's a cartel *everywhere* in Mexico. The Alianza works the Caribbean."

"So what's their affiliation with this cult?"

"None that I know of," Fred said. "That's why we're kneeling on this roof."

"I'll give you some advice from my employer: when you're dealing with cults, pretend you're on the inside looking out. My guess is not many cults or religions, including Palo Mayombe, would smile upon drug dealing. But if there is a connection, it exists for a reason."

"Ten-four."

"Speaking of connections, we have our first visitors." Grey returned the binoculars to Fred, noticing that dusk had crept up on them. "Two people approaching from the Mercedes across the street."

"C'mon," Fred said as he focused, "turn around for Daddy. That's it, that's it . . . damn. I didn't get their faces."

Mosquitoes became a constant annoyance, lizards slipped in and out of cracks in the wall. Over the next thirty minutes, Grey noticed the faint outline of four more people arriving.

Fred whistled. "I recognized three of those four. Alianza middlemen. And there's another getting out of a Jag . . . it's an Alianza happy hour in there."

Grey sat watchful beside him, one eye on the door to the roof, the other gazing on the scene below. Fred counted off twelve arrivals in total.

After an hour passed without another visitor, Fred lowered the telescopic lens. "At least seven were Alianza, and those are just the ones I recognized. My guess is all of them. Good instincts. There's definitely a connection."

Grey could smell grilled meat from somewhere below, and realized how hungry he was. Just before midnight Fred reported that all twelve had left the house. "Thirteen, counting Hector," he said. "That mean anything? You know, like a coven or something?"

"That's probably mixing metaphors," Grey said, "but who knows, I'll ask Viktor."

"Say, you find out anything on that blue lady?"

"Not yet."

Fred grunted. Grey thought he could read something in Fred's mannerisms, something he wasn't disclosing, but Grey didn't press. At this stage, Grey and Viktor were providing consultation services. If Fred wanted to play coy, that was his business.

Fred walked to the ledge, crossed his arms, and peered over. "You know what I think? I think we need to get inside that house."

Grey inverted his wrists and stretched them, a habit from the dojo. "I wouldn't disagree. Any ideas?"

"Yeah, actually. Want to grab some food and hear about it?"

"Now you're talking."

———— • ————

Fred took Grey to a bar near the river with low rafters and scuffed wooden floors. "Ain't much to look at," Fred said, "but the food's great." He proceeded to order a draft Budweiser, a plate of wings, and a double order of onion rings.

Grey opted for a burger and a Presidente, a Nicaraguan lager that was the draft special.

"At least you eat burgers," Fred said. "That makes you a little bit American."

Grey took a long swallow of beer. After a half-day stakeout in the Miami sun, it tasted like nectar.

"Not gonna bite, huh?"

"Not on that," Grey said.

"You political?"

"Nope."

"Me neither," Fred said. "But since you're a captive audience, I'll tell you what I think. Republicans are greedy people who vote their pocketbooks and will do anything to preserve the status quo. Democrats are bleeding hearts who, as soon they get enough money, become Republicans. The blacks and Latinos know the deck is stacked against them and aim for the middle class, so they're Democrats. The poor whites want to preserve their lottery-shot chance at being rich, so they're all Republicans. And that, my friend, is America in a nutshell."

Grey chuckled. "I think even most politicians are like everyone else, wondering how the hell they got there and why the world is so hard to change. Though they're also thinking *damn* that caviar tastes good, and maybe I better do what it takes to keep it coming."

Fred chortled. "Ain't that the truth. When did this world go to hell, anyway?"

Grey rolled his beer between his palms. He didn't think it was a new development. "So that's why you do what you do? To make the world a better place?"

Fred finished a wing and licked a finger. "People will tell you the war on drugs is a farce, because drugs are obviously what people want, and that's why they buy them."

"The Prohibition argument."

Fred nodded. "It used to be true. But let me tell you, nobody wants today's drugs. They don't want meth and crank and cheap pharmaceutical concoctions that eat your flesh and steal your soul. Today's drugs are destroying whole swaths of this country. They're our Black Plague." He picked up another wing and pointed it at Grey. "But that's not it, either. Honestly, I could give a damn about the adult users. They're lost causes anyway. It's the kids that get me, Grey. The kids."

Grey saw something pass across Fred's visage, a pain that went deep, deeper than anything to do with the job.

Fred continued, "All we're doing is lowering street prices, creating horrific synthetic drugs, and spawning drug dealers like salmon. You want to know my solution to the drug wars? Legalize the soft and medium drugs, and regulate the hard stuff for adults. But anyone who sells crank to a kid—put those people on an island together, cut down all the fruit trees, and sink the boat they came in on."

"That I'm on board with," Grey said softly, thinking of Sekai, as well as Charlie and his students at the shelter, most of them approached on a daily basis.

Fred pounded his beer. "Anyway. I'm still not sold on this Hansel and Gretel cult crap, but let's see where it leads. I've got someone inside the Alianza faction in Miami. Should be able to get us inside. Someone in there knows Manny's handler."

"Tell him to bone up on Palo Mayombe," Grey said. "My guess is Hector's house doubles as a drug drop and a house of worship."

"It's not a him, it's a her. She's hot as lava rocks, and has one of the major players in the Alianza slobbering all over her."

"That always helps."

"I'll get a wire on her, stick her in there and see what happens. And I'd like you around to translate the cult stuff."

Grey gave a slow nod, thinking, *Viktor is who you really need.* "Keep me posted."

16

Grey called Viktor from his balcony the next morning, the ocean breeze ruffling his hair.

"You're up early," Viktor said.

"You know me, late to bed and early to rise, insomnia in between. Thought I'd give you a ring before my run." He thought he detected a note of breathlessness in Viktor's voice. "Are you walking?"

"Indeed I am. I have to say, one cannot overestimate the benefits of fresh air and a stiff walk."

"I'm sure beautiful Alpine scenery doesn't hurt. You sound good, Viktor."

"I can't remember the last time I took this much time off work. Or any time."

"I hate to be the one to drag you back."

"Bah, you know me. It's never a bad time to discuss an intriguing belief system."

Grey heard some of the old urgency creeping back into Professor Radek's voice, the compulsion to pursue every buried secret to its final resting place. He smiled to himself and updated Viktor on recent events.

"I'm still confused by the CIA's interest," Grey said, "unless there's a terrorist angle within the Alianza Cartel."

"Politics is the sport of kings," Viktor murmured, "and kings are all too human. I prefer to play with gods. But we'll investigate the angle we were given."

Grey knew full well that if Viktor was intrigued by a case, he would investigate whatever angle he wished, government interests be damned.

"Can we agree that the CIA is likely seeking someone in the hierarchy of the Alianza Cartel?" Viktor asked.

"That's my guess. They're looking for someone and they're not getting very far."

"If this palero, Hector Fortuna, is as involved with the cartel as he seems to be, then we might be better off finding who *he* reports to."

"Not sure I follow," Grey said.

"Priests in all religions learn their trade somewhere. In modern times it's usually at seminary. But in the older religions, knowledge was passed down from teacher to student, priest to acolyte. Palo is more traditional than most; a Palo priest almost certainly has learned his craft from another, more experienced palero."

"So find the palero who trained Hector, and we might find drug dealers higher up the food chain, connected to the mentor. Interesting angle."

"If, indeed, there's a connection between this cartel and Palo Mayombe. It might be a local attraction."

"The cartel's based in Cancun. Is Mexico a country where Palo can be found?"

"Oh yes. It's in the shadows, but it's there."

Grey started to pace, shielding his eyes from the sun. "Why don't we see what happens with the DEA's informant first? This is a little out there, and they're more likely to bite if their other avenues dry up."

"Of course."

"Hey, you remember that package bound in black cloth I found at Manny's bungalow?"

"The one sealed with wax?"

"Yeah," Grey said. "I saw another one, in a park on Calle Ocho, embedded within the roots of a huge tree. Any idea what it is?"

"They're called *bilongos*. Packets that contain a variety of substances, usually blood, herbs, and animal matter. They're charms, magical bundles used for a variety of purposes."

"What about ones sealed in black cloth?"

"This one, too?"

"Yes."

A heaviness, as well as a hint of mystery, slipped into Viktor's professorial air. "Bilongos wrapped in black usually contain human hair or a personal item related to the individual a palero is seeking to affect," he said. "These bilongos are used to invite the *Nkisi*—the spirit summoned to the cauldron—to destroy one's enemy."

Grey stopped pacing and put a hand on the balcony. "Ah."

"I might have made some headway concerning our enigmatic blue lady," Viktor said. "Let's just say someone has a rather vivid imagination. I might even say sense of humor if there weren't murders involved."

"No," Grey said, remembering the night at Manny's house. "Not a sense of humor."

"One group of indigenous peoples known for using the knife and the sling-shot were the Incas. Other cultures also utilized these weapons, but it's a particular legend that has me intrigued. Incan mythology tells of a fierce warrior chieftain called Mama Huaco. As legend has it, Mama Huaco can appear anywhere in the world and vanish into the mist. She can also reincarnate."

"And she's blue?"

"Incan warriors were known to have decorated themselves with dyes of many colors."

"I don't think we can even be sure of the gender," Grey said, "based on that witness. How sure are you we're dealing with an ancient Incan legend?"

"It's my best guess from the research."

Viktor's guess, Grey knew, was usually on target. He just didn't see how it could all possibly tie together. "Well, if she doesn't appear for another decade, I suppose it's irrelevant."

"Oh, it's relevant. The question is whether we'll be able to determine why."

———————

Grey went for his morning run, took a dip in the ocean, and found a Cuban diner for breakfast. He had a delicious assortment of croquettes and fruit-filled pastries, washed down with fresh guava juice.

After breakfast, he called the homeless shelter to check in on Charlie. The staff said she had stayed there every night and was fine. Maybe next time Grey could leave one of the older students with a set of practice drills, so class could continue in his absence.

The thought caused him to drift to another time and place, when his own *shihan* had let him run the class and Grey had experienced a rare moment of youthful pride. He was the only American at the school, and the youngest black belt at fifteen. The other students had been jealous, but no one questioned his authority. Despite being undersized, he had proven his talent many times over on the mat. Jujitsu was all about skill, speed, positioning, and exploiting the weaknesses of the human body. Things at which Grey excelled.

That and mental toughness, being able to deal with pain. Grey still marveled at how intense his black belt training had been. Harder than Special Forces training. Harder than anything.

Which had been fine with Grey, because even jujitsu couldn't compare to the pain of a beating by his own father. That sort of pain coiled around the insides of a young boy like a sleeping dragon, claws inserted for life, the drool a searing acid that seeped outward and dissolved self-worth.

But enough of all that. On the walk back, sunlight glinting off the asphalt after a late morning downpour, he shook off the past and decided to call Nya. He told her it was to update her on the case, but he really just wanted to hear her voice, feel her aura beside him.

"Grey," she said when he was done talking, "you've done enough, hey? Let the government do the rest."

"It's our case now. They hired us to consult."

"I understand, but if anything happened to you, I'd feel responsible. I was the one who brought you into this."

He imagined her on her patio, sipping tea and slicing a mango from the garden, the sun warming her brown arms. "I doubt this project will last much longer," he said. "But you know how I feel. We might be helping the next Sekai."

"I know, just . . . be careful. Please. For me."

A little thrill ran through him at her words. They made small talk for a while, and as they did he wandered up and down Ocean Drive with the phone pressed to his ear, lost with her voice in a bubble of time and space, traffic and pedestrians muted around him.

———•———

Fred called later that evening, when Grey was stretching on his tatami mat, half watching an action flick, balcony doors open to the breeze.

"Things are moving fast," Fred said. "Our girl knows about this guy Hector, says she's heard his name quite a bit. Her lapdog already invited her to the next ceremony."

"How'd she play it?" Grey asked.

"She asked about the recent murders, whether the cult stuff was involved. Showed an interest in knowing more."

"Smart. When's the ceremony?"

"Two days. Same house. I'll pick you up at four."

17

After catching up on her daily reports, Lana sat cross-legged in the living room of the CIA condo. Through the open balcony door she could see the lights of Brickell, feel the nocturnal energy of Miami stirring below.

It was midnight. The memory of her meeting with Colonel Ganso still roiled in her stomach like the aftereffects of a bout of food poisoning.

It wasn't just him. After the act itself, the worst part about the rape was the unbearable feeling of helplessness with which it had left her. The rest of her life had been spent in compensation.

And she had compensated: third degree black belt in taekwondo, expert marksman, high-ranking officer in the CIA. No, Lana Valenciano would not be taken advantage of ever again. Not in that way.

Her father, always selfish and unapproachable, had cemented his status in Lana's mind by divorcing her mother a few months after the attack. Had he not understood that was when Lana needed them most?

She shook off the memories and reached for her cell. Agent Hernandez had informed her about the upcoming operation, and if this Dominic Grey person was going to participate in the investigation, she needed to know more about him. She had read his file, and it did not give her a warm and fuzzy feeling.

She had decided to call Harris Powell, Grey's direct supervisor when he had been fired from Diplomatic Security in Zimbabwe. Harris was still posted in Harare, which did not bode well for his career. The same Third World backwater for over four years?

Harris answered on the first ring, his high-pitched voice grating on Lana's nerves. "Dominic Grey, now that's a name I haven't heard in a while."

"We're using him on an investigation, and I thought I'd get a little more insight into his character. What exactly happened in Harare? Is he trustworthy? Capable?"

"Oh, Jesus!" Harris started laughing, and it was an unpleasant sound, even whinier than his voice. "You want the scoop on Grey? It's pretty simple, the guy can't take an order. Never could. Had trouble with him from day one."

"That's why he was fired?"

"I'm sure you read the file. Dominic was fired because he chose to pursue a personal investigation we forbade him to pursue. His job was to protect the interests of the United States of America, and he disobeyed a direct order and failed in that duty."

"The personal investigation that involved the case liaison officer from the Zimbabwean government, Nya Mashumba?"

"He came to us with some crazy story about a Juju cult that had kidnapped both Ms. Mashumba and a former head of Consular Affairs."

"Didn't that turn out to be true?"

"Half of Zimbabwe still believes that cult leader had supernatural powers, if that's what you mean. But Zim isn't exactly sending someone to the moon anytime soon. Anyway, you know as well as I do that's beside the point. The Zim government disallowed our involvement, and the action Grey proposed to take was in direct contradiction of an ambassadorial order. Period. End of story."

A night breeze stirred, and Lana flicked a strand of hair off her face. "So we've established his issue with chain of command, which is borne out by his service record. What about otherwise? Take out the leadership issues—would you trust him on an investigation? Or at all?"

"Look, lady, here's what you need to know. Dominic Grey doesn't do group hugs or company picnics or watercooler talk at the office. He's serious and remote and I guess you could say philosophical, though philosophy is about as relevant a skill in the State Department as owning a flower shop. Maybe I'm just not a deep guy. The point is, Grey's terrible at interpersonal relations and dealing with authority, but he's very smart and capable, and . . . let me put it this way. Dominic Grey is uncomfortable in ninety-nine percent of the situations normal people take for granted, and comfortable in ninety-nine percent of situations the rest of us aren't. If the shit hits the fan in a dark alley, there's no one I'd rather have at my back. And if he wasn't on my side, I wouldn't want to be in a *strobe-lit* alley with Dominic Grey."

"But would you trust him?"

"If we were on the same side, sure. Absolutely. Problem is, he decides what the rules are and who fits where. But you know," Harris's voice turned pensive, "I kinda feel bad about the way it played out for the guy. But hey, he put himself in that corner. I tried to tell him and he never would listen."

Lana ended the conversation. She fixed herself a martini and relaxed on the couch, her mind alert despite the alcohol, thinking about the investigation and her frustrating lack of progress, about enigmatic crime lords and men like Dominic Grey and the complicated world that had spawned them.

18

Two days later, an hour after sunset, Grey and Fred huddled in the back of an unmarked van with tinted windows. The vehicle was parked in a busy retail lot on South Dixie Highway, two blocks from Hector Fortuna's house.

DEA Agent Anthony Miller, Fred's partner, was in the driver's seat. Next to him was Agent Luis Menendez, a dark-skinned Cuban with the muscular wrists of a baseball pro.

Grey rolled his neck and flexed his own wrists. They weren't expecting any action, or there would have been a few more vans full of agents standing by. The undercover operative inside Hector's house, Cecilia Turner, was only supposed to gain a foothold in the cult and learn what she could. Listening devices were so unobtrusive these days, concealed in the hem of a blouse or disguised as a smartphone, that she was in no real danger of exposure. Still, Grey liked to stay loose.

"So Lana's on board with this?" Grey asked.

Fred was quiet for a moment. "Yeah. She knows."

"Still don't want to tell me what this is all about?"

"I did. We're looking for a bigger fish."

Grey's lips turned upward. "Sure."

"Hopefully we'll get a name at this meeting, and you can take your grand-a-day ass back to New York. I'm clearly in the wrong business," Fred muttered.

"Trust me, I'm just the hired help."

"You have any idea what they pay us to put our lives on the line? Just enough for booze and a bad divorce attorney."

"You've got an ex?" Grey asked.

"Almost. Wife can't deal with the job, kids are my universe, same broken record."

Grey nodded, said nothing.

Fred spread his hands. "Angst is a wonderfully empowering emotion. We're not really alive without it. You're single, I'm guessing? I can tell by the waistline."

"Yeah."

"Police report said you were investigating one of the African girls' deaths. What's the connection?"

"I know someone close to her."

"Old flame? New?"

Grey hesitated. "Old."

Fred grunted, and Grey was relieved when a voice came through the monitoring speaker, causing everyone to quiet. It sounded as if Agent Turner and other people were being greeted at the door and ushered inside.

The small talk kept up, and Agent Menendez turned his head towards Anthony. "You know Cecilia?"

"Met her once or twice. She's been inside the cartel most of the time I've been here."

Agent Menendez gave a two-tone whistle. "That girl's the *truth*, man. Legs like tent poles. What I wouldn't give."

Grey listened to the voices coming from the house for a few minutes, then said, "Agent Turner's Venezuelan?"

"American mother, Venezuelan father," Fred said, surprised. "How'd you know?"

"My first posting as a DSO was in Bogotá. I learned to recognize regional accents."

Fred inclined his head towards the speaker. "So you're getting all this?"

"Most of it."

Luis and Anthony kept up their chatter, until finally Fred said, "Say Luis, why don't you quit running your mouth like a hyperactive parrot and act like you've been here before? Christ, you're like one of my kids. Sometimes the devil's in the details, so listen up. Why do Cubans do everything so fast, anyway? You talk too fast and drive your cars too fast and do business too fast. Aren't you supposed to be happy island people?"

Instead of the retort Grey expected, both agents in the front quieted and turned towards the speaker as if they'd been shushed by the principal. Ever since they had picked Grey up on a street corner near his hotel, it was obvious the other two men held Fred in esteem, if not fear.

Hector's voice came through the speaker, gathering everyone together. Grey snapped to attention.

"Before we begin," Hector said in Spanish, "we have a new initiate."

The priest's voice sounded different than it had in the botánica, strong and self-assured, at home among his flock.

"I hope you don't mind if I watch," Agent Turner said from inside. "I've been to a lot of Santeria ceremonies, but never Palo. I hear they're different."

"Oh," Hector said, and Grey could sense him grinning, "they're different. And you can do much more than watch."

There was something in Hector's voice Grey didn't like. An underlying current of electricity charging his words. Grey's eyes roved the van, but the others didn't seem bothered. Maybe he was just jumpy, had been in too many dicey situations.

"Come forward," Hector said. "Give me your arm."

"Go, Carina," a male voice urged, who Grey assumed was her escort. Fred had told Grey that Agent Turner was known to the cartel as Carina Trujillo.

After a moment of silence, Agent Turner gasped as if poked by a needle.

"Good," Hector murmured. "Join your blood with the prenda. I'm curious, what is it that interests you about Palo?"

"It's a fascinating religion," she said.

"Yes, it is. But surely something in particular caught your eye, caused you to request an audience? This is not for everyone, you know. We do not embrace the casual seeker."

"I know. I'm very grateful. It's an honor."

"Well, then?" Hector said. "Is there something you wish done? A desire gained or thwarted? An enemy overcome?"

Grey thought it strange that there were no other noises in the room. No music, no drums. His research indicated that Palo Mayombe ceremonies included music and singing, or at least chanting. And there had been drums at the other ceremony. Why was it so quiet?

"Or perhaps," Hector said, this time not bothering to hide the subtle menace in his voice, "you wish to learn the secrets of a palero?"

"Oh no," Agent Turner said. "I wouldn't dare to presume."

"No? Are you not a daring woman, to come here and disguise your true nature?"

Grey and Fred sat up straight. Anthony started to speak, and Fred shushed him with a finger.

"I'm not sure what you mean," Agent Turner said. "Disguise my true nature? Will Palo help me strip away the layers and reach my potential?"

Keep it going, Grey thought. *Even if you think they suspect you, keep it going. Cause them to doubt.*

"That's exactly what I mean," Hector said softly. "We are far more alive as part of Kalunga."

Kalunga, Grey repeated to himself, trying to recall his reading. That word meant something. Something important to the religion.

He remembered what it was at the same time the drums began and they heard another gasp, and then muffled screaming and the sound of someone being dragged across a floor.

Grey sprang to his feet. "Kalunga means the realm of the dead in Palo. He's going to kill her."

Fred swore and lunged for a phone at the front of the van. "We need backup *now*. Agent in peril. Send two teams." He slammed the receiver and turned to Anthony. "*Drive.*"

Anthony screeched the van into traffic. "Shouldn't we wait for backup?"

"Fuck backup," Fred said. "Didn't you hear what Grey said?"

The van screeched out of the parking lot. "Got a spare weapon?" Grey said, eyeing the rack of firearms on the side of the van. When Fred hesitated, Grey said, "Interpol, remember? I have whatever jurisdiction you tell me I have."

Fred glanced out the windshield and back at Grey, flicking a wrist towards the weapons. "Take your pick."

Grey had enough time to select a Glock and check the cartridge before the van jerked to a stop in front of Hector's house. The DEA agents and Grey piled into the street, Fred leading the way.

Just as Fred reversed his weapon to smash the lock, the door opened halfway to reveal Hector, dressed in a wrinkled guayabera, his hands clasped in front of him.

The drums had stilled. Hector's smile, slow and sure in the face of four armed men, chilled Grey. "Can I help you?"

Fred flashed his ID without lowering his weapon. "We're searching this house."

"On what basis?"

"DEA matter," Fred said. "Step aside."

"You do realize this is a registered house of worship? I'm a licensed *santero*. We have a constitutional right to conduct our services as we see fit."

"I'm not going to ask again."

"Your warrant?"

Fred jabbed the butt of his gun into Hector's stomach, doubling him over and shoving him forward. Grey liked his call. This wasn't about procedure or preserving evidence, this was about saving an agent's life. In his opinion they had taken too long already.

They pushed their way inside, Fred leading Hector by the back of his shirt. Grey saw a two-story villa with a tiled central courtyard, where a group of seven men was gathered around an iron cauldron. A few palms and banana trees dotted the edges of the outdoor space, as well as thick clumps of foliage. A phalanx of tiki torches illuminated the scene. Even from a distance Grey could see bones and sticks poking out of the cauldron, and smears of blood on the tiles.

There was no sign of Agent Turner.

"Where is she?" Fred shouted. He prodded Hector into the group of men standing around the cauldron, then waved his gun at the group. "Keep them contained," he said to the other two agents.

Grey's eyes caught a trickle of crimson seeping out of a closed doorway on the left side of the courtyard. The stream of blood advanced, pooling around the shoes of the nearest worshipper.

Everyone saw it. Grey's adrenaline spiked, and time seemed to both stop and accelerate.

Fred pointed his gun at Hector, and the other two agents leveled their weapons at the group. Grey scanned the men and found the one he considered to be the biggest threat, a smaller man in the corner with the calm but alert stance of a predator. His face was concealed by a grey hoodie and his hand had been the first to slip inside his jacket, feeling for his weapon.

"Open the door," Fred said to Hector, his voice trembling.

Not trembling from fear, Grey realized, but from barely controlled rage, as if Fred were a whistling teakettle ready to pop. His face had reddened and a vein on his neck pulsated like a signal from a lighthouse.

"*Solo un pollo*," Hector said, grinning. *It's just a chicken.*

The blood spread farther, to the base of the cauldron. Fred gritted his teeth. "*Open* it."

Hector's grin expanded. "*Sí, señor.*"

The priest stepped to the closet. As he opened the door, he whistled and then disappeared inside, closing the door behind him. A gunshot sounded. Anthony pitched forward, blood spurting from his chest. The men around the cauldron drew weapons and dispersed.

Realizing the shot must have come from behind them, Grey dove behind a banana tree at the same time he shot the man in the grey hoodie. Out of the corner of his eye, just before he dove, he saw Fred shoot the dealer closest to him and then scurry away, and Agent Menendez firing his weapon into the crowd of men.

Grey looked up and saw someone lying on the floor of the second-story balcony. He fired at the sniper, causing him to back-crawl through a door. The sight of the wraparound balcony caused Grey to swear. Too many exposed angles.

When Grey looked back at the room, he saw five dead or unmoving bodies. Three cartel members, Agent Menendez, and Agent Miller. The stench of blood and gunpowder filled the air, mixing with the incense from the ritual. It was eerily quiet.

Grey spotted Fred behind a palm tree to his right. Hector was still behind the door, which Grey assumed was a closet or a bedroom. The other two dealers must be hidden within the foliage on the other side of the courtyard.

There was no sign of the assailant who had fired from the balcony, and that was a problem. Time was on his and Fred's side, as he assumed a strike force was on the way, but they were outnumbered and had to live long enough to greet them.

Grey caught Fred's eye and motioned with a head jerk that he was going upstairs. Fred gave a thumbs-up and started firing across the courtyard. Grey took the cue and dashed for the stairway, just ahead of the return fire.

Rising to a crouch, he sprinted for the stairs at the end of the corridor, gun gripped in two hands at chest level. He passed an open doorway just before the stairs, and almost got butchered by a wild-eyed Hector wielding a foot-long knife.

The only thing that saved Grey was his jujitsu training to move *into* an attacker wielding a short-range weapon, rather than away. As soon as he saw the glint of iron coming at him from an overhead swipe, Grey ducked under the knife thrust and into the body of his attacker, negating the strike. Hector stumbled, and Grey grabbed him and whirled both their bodies violently to the ground, dropping his gun but using his own falling body weight as momentum for the twisting sacrifice throw.

Hector was stunned by the maneuver, and Grey came up straddling him, using his knees to pin his opponent's arms and trap the knife. Then he knocked the priest senseless with an elbow to the head.

Grey heard sirens at the same time he saw a flash of movement at the top of the stairs. A gunman appeared and Grey had nowhere to go. He rolled with Hector's body, using it as a shield, and felt a round of bullets thump into the priest's flesh. One tore through Hector's face and missed Grey by inches.

Still hiding behind Hector's body, Grey managed to grab his gun and return fire, catching the shooter in the leg. The man dropped his gun, which bounced halfway down the stairs.

Grey threw off Hector's limp corpse, ready to rush up the stairs and secure the man as a witness. Another gun sounded, and the man at the top of the stairs convulsed and then pitched forward.

"What a pity," Fred said from behind Grey. "No survivors."

19

Sometime after two a.m., after Grey finished downloading to a room full of DEA agents in the South Florida Home Division office in Weston, Fred caught him on the way out the door. "Want a lift?"

"Sure."

"Grab some grub on the way?"

Grey nodded.

Weston was a muggy strip of suburb west of Fort Lauderdale, and Fred took him to a Waffle House near the Interstate. The place was packed, full of casino workers and a random assortment of nighttime denizens.

"Grease never smelled so good," Grey said.

Fred found a booth in the rear and glanced eagerly at the menu. "This place almost makes Weston bearable. Miami's too full of places where they hold your wee-wee when you pee."

They both ordered coffees and waffles with bacon. The food came quickly, and Grey dug in. When he was finished eating, Fred leaned forward and cupped his hands around his coffee mug. "Thanks for not ratting me out."

Grey knew he was talking about the unarmed man Fred had shot at the top of the stairs. Grey took a sip of coffee and eyed Fred calmly. "I got over that when I saw what they did to Agent Turner." He pushed away a mental image of the undercover agent's corpse, the hole in her chest cavity gaping like a shark's mouth. He didn't want to know where they had found her missing organ.

"What I care about was losing a potential witness," Grey said. "And how they made her. But hey, it's your case."

"He shot my partner in the back. I did what I had to."

"I'm not your boss or your priest. It's your conscience. I'm just saying he might have been a good guy to interview. How's Anthony?"

"Critical, but alive. Maybe paralyzed."

"I'm very sorry."

"Yeah." Fred stuck a toothpick in the side of his mouth, eying Grey's empty plate. "Most people wouldn't have an appetite after a night like that."

"Probably not."

"How many times you been there?"

"Too many," Grey said.

Fred gave a slow nod, flipped the toothpick over. "You know that guy in the gray hoodie you shot?"

"Yeah."

"It wasn't a guy. It was Angel Alianza."

"One of the assassin twins?" Grey pressed his lips together and returned to his coffee.

"Her brother probably won't be too happy about that," Fred said.

"Not much I can do about that now."

Fred's chuckle died almost as soon as it started. "You're one cool customer, aren't you?"

Grey set his coffee down. He didn't react because he was a professional, but the violence of the evening still filled his veins like a drug, coursing through his system as sure and swift as any narcotic. It was an addiction he fought at every turn, a patch of darkness on his soul he loathed with all of his being.

The thing was, just like a heroin addiction, violence was a path that, once trod upon, was impossible to leave behind. It could only be managed, fought against, compartmentalized.

"I thought I was the guy who made people nervous," Fred muttered. "Look, I appreciate all your help. And you're right, I screwed us. I don't know how they made Agent Turner, and we probably never will. And that other thing with Lana, the cult angle—tonight was our shot." He twirled the toothpick and smiled his confident smile. "But that's okay. You're private sector, and my career's already ruined."

The waitress cleared their plates, and Grey said, "You know the two guys I took out at Manny's place? They still in custody?"

"Nah, we had nothing on them except a few stolen bones from the cemetery. Those two are guppies. We threw them back in the sea."

"Let's go chat with one of them."

"I already have," Fred said.

"You might not have asked the right questions."

Fred stopped fiddling with the toothpick. "What're you thinking?"

"Get me an interview and I'll let you know."

Fred dropped Grey outside his hotel. On the way to his room, as the last of the adrenaline seeped away and left him feeling hollow and alone, Grey couldn't stop thinking about the expression on Fred's face during the shootout, the bloodthirsty glaze that had coated his eyes. He knew Fred was fighting a losing battle against his demons, and it pained Grey because he sensed Fred was a good man.

But Fred had seen too much or fought too long, or something else had happened, something that had taken him to the brink. He was perilously close to succumbing to the siren call of violence and slipping into those dark waters forever.

Grey didn't have many possessions, but one of them was a tiny soapstone carving of two intertwined lovers that Nya had given him. He took it off the bedside table and carried it to the balcony, feeling the need to gaze upon the beauty of the night sky before bed, a final cleansing of the events of the day. As he leaned on the railing, carving in hand and thinking of Nya, he heard a faint *thwap* and sensed rather than saw the stone ball hurtling towards him out of the darkness. He flung his body downward onto the cement.

The balcony door shattered behind him. Shards of glass punctured his skin. A scream pierced the night.

As he peered through the metal railing, a streetlight illuminated what looked like an athletic young Amerindian woman, dressed in a loincloth and a leather bra, disappearing into the darkness of Lummus Park. Her skin had a distinct blue tinge.

Grey belly-crawled inside his room, took the stairs four at a time, and sprinted into the park. Head on a swivel, he canvassed the park once, twice, three times. He ran up and down the beach, circled the hotel, checked the streets off the beach.

Nothing.

No one.

The woman who had screamed, a stripper returning to her condo, had seen nothing. The scream was a reaction to the glass shattering.

Not a single suspect or witness or clue, just wisps of warm sea breeze that caressed him like the memory of lovers past.

Or perhaps, he thought, *it wasn't the memory of lovers at all, but the ghosts of those whose lives he had taken, surrounding him like the ocean of dead souls in Kalunga, mocking him as he searched in vain for his spectral assailant.*

———————

Grey kept lookout until dawn, and stayed in bed until ten. When he woke he called Fred and updated him on the attack.

"A slingshot and a blue Indian, huh?" Fred said. "I guess this just got a bit more personal."

"Guess so."

"It could be a warning, telling you to back off."

"A warning? If I hadn't dropped, I'd be lying on a slab with a stone ball embedded in my skull."

"Still want to meet with the goon from Manny's place? I don't blame you if you don't."

"What do you think?" Grey said.

Fred grunted. "Pick you up in half an hour?"

"You've got it set up already?"

"You could say that. Listen, I dug into Hector a bit more, like you asked. He opened the botánica soon after he returned from Mexico. Before that, he worked at a gas station that pumped more drugs than gas."

"What about cult activity?" Grey asked.

"He's been a licensed santero for years, even before Mexico. Why? What're you thinking?"

"I think Hector Fortuna upped his game in Mexico."

———————

Fred drove Grey down South Dixie Highway to Cutler Bay, a jumble of seedy strip malls south of Miami. The house where Fred parked was the largest on the block, a stucco with garish yellow awnings and Roman statues on the lawn.

The property belonged to Elias Monte, one of the men Grey had taken out when the Alianza twins had disrupted the ceremony on Manny Lopez's back patio. Elias answered the door with a bandage wrapped around his head, and Grey remembered him: a snub-nosed bulldog of a man with close-set eyes and thick arms.

Elias's eyes found Fred's badge, then widened when he saw Grey. "You're the *hijo de puta* who pistol-whipped me," he said, taking a step forward.

Fred held a palm out and put his other hand on his gun. "It's time for our appointment," he said.

"What appointment?"

"The one we have right now." Fred waved his gun towards the car. "Let's go."

Elias hesitated, nervous. "I'm not going anywhere with you."

"I don't know who's inside that house, so we're going to my car. Or downtown, if you prefer. We have plenty to hold you on. Not least of which is the cocaine we found on you at Manny's house."

The nostrils of Elias's snub nose flared, and he balled his fists. He muttered to himself but let Fred lead him to the back seat of his car. Grey slid in opposite.

"I already told you everything I know. I'm not talking to any more cops without my lawyer."

"I'm not a cop," Grey said softly. Elias whipped his head around to stare him down, but ended up moving his eyes to the side.

"Hector was Manny's palero, wasn't he?" Grey asked.

He got the reaction he expected: Elias's face tightened, a shadow of both fear and surprise sweeping across his visage.

"Was Hector different when he came back from Mexico?" Grey asked.

"I no know what you mean," Elias muttered.

"I think you do. He met his own palero there, didn't he? Someone known to the cartel. Who was it?"

Elias didn't answer. His forearm was lying on the seat rest, and Grey slid his own forearm over it. Before Elias could pull away, Grey slipped his thumb against the inside of Elias's wrist and pressed.

Elias gasped. "*Coño!*"

He tried to pull away, but Grey had entwined their forearms, and when Elias twitched Grey pressed harder on the median nerve, the soft area between the radius and the ulna on the inside of the wrist. Acute pressure on the median nerve, Grey knew, caused a feeling of intense and nauseating pain.

As Elias moaned, Grey asked, "Who's Hector's palero?"

Fred's eyes were wide, but he said nothing. Grey increased the pressure, until Elias screamed and looked like he was going to be sick. Grey released enough to let him speak.

"Okay, okay, *loco*, it's not like it's a secret. But I'm telling you it's the last name on earth you want to know."

Grey found Elias's eyes again, keeping pressure on the nerve. Elias squirmed and said, "Tata Menga, okay? That's his name, I swear."

Grey watched him, found a face too brutish and simple for effective lying. What he did see was fear, swimming in Elias's engorged brown pupils.

"Where is he?" Grey asked.

"Mexico."

"That's a big country."

"Hey man, you said just his name."

Grey squeezed.

"*El Yucatan!*"

"Where in the Yucatan?"

"I don't know."

Grey pressed his thumb even deeper, feeling the tendons underneath. Elias tried to ball his fist, but Grey knew that made the pain worse, and Elias bellowed and flung his head against the seat back. "I swear I don't know. No one does. He lives somewhere in the jungle. In Palo Land." He emitted a high-pitched giggle that sprang from the pain. "Palos are sticks, you know. Sticks are trees, trees are forests. Palo Land is where the spirits roam."

Grey watched him a moment longer, then released his grip and nodded at Fred. Fred opened the door and let Elias stumble out of the car. Elias spit on the ground as he walked backwards towards his house, rubbing his wrist, finally mustering the courage to meet Grey's eyes. "Go find Tata Menga, you stupid *cabrón*. Go find him and die."

20

Want to tell me what that was all about?" Fred asked as they drove north, away from Elias's house.

"Sure," Grey said. "As soon as you tell me what the hell's going on."

Fred chuckled, then took a toothpick out and twirled it between his fingers. "You really think there's some connection to that priest in Mexico?"

Grey didn't answer, watched the traffic inch forward.

Fred took a deep breath. "Fair enough, I don't blame you. I need to okay it with Lana."

"I've got a better idea. How about I hear it from her in person? If she's interested in what I have to say, let's all talk."

Fred glanced at Grey as he drove, then reached for his cell. When Lana answered, Fred gave a rundown of the events of the last twenty-four hours, including the shootout at Hector's house, the attack on Grey, and a teaser of the conversation with Elias Monte.

Fred listened for a few seconds, grunted his assent to something, then shut his cell and looked at Grey. "How about right now?"

Lana wanted to meet at a coffee shop in Coral Gables, which Grey found odd. Why the public venue?

As they drove through the Gables, Grey's eyes rose at the display of wealth, while the natural beauty reminded him of the northern suburbs of Harare, where Nya lived. The whole neighborhood a seething jungle, jacarandas and flamboyants and mangoes and lichen-covered oaks, entire streets shaded by canopies of banyans with their vine-like tendrils swaying down like horses' tails.

They drove down a street full of upscale boutiques with red barrel-tile roofs that soaked up the sun. The café was at the end of the block. Fred led Grey through a door in the rear, to a brick courtyard surrounded by a wall draped with bougainvillea. The place smelled of lavender and coffee beans.

Except for Lana, sitting alone at a table by a gurgling fountain, the courtyard was empty. Lana ordered a cappuccino from a waiter, Grey a double espresso, Fred a cup of ice water.

Fred mopped his brow. "How do you drink coffee in the jungle?"

"We're in the shade," Lana said. "It's lovely."

"Shade doesn't help with thousand percent humidity."

Grey poured a sugar into his espresso. He didn't mind the heat.

Lana stirred her cappuccino. She was wearing white linen slacks and a sleeveless black top that revealed toned arms. "Before we begin," she said, "you should know that what I'm about to tell you is a matter of national security. That makes disclosure of this conversation a very serious crime."

"Which makes me wonder why you chose a public venue," Grey said, "and leads me to assume you're avoiding government offices. Someone tipped off the cartel about Agent Turner, and you don't know who to trust. Though as public venues go, this was a good choice. Empty, surrounded by a wall, and the fountain is loud enough to discourage listening devices."

She nodded approvingly, then cocked a grin. "That, and my cousin owns the café."

"That helps," Grey said drily.

"I understand avoiding the DEA," Fred said, "but the CIA? I doubt you broadcasted our presence at Hector Fortuna's last night."

"There must have been a leak at the CIA before," Grey guessed. "With whatever's going on."

Lana gave her assent by leaning back and regarding them with eyes as cool as the fountain.

"So why trust us?" Fred asked. "Besides the fact that we could have died last night, and that I'm too poor to be on the take. And this guy being a mole for the Alianza," he jerked his thumb at Grey, "well, that would be a stretch. Unless he's not who he says he is."

Grey didn't reply. He barely knew Fred, didn't trust Lana, and didn't care if either one of them trusted him.

"You're right," Lana said, "it would have been colossally stupid of either of you to walk into that situation as a mole. Unless, of course, everyone in that room knew who you were and purposefully avoided shooting you."

"We took out the whole room," Fred said flatly.

Lana spread her hands. "Which is why I'm here. And," she turned towards Fred, her smile slow and sure, "as we discussed before, I've seen your record and made my inquiries. Loyalty to the cause does not appear to be an issue."

"Goddamn right," Fred said, though Grey detected a note of irony.

"And you and Professor Radek," Lana said, turning to Grey, "have worked with numerous governmental agencies before, and have impeccable reputations." She placed her elbows on the table and interlaced her fingers. "What sunk you on your CIA application, you know, wasn't your background or skill set. It was your ethical profiling."

"I'm as distraught as the first time you brought this up," Grey said. "Really, I've never recovered."

"Your profile claims you suffer from a narcissistic and delusional sense of altruism—"

"Lady, if I'm a narcissist, then you're the Queen of England. I'm many things, but a narcissist isn't one of them."

"—also known as instinctive cooperative behavior complex, also known as hero syndrome. The hallmarks of which are someone who will never be comfortable accepting partisan dictates, or have the capability to put aside principle and do what is necessary for the greater good."

Fred laughed.

Lana crossed her legs and returned to her cappuccino. "A state of mind that's the polar opposite of that required of a successful government agent, especially of the clandestine variety. Fortunately, the condition *is* favorable for situations requiring trust."

Grey snorted. "Since when are my psych evaluations public record? You've obviously broken the law and disclosed it for a reason—don't worry, I couldn't care less—and I'm guessing that reason is so Fred can trust me as well."

Lana leaned forward. "I know who you are, Dominic. We're all on the same side. We all want the same thing. If you really want to do something for Sekai and Nya, if you really want to make a difference, then help us catch the man we're after."

"Don't manipulate me," Grey muttered, though he knew she just had. "Call me Grey, get to the point, and tell me what this is all about."

She told him everything: about El General, his proclivity for using a blue-painted Indian woman as a personal assassin, the CIA's fears of terrorists penetrating an uncontrolled border, her excitement at the recent appearance of the General's mysterious assassin on U.S. soil.

"That's quite a story," Grey said.

"I can vouch for some of it," Fred said grudgingly. "Or at least the legend. My informants get all weak-kneed at the mention of this guy."

Grey folded his arms. "I might be less inclined towards belief if a blue Indian woman hadn't fired a slingshot at my head last night."

"Speaking of that," Fred said, "did your guy ever come up with anything?"

"Yeah, he did." Grey told them about the legend of Mama Huaco that Viktor had found.

Fred's eyebrows lifted, and Lana's lips curled. "Moving right along," she said, and Grey shrugged. He didn't blame her.

She paused to consider her next words, and Grey's eyes flicked to the side again, to the empty courtyard. He hated not having his back against the wall, but Lana had claimed that chair.

"Fred mentioned you might have learned something from your outing today?" she said to Grey.

Grey eyed the two of them, wondering what else Lana wasn't telling him. Her claim of an insecure border seemed lacking. "Judging by your reaction the first time we met," he said to Lana, "I'm guessing your investigation has reached an impasse."

She clasped her hands on the table and said, "You would not be incorrect."

"Obviously someone in the power base in Cancun knows something," Fred said, "but we don't have anyone that deep inside. All we know is that this Palo Mayombe cult might be involved in some way, and we just lost that lead. Unless," he turned to Grey, "you think finding this priest in Mexico might help?"

"According to Professor Radek, every palero—a Palo priest—is trained individually by another palero."

"I don't doubt the scholarship," Lana said, "though I fail to see the connection to the case. Not that the Alianza Cartel members aren't involved with Palo Mayombe—they obviously are—but how will that help us locate our principal?"

"You've said you can't find a connection through the cartels," Grey said, "but what if we could backdoor our way in? Who knows how deep the connection to Palo Mayombe runs? Maybe the General himself is involved—maybe he was the original palero, or knew him, and everyone links back to him."

Lana leaned back, the doubt on her face morphing to curiosity. "You actually think you might be able to trace this cult to the General? Or somewhere close?"

"I think we can try."

She finished her cappuccino, drumming her fingers on the table as she thought. "It's worth a shot, and I've already cleared you both." She cupped her empty mug in her palms. "What if I were to engage you to go to Mexico to find this priest? Both of you."

Fred muttered something under his breath. "I'll need to clear it on my end."

"You'd do nothing of the sort," Lana said. "Remember the leak?"

Grey frowned. "You want us to go dark?"

"Just anonymous. You don't need to penetrate the cartel, just look into the cult angle."

"Which is closely tied to the cartel," Grey said.

"It's a dangerous assignment," Lana said. "We'll include fifty percent danger pay on top of the usual fee and expenses. And if you didn't have such a specialized background, I'd never consider putting you in this situation."

Right, he thought. Now he knew why she had thrown in the bit about Nya and Sekai, to secure his help in case she needed him. There was also the fact that he had just killed the twin sister of an Alianza sicario, and the General's personal assassin had tried to murder him the night before.

Like it or not, he was involved.

"I'll need to consult with Professor Radek," Grey said.

"Of course." Lana turned towards Fred. "You know there will be an investigation concerning last night." Fred didn't answer, and she continued, "Taking into account your previous record . . . frankly, I'm not sure your career will survive."

Grey thought Fred would retort, but instead he looked defeated.

"Here's what I can offer you," Lana said softly. "Take a leave of absence.

Claim you need a vacation. We both know no one will blink an eye. Work with me on this, and we'll clear your record and restore your pay grade."

Fred licked his lips. "You can't promise that."

"I report directly to the Deputy Director on this matter. He's the one who authorized the investigation. I don't have the power to clean your record, but he does. And I swear to you both, he and I are the only two people who will know about this. There will be no leak from our end. And all of *that* is classified."

Fred remained silent, though Grey could see some of the light returning to his eyes.

"No leak unless you or the Deputy Director is dirty," Grey said.

Lana looked him in the eye and held his gaze. She let the stare linger, unblinking, every muscle carefully controlled, giving him plenty of time and opportunity to gauge her body language. He saw no signs of deception, but of course, she was trained to lie.

"If he were dirty," Lana said finally, "then he wouldn't be spear-heading this investigation. And if I were turned, I wouldn't be seeking your specialized assistance."

Her points were valid, and Grey could think of no reason why she might be lying. At least not at the moment.

"I understand all of this is highly irregular," Lana said. "Believe me, we don't engage outside assistance lightly. But you both possess rare expertise, and, well, exceptional circumstances require exceptional solutions."

"What about you?" Fred asked. "You coming with us?"

"There's another angle I need to finish investigating from here— which I'll discuss as soon as we've come to an agreement. I propose that we meet here at the same time tomorrow, after I've cleared this with the Director and you've had a chance to consider. Hopefully we can move forward."

Fred gave a slow nod. "Okay."

She turned to Grey.

"Sure," he said, raising his cup. "The espresso's good."

21

Needing to think, Grey took a long drive along Collins Avenue. A barrier of palms and dunes hid the ocean. He kept an eye out for trailing vehicles, but it was broad daylight in a bustling city, and this was not the Miami of the eighties. Cartel assassins did not march into shopping malls and spray bullets into the crowd.

But they did in Mexico.

Though Grey was a risk taker, he did not willingly put himself in dangerous situations without doing some fact-checking. He knew he wouldn't find much on Lana, but he gave it a shot.

Before he left the hotel he had consulted his usual array of Internet databases that provided background checks. Lana, as Grey had guessed, was a Miami-born Cuban. Her socialite mother and prominent businessman father had divorced in 1997, Lana's senior year of high school. She dropped out of cheerleading and almost flunked her first semester that year, then rebounded in the second. College admissions advisors must have taken the divorce into account, because she graduated *summa cum laude* from Princeton and starred for the debate team. After that came an internship with the U.N., a year as an aide on Capitol Hill, and then he presumed she joined the CIA, since she dropped off the radar.

Along the way she picked up a black belt in taekwondo, which he discovered because she won her division at nationals. No property or vehicle records. Never married. No criminal history. Younger brother a heart surgeon in Tampa.

Grey had two contacts in the CIA, one he knew from his posting in Bogotá, the other an ex-girlfriend from his vagabond days in New York. The latter had been an NYU student from an uptight Boston family, attracted to Grey's gypsy lifestyle and restless anger. They met at a club where Grey worked the door. She was surprised someone as thin as he could be a bouncer, even more surprised to learn he was more well-read than she.

The former DSO didn't answer, so he tried the ex-girlfriend. Grey called her old home number and got her mother. She remembered Grey and gave out her daughter's cell, also hinting that her daughter was still single.

Grey called his long-ago ex and was surprised when she answered. The conversation was short and awkward, but it sufficed. He learned that a CIA agent named Lana Valenciano did indeed exist, and that she fit Grey's description. He also learned, through a silent acquiescence to his questions, that Lana was considered a rising star and known to report on Latin America directly to Jeffrey Lasgetone, the current Deputy Director of the CIA. Who Grey surely knew, his ex said, had recently announced he would be running for president?

Grey hadn't known. Or cared. But it did start his wheels spinning.

He got nothing else, but it was a start. He knew they were chasing a very bad operator. He knew Lana was at least who she said she was and that she had the ear of the Director.

And he knew, of course, that she wasn't telling him everything.

———

Grey rolled through a quaint little beach community called Surfside, his thoughts coalescing at a stop sign. In his mind, the benefits of going to Mexico outweighed the risks. Besides the fact that a killer had him in his sights and Lana needed his and Viktor's expertise, well, this was what he did. Grey might not be able to do much about who he was, but he could choose *what* he was.

He called Nya next, and thought of trust for the second time that day. She too had concealed things from him in the beginning, and even though it was because she hadn't trusted *him,* it had still smarted.

Which only made her human. But which had not improved his ability to trust.

Nya was not happy with his decision to pursue the case. She was Catholic and, though she struggled with faith, harbored deep superstitions. She again voiced her worry that something terrible might happen if Grey chose to continue, and it would be her fault for getting him involved.

But Grey was not superstitious, and her worry perversely drove him forward, a sign that she cared. It was a dangerous cycle and he didn't know where it would end.

———

He returned home, cracked a beer, and called to update Viktor. At the mention of Tata Menga, a flash of the old Viktor returned, a seasoned explorer stumbling upon new ruins in the jungle. "A feared palero in the Yucatan?" he said, an eager lilt to his voice. "Most intriguing."

"What's the history of Palo in Mexico?"

"The Africans taken to Mexico during the slave trade were in the vast minority, and their religious practices never established a foothold, especially not in the Mayan-controlled Yucatan. Santeria and Palo Mayombe gained a following in Mexico much later, due to Cuban immigration. The jungles of the Yucatan are the perfect place for Palo to thrive, however. Forests are sacred to Congolese religion. That's where they believe the spirits prefer to roam."

"The Yucatan's huge," Grey said. "Where do you suggest I start looking?"

"Perhaps start with the urban botánicas—*yerberías* in Mexico— and inquire discreetly about Palo."

"The Alianza Cartel is based in Cancun, so that might be a good place to look."

"Good. Yes. Though be warned, Palo and even Santeria are far less prevalent in Mexico than in Miami or Cuba. If you find you're not making progress, there is a more . . . unorthodox . . . angle you might try."

"Not sure I like the sound of that."

"A palero who is widely sought after for his magical services will need supplies. Many Palo rituals, and each new prenda, require human bones exhumed from a cemetery."

It took Grey a moment to see where Viktor was going. "You think I should stake out the cemeteries?"

"It might prove an excellent way to locate practitioners of Palo. Though my guess is that a palero with the reputation of Tata Menga will have someone collect his materials for him. A Renfield, if you'll excuse the expression."

"Thanks for the tip," Grey said drily. "I'll start with the botánicas."

"There's something else you should know."

Viktor paused, and Grey's eyes scanned the street out of habit. "I've done further research on the Mama Huaco mythology," Viktor continued. "In addition to being a legendary warrior, she was also summoned for vengeance. And legend has it that once she focused on an enemy, she never failed to destroy him."

"*Legend* being the operative word."

"I just thought you should know. Those whom the General is seeking to cow will be familiar with the myth."

"Yeah. Thanks. Anything else of interest?"

"Not as yet."

They finished up with small talk, and Grey fell asleep on the couch with his arms crossed and his eyes on the door, thinking of the blue assassin and reminding himself that he was not, indeed, a man of superstition.

22

In the old days, Fred would have agreed without hesitation to go to Mexico on the spot, ready for another adrenaline-fueled adventure. Now he had a family to think about, and a floundering career, and a pair of aching knees.

Then again, he had a paralyzed partner on his hands. Back in the day, that alone was cause enough.

He stared at the phone, knowing that if he went to Mexico, he had to make that call. The one where he told his family a story they knew was bullshit, the one where the good-byes were quiet and somber because he might be coming back in a body bag.

The wife was no longer an issue, but he'd have to call his daughters.

His son.

Lana was right. He was a true believer. Most Americans spent their lives unaware of what the cost of cheap gas truly was, or what it meant not to have religious or political freedom. What it meant to walk down the street without worrying that the son of the current dictator might decide to pluck your daughter out of the crowd and rape her.

Fred did not kid himself that Americans were any better than anyone else, or that he wasn't lucky as a leprechaun to have been born in the States, or that the American ghettos were not their own form of living hell.

He just knew his kids were safer than most around the world, and he was helping to keep them that way.

On the way home, Fred had looked for Freckles but hadn't been able to find him. He was probably holed up in a crack house somewhere.

Stranger that he hadn't been able to reach Ernesto. His secretary had confirmed the accountant's presence at the office that morning, but Ernesto usually called him back within the hour.

Fred stepped outside to smoke a cigar, offering his flesh to the creatures of the night in exchange for a hit of nicotine. Talk about an addictive substance—he'd seen people shake off meth easier than cigarettes.

A breeze stirred, keeping the bloodsuckers at bay. He could still catch the end of the Braves game, a frozen pizza was in the oven, and the fridge was full of beer. Life was good.

A buzz on his BlackBerry caught his attention. It was an email from his regional supervisor, ordering Fred to attend a meeting with the Office of Professional Responsibility on Friday morning to discuss the incident at Hector Fortuna's house.

The Office of Professional Responsibility was DEA internal affairs. This was not routine.

This was the Inquisition.

Fred crushed his beer can. "Goddammit."

Lana had been right. He wasn't surprised, just disappointed. The better he did his job, the more heat he got. What had the Suits thought was going to happen when Fred rang Hector Fortuna's doorbell? Those monsters had killed Agent Turner and stuffed her in a *closet*.

He ran a hand through his hair and called the wife. He needed to hear his daughters' voices.

No one answered, and Fred spewed more curses. He knew they were home.

After popping another beer, he sat on the couch with the phone in his lap, staring at it while grown men ran circles around a patch of dirt. He finished the beer in minutes, gathering the nerve to push and hold the "1" button on his cell. Speed dial for the methamphetamine clinic.

A nurse answered, and Fred said, "I'd like to speak to my son. Danny Hernandez."

"Let me see if he's available."

Fred paced the living room while he waited. Danny was four months deep into the six-month recovery program, his third in three years. Meth addiction was notoriously difficult to treat. Unlike heroin addicts, who can use methadone to wean themselves off the drug, meth had no known pharmacological treatment. The only relief was an uncertain mix of behavioral therapy, family support, and luck.

Moreover, withdrawal from meth was insidious: not a physical reaction, but a condition called anhedonia—an inability to experience pleasure that could last up to six months, induce deep depression, and cause users to crave another hit. The brain's response to the manufactured highs of prolonged meth abuse.

What that meant to Fred was that his seventeen-year-old son was a robot, an empty shell of the curly-headed boy he had raised and loved, who he had taken to soccer games and taught to ride a bike and held in his arms after a bad dream, who he would die a thousand terrible deaths for and smile while he did it.

A boy whose chances of beating the drug for good, while never high, were sinking with each relapse.

"Dad?"

The same wooden voice to which Fred had grown accustomed. The new normal.

Fred forced himself to sound upbeat. "Hey, son. How are things? I mean, are you doing okay this week? Have you talked to Mom?"

"Yeah, she called."

Fred waited for him to say more, knowing he wouldn't.

"You been sleeping okay?" Fred asked.

"Yeah. Sure."

"Eating?"

"Mm."

"Exercising?"

"Nah," his son muttered, as if his energy was already sapped.

"Still turning girls' heads at the Center?"

Danny didn't even muster a response.

The reason Fred dreaded calling his son, besides the obvious pain it caused, was because he never knew what to say. They couldn't talk about normal life, because it didn't exist. They couldn't talk about treatment, because Danny would freeze up. So the conversations would go from awkward to silent, and Fred would mumble his good-byes and then lie on his side and stare through the TV for the rest of the night.

"Son," Fred said, "there's something I need to tell you. I might be going away for a while, probably a week or so, just a little getaway."

Silence.

"You'll be okay if I don't call for a few days?"

"Mm."

"Son, I just needed to say . . . I just wanted to let you know that I . . ."

Fred tried to get the words out, but his voice cracked. Embarrassed, he tried to speak again and failed.

Danny mumbled a good-bye and hung up. After a prolonged silence, a sob escaped Fred, a brief hiccup that he choked off as if it were rising bile. He held the phone in his hand for a moment, then cursed and threw it against the TV. He stalked across the room and punched a hole in the drywall, kicked the foot hammock down the hallway, and then stood with his arms extended against the bedroom door, deep shuddering breaths heaving out of him, his rage and pain pressing down on him like the weight of an ocean.

When he calmed enough to speak, he retrieved his phone and called the number Lana had given him.

"Agent Hernandez?" she said. "Everything okay?"

"Put me on the first plane to Mexico."

23

When Grey and Fred returned the next day, to the same table at the same café, Lana greeted Grey by lifting her eyebrows, her chestnut eyes intense.

"I'm already in," Fred muttered.

Grey gave Lana a single, curt nod.

She leaned back and pushed a thin black folder across the table to each of them. A beige "Classified" stamp was splayed across the front.

"It's what we know about the General's activities over the years. It isn't much. There are two notable items I wanted to bring to your attention, one of which isn't included in the dossier." She waited until Grey and Fred had ordered coffees before continuing. "We know he has a right-hand man, a Colombian named Señor Guiñol. We don't have a photograph of him either. He only meets with high-level cartel leaders, usually in a neutral location, to hand out instructions or reprimands from his boss."

"Reprimands to cartel leaders," Fred said. "Jesus."

"What else do we know about him?" Grey asked.

"Almost nothing, except he was known in Colombia as Doctor Zombie."

"Excuse me?" Fred said.

"In his former life, he was a pharmacist known for experimenting with scopolamine on his patients."

Grey had been briefed on scopolamine during the Bogotá posting. It was a substance derived from the *borrachero* tree, native to Colombia. In high doses, it was lethal. In lower doses, it robbed victims of their free will and erased memory. It was used in rapes and street crime in the larger Colombian cities, especially Bogotá.

"It's been called the most dangerous drug in the world," Lana continued, "but Agent Hernandez would know more about that than I."

"It's the real deal," Fred said. "Frightening."

Grey smacked at a mosquito. "So he gets off on turning people into zombies?"

"Something like that," Lana said. "Though those who've seen his handiwork swear he doesn't use any drugs. Obviously, they're misinformed."

"This is some organization this General's got going," Fred said. "Anything else on Guiñol?"

"Just that he's the only known associate. Finding him might be almost as good as finding El General."

Grey took a sip of coffee. "You mentioned a second item?"

Lana pressed her lips together, her head bobbing almost imperceptibly. "We think he's one of ours."

"Guiñol?"

"The General."

Grey's eyebrows rose, and Fred spluttered ice water back into his cup.

"No one could operate like he does without inside knowledge," Lana said. "*Continuing* inside knowledge. And what we know of the way he works . . . he acts like one of us. Thinks like one of us."

"Not to burst your bubble," Grey said, "but there are other intelligence services around the world with some pretty talented operatives."

"Every agency has distinctions, its own idiosyncratic methods, and he follows ours."

"Still," Grey said, "couldn't it be a rival agency or a cartel playing games, using info from a captured CIA operative to lead you on a goose chase?"

Lana crossed her legs and smoothed her skirt. "Anything's possible."

"It's starting to make sense," Fred said. "You've kept it under wraps because of the potential for embarrassment?"

"The threat to national security is real," Lana said. "That's all I can say. I'm doing my best to probe the angle of his past identity."

"We're putting our lives on the line," Grey said. "I don't want to find out you've kept something to yourself that might help."

"You have my word," Lana said. "You're doing the right thing."

Grey's smile was thin.

"Remember, we're not asking you to penetrate the cartel. We just want to see where the cult angle leads."

Fine advice, Grey thought, *except that judging from past experience, the cult might be the more dangerous of the two.*

On the ride home, Fred took a call on his cell and then did a U-turn in the middle of the highway.

"What's up?" Grey said.

"Someone found a corpse in the Everglades with my business card in the pocket. They want me to come identify. You mind coming, in case there's something we need to see? Or you got evening plans?"

"My only plans involved not seeing any more dead bodies."

Fred cranked the A/C. "Yeah, sorry about that."

It took them an hour to pass through the dregs of Homestead and Florida City and reach the entrance to the Everglades. As soon as they passed through the gate and entered the park, minutes from the strip malls of South Dixie Highway, all pretense of civilization disappeared. The saw grass and endless vistas of the Everglades sprawled to the horizon, reminding Grey of an African savannah.

They had the road to themselves. Dusk approached, and Grey didn't need a park ranger to tell him it was a bad idea to be caught out there after hours. The din from the insects was stunning, not a soft concerto but a violent throbbing of sound, an assault of the night. Alligators lined the muddy watering holes, and Grey whistled when he spotted a twenty-foot snake slithering into a canal.

"Did I just see a python?"

Fred shuddered. "They're taking over the Everglades. That's what happens when people buy pet snakes that get bigger than they are."

There was beauty as well, visceral and intense. Brilliant roseate spoonbills swooping over a hardwood hammock, the symmetry of a grove of dwarf cypress, a sky that spanned worlds. *Nya would love it here*, Grey thought. *Find it spiritual.*

The spell was broken by a bevy of police cars parked alongside a sign that read snake bight. Behind the sign, a footpath led into the swamp. Grey could see more officers farther down the path.

When they left the car, the rush of humid air made Grey feel as if he had been lowered into a volcano. Fred flashed his identification at a uniformed policeman and nudged his head towards the trail. "The body's down there?"

"Yeah," the officer said, "but you don't want to go in there like that."

"Like what?"

"Look at your arms."

Grey saw Fred look down at his bare forearms, then start cursing and slapping at his skin. Grey looked at his own arms and noticed they were covered in black dots.

The officer grinned and thrust a bottle of mosquito repellent at Fred. Grey blanched and snatched it as soon as Fred was finished.

"A few hundred yards down the path," the officer said. "Trust me, you won't miss it."

He was right. Deep into the mangroves, surrounded by cops and medical examiners, bound with rope to a bald cypress, was a corpse with a face so swollen from insect bites that it was unrecognizable. It was also missing one of its legs below the knee, and the skin was flaccid and sagging.

A plainclothes detective approached Fred, who was chewing furiously on a toothpick. The detective handed Fred a business card sealed in a plastic bag. "This yours?"

Fred looked down. "Yeah," he said softly. "The guy's name was Ernesto Reinas. He's an accountant on our payroll. We turned him a while back, had him looking into the cartels."

"Apparently they didn't like it."

Trying not to gag from the stench, Grey breathed through his mouth and waved mosquitoes off the body as he checked for signs the murder might be cult related. "Body was found like this?" he asked.

"With the business card halfway out of his pocket."

A medical examiner stepped forward. "The body's been here overnight. My guess is a gator got the leg, and take your pick as to cause of death: blood loss from the missing limb, dehydration, allergic reaction to a million insect bites. Another twenty-four hours and bones are all we'd have left."

"No one found him sooner?" Grey asked.

The detective chuckled. "Not from around here? Let's just say summer is not tourist season in the Everglades. Imagine this place at noon. These mangroves are *infested* with mosquitoes." He turned to Fred. "You got any idea who dragged him out here?"

Fred flicked the sweat off his brow, and exchanged a glance with Grey.

MEXICO CITY
1983

His handlers had called it "situational flexibility," the ability to convince oneself that normal ethical standards did not apply in certain self-serving scenarios. The textbooks referred to it as "moral disengagement." Nietzsche termed it the concept of the Superman.

John Wolverton called it The Mirror.

He had been a young man before Jonestown. Two years out of Yale, two years into the Company. Still a man of society, of the Western world, though too brilliant and restless for a normal life to be of interest. Possessed of an intellect so keen it seemed as if everyone else spoke too slowly, lived far below the human potential.

They sent him to Guyana because he had exhibited the same psychological traits as the leader of the Peoples Temple, Reverend Jim Jones.

High charisma. Rhetorical gifts. Situational flexibility.

Yes, he was morally ambiguous, at least according to societal standards. Not vacant, which he realized after kneeling beside the corpse of his beloved and their infant child. Just ambiguous. Weren't we all, except for a select few misguided souls on either end of the spectrum? Wasn't that the point of evolution? To adapt and survive the best we can?

Besides, those societal standards had produced My Lai and irreversible ghettos and the School of the Americas, along with a million other atrocities.

The drug deals with Hilltown and Rabbi Washington had started the connections. John Wolverton began using a variety of pseudonyms and business fronts, both when dealing with the CIA and with other entities, which ranged from South American governments to drug cartels to the Mafia. He had to be especially careful with the CIA, who might connect the note he had left at Jonestown with the rising gringo crime lord in Guyana. While the Jonestown tape was a powerful piece of leverage, anonymity was even better.

The deals and alliances, the orchestral chess moves in the underworld, came easy to him. Within three years he was a wealthy man, possessor of a million dollars of cash and real estate in Guyana, Venezuela, and northern Brazil. His ambition was as vast as the Argentinean pampas, yet he felt as if he were missing a key ingredient, something that set him apart.

He needed an angle. He needed a name. He needed an *identity*.

Deciding to follow in the footsteps of countless philosopher kings before him, he set out on a journey to explore the continent, a pilgrimage of personal enlightenment.

He started with Venezuela, from its sultry Caribbean islands to the high society shoreline of oil-soaked Lake Maracaibo, up to the cozy Andean mountain resorts and then down to his personal favorite, the flat-topped jungle mesas known as *tepuis*, their prehistoric eco-systems immortalized by Sir Arthur Conan Doyle's *The Lost World*.

And the women—ah, if only he were a bard as well, the ballads he would compose! Suffice it to say he could have lingered in the salsa and merengue clubs of Caracas forever, rum-soaked and dazed, lost in a fever dream of dark eyes and lilting Spanish voices.

It was a blur after that. Absorbing the otherworldly beauty of Rio, hearing the roar of Iguaçu Falls, swept along by the hypnotic current of the Amazon, drifting across a glacial lake in Chile, mesmerized by street tango in the colorful streets of Buenos Aires, tumbling down sand dunes on the coast of Peru, staring agog at Machu Picchu. And all along the way, with his money and charisma and swarthy good looks, he lived the life of the most indulgent of rock stars, gobbling up exotic cuisines and drugs and women.

Months went by, then a year. An entire continent split open and savored like a ripe papaya. Still, as enjoyable as it all was, nothing and no one moved him as had Tashmeni. He wasn't sure what to think about that. Was he seeking to forget, or remember?

Youthful passions satiated, he was ready to build his empire. Still lacking an identity, he traveled north, through the beauty and poverty of Central America, a true lost world, misted green volcanoes crouching above bubbling fumaroles and black sand beaches, ramshackle cities draped over the ruins of ancient civilizations, villages infused with the aroma of coffee beans.

Weary but brimming with life, he stumbled into Mexico City, stunned by its sophistication and the crush of humanity. It was at a party in the *Colonia Roma* where he met the man who would change the course of his life.

———◆———

Through one of his connections, the man once known as John Wolverton ended up at a mansion full of fashion models, wealthy businessmen, and film stars. One of the attendees, Adolfo Constanzo, was known to him. Adolfo was a Cuban-American drug dealer from Miami who was making inroads into the burgeoning Mexican-American pipeline.

Adolfo was lounging on a sofa with his arm draped around two women, though his gaze lingered on the men in the room. John Wolverton knew him at once. The striking good looks, the confidence held loose in his broad shoulders, the infectious laughter, the gravity of his eyes that seemed to suck in the entire room.

Adolfo was someone just like him.

John Wolverton watched him throughout the evening, and knew that he in turn was being watched. He pictured himself through Adolfo's eyes: a man with a leonine head and midnight-blue eyes, skin tinged beige from his mixed Latino heritage, wearing white slacks and a black V-neck shirt and wire-framed glasses, his fierce intelligence coexisting with a raw physical competency. A man who looked as comfortable in jungle fatigues as in the boardroom.

At the end of the night, Adolfo approached him, and John Wolverton assumed an identity Adolfo would recognize, that of a prosperous Caribbean smuggler.

They spent the next week dissecting the city together, an endless string of parties and society events. Eventually the time for business came, and they discussed the convenience of the Cold War to the drug trade, as well as their mutual connections inside the CIA.

Both men knew the friendship wouldn't last, for two people of such towering ego and personal magnetism can never exist in the same space for long. At the end of the week, perhaps still trying to sway the man who had fended off his sexual advances, Adolfo told him there was someone he wanted him to meet.

"Do you know what Palo Mayombe is?" Adolfo asked.

John Wolverton did not.

Adolfo described the religion, and asked him if he would like to attend a ceremony.

"Why not?" John Wolverton said, intrigued.

"It's a special ceremony," Adolfo confided. "I'm a palero myself— a sorcerer—and the real reason I've come to Mexico City is not for the parties, but to train under someone, a palero much stronger even than I. Do you believe in sorcery?"

"I believe in the power of many things."

"This palero, you've got to meet him, man. You can feel his power radiating off him. I've seen a lot and I've never seen anything like it. He's a Pied Piper of the dead. The whole city's afraid of him."

"Interesting," John Wolverton said. "I'd indeed like to meet him. What's his name?"

Adolfo's grin implied a gift both secret and delicious. "Tata Menga."

"He's in the business?"

"Oh yeah," Adolfo said. "Doesn't deal himself or anything. He provides spiritual protection to the cartels in exchange for a cut of the profits. I've adopted the model myself. Works like a charm. The cartels are believers, man. They're all former Catholics who can't shake it off. Might as well embrace the dark side and seek its protection, right?"

The gears in John Wolverton's mind whirred furiously, alive with the possibilities, connecting the past to the present.

"That's right," he murmured.

24

DER HEILIGKEIT DES LUFT SANATORIUM
PRESENT DAY

Viktor stood at the edge of the lookout, arms folded, peering into the layers of fog that swirled like restless phantoms above the chasm. It was nearly dusk. He was alone.

The altitude was high enough to warrant a coat, but Viktor preferred the chill pressing through his sweater, the cleansing briskness of the mountain air. It was liberating.

Shuffling forward until he felt empty space beneath his toes, the fog made him feel as if he were drifting in midair, lost in a white abyss. What lay below, he wondered, in the realm of mist and death? Heaven? Hell? Nothing? Everything? If he were to take another step, he would know.

He stepped back, his smile quick and fierce. Suicide had never tempted him.

Those kinds of answers he would discover in time, as would we all. What Viktor desired, the object of his lifelong search, was to circumvent the wait. To know the unknowable, to crack open the door of doors, to see beyond the veil before it fluttered and settled over his corpse, separating the two realms forever.

Perhaps, just perhaps, to learn something that might affect the outcome.

His thoughts drifted to the case. To Palo Mayombe. Though aware of the religion for years, the last time he had encountered it during the course of an investigation was in Matamoros, Mexico. It had not been a pleasant experience.

"Cult" and "religion" were terms of art whose definitions depended on the user. To Viktor, religion was simply veneration of a person, ideal, or thing. Thus, all cults could be considered religions.

Oh, Viktor could hear the proponents of the major faiths clamoring for supremacy, and it was true that the weight of history lent a movement a certain gravitas. Still, since no one could actually prove the validity of any religion based on the concept of the divine, there was no real barometer.

Moreover, no one within a cult actually thought of themselves as belonging to a cult—to them, whatever belief system they were engaged in was as valid as any other. More so.

But if there was ever a case for the vernacular, Western definition of a cult, that of deviation from the religious and societal norm, then it would be the crime scene Viktor had been called to examine in Matamoros.

The year was 1989. The call from Interpol was frantic. Mexican authorities had uncovered a horrific crime scene just south of the Texas border, and one of the victims, Mark Kilroy, was an American pre-med student on spring break. DEA needed help piecing together the puzzle before the public went berserk.

When Viktor arrived at the scene, a ranch in the Mexican desert twenty miles outside Matamoros, law enforcement officials with eyes that looked ready to slip out of their sockets led him to the unearthed remains of fifteen bodies, clearly victims of ritual sacrifice. Beheaded corpses, digits missing, organs excised, spines and brains removed.

On the property they found drugs, guns, votive candles, wax skulls, and a plethora of homemade religious icons. And in a wooden shed hidden behind a corral, they found cigar butts, torture implements, discarded rum and tequila bottles, a rotting turtle—and a cast-iron cauldron filled with human and animal body parts stewing inside. The Mexican *federales* brought in a *curandero*—a Mexican folk healer—to exorcise the contents of the shed before they would continue the investigation.

The property was Rancho Santa Elena, and it belonged to the Hernandez drug family. A man named Adolfo Constanzo, a Cuban-American from Miami and a known practitioner of Palo and Santeria, had convinced the Hernandez Cartel that his sorcery could protect their illegal enterprise. A group of disciples lived at the ranch with Constanzo, and they had tortured and sacrificed dozens of victims.

The eeriest thing of all about the case, and the most interesting from a professional standpoint to Viktor, was that when interrogated, all of the cartel members they had rounded up, right up to the leaders, admitted the slayings had been human sacrifices carried out to protect the cartel. They also told the authorities that Constanzo's powers could render them bulletproof and invisible, and nothing the police could do would harm them.

In short, they were utterly convinced that they were, even while sitting in jail, under the protection of the sorcery of Adolfo Constanzo.

Viktor shook his head at the memory. He would never cease to be amazed at the ability of ultra-charismatic individuals to coax a sliver of evil out of otherwise normal human beings and expand it to grotesque proportions, like winding a tapeworm around a stick.

As with most of the criminal factions with which Viktor dealt, Adolfo Constanzo's cult was a derivation, a perversion of traditional religion. Whether or not Constanzo could actually do what he claimed to do . . . well, that had not been within the sphere of Viktor's professional ambit. What mattered was that Constanzo's followers *believed* he could.

Viktor sighed and rubbed his arms against the Alpine chill. None of the law enforcement officials at Matamoros had understood Palo Mayombe. Viktor understood the Western aversion, since Palo was so closely aligned with the realm of the dead, but he also appreciated the Congolese theology. While Viktor claimed no religion, he did believe in the concept of life force or bodily energy or the soul— he had witnessed too many affirmative demonstrations to come to any other conclusion.

And if science was to be believed and matter could not be destroyed, only transmuted into other forms, then the life force of the living had to go *somewhere* after death.

Turning to walk back to the sanatorium, he bumped into a large man standing inches behind him. The contact made Viktor scramble to right himself, almost causing him to plummet off the cliff. The person behind him was someone he had never seen before, and Viktor hadn't heard him approach.

Someone dressed in white scrubs and standing inches from Viktor's face, staring at him with a blank expression, a push away from sending him off the edge of the chasm.

25

As the plane flew over the Gulf of Mexico, Grey pored over Lana's file on the General. It didn't take long.

The report was a dry description of a dozen busted drug transactions from several government agencies over the last thirty years. In each case, one or more suspects had mentioned the General during interrogation—or at least had mentioned a faceless entity fitting the description. The evidence was all hearsay, as not a single witness claimed to have dealt with the crime lord himself. Some of the witnesses thought he was based somewhere in Colombia. Some said Peru. Others said Mexico, Bolivia, Argentina, Chile, Nicaragua, Panama. One claimed he lived on a yacht in Antarctica.

As Lana had intimated, the report was vanilla, whitewashed, and unhelpful. Nothing new on Guiñol. Not a word about Palo Mayombe. The five known victims of the blue lady were mentioned, each of them a former member of a different criminal organization.

Could it be, Grey thought, *that Palo Mayombe was the key?* Did the General control the cartels through the cult? Through fear of torture, human sacrifice, and supernatural reprisal?

Grey had seen firsthand the power of charismatic cult leaders, from his mother's death to his string of cases with Viktor that illustrated, in graphic detail, just how far a human being could be persuaded to go. But could Palo Mayombe be that widespread, touching all corners of the Americas? The thought chilled him. At first he found it unbelievable, but then he thought of the conviction in Elias Monte's eyes, and of Hector Fortuna's disciples standing around an iron cauldron after stuffing a dead DEA agent in the closet.

Yet how did the blue lady fit? Her appearance seemed unrelated to the cult. And surely at least one of the suspects in the file would have mentioned the General's involvement in Palo Mayombe, if they had been brave or foolhardy enough to name him in the first place.

Grey sighed. Mexico was the right call. He closed the file and saw Fred watching him.

"I've seen IKEA instructions with more substance," Fred said, flicking his eyes to the file.

Grey relaxed the seat rest and crossed his arms. "Yeah."

"So you know what you're getting into down there?"

"I suppose it's a bunch of extremely ruthless men making stacks of money pushing drugs across the border to willing consumers."

"You're right about that." Fred cracked his knuckles with a vengeance. "Look, I get it. Americans want drugs, a young dealer in the ghetto will risk a dime in prison versus a lifetime of poverty, and an illiterate Mexican peasant is going to do whatever it takes to feed his family. It all sucks. Both countries need to get their shit together. But still. I don't care what's happened in your life—you do *not* deal drugs to kids. You don't ruin someone else's family. If we ever find this General, I'll shove a kilo down his throat myself and watch his heart explode."

By the time he finished his off-topic rant, Fred's face had flushed, his voice had risen almost to a shout, and Grey saw the same dangerous look in his eye he had seen at Hector Fortuna's house.

Fred swallowed and worked his jaw back and forth, his voice lowering. "Anyway, the system isn't our concern. The cartels it spawned are."

"And the Mexicans are particularly ruthless."

"The Mexican cartels are country clubs who only admit psychopaths. The Colombians are smarter and have the coca fields, but the Mexicans will do anything it takes. And I do mean anything. You don't even want to hear the stories."

"Let's bring it down to eye level," Grey said. "What's the hierarchy of a cartel like the Alianza, and how does it all relate to this stage of the investigation?"

"Cartels are like pyramid schemes. At the bottom are the foot soldiers, the kids dealing crack on the corners. A step up are the local retailers—the Manny Lopezes of the world. There're usually a few levels of retailers under the domestic distributors, which is where the serious money starts to flow. Then you have the stateside kingpins, the international smugglers with the overseas connections. These guys are often inducted into the parent cartel."

"Vertical control of distribution," Grey said.

"That's right. But even the L.A. and Miami kingpins are small fry compared to the fat cats south of the border. Those guys *mint* money. Production is everything, and that's why the Mexicans are gaining ground. Cocaine is still king, but our friendly neighbors are funneling homegrown weed and meth and heroin and prescription drugs into the States like grain pouring into a harvester."

"And the General?"

"A new level, if he's real. Someone working behind the scenes but who has some weird hold on the organizations he deals with. A shadow cartel." He reached up to crank the air conditioner above his seat and said, "You really think this cult is involved at that level? It just seems so . . . I don't know, surreal. Grown men stirring bones in a pot? Robbing graves?"

Grey stared at the seat back in front of him as the pilot announced the initial descent into Cancun. "I've seen some things while working with Professor Radek that . . . well, you wouldn't believe me, unless you'd seen them yourself. I'm not sure what I think about it all yet, but there's one thing I know for sure: never underestimate the power of the mind, especially the ability of a master manipulator to influence and control. Think of the world's major religious figures, its cultural icons, its politicians. Think of the power they wield. Think of that applied to a criminal organization. Think of Adolf Hitler."

Fred was staring out the window, where the coral reefs created shadow patterns along the bottom of the sea. "So it's not like you're telling me there's anything to this Palo Mayombe insanity, just that our guy's maybe using it to stay in control."

When Grey didn't respond right away, Fred turned his head and said, "You don't actually believe any of that crap, right? I didn't take you for that kind of guy."

"No," Grey murmured, his voice drowned by the sound of the plane hitting the runway, "I suppose I'm not."

26

DER HEILIGKEIT DES LUFT SANATORIUM

His heart a set of fists hammering against a speed bag inside his chest, Viktor settled the weight of his seven-foot frame into his heels, rooting himself to the ground. He could feel the wind from the thousand-foot chasm behind him, whisking across his back. The best he could do, if pushed by the mental patient standing inches from his face, would be to take them down together.

The man's hands were hidden behind his back, as if concealing something. He hadn't moved, but kept staring at Viktor with a vacant, almost bovine expression. There was an asylum for the criminally insane on the property, lower down the mountain, though none of the inmates should be out alone.

Viktor edged sideways, debating rushing forward to drive them both away from the cliff. The man made no movement, and when Viktor moved far enough away to feel safe, he stepped rapidly away from the drop-off and over the guardrail, his heart pumping so fast it felt like a bellows in the hands of a grinning Hephaestus.

After backing well away from the cliff, his eyes never leaving the face of the man in white scrubs, Viktor subconsciously reached for his *kris*, the asymmetrical dagger he normally carried at all times. He never dreamed he would need it at the sanatorium.

The man looked about Viktor's age, and though not nearly as tall, he was thick, with hunched shoulders that sloped to a bloated neck. His face was shaped like a watermelon and sported facial features so small they looked etched. Splotched in the upper third of his forehead, below the receding hairline, was a purple birthmark.

Security was fierce on the mountain. Even Viktor's building, which housed voluntary patients, was controlled by key card access and patrolled by the finest guards money could buy. The only road was watched by CCTV and secured by three different gatehouses. The Swiss treated this sanatorium like they treated their banks: catering to the wealthy, clandestine, and unassailable.

"Do I know you?" Viktor asked in German.

The man looked startled that Viktor had spoken. Viktor repeated the question in French, and then English.

Some of the glaze lifted from the man's eyes. "I don't think so," he answered in German.

Viktor grimaced. "Then why were you standing right behind me at the edge of the cliff?"

"Was I?" The man smiled, though the thinness of his lips made the smile look too narrow, as if half-formed.

"What's your name?" Viktor asked, as if addressing a student.

"Glen. And yours?"

"Professor Viktor Radek."

"You're German?"

"Czech."

The man shuffled forward, and Viktor took a step back. The man didn't seem to notice.

"Are you returning to the East Wing?" Viktor asked. "I'm going that way, if you'd like to join."

The man's smile was sad, as if he had lost something he could never retrieve. He turned to back away from Viktor, still concealing whatever was behind his back, then headed down a footpath opposite the cliff that descended into a copse of pine.

After watching the man disappear into the forest, Viktor strode down the mountain road, passing a gatehouse and taking a smaller road that led to the criminal sanatorium. Two men with rifles stood in front of a guard shack just off the road.

Viktor showed his identification, explained the situation, and asked the guards if they recognized the description of the man who'd approached him on the cliff. He could tell by the lift of their brows that they had.

One of the guards went inside the gatehouse, and the other, a stern-faced man with graying temples, waited with Viktor.

"I understand you can't reveal names," Viktor said. "I'm just letting you know you might have an escaped patient on your hands."

The guard held up a finger, saying nothing. A few moments later the other guard returned and spoke in a low voice to the guard who had waited with Viktor. Both of the guards' faces relaxed, though they looked askance at Viktor, as if he might need to be put away.

"Not to worry," said the stern-faced man. "Everyone is accounted for. Would you care for an escort back to the East Wing?"

"Sure," Viktor said.

Though Viktor accepted the ride in the jeep without a word, he had understood what the first guard had told the second. The guard had spoken in rapid-fire, slangy Swiss-German, but Viktor had attended boarding school in Switzerland and was familiar with the dialect.

Don't worry, the guard had said, *Glen's been in isolation for the last three days. This tall guy must be off his meds.*

27

ZONA HOTELERA
CANCUN, MEXICO

Glass of Don Julio Real in hand, a tequila as smooth as the curve of a virgin's thigh, Ricky Orizaga surveyed his fiefdom: Caribbean waters the pale blue of a robin's egg, golden sands the texture of flour, a fifteen-kilometer spit of land pregnant with mega-hotels and worth as much as the rest of Mexico put together.

Life was good. Business was booming. Ricky's place in the cartel was secure, his village provided for.

The Alianza owned the hotel, and Ricky lived in the penthouse suite. Handmade Indonesian furnishings surrounded him. A wall of glass showcased the Caribbean. Two women lounged in his bed in the next room.

He couldn't ask for anything more. Nothing, that was, except a replacement for the missing finger on his left hand.

In order not to anger El General, his superiors had not allowed Ricky to reattach the finger Señor Guiñol had removed with a knife. More than the missing finger, Ricky shuddered at the memory of the event.

Or the lack thereof, since he remembered none of it.

He had awakened in a hospital bed, screaming for pain meds, his memory of the preceding days a slab of unfinished concrete. All he knew was what he had been told: that after the meeting with Señor Guiñol, he had returned to Alianza headquarters, where he had calmly handed over his blood-soaked finger to the leader of the cartel, and informed him that it was his punishment for Miami. That if it happened again, there would be more than just a severed finger.

Relieved he had escaped with his life, Ricky had moved on. He was the highest-ranking member of Alianza living in Cancun, as the few men above him preferred their heavily guarded compounds outside the city. Ricky was someone the cartel leadership wanted to have a direct hand in the day-to-day business, high enough in the hierarchy to command attention yet low enough to replace.

Ricky didn't mind. He knew the score.

A bell chimed, signaling the arrival of someone on the suite's private elevator. His bodyguards hustled to the door, returning with a gilt-edged envelope bearing Ricky's name. He blanched when he saw it, and started tugging on his goatee. The last such envelope had been an invitation to the meeting with Señor Guiñol.

Feeling a stab of phantom pain in the stub of his finger, he downed the tequila and used a penknife to slit open the envelope, needing a few tries before his hand stopped shaking. Ricky had ordered hits across the Americas, stared down *federales*, exchanged gunfire with rival cartels—yet it took him three attempts to open a goddamn envelope.

Inside was a sheet of paper made of thick cream stock.

Agent Federico Hernandez just landed at Cancun Airport. With him is a man named Dominic Grey. It would be best if they did not leave the country.

Ricky's sigh of relief coursed through him like an orgasm. He would not have to meet with Señor Guiñol. He merely had to kill two men. If so asked, he would have tried to assassinate the President of Mexico rather than face El General's spokesman again, handing over his own body parts to his superiors like some mindless golem.

Ricky knew the two men named in the letter; his cartel already wanted them dead. Their arrival was a stroke of luck. DEA agents were untouchable in the States, but Mexico was a different story.

His cartel's best sicario, Lucho, would be especially interested in the news. As far as Ricky knew, Lucho had loved nothing in life except for his sister. Ricky would not want to be either of those two gringos, oh no.

He gave instructions to his men, then held the letter aloft on the balcony and lit it with his lighter. Ricky's last thought before the letter flamed and then crumbled, ashes drifting to the beach, was not a pleasant one.

Agent Hernandez would have taken steps to disguise their arrival. Fake passports, bribed officials, the usual. Otherwise, the Alianza would have known of the visit before they left Miami.

The fact that El General knew of Agent Hernandez's and Dominic Grey's arrival before the Alianza did, in their own town, caused another ache where the missing finger should be, this one duller, deeper, and much more prolonged.

28

CANCUN, MEXICO

Fred drove away from the car rental agency in a sedan he had reserved under a false name. Their plan was to spend a day in Cancun checking out the yerberías, then head down the coast to hook up with an ex-DEA agent who could provide information and weapons.

Grey lowered the passenger side window. "You know Cancun? I've never been."

"Too well."

Five minutes later they entered Cancun's *Zona Hotelera*, a rapier of land poised between an emerald lagoon and the Caribbean. In between the beachfront hotels whose entrances looked built for a race of giants, Grey got tantalizing glimpses of golden sands and azure water.

The car windows were down, a pleasant breeze rushing in. "Can you believe this was a coconut plantation in the seventies?" Fred said.

Grey leaned an arm out the window. "Not really."

"The Mexican government decided to turn this place into a world-class resort and, well, it's one of the few things they got right. Don't worry, we'll be back in the real Mexico in, oh, about thirty seconds. So what's on deck first, finding one of these yerberías?"

"You know where to look?"

"I think so. You know what to say when we get there?"

"Not a clue."

The change was immediate and visceral. One minute they were gliding through one of the most impressive tourist centers in the world, the next they were delving into the actual city of Cancun, a sprawling montage of concrete eyesores, chaotic traffic, and weedy abandoned lots. Though a stark contrast to the Zona Hotelera, Grey did not find it impoverished, at least in Latin American terms. Just scruffy and real.

"First order of business," Fred said, pulling into a McDonald's drive through, "lunch."

Grey chuckled as he watched Fred order three cheeseburgers with fries. Though Grey downed a quarter pounder, he would have preferred a couple of fish tacos from one of the enticing food carts along the highway.

Fred sucked fry salt off a fingertip. "How come Micky D's is always better abroad? I guess the pink slime factories haven't made it overseas." He pointed at a sign for mercado veintiocho. *Market Twenty-Eight.* "That's the one we want."

A few minutes later they were parking near an open-air marketplace with tiled walkways and a warren of contiguous stalls. The humidity was oppressive, the covered stalls steaming the market like the lid on a crock-pot.

"Pretty sure I've seen a yerbería here before," Fred said. "This is the main downtown market."

There was a plethora of indigenous wares: ceramics and leather goods, jewelry, pottery, wooden toys, wedding dresses, colorful *luchador* masks. Grey led Fred deep inside, stopping to eye a knickknack now and then so as not to attract attention. The smell of stale lard emanated from a collection of food stalls near the center, and at times the chords of a roving mariachi band rose above the din.

Grey didn't like the feel of the place. There were far too many vendors vying for the attention of a handful of patrons. The vendors were aggressive and accosted Grey and Fred in the narrow corridors of the bazaar, honing in on the promise of American dollars like birds of prey clawing at a pair of mice.

He could also sense the vice and the promise of illicit goods lurking just beneath the surface, behind the hard stares of the men, sticking to the honey-eyed smiles and beckoning fingers of the women. Normally Grey would have stalked through such a place, his own hard eyes and dangerous aura warding off aggressors. But he didn't want to attract attention, so he played the part of the innocent tourist, eying a hand-woven shirt here, testing the strands of a hammock there.

A burly man in a soiled guayabera shoved a toy in Grey's face, a rubber ball attached to a paddle that the man ping-ponged back and forth. "Mexican PlayStation?" he asked. He was so close Grey could see the dirt underneath his fingernails.

Grey let out a slow breath, resisting the urge to twist the man's arm behind his back and shove his face into the stall. "I don't have kids."

As they walked away, Fred said, "Good times, huh? We should shop together more often."

Half an hour later, just as Grey was starting to wonder if Fred had been mistaken or if the yerbería had relocated, Fred touched his arm and nudged his head towards a stall the size of a walk-in closet. The front counter displayed a collection of painted ceramic skulls.

Grey felt a buzz of excitement when he saw what filled the shelves lining the walls behind the skulls. Glass jars of dirt with taped-on labels, bead necklaces, religious icons, railroad spikes, and a few other items he recognized from the botánica in Miami.

Fred twisted the lid off a soda as Grey sidled to the counter. A middle-aged woman in a red-and-green patterned dress, her hair in a bun, rose from a folding chair.

"*Sí?*"

Grey spoke in formal Spanish, deciding on a different tactic than the one he had tried in Miami. "Good afternoon, Señora. You have a nice selection."

"*Gracias.* There is something in particular you're looking for?"

"Yes, there is. I need something for my palero."

Her gaze remained steady, a slight lifting of her eyebrows the only sign of surprise. "We have a few items, *sí.* Candles, herbs, dirt, animal skulls."

"Do you have any cauldrons?"

This time her gaze lingered on Grey, wondering what the gringo in the cargo pants and black T-shirt was doing in a street market in Mexico asking about a prenda. She leaned down and pulled out two pumpkin-size cast-iron cauldrons from beneath the counter, saying nothing, her thin eyebrows arching towards Grey.

"Do you have anything larger?"

She replaced the prendas and stood. Her eyes flicked to the sides of the walkway fronting the stall, rested on Fred, and then returned to Grey. "No, señor."

"Is there anyone else in town?" Grey asked with a touch of scorn, as if it was the woman, not Grey, who was falling short.

"You would have to go to Merida."

Merida was three hours west of Cancun, all the way across the Yucatan. Grey placed his hands on the counter. "I need it," he said, his voice low and with a hint of menace, "for Tata Menga. Tonight."

He half expected her to laugh at him, but instead she took a step back, her hands pressed against her sides.

Grey leaned forward. "Surely you can help me?"

Her lips moved before she spoke. "I wish that I could. I have only the two. No one local sells larger prendas."

"Do you realize how far it is to Tata Menga?" Grey said.

"No, señor."

"I don't have time for Merida."

Her face had paled, and her voice was almost a whisper. "I am sorry, señor. Very sorry."

"Do you know anyone who can help me?"

"No, señor."

Grey let his stare linger, then eased his hands off the counter and backed away.

----·----

Waiting until they reached the outskirts of the market, Fred muttered, "That poor woman looked ready to sell you her firstborn."

"I needed to know if the name Tata Menga was real, and if she knew where I could find him. I think we got our answers." A dozen men eyed them as they returned to their car. "We should go."

"Yeah. We should."

They spent the rest of the day at different markets in town, having similar experiences. Not all of the markets had a yerbería, and not many that did dealt in Palo. After a few more inquiries about Tata Menga, more discreet than the first but just as fruitless, they decided to call it a day. Night had fallen and the markets had wound down.

They jumped in the car and found a cheap motel near a shopping mall. Paid cash and found a *taquería* a block from the hotel. After ordering Negro Modelos with limes, they kicked back in plastic chairs.

"Time to move on," Fred said. "It's getting a bit hot in this pueblo."

"At least we know we're on the right track."

"So what's next?"

Grey took a swallow of beer. "I thought we'd stake out a few cemeteries."

Fred looked as if he were waiting for Grey to laugh. "You're joking, right?"

"Viktor tells me every good palero either digs up bones from a cemetery or has someone do it for him. With an outfit like Tata Menga seems to have, I'm guessing he outsources his grave robbing."

"You're not actually proposing going door to door at cemeteries in the Yucatan?"

"Not yet," Grey said. "I thought about approaching caretakers, but they might be on the take, or the cemetery we're looking for might not employ a caretaker." The food arrived, mahi mahi tacos covered with jicama and poblano cream sauce. "This is more like it," Grey said after taking a bite.

Fred munched on his own tacos and agreed. "Should we try Merida?"

"Not yet. According to Elias, Tata Menga's somewhere in the jungle. I think he at least believed he was telling the truth about that." Grey rolled the beer between his palms. "We need local information. Someone who can ask around without raising as many eyebrows."

Fred wiped a dollop of sauce off his mouth. "My guy should be able to help with that. I hope he's got our hardware, too. I feel a little naked in this country, if you know what I mean."

Grey nodded, in full agreement. He had no affinity for guns but he understood their place.

Never focusing too long in one direction, Grey's eyes roamed the taquería as they ate, searching for signs of anyone or anything that didn't fit, flicking back to the entrance every few seconds for the trouble he sensed would find them one way or another before they left Mexico.

29

MIAMI

Lana woke to a feeling of suffocation. Something was covering her mouth and nose, something fleshy and foul. After gasping for breath and moving her head to the side to find air, she realized with a stab of terror that a heavy body, damp with sweat, was pressed against her in the bed, groping her as she struggled to move. A geyser of dread welled up inside her, flooding her pores when it erupted, the kind of fear that can only come from foreknowledge of one's fate, from past experience of something so terrible that even the thought of it was paralytic.

Lana screamed.

Rough hands slid up her thighs and yanked at her underwear.

She pushed as hard as she could against the crush of the man's weight, gagging on the stale body odor. Why couldn't she shove him off? She found enough focus to grasp the headboard and try to leverage him off the bed, but nothing worked. It were as if he weighed a thousand pounds and she were a child.

Panic overcame her, her mind a helium balloon filled with horrors from the past. She pushed and she pinched and she bit and she screamed and yet nothing could make him stop and he was closer to being inside her and this time Lana screamed so loud her soul ripped even further apart from her body than it had the last time and—

She jerked up in bed, shaking from the intensity of the dream. A nightmare of the worst kind, when one thinks one is awake but isn't, the mind's complicity lending the dream a terrifying reality.

It was five in the morning. Lana wasn't about to face the possibility of another nightmare. Still in a cold sweat, she shuddered to her feet, turned on all the lights, and prepared coffee.

She hadn't had that dream in years. Was it Miami? The conversation with Colonel Ganso? The current case and the bizarre cult?

All of the above?

She needed to cleanse. As soon as dawn arrived, she went for a long run across the Rickenbacker Causeway, past Virginia Key and all the way to Crandon Park. She walked beside the ocean, curled her toes in the sand, let the breeze caress her, and then ran back. She showered and dressed before driving to her favorite spot after a run, the Pinecrest Market.

Fresh pineapple shake in hand, she sat on a bench and let the sun burn away the memories, let the canopy of jacarandas and the chitter of tropical birds and the unfurling of a peach hibiscus restore her sanity.

She didn't berate herself for her reaction to the dream. Being brave did not mean being fearless, she knew.

It meant being able to overcome the fear.

After breakfast she took refuge in her work. She sat in front of her laptop and put her index fingers to her temples. In the age of Internet and drones, of CCTV cameras and NSA wiretaps, in an almost limitless informational society, why couldn't they find the General?

Fine, he was ex-CIA and knew their tricks. It had to go deeper than that. He was old school, an avoider of technology, able to live and thrive off the grid. An Osama bin Laden, living in a cave and avoiding the world as the might of the United States crashed against his mountain.

Where was the General's cave? How did he run his empire?

He kept his money off the books, easy to do with drugs. He probably had billions hidden in a jungle hut in the Amazon. But it was as if he ran a two-man organization, himself and Guiñol, giving orders to a dozen cartels. Where were his lieutenants, his foot soldiers? How did he do it?

Could the cult angle have merit? It wasn't the subject matter that gave Lana pause—the CIA knew better than most just how susceptible human beings were to the power of coercion—it was the scope. Palo Mayombe was one cult, and the General had his hand in multiple organizations. Could Palo be that widespread?

If Grey and Fred's investigation brought her even one step closer, then it was worth it. To advance to the highest ranks of the CIA, it took something extraordinary, and she didn't have the luxury of nepotism or a Cold War. Because of her Spanish, her career had been focused on Latin America, outside the front lines of the war on terror, limited in opportunity for an ambitious young agent.

She stopped alongside a canal, eying a red-and-black alien insect hive clinging to a tree. Miami had bugs that hadn't even been catalogued.

Forcing the memory of the dream to return, she confronted it headlong, laughing in its face until it disintegrated in the sunlight, motes of greasy subconscious scattering in the breeze.

Then she wheeled and went to see Colonel Ganso.

———— • ————

She found him in his garden, legs crossed, sipping coffee and stacking a handful of dominoes. He waved her over, beaming like a golf pro after an eagle putt.

What does he do all day? she wondered, then wished she hadn't. An image of the Colonel in his study late at night came to her, cognac in hand, surrounded by the chittering ghosts of his victims.

"Any progress?" she asked, walking to the edge of the sitting area and folding her arms.

"Sit, sit."

"I'll stand today."

He rubbed his chin with his thumb and forefinger. "As you wish. Unfortunately, Lana, despite the sifting of many . . . memories . . . I can remember nothing else of value on this topic."

Lana shifted from left to right. The dominoes rose and fell from Colonel Ganso's fingers, a rhythmic series of clicks. "I will not bother asking why you seek him, since it is not my place. But some advice, if I may?"

Lana eyed him warily. In the foliage draping the wall behind the Colonel, a golden orb weaver squatted in its web like some fat prince of death. The imagery was not lost on her.

"Were I seeking someone hidden," he said, "I would think like someone trained to elicit such information. I would think like a torturer."

"You mean think like yourself?"

The Colonel spread his hands in admission, his groomed hair and patrician face a model of colonial charm. "A good torturer does not simply elicit pain—he seeks points of pressure. These are two very distinct things, and they are different for everyone. Yes, physical pain will eventually break most people, but you cannot trust information given by a broken man. A man who *fears* something, however—such information is far more reliable. A selfish man fears for himself, and is easy to read. A better man fears for others. If possible, when dealing with a better man, one will find a loved one and bring them close. The very thought of torture befalling a family member was often enough to loosen a tongue—or to cause someone in hiding to emerge."

"Lovely advice," she said.

"Were we not neighbors once, Lana? I wish only to help. We both have done what is expedient to our aims, so let us not be squeamish."

"You have to find someone before you can torture them."

He shifted forward in his seat. She tensed, resisting the urge to snap a front kick to his face.

"What I am trying to impart is that everyone has their pressure point, someone or something they love. *Everyone.* Why focus on going to him? Find his pressure point, that which he loves or fears, and perhaps he will come to you."

Lana couldn't stand to be in this reptile's presence for another second. She gave him a thin smile, dismissed him, and walked away.

She was thoughtful, however, as she drove by the stately palms of Merrick Park on her way home. While she would never let Colonel Ganso know it, and had no idea what to do about it, she had to admit his twisted little speech was not devoid of merit.

30

Grey barred the door and slept in a semiconscious state, but the night passed without incident. After breakfast, he and Fred drove down Highway 307, the principal artery—the only artery—along the coast south of Cancun.

This was the Mayan Riviera, though the moniker made Grey chuckle. The road was newly paved, but it was still Mexico: a series of spooky police checkpoints along the way, workers eating lunch and urinating along the side of the road, colorfully dressed Mayan women walking to work with baskets on their heads, a dog with a tumor the size of a baseball waiting to die beside a bus stop, palatial resorts on the Caribbean side and a vast stunted jungle stretching to the horizon on the other.

Occasionally a village would interrupt the jungle, dusty little hovels built to service the mega-resorts, withering in the sun as if the all-inclusives had sucked the life and raw materials out of the land, leaving husks of towns and people.

Two hours later, they turned off the highway into Akumal, a tasteful enclave of condos fronting a beautiful rocky bay. The village where Carson Young, ex-DEA agent and Fred's contact, owned a condo.

"What's the story on your guy?" Grey asked, as Fred navigated the potholed road through a handful of shops and restaurants in the village center. Thick dark clouds filled the sky.

"One of those agents who retired but could never leave. No family back home, didn't want a normal life in the States, and hell, they don't pay us enough to retire there anyway. We worked on a few cases together in South Texas. Stand-up guy, very old school. He'd as soon jump off a bridge as break his word."

"Isn't he worried about retiring down here?"

"He was never undercover in Mexico. You're right, still maybe not the smart-est play, but he's been down here a while, probably picked up his pad for a song."

Fred parked in front of a three-story stucco building, painted soft yellow. They climbed to the top floor and rang the bell. A broad-shouldered older man with a moustache opened the door. Carson embraced Fred with a hearty grin and led them to a balcony overlooking the bay.

Their host disappeared inside to retrieve a cooler full of Dos Equis and limes. Down below, Grey saw a honey-colored beach and an aquamarine bay so clear he could see the bottom. *Palapa* huts dotted the sand.

They relaxed in lounge chairs as Fred brought Carson up to speed on the situation, leaving out the CIA's involvement, telling him they were pursuing a lead on a big shot in the Southern Cone. When Fred mentioned the General, Carson didn't react.

"Ever hear anything about that down here?" Fred asked. "Rumors, myths, urban legends?"

Carson wiped beer off his moustache. "Nope, but I wouldn't be the guy. I still do a little go-between work here and there for headquarters, got to keep gas in my boat, but other than that I stay off the radar. Alianza has the Yucatan on lockdown, though every month or so some upstart crew makes a play in Cancun, and the Alianza leaves a pile of headless bodies in a disco. The tourists never hear about it, but it's here."

Fred told him about the Palo Mayombe angle, and Carson started nodding along with the narrative. "That's down here, for sure," he said. "I don't know the extent, and you'll never see it out in the open, but I hear the Alianza's pretty steeped in the stuff." His thumb caressed the neck of his beer bottle. "Now *that's* something I don't poke my nose into."

"What about someone named Tata Menga?" Grey asked. "A big-time cult boss living somewhere in the jungle? Ever hear of anyone like that?"

Carson's hand tightened around his beer. He took a long sip and wiped his moustache. "I don't know any names, but there are plenty of rumors. They say there's shit in the jungle you don't even want to think about, not in your worst nightmares." He turned to Fred. "You heard about Adolfo Constanzo's cult up in Matamoros years back, right? If you haven't, I suggest you look it up. And that was Northern Mexico, close to the border. This is the Yucatan. Nothing but scrub and vines and ruins between here and Merida."

"You mentioned you might know someone to talk to?" Fred said. "Someone local?"

Carson plucked at his moustache. "Yeah, I know a guy. He spooks easily, but I can probably find him tonight, if you can stick around."

"You sure it's okay?" Fred said.

"Don't insult me, Freddie." He reached for another beer. "So how're the kids?"

Fred mumbled a reply, avoided eye contact, and went to use the restroom.

Grey watched him as he walked away.

————•——

The afternoon squall moved across the bay like an angered god. When the weather settled, Grey and Fred walked down the beach for dinner, past white-washed villas and little wooden signs marking turtle nests. They dined next to a pair of Swedes bemoaning the new construction spoiling the Mayan Riviera.

What they really mean, Grey thought, *is that they'd like the level of spoliation to remain exactly where it is, so they can continue to enjoy their low cost of living while the impoverished locals wait on them hand and foot.*

Carson returned after dinner with no success at reaching his contact, rolling his eyes at the impossibility of doing business in Mexico. He said he would try again the next evening, but Grey was nervous. Every hour they spent in Mexico was on borrowed time.

Just as Grey settled into bed, he spotted a flashlight bobbing on the beach, outside his window. He rushed to the balcony in a crouch.

Carson, who was sitting in the dark, stopped him with a hand on the arm and pointed out an elderly man shuffling along the beach, a handful of sticks in one hand and a flashlight in the other.

"He walks the beach every night during turtle season," Carson said. "Marks where they lay their eggs."

Grey watched the old man disappear down the beach, then returned to his room. After his adrenaline calmed, Grey had a peaceful sleep, drifting off to the sound of waves thumping against the shore. He dreamed of long walks on the misty peaks of the Vumba, hand in hand with Nya, the whole of Zimbabwe cradled below.

————•——

Grey spent the next day in the condo, restless, risking a run along the beach to settle his nerves. An even more serious afternoon storm swept through, bending palms and frothing the water, but then the rain stopped and the evening sunset mottled through the clouds, turning the bay into a smudged silver dollar.

Just before dinner, Carson returned from an outing and ushered them into his battered Land Cruiser. "Got good news for you, gentlemen. Hop in. I'll tell you over dinner."

Grey was surprised when he took them across the highway to Akumal Pueblo. He was even more surprised at the chill feel of the place. Some of the concrete houses lining the single paved road had fresh coats of paint, plants and herbs adorned the windowsills, people laughed and smiled as they took their evening walks. There was even a well-maintained soccer field for the kids.

Carson parked alongside a chicken rotisserie joint that consisted of a rusted black smoker, five plastic tables, and a waddling Mayan woman as tall as Grey's chest who greeted them like they were her nephews. The smell of roasting chicken almost made Grey swoon.

Carson noticed his approval, slapped him on the back, and ordered a round of beers. Fred looked uncomfortable and kept eying the pueblo.

"Never could take you anywhere," Carson said. "Don't worry, this place is narco free."

"No place is narco free," Fred said.

Carson wagged a finger. "Don't let their size fool you—Yucatan Mayans are a tough breed. Held out longer than anyone against Mexican rule, you know." The proprietress brought out a plate of *chicharrones*, crispy nuggets of pig fat, and Carson crunched into one. "So my guy," he rumbled between bites, "wants to meet tonight after dinner, at a nightclub he likes to frequent. Bring five hundred in cash."

"Lana better reimburse me," Fred muttered.

"Who's the guy?" Grey asked, munching on a chicharon. His eyes swept the village, but he hadn't gotten a danger vibe, even before Carson's reassurance.

"His name's Checo, an informant out of Playa del Carmen. Been here all his life, has his ear to the ground. He's a rat-faced mestizo with spiderweb prison tats on the backs of his hands. You'll find him by the pool table."

Mexican folk music blared from down the street, and the tables filled with families. The roasted chicken tasted even better than it looked, soaked in its own juices, and the rice and black beans were some of the best Grey had ever had. Washed down with cold beer, Grey thought it the perfect meal.

"What about that other thing we discussed?" Fred asked, forming a gun with his thumb and forefinger on the table.

Carson looked embarrassed. "My guy's bringing them by tomorrow. Sorry, nothing gets done around here on time."

Fred mashed his lips together, and Grey could tell he was trying to control his temper. "How much?" Fred asked.

"Two bills."

"Apiece?"

"Total."

"Jesus," Fred said.

"Any chance this guy Checo turns on us?" Grey said quietly. "We did a few things in Miami the Alianza won't have approved of."

Carson's moustache bristled as he turned to Grey. "I'd never compromise you. This guy *hates* the Alianza. He had two brothers who were selling blow to tourists because their mother needed surgery, and the Alianza got wind of it. A sicario paid them a visit, tortured and killed the brothers and one of Checo's nephews, then left all three hanging from a bridge on the highway. Checo was in jail at the time, or he'd be dead, too." He pushed his plate away, wiped his hands, and stood. "Shall we?"

———·———

Carson took them back to their car and retired to his condo. After stopping at an ATM by the grocery store, Grey and Fred headed to the nightclub where they were supposed to meet Checo. It was only a few miles down the road, just off the highway, a rotting yellow shack at the edge of the scrub line.

A dozen or so cars were parked haphazardly in the grass. Night had settled over the jungle like a billowy black shroud coming to rest on a corpse. There were no windows in the shack, no ambient light, no other buildings in sight. A sign on top of the bar read cervezas frías. *Cold beer.*

Grey exchanged a grimace with Fred as the rental car idled just off the road. Carson had an interesting definition of a nightclub.

"Carson wouldn't send us into the lion's den," Fred said.

"Too bad he didn't come through with the guns on time."

"Yeah, too bad. Come back tomorrow night?"

Grey opened the passenger door. "The longer we wait, the more time we give the cartel to find us. And then the guns won't matter."

31

As soon as Grey cracked the door, a jumble of male voices poured out of the bar, along with the maudlin guitar chords of Mexican folk music. By the time he and Fred stepped through the entrance, the voices had quieted, and each of the twenty or so men inside had stopped to stare at the two gringos.

The ceiling was so low Grey could reach up and touch it. There was a rickety wooden bar along the opposite wall, two pool tables to Grey's left, and a few plastic tables with chairs to his right. Most of the men stood around the pool tables or leaned against the bar.

Too many hard eyes, Grey thought, *and not enough exits.* There were no openly displayed firearms, but he noticed a pair of machetes in the corner, and a knife scabbard hanging from a belt. None of the men stood like trained fighters, but nearly all of them had the look of someone who would mix it up on the street. Real fighters or not, twenty to two were losing odds.

He saw Fred catch the eye of a skinny man at one of the pool tables, standing beneath a neon Tecate sign. The man nudged his head towards the right side of the room. Fred headed to the bar as Grey took a seat at one of the tables. The talking among the patrons resumed, but one man was still glancing at him and Fred out of the corner of his eye, a bulky man about Grey's height, with soil-stained hands and sleepy eyes. He was talking to a short but even thicker guy at the end of the bar, the one with the knife.

The tension in the room eased from a boil to a simmer. Fred returned with two bottles of beer.

"We've got some eyes," Grey said quietly.

"Keep scoping, but this place looks too low rent for narcos," Fred said. "Probably locals who won't buy in."

The skinny man joined them a few minutes later, when his game was finished. His face did resemble a rodent's, long and narrow and sly. Spiderweb tattoos dissected his hands, and his eyes were wary.

"*Hola. Soy Checo. Carson les mandó?*" *I'm Checo. Carson sent you?*

"*Claro,*" Fred said. *That's right.*

As Fred and Checo made small talk, Grey remained silent, playing the part of the unassuming gringo. He got a strong whiff of stale lard again, mixing with the cigarette smoke drifting above the pool tables. A ceiling fan circulated the nauseating odors throughout the room.

Checo had an easy, confident air, but when Fred got around to asking about Palo Mayombe, his eyes withdrew.

"*Por que quieres tratar con esto basura?*" Checo said, and Grey had to concentrate to understand his dialect. *Why would you want to deal with that garbage?*

Grey was wearing jeans and a forest-green T-shirt, Fred khaki shorts and a short-sleeved white linen shirt. Fred eased the corner of an envelope out of his shirt pocket, still speaking in Spanish. "Does it matter why?"

Checo glanced at the envelope and then met Fred's eyes. "Yes. It matters."

Fred grinned. "Okay, I hear you. We're on the same side, my friend. Opposite the narcos."

Checo's upper lip curled when he smiled, showing too much teeth, reinforcing the imagery of a rat. "In that case, let's do some business."

"We're looking for someone called Tata Menga," Fred said.

The smile disappeared. "Are you crazy? Why would you want to look for someone like that?"

"I thought you said let's do some business?" Fred said. "Do you know where he is or not?"

"No."

"*No* you have no idea, or *no* you won't tell me?"

"Somewhere in the jungle. That's all I know."

Fred rolled his eyes. "Yeah, we know that."

Grey decided it was time to be more direct. "Look. There's got to be some rumors about a man like him. Just get us close. I know a palero needs bones, where does he get his? Who does his dirty work?"

Checo looked surprised that Grey spoke such good Spanish, but at the mention of the word *bones*, Checo lowered his eyes.

"You need some time?" Fred asked. "A day?"

Checo eyed the pocket with the envelope and fidgeted his hands. "I don't know anything about that. Truly. All I know is that Tata Menga comes from Puerto Huelva, a village on the road to Cancun. This pueblo, it's bad."

"Bad?"

"There's lots of Palo there. Maybe Tata Menga lives in the jungle nearby. I don't know."

The door opened, and Grey's eyes lasered to it. The sleepy-eyed man and his friend with the knife walked back inside. Grey cursed himself for his lapse of concentration.

Grey watched the smaller man with the knife ease a cell phone back into his pocket. Their eyes flicked to Grey's table.

Grey whipped the envelope of cash out of Fred's pocket and thrust it at Checo. "We're leaving," he said to Fred, who hadn't seen the two men. "Now."

"What's up?"

Grey jumped to his feet and started for the door. The two thugs moved to block his path, arms folded. Grey had no idea how long it would be before whoever they had called would arrive, or how many men in the room were sympathetic to the cause, but he wasn't about to find out.

"Move," Grey said in Spanish as he approached, without slowing down.

The larger man unfolded his arms, the smaller man slid his hand over the hilt of his knife. Neither looked as if they expected Grey to actually keep walking. Out of the corner of his eye, Grey noticed Fred a step behind him.

Grey attacked without warning. Since the knife posed the most threat, he went for the smaller man first, snapping a front kick to the groin. When the man groaned and lowered, Grey closed like a pouncing lion and threw a hard elbow to the temple, knocking his opponent unconscious before he could pull the knife.

The larger man swung at him from the side. Grey crouched as he leaned back and brush-blocked the punch away, then quick as a mamba, he uncurled his body and went straight up the middle with his strike, jabbing the man in the throat with the web between thumb and forefinger. When the man gagged and reached for his throat, Grey stepped back and threw a side kick, sending him crashing through the door. Grey stomped on his face on his way out of the bar.

Shouting broke out behind them, some of it directed at Grey and Fred, though Grey heard Checo yelling in anger. Grey pulled Fred into a sprint.

They reached the car and Grey jumped into the driver's seat. Breathless, Fred tossed him the keys. "What was that about?"

Grey pulled onto the road just as two pickup trucks full of men crossed the highway, passing them on the way to the bar. The men looked tense and most had a hand on a machete.

"Oh, shit," Fred said. "That's what. How'd you know?"

"Saw a couple of guys behind you on a cell phone."

Grey waited before he floored it, increasing the distance as much as he could before startling the men in the truck. Once he heard the screech of tires and rough shouting behind him, he jammed the accelerator.

A shotgun blast echoed behind them.

"They won't hit us with that," Fred said.

The two trucks were a few hundred feet behind them, most of the men standing in the truck beds. Grey gripped the wheel and covered a mile before he answered. "They're not gaining any ground, but we're going in the wrong direction, and they're gonna jump on their phones and call for help."

"How's gas?" Fred asked.

"Quarter tank. This won't last that long."

More gunshots sounded behind them, this time the staccato punch of a handgun. Grey grimaced. "They'll get lucky eventually."

Up ahead they saw lights, and Fred swore.

"What?" Grey asked.

"Police roadblock. Our fate's about to be sealed one way or the other."

"What are the chances the cops are dirty?"

"I'd say fifty-fifty. Good news is, they're the best odds in Mexico."

They hit a line of speed bumps as they approached the roadblock, which consisted of a guard shack in the median and a few shadowy figures in black combat gear on the side of the road, waving cars over.

When Grey's eyes returned to the rearview, he saw no sign of their pursuers. Fred turned and watched the road. "They killed their lights and crossed the median. Now they're heading back. Still doesn't put us in the clear, though. This riot gear means anti-narco police, but down here you never know."

Grey slowed even further as the first cop approached their car, hoisting a flashlight and a machine gun. "Not much we can do about it now," Grey said.

The cop glanced at Grey and Fred, then waved them over and ordered Grey to step outside. Grey eased out of the vehicle, hands open and in front of him, not saying a word. The cop approached from behind, a hulking Mexican even taller than Grey.

He stuck the barrel of his gun in Grey's back and shoved him over, so that Grey had his hands on the roof of the car, feet spread. Grey could smell the garlic on his breath. Grey's pulse increased, and he resisted the urge to back-heel the cop in the groin, spin and grab the gun, and smack him with it. There was nothing Grey hated worse than an abuser of power.

Nothing, that was, except getting shot in the face by the abuser's friends.

The cop patted him down slowly, then did the same with Fred. Grey kept quiet, wondering if the cop was working with the men in the truck. Buying time for someone else to hunt them down when they left the guard station.

After checking the trunk and the inside of the car, then eying their passports, the cop waved them through without a word, turning to the next car in line before Grey had the car started.

"How routine was that?" Grey asked, as they pulled away.

"Not very. My guess is we have about five minutes before more visitors arrive."

"What's the closest town? Playa del Carmen?"

"Yep, five minutes away."

Grey sped up, his eyes alternating from the rearview mirror to the tiny dirt roads feeding onto the highway.

"Here's the first Carmen exit," Fred said.

Up ahead, Grey saw a paved exit ramp leading to a darkened collection of buildings. Grey pursed his lips and kept driving. There might be someone waiting just off the highway. Playa del Carmen was a sizeable town, and he wanted to get lost in a crowd. "Let's wait for a little more civilization."

They passed a dirt road leading to a lightless factory. A few moments later, headlights popped onto the road behind them, closing fast. Grey swore and jammed the accelerator of the tiny import.

Fred pointed. "Next exit! Lots of lights."

Just after crossing an overpass, Grey veered off the highway onto the next exit. The other vehicle, a dark SUV, was a few hundred feet back. Grey made a quick right, taking a narrow road into a poorly lit neighborhood.

"What the hell?" Fred said.

"I saw something, if we can get to it."

With the SUV two blocks behind them, Grey delved deeper into the barrio, hands stitched to the steering wheel. The occasional streetlight revealed corridors of concrete block homes with iron bars guarding doors and windows. Low wires crisscrossed above the street, and graffiti defaced the storefronts.

Grey ran over a dead rat and sped through a stop sign, dodging potholes the size of bathtubs and the occasional group of street thugs. Every time they rounded a corner, the SUV fell out of sight, only to reappear by the end of the block.

Just as Grey started to worry he was lost in the barrio, they reached the other side of the neighborhood and Grey found what he had seen from the highway: an expansive dirt lot full of cars and set just off the road, in front of a warehouse. A line of local teenagers waited near the front of the building, and a sign at the top read CLUB LOCO.

The road kept going past the club, hitting a busier intersection up ahead. There was no sign of the SUV. Grey whipped the car into the lot, went a few rows deep, then parked in a tight space between two pickups.

Grey opened the door, got out and eased it shut, then dropped to the ground. Fred followed suit. Crouched in a squat, Grey moved a few rows over before he started trying car doors. Headlights swung into the lot behind him, and he heard a car coming to a stop and the sound of footsteps running through the lot.

Grey kept looking for an open door. The footsteps drew closer, a few rows away. "Over here," Fred whispered. Grey scurried to the door Fred had cracked, a dented beige Renault Alliance, one of the low and boxy older models. Both men scrambled inside.

Grey hunched down on the driver's side, Fred lay across the back seat. Flashlight beams swung back and forth across the lot. With any luck, the narcos wouldn't spot their rental car fast enough and would assume they had driven farther into town.

As he waited, Grey's hands went to work, relieved beyond words the car was an older model and susceptible to hotwiring. He felt under the steering wheel and ripped the access cover off, found the two red wires, stripped off an inch of insulation, and twisted the exposed ends together.

After he stripped the brown ignition wire, a beam of light swept across the windshield. Grey tensed and then stilled, his hands poised to connect the wires. The light bobbed all around them, and Grey couldn't tell if the wielder of the flashlight was moving forward to get a closer look, or checking the other cars. His palms started to sweat, and he had stopped breathing.

Finally the light retreated. Grey heard the roar of engines, followed by a prolonged silence.

Two minutes later, Grey slid up in the seat and risked a glance around, seeing nothing. "Time to go," he said.

"They might be waiting for us to start up and pull away," Fred said.

"That's a chance we have to take. I'd rather take the initiative than risk getting trapped here."

"I don't disagree."

Grey reached down and connected the wires. The engine came to life with a rough purr. There was still no sign of the SUV, and Grey eased out of the parking lot with his lights off. He didn't realize how quiet they had been until they reached the highway and Fred let out a slow breath. "I guess I was wrong about some of the people in that club."

"It happens," Grey said.

Fred pulled out his cell and tried Carson's number. There was no answer and he left a message to warn him about the heat.

Grey mashed his lips together and kept checking the rearview. Fred stared at him. "You're thinking about that cemetery in Puerto Huelva, aren't you?"

Grey kept his eyes on the road, nerve endings still buzzing. "There's no reason they'd look for us there. If Checo has any sense at all, he'll go underground, and we'll have a small window. Tomorrow might be too late."

Fred let out a breath and ran a hand through his receding hairline, then left it palming the top of his head as he checked the rearview. "Puerto Huelva's on the way to the airport. We give it a look, then take the first flight out. I don't care where it goes."

32

For as long as Lana could remember, the best ceviche in Miami had come from an old man selling fresh seafood out of the back of his truck near Thirty-Seventh Avenue Southwest and Ponce de Leon. She had just come from there, and was now sitting on her balcony, spooning lime-marinated shrimp and red snapper out of a Styrofoam cup.

She washed it down with mango juice and thought about the case as the breeze ruffled the tops of the trees lining Brickell. Their investigation must be troubling the General, or he wouldn't have sent the blue lady after Grey. Colonel Ganso's words drifted back to her. *Find his pressure point, and maybe he will come to you.*

She assumed the General, like any über-criminal, was a supremely selfish man. They knew too little about him to have a clue as to *who* might be his pressure point.

But they might have a *what.*

It had to be Palo Mayombe. Something about their investigation, about Dominic Grey's involvement and the potential for exposure, had spurred the General to send his favored assassin twice in one month.

She set down her spoon. Were Grey and Fred onto something important in Mexico?

The thought gave her hope. She would renew her search into the General's background, this time concentrating on a cult angle among missing CIA agents.

Head spinning with possibilities, she finished the ceviche and started pacing the living room. If only she could bring this man home and stick him in Guantanamo Bay. Imagine the intel they might gather. The CIA could even replace him with someone else, someone under their thumb. Someone who wouldn't sell the border to the jihadists, and who understood the CIA offered better employee benefits and life insurance.

There was something else she could do from her end. Something to further their cause and distract the General's attention while Grey and Fred searched. An image of the golden orb weaver in the Colonel's garden sprang to mind.

Yes, it was time to exert pressure on that which their adversary feared.

It was time to cast light on his carefully hidden world.

It was time to set a trap.

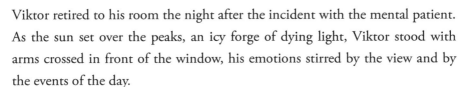

33

Viktor retired to his room the night after the incident with the mental patient. As the sun set over the peaks, an icy forge of dying light, Viktor stood with arms crossed in front of the window, his emotions stirred by the view and by the events of the day.

He felt as if he had just had a near-death experience. Something, an intuition gained from decades of investigations, told him that the man in white had wanted to kill him. And that, had Viktor not turned when he did, the attempt would have been successful.

Why the man had stopped, Viktor wasn't sure. Had this automaton been given very specific orders, which Viktor's movement at the last moment had disrupted?

Or maybe Viktor was wrong, and the man had only been sent to spook him, to deliver a warning.

Warning: received.

But from whom had it come?

There was something else. Contrary to his initial impression, Viktor now had the nagging suspicion that he had seen this mental patient before. It wasn't anyone important in his life, no one he had personally apprehended. It might have been someone ancillary to an investigation, or something else altogether. But Viktor was sure he had laid eyes on that man.

The guard had said the patient's name was Glen, and that he was housed in the criminal wing. In the morning, Viktor would pull some strings. He doubted an Interpol request would be enough to force the Swiss to reveal the patient's identity, especially without knowledge of an impending crime, but his description might be enough for a behind the scenes identification. The man was a criminal and should be in the system.

Could the patient be involved in Palo Mayombe? Perhaps. It didn't seem to fit, however. Palo wasn't known for mind control. Palo was known for consultation of the dead and the unleashing of Kalunga, the spirits of the dead, to do the bidding of a palero.

Still, it was possible. It was always possible.

The sun sank behind the mountains. With darkness came a heaviness Viktor had not felt in weeks, the oppressive weight of memory. His thoughts turned to his investigation into Adolfo Constanzo's cult at Matamoros. To the abominations he had seen.

Why, he whispered to himself? *Why are some men attracted to darkness and violence like the proverbial moths to a flame, batting their mottled wings faster and faster and faster until creating a vacuum that sucks everything around them inside?*

The thumb of Viktor's left hand quivered, the vibrations spreading throughout his body until he was tingling with desire. He could almost taste the soft burn of the wormwood sliding into his throat, easing his troubled soul and taking his mind elsewhere. He had seen a liquor store on the way in, at the bottom of the mountain.

This place had no hold on him. He was there voluntarily. He could walk out of this room, procure a ride down the mountain, purchase what he needed, and be in a better place.

A place apart from himself, far above the mud-filled gully that was the bottom of the human soul. Somewhere lucid and dreamy, drifting above the fray, the sludge from below mere speckles of brown on his Italian leather shoes.

He put his hands on the windowsill and bowed his head. Grey had once spoken of the demons within, of how he fought against them. Viktor had thought he understood, but he was wrong. He hadn't known what it meant to feel those demons living inside you, growing and feeding, inserting their claws into your psyche, urging you onward.

The trembling increased, the need for escape, until Viktor could hardly bear it. He moved for the phone, ready to call for a car.

One hand on the receiver, he slammed his other palm on the table as he remembered the rest of what Grey had said. How he had to face those demons head on, daily, to even stand a chance. How if he tried to forget them or placate them or seek escape through other means, then they would cackle and sink those claws deeper.

Viktor shuddered, a long and visceral contraction of his will. He had broken into a cold sweat. Mouth tight, he pushed away from the phone and grabbed his coat. Fight he would, but not trapped within those four silent walls. He was not yet strong enough to face an empty room and a head full of memories. He would request a guard and walk into the night, into the cold, until numb to desire.

After grabbing his knife, he looked in the mirror on the way out, at the heavy brow and the strength of will reflected deep inside his eyes, struggling to re-emerge.

He had seen that man before. He would see him again.

34

An hour after leaving the roadblock, Grey exited the highway at Puerto Huelva. Signs and a well-maintained road led to the right, towards the beach.

"Go left, into the pueblo," Fred said.

The road to the left took them to a collection of tin-roofed homes on cinderblocks. Pools of stagnant water spotted the road where the roots of scruffy jacarandas and ficus trees had cracked the pavement.

It wasn't so much the scenery that was different from other impoverished Latin American villages Grey had visited, because it had the same half-finished concrete houses, disease-ridden dogs, and impromptu trash heaps. What caused Grey's knuckles to tighten on the steering wheel were the wary stares of the villagers, the lack of crosses and other Christian iconography on the doors and windows, and the sense of menace that filled the air, festering in the water-logged potholes and the decaying coconuts littering the ground.

"What a cesspool," Fred said. "God, the Spanish really did a number on Latin America."

Here and there Grey saw pairs of teenage boys in grimy tank tops, staring at them as they passed. "Any idea where we're going?"

"Make your way to the back of the village," Fred said. "That's usually where the cemeteries are."

A few streets into the pueblo, the broken pavement turned to dirt, and the concrete block dwellings were replaced by wooden and tar paper shacks, some of them built into the low-hanging canopies of the trees. Grey lowered the window and got a whiff of diesel fumes and swamp water.

On the last road of the village, at the edge of the jungle, they spotted a footpath leading into the brush. A wooden sign next to the path read CEMENTERIO.

Grey drove two streets over to where he had seen an empty lot shielded by a pile of rubble. He hid the car as best he could, stalled the engine, then looked at Fred. "Ready?"

"As I'll ever be."

Grey gazed upward at the bloated circle whose light shone dull and gray against the cinderblocks. "Seems like a good night to gather bones in a cemetery."

Fred swiveled his head to take in the silent village. "Is there ever a good night for such a thing?"

Grey felt sure no one had seen them park the car, and they crept unnoticed down the footpath to the cemetery. Beer bottles, soda cans, and empty bags of chips pockmarked the sides of the path. After a hundred feet the path emerged into a sizeable cemetery that was in better shape than the village.

Though the grass was high, and stray vines snaked down from the trees, neat rows of miniature funereal houses comprised the cemetery, cinderblocks painted in bright pastel hues and topped with peaked barrel-tile roofs. Some of the crypts had flat roofs with dollhouses on top, which Grey assumed signified the resting place of a child.

Then he looked closer, and grew uneasy. Some of the tops of the tombs were off kilter, as if they had been opened and not fully closed. Outside of the center, hundreds of smaller graves merged with the encroaching edge of the jungle, and mounds of dirt and discarded headstones riddled these peripheral graves.

Grey grimaced. "I think we're in the right place."

"Yeah," Fred said, eyes wide as he surveyed the desecration.

Their footsteps crunched into gravel-strewn ground. White crosses topped some of the crypts like Catholic weathervanes, but Grey saw evidence of another religion: candles and half-empty bottles of rum placed on tombstones, chalked markings on the sides of sarcophagi, cowrie shells and beads and animal skulls left on a blanket under a tree.

By the light of the moon, Grey pulled Fred into the jungle, near an overgrown portion of the cemetery far enough from the center to be invisible but close enough to observe any action.

The wait was not a fun one. Mosquitoes gnawed at Grey's exposed forearms, and every now and then something multi-legged and unseen would skitter through his hair. He kept expecting a snake to slither down his back.

An hour after they arrived, just before midnight, someone emerged from the path. Grey hunkered lower as a thin Mexican woman strode into the cemetery, dressed in ragged jeans, a loose T-shirt, and a head scarf. She was carrying a canvas bag and wearing a rucksack. Fluid and sure, she did not look in the least bit uncomfortable strolling alone into a graveyard in the middle of the night.

Hands clenched, Grey watched the woman retrieve a crowbar from behind one of the crypts. Then she made her way to the center, stopping in front of one of the miniature houses. He didn't see a cross on the tomb. Looking around, he noticed that most of the graves with crosses had been left undisturbed.

She gouged the door with the crowbar and pried it open, then disappeared inside. When she emerged half an hour later, the canvas bag was full, and he could see the knobby white ends of bones poking out of the top.

The woman replaced the crowbar, then lugged the bag of bones to the overgrown section of the cemetery. Grey tensed, thinking she was coming their way, but she stopped a few feet from the jungle, setting down the canvas bag and rucksack. In the moonlight, he saw an attractive face with sunken cheekbones, her body long and narrow as a reed, like a fashion model fallen on hard times.

Brown toes curling out of her sandals, the woman bent over a grave and set the rucksack beside it. After taking out three glass jars, she set a lit candle on a teacup beside the grave, then started singing in a low voice. The language sounded West African, with a few Spanish words thrown in. As she sang, she took a handful of what looked like wooden quarters out of the backpack, shook them in her hands, and tossed them on the grave. After peering at the tokens, she took a spade out of the rucksack and started filling the three jars with dirt.

When she finished singing, she placed the glass jars in the canvas bag, shouldered the rucksack in a workmanlike manner, and left the cemetery.

Grey and Fred exchanged a look as they stepped out from behind the trees. "Well," Fred said, "that was creepy."

Grey started walking through the cemetery, averting his eyes from the contents of the newly desecrated tomb. "We should go before we lose her. She could be the key."

Fred caught up to him, one hand gripping a broken beer bottle he had picked up on the way in. "You used to this sort of thing?"

"I wouldn't say it's outside the job description."

Checo sat with his back against the rear wall of the bar, one hand wrapped around a bottle of tequila, the other clutching a gun. No one, of course, had stuck around after the gringos left. The only noise was the cacophony of insects outside.

It wasn't a matter of *if* someone would come to avenge the two Alianza informants he had just killed. It was a matter of when. He had always known he would lose this battle, and he didn't care. Some things in life were worth dying for. Stringing his brothers and nephew from a bridge was one of them.

The owner of the bar was friendly to the cause and let him stay the night. Checo couldn't go home and risk the safety of his neighbors. The Alianza had been known to burn an entire pueblo to make their point.

The two gringos were probably dead. Carson was dead, or, if he was smart, on the first plane back to his own country.

Checo had no such luxury. He had no second home in the mountains, no car, no escape plan, no savings. Checo was born into a pueblo so poor that a flush toilet was a myth and a third-grade education was the equivalent of a PhD. The far, far easier thing to do had been to heed the siren call of the narco life. These days the children sang *narcocorridos* glorifying the life of the drug dealer, they played games simulating elaborate kidnapping schemes.

Checo had been to prison; he was no saint. But some things were a different kind of wrong.

After swigging the last of the tequila, he reached for another bottle. The *hijos de putas* narcos had ruined his family, his life, his country. The drunker Checo got, the angrier he grew, until he was pacing the bar, waving the gun and hoping someone would burst through the door. He would take out as many of them as he could, he promised, then spit in the face of the new *conquistadores* and laugh as they tortured him.

Checo heard the sound of a vehicle pulling off the highway and coming to a stop outside the bar. Nerves fortified by alcohol, he gripped the rosary in his pocket, cackling as he set down the bottle of tequila and aimed the gun at the door.

The door cracked, and Checo started firing. It swung all the way open, but no one appeared in the entrance.

Checo fired twice more, then shouted, "Come in, pig!"

A pellet rolled through the door and came to a stop near Checo, pouring smoke. He tried to keep his gaze focused on the door, but his eyes stung and he was forced to bury his face in his sleeve.

When he looked up, eyes still burning, there was a blur of movement near the entrance. Checo fired twice more into the haze of smoke, and then someone ripped the gun out of his grasp and struck him in the head. Checo tried to fight back, but his assailant struck him a few more times, handcuffed his hands behind his back, and shackled his feet.

The man took Checo outside and shoved him against the rear wall of the bar. When the stars in his vision cleared, Checo saw a well-built young man with soft skin, a thick brow that almost met in the middle, and a handsome but lifeless face.

He knew this man, and despite his self-proclamations of bravado, Checo paled at the knowledge. The sicario standing before him was Lucho, one of the most feared men in the Yucatan.

Lucho sat on his haunches two feet away, facing him. The sicario's eyes were red from the smoke, and the intensity of his gaze exacerbated the redness, making it appear as if a ghoul from hell had arrived to extract vengeance.

Checo whispered words of courage to himself as Lucho interlaced his fingers in front of him, elbows resting on his knees. His Spanish was as smooth and menacing as the glide of a cobra. "What did you tell the gringos?"

Checo spat in his face.

His eyes never leaving his captive, Lucho reached up and wiped the spittle off his cheek. "Do you know who I am?"

"Yes, pig."

"Then you know of my reputation."

Checo didn't answer.

"What you may not know is that one of the gringos you spoke to killed my sister. So, this man took my life, too. But one way or another, tonight, you're going to tell me what I want to know."

Checo thrust his face forward. "The Alianza took *my* family. Now you know how it feels. I hope you like it."

Lucho had a large black gun in his right hand. Expressionless, he set it down and took out a knife. He also lifted two vials from his pockets, and set them on the ground.

Still in a squat, Lucho placed the knife lengthwise across his lap and leveled his gaze at Checo, each word quietly spoken, but ringing with the power of truth. "First I will take your eyes, your nose, your lips, your ears. I will leave your tongue, so you can tell me what I wish to know. If you still refuse to speak, I will cut off your limbs and flay you alive and roll your skinless torso into the jungle. If you believe that any of this is an exaggeration, then you do not know me."

Checo passed out when Lucho took the first eye, but Lucho woke him with a dose in the other eye from a vial filled with Tabasco-laced soda water. After Checo finished screaming and Lucho put the tip of the knife on his other eye-ball, Checo told him everything.

Even this they take from me, he thought. *Even this.*

———————

Grey and Fred emerged from the cemetery path just as a yellow Jeep Wrangler revved to life. They waited at the edge of the brush until the jeep disappeared.

"There's only one road out of the village," Fred said as they raced to their Renault.

Grey leaned over to hotwire the car again. "Let's hope she takes that bag to Tata Menga tonight. Sticking around another day is too risky."

"*This* is too risky." Fred reached into his pocket and pulled out a plastic black circle the size of a dime. "I brought a little something from home, if we can get close enough."

"Tracking device? Good thinking."

The village was asleep, but Grey cut his lights until he reached the highway. There was no sign of the jeep, and he worried he had waited too long. Then he saw a flash of yellow in the distance.

"She's on the road to the beach," Fred said.

Grey eased out of the village and crossed the highway. "Good thing she's a careful driver," he said as the Renault slowly gained speed, despite the accelerator pressed to the floor. "We don't exactly have a getaway car."

After crossing the highway, the two-lane road cut through the jungle for five minutes before emerging into the outskirts of Puerto Huelva. They eased into the town square of the little fishing community, a few blocks of shuttered restaurants and tourist shops backed by the sticklike tops of sailboats jutting out of the harbor.

Fred pointed. "There she is."

The jeep turned left on the last street before the waterfront. Grey waited a few seconds and did the same. The gravedigger rolled through a few more streets, into a tony neighborhood of stone-walled houses and landscaped lawns. When she parked, Grey turned left and stopped two blocks away.

He turned towards Fred. "Shall I do the honors?"

Fred handed him the tracking device. "Be my guest."

Grey took the black dot and stepped out of the car, leaving the engine running. He slipped around the corner, staying to the shadows and hunching as he walked. He spotted the jeep a block away and increased his pace, on constant alert for movement. For all he knew, the woman had gone to an Alianza safe house and Grey's photo was plastered on the wall.

As he closed on the jeep, he peeled off the back of the tracking device and held it between thumb and forefinger. The house the jeep had parked in front of was the largest on the block, a two-story Mediterranean villa with an iron fence enclosing the property. The windows were shuttered.

Grey brushed right past the jeep, not stopping as he affixed the tracking device to the inside of the left rear wheel well. He glimpsed the canvas bag of bones in the back seat, bulging at unnatural angles.

Just as he finished placing the tracker, the door to the villa opened, and the woman from the cemetery stepped outside, along with an older man in a suit and a trimmed white beard.

Out of the corner of his eye, Grey saw the woman and the man stop talking and watch him. Hands in his pockets, heart slapping against his chest, Grey kept walking until he reached the end of the block. He turned left, away from the beach, and as soon as he was out of sight, he broke into a sprint, turning left three times until he reached the Renault.

Fred had moved to the driver's seat. Grey jumped in the passenger side. "Go!"

Fred pulled away from the curb. "Where?"

"Doesn't matter. Away. The device is on."

"Someone see you?"

"Yeah, but not planting the device. I've no idea if they know who I am."

They sped out of Puerto Huelva, waiting at a gas station down the road until the jeep left town. Eying the vehicle's progress on Fred's handheld tracking device, staying well behind their quarry, they followed her to three more stops: one in the ritzy downtown section of Playa del Carmen, one in a much poorer neighborhood in the same area, and one just off the highway on the road to Tulum, disappearing into a gated community for half an hour.

After that, the jeep traveled down a bumpy paved road that cut straight into the jungle, perpendicular to the ocean. Staying at least a mile behind, Grey and Fred followed the jeep for forty-five minutes, tunneling into the darkness, the jungle a towering shadow on either side.

Finally the tracking device indicated a right turn, onto a dirt road that they followed for another fifteen minutes, slowing to a crawl as they bounced over potholes and rocks. Grey worried the Renault would hit a bump they couldn't handle and leave them stranded.

When the beeping stopped, Fred stopped with it, waiting to see if the tracker picked up again. Ten minutes later, when their quarry still hadn't moved, Fred coasted a bit farther, until they were half a mile from the signal.

He pulled as far off the road as he could, killed the engine, and put his hands on the steering wheel. "How far do we take this? We don't even have a piece."

Grey rubbed at his stubble with both hands. "If there's anything to find, I have the feeling this is our shot. But who knows, maybe that lady lives out here. Or her boyfriend does."

"You didn't answer my question. And you and I both know who lives out here."

Grey put a fist to his mouth and eyed the sliver of dirt road snaking into the unknown. He knew it was risky, but he felt in his gut they were in the right place, and he didn't want to go home empty-handed. Not to Nya, not to himself. "Just a look, and that's it. You want to wait in the car? Be ready to roll when I come back?"

Fred bared his teeth and reached for the door handle. "Hell, no."

35

Lana set the trap swiftly. First, on internal DEA channels, she circulated that the murdered accountant, Ernesto Reinas, had orchestrated a little surprise for the Alianza. That through his attorney, in the event of an untimely death, Ernesto had arranged for a USB drive to be sent to the Miami DEA office with unreleased information on the cartel, including "constructive financial evidence" indicating that the Alianza made payments to a behind-the-scenes entity in the Southern Cone.

It was a risky maneuver, because the Deputy Director had warned Lana not to tip their hand to the General. Not only were they dealing with a leak, but the CIA preached secrecy and the element of surprise. The less an enemy knew he or she was being targeted, the better.

After fabricating the USB drive, Lana had the DEA bring in a mid-level Alianza suspect for questioning, on the basis that he was someone who Ernesto Reinas claimed had knowledge of the shadow entity. She clued in the ranking DEA officer in Miami to the scheme, and no one else. The risk of blowback was minimal, and she kept her own name out of it, using the authority of the Deputy Director's office to issue a memorandum to the DEA chief.

In the interview room, the unknowing DEA officer questioned the unknowing Alianza suspect, Ollie Fortuna, about a minor coke deal that had gone down the week before. Ollie left perplexed by the interrogation. He would no doubt relay everything to his superiors, claiming he had no idea why he was picked up. That information would reach the General or his people, who would have heard about the incriminating USB drive and would not believe a word of Ollie's story.

Banking on this outcome, Lana was now parked in a surveillance vehicle a few blocks from Ollie Fortuna's house in Kendall. This was her second night on stakeout, and a DEA surveillance team was with her, unaware of the true nature of the mission. She was surprised the General hadn't already sent someone to eliminate Ollie.

Thoughts crowded her mind while she waited. As off the grid as the General liked to roam, he couldn't escape the age of information. Everyone slipped up and sent the wrong email, or used the wrong phone, or, as most often happened, trusted the wrong person.

One way or another, Lana was going to find him.

She had already started her search for missing-in-action CIA officers connected to cults, especially someone who might have been exposed to Palo Mayombe along the way. A mole inside the Falun Gong movement in China had dropped off the radar five years ago, numerous undercover operatives in Muslim fundamentalist movements had disappeared without a trace, and in one case, a spy within the disgusting Children of God cult had taken his assignment too far, embracing the practices of the cult and relocating to Thailand.

Nothing promising enough to pursue, and none connected to Palo Mayombe. Maybe the cult angle was a red herring after all, a quirk of the Alianza. The thought depressed her.

Was there anything else the General cared about besides exposure? A lover, a prized possession, a relative—Colonel Ganso was right on that one. Everyone had a pressure point.

Ollie returned home at midnight. Two a.m. came and went, and then four a.m., with no activity. Statistically speaking, very few hits occurred between four a.m. and daylight. Lana sighed and left the stakeout, leaving two team members in place.

She flipped through the radio as she navigated the silent streets, taking a circuitous route through the leafy neighborhoods of South Miami to avoid detection.

Sure no one had followed, she entered her building's garage through a secure gated entrance, then took the elevator to her apartment. On the way down the hallway she cranked the volume on her cell. She wanted to know the instant something went down.

Though physically exhausted, her mind was piqued, and she set her gun on the dining-room table and poured a glass of pinot noir. As was her custom, she walked through the apartment before entering her bedroom, checking all rooms and closets.

On the way through the living room she paused. Something didn't look right. Setting her wine glass down, she backed towards the gun as her eyes swept the room.

She relaxed when she realized what was different: the night before she had moved the lamp beside the couch to the bedroom. *Lana*, she berated herself, *take it easy.*

After checking the balcony, she finally headed for the bedroom. When Lana had been raped, she had been house-sitting for a neighbor. She had walked into a bedroom and a man had shoved a chloroform-filled rag over her mouth. Since that night, she never entered a bedroom alone without putting her hands in front of her face, ready for defensive action. Unworried, but out of habit, she did the same as she opened the door of the safe house bedroom, holding her wine glass a foot in front of her.

Crack.

Her glass shattered, spraying her with wine and shards. Out of instincts honed over a lifetime of self-defense training, Lana didn't stop to look or wipe her eyes, but rolled to her right on a diagonal, coming up with hands at the ready.

The knife came at her so fast, Lana had no time to think. She lurched to the side, narrowly avoiding the thrust, then snapped a front kick at her opponent. The kick was too weak to be anything but a distraction, but it connected and bought Lana the second she needed. Despite the terror of the attack, her training took over, and she cleared her mind to face the indigenous Indian woman weaving a dagger in front of her, a slingshot at her feet, her exposed skin painted blue, and her long black hair pleated in a braid.

She lunged for Lana with skill, her movements tight and precise, jabbing forward with the knife without overexposing. Lana managed to block the thrust and scramble away, looking for a weapon. A knife was exceedingly dangerous in tight quarters, able to cut from any angle.

Lana dove across the bed and went for the spare gun she kept in her bedside drawer. She managed to reach the gun, but not in time to use it. The Indian woman jumped across the bed and thrust the knife straight at Lana's chest. If Lana had tried to raise the gun, she would have been gutted. Instead, she dropped the weapon and grabbed on to the wrist holding the knife.

As the Indian woman struggled to free her blade, Lana kneed her in the ribs, then stepped back and threw a side kick, her hands still holding on to her assailant's wrist. She yanked on the wrist as she threw the kick, ripping the knife away. The Indian woman gasped from the blow but came back just as fast, striking Lana in the face and then lowering to trip her with an ankle grab.

Lana lost the knife when she struck the ground. Both women lunged for it, and it slid under the bed. Lana scrambled on top of the woman, jabbing at her eyes and then securing a chokehold. She dragged the intruder into the living room, trying to distract her while she leeched her air.

The Indian woman twisted and bucked, managing to insert a hand into the chokehold. Lana stepped back and threw another kick, this one powerful enough to send the woman crashing through the balcony door. Someone on the street below screamed at the sound of breaking glass.

With her back against the waist-high railing, the woman matched Lana blow for blow, using a stance and a fighting method similar to Lana's. Both their faces streamed with blood from glass cuts.

Lana debated making a run for the gun on the dining-room table, but she couldn't risk turning her back. The Indian woman let loose a barrage of open-palmed strikes to the face, which Lana parried. Then her opponent surprised Lana by closing the gap and clenching their bodies together. Before Lana could free herself, her opponent spun and backed Lana against the railing, leaning her backwards. Lana got in a few knees and elbows to the face, but the Indian woman shook them off and pushed on Lana's chest, trying to flip her over the railing.

Bent over the metal bars, in danger of plummeting twenty stories, Lana wrapped her legs around her opponent's waist and squeezed. Her opponent was no longer able to tip her over without falling herself, but a bolt popped loose and Lana felt the cheap railing start to give. She worked furiously to regain her feet, striking blow after blow into the face of the Indian woman, but nothing made her loosen her grip.

With a screech, the railing gave another few inches. Lana had to do something or they were both going over. Realizing what her legs were close to, she shifted her grip to wrap them around her opponent's ribs, squeezing until the Indian woman screamed and stopped pushing on Lana's chest.

The railing slipped farther, then gave way beneath Lana's back. Lana squeezed even harder on the ribs as she twisted her body, reaching for the balcony floor with her hands and trying to catapult the Indian woman off the ledge. When Lana released her legs to grip the ledge, both women ended up hanging off the balcony by their hands.

While the Indian woman tried to pull herself to safety, Lana opted for a different tactic, lifting her body with her abdominals and throwing a devastating side kick into the cracked ribs of her opponent.

The woman screamed and dropped back down, hanging from her fingertips. Lana kicked again, utilizing every ounce of strength she possessed, every ounce of training, every ounce of rage at the attack. She felt the ribs buckle when she kicked, and the Indian woman screamed a final time, lost her grip, and plunged into the darkness.

36

A few hundred yards down the dirt road, after passing two footpaths leading into the jungle, Grey and Fred came to an iron gate set into a high chain-link fence topped by razor wire. The fence extended into the jungle on both sides.

The gate was padlocked and wide enough to accommodate a vehicle. A prohibido el paso sign warded off trespassers.

Grey turned back the way they had come, feeling as if someone were watching, but there was no sign of movement.

Fred gripped the tire iron he had taken out of the trunk. "I wish I had my wire cutters. And my piece."

Grey sat and twisted the sole of his left boot, then slid his slender ceramic lock-picking tools—designed to avoid airport security—out of their hiding place. A minute later he had the padlock dangling from his fingertips while Fred pushed the gate open. "Nifty skill," Fred said. "We shoot the locks and kick 'em in."

On the other side, Grey shut the gate and replaced the padlock. The bulk of the forest stretched into the darkness, broken only by the dirt road. The jungle was dry and low and dense, nearly impenetrable, tough and stunted like the Mayans.

Grey thought of Palo Mayombe and how its practitioners believed that spirits thrived in places such as these, roaming the night, the empty dark between the trees echoing their soundless cries.

Fred swore and spun in a circle, slapping at his back and arms. He shone his penlight on the road as a stick insect as long as Grey's hand scuttled into the brush.

"Let's hope we don't have to go in there," Fred muttered.

Grey eyed the disappearing insect with revulsion. "Let's."

As close as it was beside them, the jungle was still a distant thing, its vine-covered depths daring them to step off the road. There was enough moonlight to see twenty feet ahead on the road, and like most predators, Grey felt comfortable in the near-darkness, knowing it worked to his advantage.

Nothing about their present situation, however, made Grey feel comfortable. The dirt road ended a quarter mile later at a grassy clearing filled with a handful of cars and SUVs—including a yellow Jeep Wrangler. Beyond the car park was a wooden fence, waist high and stretching in a wide perimeter. Inside the fence loomed the outline of a haphazard group of structures, low and long like farmhouses.

They approached on the balls of their feet, Grey crouched with his hands loose at his sides, Fred gripping the tire iron. As they neared the fence, Grey could hear the murmur of a low voice, a ritualistic tone somewhere between singing and chanting. The language sounded the same as the one used by Hector Fortuna and the woman at the cemetery.

Another locked gate. When Fred put his hand on the fence post, ready to step over, Grey grabbed the back of his shirt. Fred looked back at him. Grey flicked his eyes downward.

Fred yanked his hand away, seeing what Grey had noticed: the "fence posts" were fleshless spinal columns, straightened and braced with wooden slats. Each column was spaced six feet apart, and each rested on a sacrum with a sheared base.

"Tell me this fence is not made of human spines," Fred whispered, then looked to his left and right, where the fence disappeared into the darkness surrounding the compound. "Holy Mother of Christ, how many are there?"

Grey took a step back and hopped the fence without touching it, landing catlike on the other side. After eying the fence, Fred grimaced and put his hand on top of the nearest spine, using it for balance as he stepped over.

The nearest building was a single-story rectangular house with a screen door on the front. They approached and found the door unlocked.

Instead of going inside, Grey risked a glance between the buildings. Torchlight revealed the backs of a line of men standing in a circle. The singing continued unabated, now joined by the steady thump of a conga drum.

Grey could see movement inside the circle. He pulled back.

"What is it?" Fred asked.

"My guess is a Palo ceremony."

"Any idea how long it might last?"

"All night, five minutes, who knows?"

The buildings were wooden, aged, all with doors and windows unlocked. Grey and Fred darted across the gaps, and when they were opposite the car park, they risked taking a look inside one of the houses.

After letting their eyes adjust to the dark interior, they hurried through the simple house, finding nothing of interest. Pausing by the kitchen window, Grey decided to steal a glimpse of the ceremony. Fred crept up behind him.

In an open space between the compound's buildings, nineteen people stood in a rough oblong circle. Torches in iron stands lined the perimeter, dirt and scraggly grass covered the ground. Spaced between the torches were tall stakes topped by hollowed-out coconuts, each carved and painted into a different grotesque face.

Two more people, a man and a woman, stood in the center of the circle, next to a gigantic terra cotta cauldron, easily four feet across at the lip, filled to bursting with sticks and dirt and bones. The thin and shirtless man in the center, an older man with wrinkled cinnamon skin and wild and uneven dreadlocks, had two live black snakes wrapped around each arm. He was barefoot and pushing a long pole around the pot, chanting as he stirred.

The woman in the middle, the gravedigger Grey and Fred had seen at the cemetery, had stripped to jeans and a bra, and was singing and gyrating around the pot, her limbs flailing as if dancing to ten different tunes. Her eyes were rolled back, her hair loose and spinning in her face.

Except for the man thumping the heel of his hand on the conga drum, the people on the perimeter looked divided into two groups: three well-dressed men with hulking bodyguard types on either side of them, and a collection of emaciated men and women dressed in tattered clothing. Grey guessed the people in rags were acolytes of the palero with live snakes on his arms, who could only be Tata Menga.

"Holy shit," Fred said, in a voice so low and hoarse Grey could barely hear him. "The man in the sport coat? That's the Alianza's number two guy. The jackal with the goatee is Ricky Orizaga, he runs the South Florida arm from Cancun. The other guy, I forget his name, he's a big deal too."

Tata Menga stopped stirring the pot and sat cross-legged on the ground in front of a low table. Grey took a closer look and saw two open bilongos sitting side by side, the black wax paper spread open like the wings of some foul carrion bird.

Grey clenched his hands when he saw what was inside the first bilongo, ready to be stuffed into the bundle of black magic. Nestled among the blood and dirt and dried lizards, Grey could see the soapstone carving Nya had given him, missing since the night the blue lady had tried to kill him. When Grey had failed to find it the next morning, he assumed he had knocked it off the balcony.

Which meant someone was in his hotel room when he chased after the blue lady.

Tata Menga opened his hands. Grey noticed his fingernails were incredibly long, curving in a limp sickle away from his palms. The palero bared his teeth, then moved his hands back and forth, as if showcasing the contents of the bilongo. He wriggled his fingers, the six-inch fingernails bending under their own weight, and started to close the first package. The long fingernails and waxy black bundle made Grey think of a spider wrapping its prey.

"What the—that's my lucky blue and red baseball," Fred said, "inside that second whatever it is. I had it in Miami, they must have broken into my place."

"The soapstone carving's mine," Grey said quietly.

As Tata Menga wrapped the bilongos, one of his disciples stepped forward, took a swig from a plastic bottle, and spewed liquid over the cauldron. He then inverted the cigar he was smoking, ashed, put the glowing tip in his mouth, and blew a cloud of smoke.

"What the hell is this?" Fred said.

"You don't want to know. C'mon, we've seen enough."

"This night, this ritual, it's about us, isn't it?"

Grey didn't answer, and Fred crossed himself as they backed out of the house.

When they had almost circled back to the car park, Grey noticed a footpath branching away from the compound. They followed it to a shed a hundred yards from the buildings, backed against the spine fence.

The metal shed had no windows and was padlocked. Leaning against the door was a stick with a doll's head stuck on top, eyes missing and blond tresses in tatters, as if a willful child had plucked out chunks of hair.

"We're pushing our luck," Fred said.

"This could be the prize."

"Just hurry," Fred muttered.

The noise of the ritual had faded, leaving only the din of insects. Grey moved the stick and went to work on the lock. He had the intense feeling of sand pouring out of a broken hourglass.

The padlock was an enormous seven-pin lock, rare and hard to conquer. Lock picking had been one of Grey's specialties in Recon, however, and a few minutes later he heard the final pin click as the lock popped open.

They stepped inside and shut the door behind them. Both men turned on their penlights. Small as it was, the shed was climate controlled with a dehumidifier, the air cool and dry.

Expecting the worst, piles of dead bodies or more cauldrons overflowing with vile materials, Grey was surprised to find an orderly room, half-filled with locked bronze chests. Grey opened three of them. All were filled with American dollars arranged in neat stacks of twenties, fifties, and hundreds.

Fred whistled. "Must be a few million in here. I'll get this in for analysis." He pocketed a stack, then surveyed the shed with crossed arms.

"I was hoping for something more informative," Grey said. "We still don't have the link."

"We're staring at the link, though who knows if it ultimately connects to the General."

Grey glanced at the door. "I want to search more of the houses, but I think we've overstayed our welcome."

Fred swore softly. "Maybe the money's dirty, and will lead us somewhere."

"That's a long shot."

"There's one more thing I can do," Fred said. He took out a slender, rectangular case from his pocket. "Emergency fingerprint kit."

Fred dusted various parts of the metal shed, including the door handle on both sides. After sticking fingerprint tape over the best prints, he removed the tape and placed it on small backing cards, then stored them in a tiny plastic case.

After dusting off their own prints, they heard Tata Menga's voice rising in volume, more forceful than before. A few seconds later, the drums accompanied the chanting of the palero.

"Time to go," Grey said.

He knew the reason security wasn't tighter on the shed was because they were deep inside the jungle, and no one in Mexico was foolish enough to visit Tata Menga's compound without an invite.

Or almost no one.

Grey and Fred sprinted along the darkened fronts of the buildings, crouching whenever they traversed a gap. They reached the spine fence, but just as Grey started to vault the disturbing barrier, truck headlights swung into view.

They scrambled behind a building. The vehicle, an old but rugged-looking Bronco, pulled into the car park. Grey figured whoever was in the truck was headed to the ceremony, and as soon as the occupant disappeared inside the compound, Grey and Fred could slip back to their car.

When Grey saw who was stepping out of the truck with purpose, a man with hooded eyes and a muscular build, he knew his assumption was wrong, and that everything had changed.

Lucho.

Fred was brushed up against Grey, and Grey could feel him tensing. Lucho took a rifle out of the passenger seat, slammed the door, and strode towards the ceremony. As soon as he passed the first building, Grey pulled Fred into a run.

Fred stopped to climb over the spine fence, and as soon as they hit the other side, they heard shouting as floodlights popped on above the compound, staining it with yellow light.

37

Grey raced into the darkness past the car park, Fred right behind him, slower but pushing hard. Grey thought it was fifty-fifty as to whether they would make the main gate in time.

Car engines started behind them. "I'm going ahead to work the lock," Grey said.

"Go, man!"

As soon as he reached the gate, Grey grabbed for his heel and pulled out his tools. Car lights swung into view and lit the gate from behind.

Fred caught up, laboring to breathe. "A hundred yards away," he said. "At least three vehicles."

The engines roared closer, the headlights pinning Grey and Fred against the gate like butterflies on a board. Grey opened the lock and shoved Fred through, then slammed the gate shut on the other side, replaced the padlock, and broke his thinnest pick off in it.

They sprinted down the dirt road to the sound of cursing and shouting behind them. Someone took a shot at them through the fence, spraying dirt two feet to Grey's left. Grey wove and ducked until he was a hundred yards down the road, out of range in the darkness.

Moments later Grey heard a shotgun blast, and then another. "They just shot the lock," he guessed, confirmed by the sound of engines revving. From his recollection, they were still a few hundred yards from the car. "We're not going to make it."

Fred huffed. "Remember those footpaths on the way in? As bad as it sounds, it may be our only option."

Grey looked over his shoulder and saw the Bronco leading the charge, rapidly closing the gap. A shudder of adrenaline rolled through him. "You remember where they were?"

Fred shone his penlight along the left side of the path, and he pointed up ahead, where a break in the foliage revealed an occluded passage through the trees. "Right about there."

They darted down the path. Grey wiped sweat from his eyes and moved forward as fast as he could. He debated hiding in the jungle, but the foliage was too thick and it would be impossible to get far enough off the path in time.

Shouting from behind spurred them forward. After passing a fork on the left, they saw another path on the right, and then two more on either side.

A maze which they had no hope of solving in time.

"Either they'll cut us off from another direction," Fred said, "or we'll end up back at the compound."

"Save your breath and keep running."

"I'm slowing you down. You go ahead, I'll distract them as long as I can. Bring Lana and the feds if you get out."

"Like I said, save your breath."

They heard voices behind them, keeping even with their pace. Less than a minute later, the path dead-ended at a three-foot wide hole in the ground with a rusty aluminum ladder set into the side of it. On the other side of the hole was a wall of trees and foliage.

Grey shone his light into the hole but couldn't tell what lay below. Fred peered in beside him. "It's probably where they throw the bodies."

Grey started down the ladder. They didn't have a choice.

The ladder ended twenty feet underground. Grey was surprised at what his penlight revealed: a sprawling cavern covered in stalactites and stalagmites. An underground lake stretched almost the length of the fifty-yard grotto, and water dripped from multiple points along the ceiling into the pool.

"Some type of sinkhole?" Grey asked.

"Cenote," Fred said. "The Yucatan is a big piece of limestone Swiss cheese."

Grey stepped to the edge of the pool and shone his light into the blueberry-colored water. It wasn't that deep, and Grey could see the bottom. And on that bottom, he saw hundreds, if not thousands, of bones. A few were intact human skeletons.

Grey followed Fred's penlight to the far side of the pool, where it illuminated a decomposing female corpse floating face up in the water. A note of hysteria permeated Fred's chuckle. "Guess I was right about the bodies."

Grey walked along the edge of the pool and found four different exit passages, then started down the passage farthest from the entrance.

"This is crazy," Fred muttered.

The passage was slippery and uneven, beset by jagged limestone protrusions, muddy pools, and piles of pebbles. At times the ceiling lowered to chest or even waist height, and they had to crawl through the mud on their hands and knees. In some of the passages with higher ceilings and in most of the caverns, holes of varying size allowed moonlight to sneak through, illuminating the merger of cave and jungle as if through a viewfinder.

The underground habitat was a living and breathing organism, warm and humid and smelling faintly of vinegar. The vines and tendrils of giant tree roots hung down through the holes or draped like snakes against the sides of the caverns, though none were low enough to climb. Colonies of bats tucked against the ceiling, insects scuttled across the floor, and their penlights illuminated more than one tarantula.

They quickly lost their bearings. With no choice but to plow ahead, they peered in vain for a good place to climb out, hoping against hope they had thrown Tata Menga's men off their trail.

"This looks promising," Fred said, as they rounded a bend and saw a large cavern up ahead. "One of these has got to lead to the surface."

Grey led the way into the grotto, illuminating yet another large pool. He was about to tell Fred he thought the cavern looked familiar, when Fred aimed his light at a ladder ascending to the surface through a narrow hole.

"Mother of Christ," Fred said. "We're back where we started. If we hurry, maybe we can—"

A light emerged from one of the other tunnels, followed by shouting voices and gunshots. Just before he scrambled back into the tunnel with Fred, Grey got a glimpse of Lucho and the goateed drug lord leading the charge.

The confident tenor of Tata Menga followed them, echoing off the walls, rising in volume with each word. "*No tienen que correr, es demasiado tarde por ustedes. Ya les hecho una brujería. La muerte les seguirá como el más fiel de los perros.*" *You don't have to run, it's too late for you. I've already cursed you. Death will follow you like the most loyal of dogs.*

Fear wormed its way into Grey's marrow, spiking his adrenaline. They were out of options, lost in the enemy's backyard, and he knew what fate awaited if Tata Menga caught them.

They careened down a new tunnel that revealed a nest of side passages honeycombed into the limestone. Shouting echoed from multiple directions, and it was impossible to discern the source. Grey wondered if there was even an exit to be found, or whether they were being flushed like rats back to the entrance.

They entered a large cavern filled with beehive towers of calcium deposits rising from the floor. The cathedral ceiling was studded with millions of spaghetti-thin stalactites, and a group of pointed stalagmites bunched on the far side of the cavern resembled a field of swords. Just as they cleared the stalagmites, three men rounded the corner in front of them. Grey saw the light from their flashlights swing into the passage a split second before he saw them.

Grey and Fred rushed them before the men had a chance to fire. The first man was bulky and had a ponytail, one of the bodyguards. Grey chopped down on the forearm holding the gun, sending the weapon flying. Before the man could recover, Grey followed through with a side elbow to the face, a rising elbow to the jaw, and then a throat chop with the opposite forearm, dropping the man as he grasped at his crushed windpipe.

When Grey saw the next man raise his gun, he crouched low and rushed him, feeling a bullet whizz over his head as the crack of gunfire exploded in his ears. Out of the corner of his eye, he saw Fred fighting for his life with another of the men, both struggling for control of a gun.

Grey's new opponent, the drug lord with the goatee, smacked Grey on the side of the head with his gun as Grey closed the gap. The sound of a clanging bell erupted inside Grey's head, but he gritted through the pain and grabbed the shooting arm with both hands.

Instead of yanking on the gun, Grey pushed it towards the man to create muscle confusion, then spun him in the opposite direction. While the off-balance drug lord kept a desperate focus on maintaining control of the weapon, Grey twisted and crouched deep into the drug lord's center of gravity, lifted him in the air with his hips and one arm, then uncoiled and impaled him on one of the spear-like stalagmites. Only then did Grey rip the weapon out of his grasp.

The man Grey had first engaged was gurgling his last few breaths. Grey turned to see Fred strike his adversary in the face with the tire iron. The man fell, and Fred hit him over and over, until Grey rushed over and laid a hand on his arm. "He's dead."

Fred spit and shone his light on the ground, until he found the other gun. He pointed the weapon at the man Grey had impaled. "You just killed Ricky Orizaga. The world is now a better place."

Grey checked the magazine of the nine-millimeter Beretta he had grabbed, then clicked it back into place. "Let's go."

Just past the field of swords, the passage took a quick turn to the right. After another few minutes, it straightened and they were able to sprint a few hundred yards until they came to a cavern submerged in a pool of water.

A bridge led across the sump, though the wooden slats were two feet underwater. "I say we cross," Grey said. "The last side passage was too far back."

Just before they reached the other side of the pool, light from a flashlight appeared and the sound of gunshots came from behind. One of the bullets hit Fred in the shoulder, and he cried out and dropped his gun in the water. Grey turned and fired, seeing two men but missing them both. He pushed Fred forward. "Go!"

They cleared the bridge and dashed into the next cavern. Grey stopped and held his gun out. "Can you shoot?"

Fred winced but took the gun. "I'll manage."

"Go twenty feet down the passage," Grey said, "wait till the first man passes me, and shoot the lead man. I'll take care of the second."

Hands at the ready, Grey stepped behind a cone-shaped stalagmite. The men came seconds later, leading with gunfire as they barreled down the corridor. Fred got the first man in the chest, and Grey jumped on the second, Lucho, before he could return fire.

Grey drove Lucho backwards onto the bridge in a football tackle, and they crashed into the water. Grey had grabbed the sicario's shooting arm during the tackle, but unlike Ricky, Lucho wisely let the gun go. Instead he slammed his other fist down on Grey's back, then kneed him in the face and pushed his head under.

Freezing water poured into Grey's mouth and nose. Choking and unable to see, he flailed to find a grip, finally managing to drag Lucho underwater by his shirt. Lucho scrambled for the surface, but Grey kept pulling on his clothes until he found an elbow and then a hand, isolating the pinky until he felt it snap backwards.

Lucho thrashed from the pain, but Grey found the back of his hair and pulled him under, curling his legs around Lucho like a vine. As they sank towards the bottom, Grey reaching for a choke, he felt a stabbing pain in his side.

Grey knew that sort of pain from experience. Lucho had knifed him.

It would have been a far more serious blow on the surface. Underwater, it hurt like hell, but Lucho didn't have enough momentum to thrust very deep. Grey grabbed Lucho's wrist with both hands and pulled the knife out by pushing off the sicario's stomach with his foot. Grey flipped Lucho's wrist and broke his hold on the weapon, and Lucho let the knife go instead of letting Grey rip it out of his grasp.

The knife thrust had caused Grey to expel his breath, and he was running out of air. He forced himself to remain calm and preserve his oxygen. He kneed Lucho in the stomach, fended off his blows, and wormed his way into a front choke. Grey used Lucho's knife arm as part of the choke, bending it around his own throat. Lucho thrashed like a spooked stallion, but Grey held on, head-butting him at close range a few times and then corkscrewing the blood choke deeper, cutting off the oxygen from both sides, until Lucho finally went limp.

Grey would have held on longer, to make sure Lucho was dead, but spots of black were entering his vision. He kicked away and broke the surface, gulping in air. Fred was there to pull him out of the water.

"It was Lucho," Grey said, inspecting the stab wound in his left obliques. Though dripping blood, the wound wasn't that deep. "I doubt he's coming back up."

Fred started to fire into the water, though it was cloudy with blood. Grey stayed his hand and put his finger to his lips. Voices drifted through the cavern from the opposite end of the bridge.

They hurried back to the intersection. Fred guided Grey down the passage to the left, saying he had seen moonlight.

"We need something dry to bind your arm," Grey said.

"It just grazed me. If I survive these caves, I'll survive the wound. What about yours?"

"The same."

Fred whistled as they rounded a corner. "Thank God."

Grey sagged with relief when he saw inside the next cavern. Moonlight poured through a huge hole in the ceiling, revealing a nest of thick roots tumbling down to the cavern floor.

COLONIA DIGNIDAD, CHILE
1984

Backlit by the setting sun, the snowcapped peaks of the Andes appeared on the horizon like a line of melting ice cream cones. It was a windswept evening, chilly and clear. The man once known as John Wolverton, still putting the finishing touches on his identity, exited his hired car at the entrance to Colonia Dignidad, a utopian community nestled in the foothills of Chile's central valley.

He was on a mission to find a man, a German named Paul Schaefer, who was something of a legend in the tight-knit club of South American cult leaders and criminal overlords. Like most of his peers, Schaefer had deep ties with the CIA and the local government, but Colonia Dignidad was particularly successful, known for its stores of money and weapons, as well as the absolute devotion of its members to the godlike reign of Schaefer. Moreover, unlike most of its cousin communities that had leeched on to South America like ticks on a dog, growing fat on the blood of their hosts and then popping, Colonia Dignidad had prospered for more than two decades.

As the violet sky faded to black, John Wolverton passed through an eight-foot fence topped with coils of barbed wire and manned by armed guards with German shepherds. He could see cameras and observation posts along the perimeter, men with binoculars peering out of towers.

To pass through that fence was to step into another universe. Two guards, fawning over John Wolverton as if he were a visiting captain of industry, led him into a hamlet ripped straight out of Bavaria.

With calm detachment, but filing away every detail, John Wolverton noticed the wool pants and suspenders worn by the men, the homely gray dresses and head scarves assigned to the women, the hairstyles from four decades ago.

Flowerbeds arranged in neat rows, bike paths and bridges, immaculate streets, fresh paint on the red-roofed homes. Perfect, perfect, perfect.

On the way in he noticed signs for an airport, a hospital, and a hydroelectric power station. He also noticed the sign that read WORK IS DIVINE SERVICE, an eerie parallel to the *arbeit macht frei* sign he had once seen at the entrance to Auschwitz.

Under the hum of an electric generator, the guards passed him to a teenage boy, who led him to a sitting room in the largest home in the compound. After guiding him to a leather chair and plying him with Scotch, the boy stood in the room with him until Paul Schaefer finished his nightly duties.

Tall and lean, Schaefer entered the room in a crisp white suit set off by his tanned skin. His stride was confident, but his lips and eyes appeared sunken, dissipated. As if some terrible disease were ravaging him from within.

Schaefer patted the boy on the rear before excusing him, eying John Wolverton as his hand lingered longer than appropriate, demonstrating his control over his flock.

The boy left, and all signs of internal conflict were consumed by the flare of Schaefer's smile. John Wolverton greeted him with his most well-known alias, a smuggler of drugs and guns from Guyana. Schaefer was a far bigger player on the international crime scene, and Wolverton let him assume the role of mentor.

"I am so pleased you could visit," Schaefer said, his English thick and chewy from the German accent. "You must be starving, weary beyond belief from your travels. My chef is preparing dinner, and please let me know if there is anything you desire during your stay. We have full amenities at the colony."

"Too kind," John Wolverton murmured.

"Well," Schaefer swept a hand towards the window showcasing the compound, "what do you think?"

"Most impressive, I must say. A little slice of Germany in South America, exhibiting all of the excellent Teutonic traits. Order, discipline, beauty, invention. I look forward to seeing more."

Schaefer beamed. "And you shall, you shall. You are young, but wise to recognize the value of relationships in a business such as ours. As you know, on this continent, if one is isolated from the local government one becomes vulnerable. And if one does gain the favor of the local authorities"—he paused, his lips curled in a conspiratorial expression that John Wolverton found weak and distasteful—"one may do as one . . . pleases."

John Wolverton returned the expression, because he knew that was what

Schaefer wished him to do. He had already formed the opinion that while charismatic, Schaefer was not overly bright.

Which made his visit even more interesting. For how did a man of limited intellect and voracious passions manage such an impressive project as Colonia Dignidad? Imagine the possibilities in the hands of someone more like him.

Then again, he thought, *do any of us ever truly shed our passions?*

He thought not. It was just that some passions were more overt than others.

"And how is the local climate at present?"

"You may know," Schaefer said, "that when Pinochet seized power, there was a moment of indecision about the fate of our colony. I took matters into my own hands and let it be known that I was well disposed to the regime."

He understood Schaefer's allusion: it was known in certain circles that Pinochet had needed secure locations for the torture of political dissenters, and Colonia Dignidad was just such a place.

A clever move, he thought. Maybe Schaefer wasn't so simple after all. In the underworld, cunning often trumped intelligence.

"Of course," Schaefer continued, "our mutual business partner from the north is supportive of Pinochet. Everyone, it seems, is pleased by the arrangement. Business has been good. And you? I understand the other side of the continent thrives as well?"

John Wolverton let a swallow of Scotch slide down his throat, enjoying the burn. "As never before. I believe our industries are poised to explode."

Schaefer's nod was vigorous. "Indeed, indeed. The pipeline you've proposed is exceedingly timely." He rose to his feet. "But let's wait until tomorrow to discuss details. I've a bit of business to attend to. Enjoy your dinner, and one of my boys will see you to your room. Would you like companionship for the evening?"

"I would not object."

"Male or female?"

"Female. Indigenous, please."

"Excellent. I keep the libidos of my women under strict regulation, and I think you will find that, once loosed, they are . . . quite uninhibited. Your consort will view her duties as penance owed to the colony, punishment for her gross sins of the week."

Schaefer's smile was a handful of snow stuffed under the collar of a winter coat. "She will be eager to perform."

———◆———

As promised, a woman came to John Wolverton's bed that night. She performed admirably and with good cheer, and allowed him to fantasize about Tashmeni. He was impressed by the absolute control exhibited by Schaefer over his subjects.

Over the next few days, Schaefer entertained him with gourmet food and fine wine and children's choirs, putting on theatre plays and taking him for long walks in the countryside. As John Wolverton studied Schaefer, he kept in mind the man's background.

What he knew about Paul Schaefer: a gifted orator born in 1921 in a small town in Germany, a terrible student by all accounts, rejected from the Nazi SS due to an eye injury, fired from his position as a church youth leader on suspicion of child molestation. Later he became an itinerant preacher who founded an orphanage for war widows and their children.

After more accusations of child molestation at the orphanage, Schaefer used donations from the war widows to move his community to Chile in 1963, buying a ranch that would eventually grow to more than seventy thousand acres.

Once on foreign soil, Schaefer moved quickly to establish control. He forbade private conversations as tools of the devil, prohibited anyone from leaving the compound without permission, limited and even faked news from outside, required confessions of sin on a daily basis, and separated the men and women, banning marriage or reproduction without his consent.

Violence and torture were commonplace punishments, including electroshock, pharmaceutical concoctions, beatings, and starvation. Schaefer also kept a troop of young boys called "sprinters" at his beck and call, automatons who followed him around the compound and were subject to frequent sexual abuse.

Though it was not to his personal taste, John Wolverton noted the sexual abuse in a clinical manner, weighing the effects on the community. It was obvious everyone knew of Schaefer's proclivities, and what intrigued John Wolverton was *why the members allowed him to get away with it.*

It took two to tango, as they said in Buenos Aires, and the members of the utopian community bore personal responsibility for letting their demigod run rampant, for letting a warped man such as Paul Schaefer touch their children.

Yet this was why he had come: to unlock the secrets of Paul Schaefer's power over these people.

To study.

To learn.

He had begun the inquiry in Jonestown, watching every move made by the Reverend Jim Jones. Influential as he was, his community in Guyana had barely lasted two years.

And in Mexico City, after witnessing the absolute terror Tata Menga inspired among the citizenry, John Wolverton had lingered until gaining the confidence of the feared palero, studying his religion and discussing how they might mutually benefit from a partnership.

Schaefer was something else entirely. He had an industrious work force in his thrall, which produced a considerable income. He treated the local community well, establishing a hospital and giving to the poor. He went to great lengths to ingratiate himself to local government and the wealthy private sector.

Yet there were negatives. Schaefer's empire was local, his international influence limited. He was too visible, easy to find if things took a turn for the worse. And it was obvious he was more concerned with playing God and maintaining a personal pleasure palace than with expanding his territory. Yet perhaps that was the limit of his ambition, and what worked for him.

It did not work for John Wolverton.

———◆———

The night before he was scheduled to leave, he played a final game of chess against Schaefer, a nightly ritual. While John Wolverton made many concessions to the ego of his host, chess was not one of them. To his credit, Schaefer didn't seem to mind losing. He even invited the best players from the colony to play against his guest, promising great privileges if they bested him. No one had come close.

During the game, one of the guards burst into the private dining room. He had a rapid exchange with Schaefer, waving his rifle as he spoke. Schaefer's face paled at the news, the first sign of stress he had exhibited during the visit.

John Wolverton understood enough German to catch the gist: one of Schaefer's favorite sprinters, a Chilean boy sent to the colony by his impoverished parents from a nearby village, had managed to slip a note to someone on the outside. Though the guard danced around his words, the note was apparently a cry for help, alleging that Schaefer was molesting the boy. In response, an angry mob of peasants had gathered around the gate, threatening reprisal if the boy was not released.

Schaefer released the guard with a flick of his wrist, clenched his fists, and shuddered. Once in control of his emotions, he looked across the table at John Wolverton. "Well, my young friend, it seems we have a predicament. You understood?"

"Enough."

"Then tell me, what should I do?" He asked the question not as a plea for assistance, but as a test.

John Wolverton cradled his tumbler between thumb and forefinger. "The obvious options are to let the boy go, deal with the crowd, or do nothing."

"Yes."

"If you let the boy go, it sets a bad precedent. Moreover, he might accuse you before a court of law. That can be dealt with, but it's bad publicity." He swirled his Scotch. "Dealing with the crowd is even riskier. The protection of the regime only goes so far, and might not extend to the slaughter of a crowd of villagers. Perhaps shooting one of them would disperse the mob. Perhaps not."

John Wolverton rattled his ice and took a sip. "Doing nothing is probably the best option of the three, as I am guessing the villagers are not equipped to force their way inside. Eventually they will leave, disgruntled but impotent, their only recourse a plea to the authorities based on a note whose author is unavailable for testimony. Yet another option," he showcased a palm, "is to let a few of them slip through the gate, where you will be well within your right to respond with force."

Schaefer's eyes had grown brighter and brighter. "You would have made quite the SS officer."

John Wolverton had been regaled with many tales of Schaefer's exploits in the Nazi unit in which he had never served.

"And were you me," Schaefer continued, "which of those would you choose?"

John Wolverton leaned back, the arm holding the Scotch extended on the table. "None."

"Is that so? What, then?"

"Who is the boy's closest companion inside the colony?"

"His sister."

"How old is she?" Schaefer asked.

"Ten."

"Let the boy return to his family. Tonight. Before he goes, have a little chat with him, perhaps a small demonstration, and let him know exactly what will befall his sister should he do anything other than return home, confess his lie, extol the virtues of Colonia Dignidad, and return for good on the weekend."

Schaefer's thin lips parted, then broke into a cruel grin. "A master of the chess board, orchestrator of cross-continental business relations, and now this." He raised his glass. "An officer is too pedestrian a title for one such as you. A general, you are. *Ja, ja,* my young friend. Perhaps that is what we should call you. The General."

38

YUCATAN JUNGLE
PRESENT DAY

The enormous ficus roots reached into the cave like the tentacles of some mythological beast. A few bats circled the opening, and spiderwebs stretched twenty feet across the diameter of the hole.

Wincing at the shallow knife wound in his side, ears cocked for sounds of pursuit, Grey helped Fred climb out of the hole, pulling down spiderwebs with the tire iron as they went. They surfaced to find palm fronds as big as cars surrounding the rough edges of the sinkhole. Moonlight revealed the pitted gray surfaces of Mayan ruins crumbling in the jungle, as well as a footpath leading into the darkness.

They caught their breath sitting on a block of limestone stained green with moss. Exposed pieces of statues and columns lay scattered in the jungle around them.

Fred slumped against the stone. "I always wanted to be Indiana Jones."

"We should keep moving," Grey said. "We might still be on Tata Menga's property."

Grey eyed the quarter-size hole on the side of Fred's shoulder. It didn't look life threatening, though he worried about infection and blood loss. Grey's own wound was an ugly gash in the middle of his left obliques.

"Why don't we just stay here until first light, and shoot anyone who climbs out?"

Grey helped Fred to his feet. "C'mon. You need medical care."

Fred kept his hand clasped on to Grey's forearm. "Thanks for sticking by me. Lots of men wouldn't have."

Grey took the gun and stuck it in his belt, then led the way down the path, praying it didn't lead them back to Tata Menga's compound.

They followed the trail for over an hour. This part of the jungle was much damper, a different ecosystem. Grey was wary of the constant rustling in the trees and hoped nothing decided to see how they tasted. He wished Nya were there to guide them. She was an expert tracker and comfortable in the wild.

Both Grey and Fred jumped when a deep-throated roar shattered the lull of insect chatter. It sounded like it had come from right beside them, but Grey knew from other jungles that the source of the noise could have been up to three miles away, and belonged to a primate the size of a baby bear.

Fred was peering into the jungle. "Was that a dinosaur?"

"Howler monkey," Grey said. "Nothing to worry about. I thought you knew this area?"

"Are you kidding? I know the cities and the coast. I've never stepped foot in a jungle in my life."

Near another cenote they saw a wild boar snorting and snuffing in the brush, and Grey thought he heard the throaty grunts of a jaguar in the distance, but nothing approached them. As the sky began to lighten, filling the jungle with dappled shadows, he thought of the parting words of Tata Menga and then again of the spirits of Palo Mayombe, flitting through the trees and vines, a mass of dead souls saturating the spaces in between.

With the dawn came visibility, but also biting insects and flat humid air. Grey's legs felt like twin blocks of cement. Fred was putting one foot in front of the other like an automaton, head bowed.

Grey felt a burst of energy when the path widened and the jungle became less dense, as if pruned. A hundred feet later they spied two palapas in a clearing through the trees. They approached warily, but the huts looked abandoned. On the other side of the outpost they found a rusty four-wheeler underneath a canopy, and Grey felt a surge of hope when he connected the wires on the engine and it roared to life.

———— ◆ ————

The aging ATV was not much faster than a bicycle, but it did the job. Grey couldn't imagine how ridiculous they looked as they followed the tiny dirt road on the other side of the clearing to a larger dirt road, and then to a one-lane sliver of blacktop.

Eventually they merged into a two-lane highway, and a sign announced they were on the road to Tulum, an hour south of Playa del Carmen along the coast. They ditched the ATV once they flagged a taxi, and rode unmolested to the tiny town built to service the ruins at Tulum. Fred found a triage center using his cell phone.

The doctor stitched them up without a word, as if knife and gunshot wounds were normal occurrences in the jungle. After grabbing a prescription for pain-killers, Grey and Fred sat on a bench in the courtyard. Grey's cell phone was ruined from the fight with Lucho, but his pants had finally dried.

"The Alianza's going to be looking for us everywhere," Grey said. "I don't even trust the airports now."

"Agreed." Fred extracted a toothpick and gnawed on the end. "I know a guy who flies crop planes out of Merida. I say we hire another taxi across the peninsula and fly our asses back to Miami."

Grey slapped at a mosquito and gave a slow nod.

———•———

Fred's contact agreed to fly them out that same evening, so they hired a taxi for the long drive to Merida, took a Cessna to Belize, and then caught a late flight to Miami. Both men were so tired they fought to stay awake on the taxi ride to an anonymous hotel near the Miami airport. They didn't trust Fred's house, or anyone in the system.

The next morning Fred called Lana and arranged to meet. She wasn't available until the evening, but she instructed Fred to drop the fingerprints off at the FBI office in town, saying she would expedite results.

———•———

In the morning, Grey called Viktor to update him. There was no answer and he left a message.

Grey and Fred had an early dinner at Titanic, a brew pub near the University of Miami. Soon after the sun went down, they drove over to Lana's coffee shop. This time a handful of patrons dotted the patio and they had to talk in low voices near the fountain.

Though Mexico was in the rearview, Grey knew the cartels had eyes and ears in Miami. He sat with arms crossed and his back against the fountain, eyes sweeping the café.

It took the better part of an hour to update Lana on everything that had happened. Her eyebrows stayed raised the entire time.

When Fred finished the story, Lana brought her cup of green tea to her lips. "That's quite an adventure."

"Adventure? Lady," Fred said, his hand moving to the edge of his stitches, just visible through the open collar of his short-sleeved polo, "that's the understatement of the decade. In all my years . . . a fence made out of human spines . . . goddamn." He crossed himself. "God*damn*."

She turned to Grey. "Any thoughts?"

Grey gave a low chuckle. What a question. "I just hope the trip wasn't in vain. What's the ETA on those prints?"

Her face expressionless, Lana reached into her shoulder bag and placed a manila folder stamped *CIA* on the table. "Delivered."

Fred clucked. "Half a day?"

"As I said, I expedited."

Grey cocked his head. "Well?"

Lana drummed her fingers on the table, then told them about her fight to the death in the CIA safe house. It was Grey's and Fred's turn for widened eyes.

"I assume no ID on her?" Grey asked.

"Completely outside the system. And believe me, we checked them all. Approximately thirty-year-old woman of Quechuan origin, no identifying marks. Clothes handwoven. The knife was clean, no residual DNA. Oh, and it was a bronze alloy ceremonial knife that forensics pegged at about seven hundred years old."

"Say what?" Fred said. "You're kidding, right?"

"I'm afraid not."

"Quechuan: so we're talking Bolivian, Colombian, Peruvian?" Grey asked.

"Possibly Chilean or Ecuadorian as well."

Fred leaned back in his seat. "So how does some peasant sicario in blue paint with no ID get all the way to Miami, kill a couple of hardened drug dealers, then stick around and infiltrate a CIA safe house? Incan spirit of vengeance, huh? After what we saw in Mexico, I'm starting to think we need an exorcist."

"The prints?" Grey asked.

Lana pressed her lips together and folded her hands on top of the manila folder. "Your trip was not in vain. We have a match."

Grey uncrossed his arms and leaned forward. "Is it him?"

"No, it's not the General. Or if so, I would be highly surprised. The man to whom the fingerprints belong is a man named Julio Ganador, the son of a former powerful member of the Escobar Cartel. Julio himself has a minor arrest record. Juvenile infractions, no drug offenses."

Fred spread his hands. "The apple never falls far from the tree."

"So they say."

"But the real curiosity," Fred said as he bit into his toothpick, "is why the son of a Medellín bigwig is delivering money to a Mexican cult leader."

"I don't think he's delivering," Grey said.

Lana turned towards Grey, eyes sharp.

"I think he's picking up," Grey continued. "He's got a pyramid scheme going, doesn't he? Tata Menga takes money from the Alianza for ritual protection, and pays out to the General. Which means the General," Grey mused, "might be Tata Menga's palero."

"I had the same thought," Lana said. "And the import of the Colombian connection?"

Fred whistled. "It must be where he's based. We're closing in on the bastard."

Lana looked from one man to the other, then said, "Agent Hernandez, you've fulfilled your part of the bargain. I'll have you reinstated regardless of what you choose next. And Grey, you're of course free to do as you choose. But I can't speak further unless you wish to continue. This assignment still needs to stay dark. We have an unprecedented opportunity to find this man, but the window will be miniscule, and the time is now."

"They may not figure out the fingerprint angle for a while," Grey said, "but everyone's going to be on high alert. Enough that they'll change their routine."

"Exactly. I believe we have days, at best, to act on this information."

"What do you propose?" Grey said.

"Same as before. Follow the Palo Mayombe link in Colombia. Stay out of the way and report back if you find something. Julio Ganador has two residences on file. One is in Bogotá, the primary. The other is a second home in a small town a few hours outside Medellín, in coffee country. I believe both bear investigation." She cupped her tea in her hands. "I know it's asking a lot—"

"Are you kidding?" Fred said. "This is what I signed up for, catching some-one who matters. Not pushing paperwork around the suburbs or chasing two-bit gangbangers in this swamp of a city. Just get me a piece on arrival this time."

Grey eyed Fred, thinking he had acquiesced a bit too quickly. Then again, Grey had already considered the prospect himself and come to the same con-clusion.

Lana gave Fred a thin smile. "That can most definitely be arranged. Grey, what do you say to extending your consultancy a bit longer?"

Grey rested his thumbs against the sides of his coffee cup, eying Lana before he spoke. She eyed him back without a twitch. One cool customer, this Lana.

"What I think," Grey said, "is that I don't like drug dealers, I don't like black magic rituals involving myself, and most of all, I don't like being on someone's hit list."

Lana's smile expanded, though still hard around the edges. "Then welcome to the team again. Due to the time constraint, I propose a division of duties."

"I was posted in Bogotá," Grey said. "I can get around."

"I've been to Bogotá as well," Lana said, "and I was thinking the Palo angle might be more pronounced in the countryside."

Grey bobbed his head back and forth as he considered the idea. "Maybe, maybe not. Cults thrive just as easily in the cities."

"In any event, Señor Guiñol's last-known residence was Bogotá. I think it's the more dangerous play, and I'd feel more comfortable going there myself."

The corners of Grey's mouth lifted. "Up to you."

"Bogotá and Medellín are an hour's flight away should one of us find some-thing. And remember, again, your goal is information. There's no need to en-gage."

Fred rolled his eyes. "Yeah, because that worked out so well in Mexico. But this time it's Colombia, land of peace and honey. What could go wrong?"

Lana began drumming her fingers again, this time on the folder. "There's one more thing you should know. Just before I arrived here, I received a call from the DEA station chief. The body of the blue indigenous woman I killed has disappeared from the morgue."

39

Grey took the couch, Fred the bedroom. After Fred turned in, Grey paced the suite, unable to wind down. He was still buzzing from the flight through the cenote, thinking about Nya, thinking about the case.

Thinking about the wooden Incan cross Lana said the coroner had found on the empty slab in the morgue where the blue lady's body should have been.

Thinking about Fred's closed bedroom door and wondering how the cartel had found them so quickly in Mexico.

He eyed Fred's cell on the kitchen table. After listening by his door until sure he heard the soft breath of sleep, Grey padded back to the phone and checked it for suspicious calls.

Finding nothing, he stepped into the parking lot and dialed Lana's number. It was almost midnight. She answered on the first ring. "Everything okay?"

"It's Grey. We need to chat." The cell phone was DEA issue, and Grey knew everything he said might be played back in the future. "In person."

A moment of silence. "Just us, I take it?"

"Yeah. Can you pick me up?"

"Where are you?"

After a pause, he told her.

"Be there in twenty."

After ringing off, Grey's fingers hovered over the keypad, his mind calculating the time difference for Harare.

Seven a.m. Zimbabweans rose early to take advantage of the morning light. Nya would be having tea in her garden, or perhaps taking an early morning stroll through the riotous foliage in her neighborhood, as lush as any zip code in Miami. Birds would be chattering above, spots of color in the shimmery morning light, wheeling through Nya's piece of the vast African sky.

If he were there, maybe there would be a power cut that night after work, and Grey and Nya would have dinner by candlelight, boiling water for the pasta on the propane gas burner, lingering with wine on the patio, a pleasant chill in the air, hand in hand under a canopy of starlight, lost in the feeling that the bottomless night sky and that red earth below, the two of them, had always been there.

He knew he wanted her as much as he had before, perhaps more so. More than he had ever wanted anything.

Too much.

He left the phone on the table and waited for Lana outside.

———•———

When he got in the sedan, Lana eyed his clothing—jeans and a black T-shirt and boots—as if making a decision. "Hungry?" she asked.

"Not really."

"Thirsty?"

"Sure."

She took him to a Spanish joint on Calle Ocho, a relaxed tapas bar with a dozen tables and a small stage in the corner. Lana ordered white sangria, Grey a draft Estrella.

Grey leaned back and eyed the crowd, surprisingly diverse in age and socioeconomic status. Except for him, however, it looked one hundred percent Latino. "Another cousin's place?"

Lana chuckled. "A high school friend, actually. Old Miami's a small town." Once their drinks arrived, she said, "You don't trust Fred."

"You don't beat around the bush, do you?"

She smirked. "You're not exactly Mr. Small Talk."

"True."

"So what makes you trust me?" she said.

"I don't."

She waited as if expecting him to add something, then raised her glass. "Touché."

"I wouldn't say that I don't trust Fred," Grey said. "What I don't trust is the situation. The Alianza found us awfully fast, even if they were passing our photo around." He took a swig of beer. "And how'd they get to you in the safe house?"

"Someone must have noticed me staking out the informant's house and followed me back. Someone very good at avoiding detection, because I'm one of the best."

She said it immodestly, but offhand, without bravado. Grey took her at her word.

"Needless to say," she continued, "I've cut off all communication with the DEA. No one but us knows where we're going next."

"No one but the Deputy Director."

"Only him," Lana said evenly, "and it was a secure line. If he were turned, he would have absolutely no reason to initiate or continue this investigation."

"No reason you can fathom."

She spread her hands. "Give me one."

"He practices Palo Mayombe. He's doing as he's told by his palero."

Lana started to laugh, then cut it off. "You're serious."

"I've seen it before. Ambassadors, ministers of state. Maybe not for the same reasons as villagers, but the end result is the same."

She shook her head. "He's a family man, staunch Catholic, a deacon at his church."

Grey laughed. "So? You *train* people to lead double lives."

"When would he have the time? Look, I applaud you for seeing all the angles, you're clearly a smart and careful guy. But I'm not buying it. And it begs the same question: even if he's under someone's thumb, which is highly improbable, why initiate the investigation?"

Grey tipped his bottle. "That, I'll give you. It seems illogical, and there's no reason I can think of. Which is why I agreed to go to Colombia. But you still shouldn't dismiss it."

She shifted closer to him, tilting her chin down and raising her eyes. "The same goes for any of us. Me. Fred. You. Your file's a bit strange, you know. Between when you lived with your father in Japan and when you joined the Marines, you're a blank. Half a decade off the grid? That's awful young for a blank."

A blank, Grey repeated to himself. A pretty good description of his years of living on the streets and in seedy hotels in sketchy cities across Asia and Europe, earning his way by street fighting and the odd security job at bars and night clubs.

Grey met her eyes. "I know the leak's not me. And I was there when Fred was shot in the arm and chased through the jungle by an angry mob."

Lana's curvy lips formed a half-frown, not an unattractive gesture. "And I came within inches of dying in my apartment. You didn't ask me to meet to talk about Fred, did you? You've already formed your opinion on him. You wanted to look me in the eye and ask your questions."

"I want to make sure I'm not walking into an ambush in Colombia."

"You can never be sure. So why go at all?"

"You know why," he said. "You profiled me."

Her head tilted back, though her body was still shifted towards his. "There're a few things I'm wondering about, that weren't in the profile."

"Such as?"

"What was your mother like?"

Grey didn't reply, unwilling to play her psych games. Despite himself, he thought, *My mother was the type of person who made everyone else feel glad to be alive.*

"I thought so," she murmured, looking in his eyes.

"You shouldn't think so much."

Grey turned his beer up for the last swallow. Lana gestured to the waiter for two more. "Tell me one thing you regret," she said. "I'll even go first. I regret sleeping with my crim law professor."

"Was he married?"

She nodded, her grin wicked. "His wife found out and he gave me a D. Knocked me out of valedictorian."

Grey wrapped his hand around the fresh glass when it came, enjoying the cool feel. The air in the bar was hot and sticky. "I wish I knew how to build a house."

"A carpenter?" she said, amused. "A killer with a Jesus complex?"

He waved a hand in dismissal. "I don't have any real-life skills. You know, fixing a sink, building a tree house for the kids. I've never even mowed the grass. Though I could probably figure that one out."

"Your skills are pretty sought after in my world."

"If this world was anything like it should be, I'd be out of a job."

"Well, it's not. You've never been raped, have you?"

Lana said it with such calm that Grey's eyes snapped over.

"If you'd been raped," she said, "you wouldn't wish things were different. You'd be glad you're exactly who you are."

Grey tried to figure out her angle for telling him that information. Was she opening up so he would do the same? Or was it a fabricated claim, designed to elicit a response?

Judging by her face, the look of pain and anger and lost innocence in her eyes, maybe the first true emotion he had seen, he didn't think it was a fabrication. "That's not what I said. I said I wished the world were different. When were you . . . I'm sorry."

"In high school. Look, if it hadn't happened I'd be some silly divorced society woman like my mother, shopping and playing tennis and serving on the board of her country club to try to plug the bitterness. Hey, don't say I can't put a positive spin on things."

Grey touched her arm. "I can tell it will never happen again."

"You're damn right it won't." She looked up at him. "That wasn't in the psych eval either."

"What?"

"That when you want to, you know exactly what to say."

He removed his hand from her arm, but she had shifted close enough that her leg was brushing his. "Did they catch the guy?" he asked.

"Someone did," she said, and Grey could tell there was a story there. "Some local tough guys, Mariel boatlift types, found me and disappeared with the rapist. He turned up a week later in a dumpster. Someone killed him very slowly."

"Good," Grey said, and then a loud clang sounded from the corner of the restaurant. Before Lana could react, Grey had palmed a dinner knife and sprung to his feet, eyes sweeping the place for the source of the noise.

Lana was pulling him down. "Sit down," she whispered, at the same time he saw a flamenco dancer emerge onstage, wrists turning and gypsy skirts twirling, more cymbals clanging in the background.

Grey returned to his beer with an embarrassed shrug. The people at the tables around them were stifling laughs.

"God, you're fast," Lana said, her thigh now pressed into Grey's leg. "Though maybe you should try not to take out the entertainment."

"Probably a good idea."

"Two more questions," she said.

"Please tell me they're situational behavior scenarios and not personal questions."

"Sorry. Do you still love Nya?"

Grey started. "Seriously? I get it now, you're trying to find my pressure points in case things go south. Congratulations."

"As someone who understands physiological responses, I'm sure you realized that your eyes moved to the side and you swallowed imperceptibly before responding. So you still love her. Good to know. Final question," she said, moving a hand on top of his and looking him in the eye, her gaze challenging. The scent of her perfume cut through the smell of tarragon and fried potatoes from the next table over, and the skin of her hand felt callused but warm. "Does it make any difference?"

He held her gaze for a long moment. "Yeah," he said softly, not bothering to hide either his conviction or the undercurrent of regret. "It does."

40

DER HEILIGKEIT DES LUFT SANATORIUM

Viktor woke the next morning stiff from the long walk, but with the satisfaction of an obstacle overcome. Still, despite his present condition, he didn't long for sobriety. He missed his emerald muse and the places it took him. Life was too complex to label such things as alcohol or wormwood bad, to not appreciate and explore the different states of reality they offered. Absinthe was a part of him and he hoped they could coexist again one day.

Just not quite yet—and on his own terms.

He listened to the message from Grey and absorbed the information. Later that day, Grey would step on a plane to Bogotá in pursuit of the link to the General.

Viktor frowned. While Palo was present in Colombia, especially near Cali, it was not prevalent. Then again, neither was it widespread in Mexico.

Palo priests were highly territorial and stayed in one location. They did not control international drug rings and send out blue-painted assassins. On the other hand, it was clear that Tata Menga was involved in drug activity, and connected to the General.

Viktor felt as if they were missing something important. That this case was not as it seemed.

He thought back to Grey's description of the cemetery. The fact that the graves bearing crosses had been untouched by the gravedigger meant that Tata Menga worked with Palo Judeo, the type of Palo Mayombe untouched by Christianity.

Palo of the purest form, the kind that traced its lineage straight from the ancient forests of the Congo.

The kind used to kill.

About the time Grey would be dashing to the airport, just after Viktor finished a late lunch of apple- and fig-stuffed pheasant with crisp *rösti* potatoes, he received a response to his Interpol inquiry.

The name of the mental patient who had startled Viktor was Glen von Reisenberg. Viktor was correct, he had been imprisoned once before, in a local jail near Santiago, Chile. The charge had been assault and attempted murder.

What, Viktor wondered, had a German with mental health issues and obvious means been doing in Santiago? Viktor slapped a hand on the table, causing a stir among the other diners.

Germany, Chile, *of course!* He remembered where he had seen this man. He remembered it well.

Colonia Dignidad. 2006. One of the most disturbing utopian cults with which Viktor had dealt. The leader, Paul Schaefer, was an émigré from Germany, a notorious pedophile and puppet of Pinochet. After the Pinochet regime folded in the early 1990s, public pressure led to an investigation of the colony, and Schaefer was forced to flee the country. He was arrested in Argentina in 2005, extradited to Chile the next year, and Viktor was called in to help cement his prosecution.

After cataloguing the torture chambers and assisting in the search for mass graves, Viktor had interviewed dozens of colony members. Glen von Reisenberg had been one of them. Viktor remembered now the purple birthmark. He also remembered the lack of emotion, the eerie movements of an automaton, the inability to relate to normal human motive.

He almost smacked himself. Glen von Reisenberg wasn't mentally ill—he was brainwashed. In the heat of the attack and because Glen was a patient at the sanatorium, Viktor had missed the signs.

One of the remarkable things about Colonia Dignidad was that a decade after the departure of their leader, not much had changed inside the colony. The residents were still loyal to Schaefer, still followed the mandates of his lieutenants, still followed the same lifestyle. And why shouldn't they? For most, it was all they had ever known.

Glen was one of these. Born and raised in the colony. At the time Viktor interviewed him, he had never set foot outside its walls. Viktor remembered a hollow puppet of a man so indoctrinated into the cult that he hadn't been able to tell Viktor the current president of Chile, or even the identity of his own birth parents, who were also members of the cult.

Yes, Viktor remembered Glen, but what was the possible connection among Colonia Dignidad, the recent threat against Viktor, and Grey's investigation into the General?

Viktor returned to his room and fired off another Interpol request, this one for a more detailed report of Glen von Reisenberg's actions and whereabouts since 2006. How did he afford the sanatorium? Did he come from a wealthy family? Did he have drug connections?

After spending the afternoon pacing back and forth in his room awaiting an answer, he decided to go ask the man himself.

———◆———

An hour later, after surprising the guards at the gate to the criminal asylum by flashing his Interpol identification, he secured a visitation window with Glen von Reisenberg, who had mysteriously returned to the asylum.

Though Glen sat across the visitation table with his hands unbound—at Viktor's request—a pair of guards waited at the rear of the room, electric batons and syringes at the ready.

Viktor spoke in German. "Hello, Glen."

The bovine head lifted to regard Viktor.

"Don't worry, I won't tell them about your excursion yesterday. It shall remain our little secret."

Still no response.

"We've met once before. Do you remember?"

This elicited a squinting of Glen's tiny eyes, making them almost disappear.

"Colonia Dignidad," Viktor said. "Eight years ago."

Glen's lips parted, and Viktor saw a glimmer of intelligence behind the foggy vision. "I remember," Glen said. "The investigator."

"That's correct. I understand, you know," Viktor said quietly. "You've no idea how many people I've seen in your position. You're just following orders. Someone let you out, someone told you to find and hurt me, and someone told you never to speak about it. Someone told you it was for the good of the colony."

Viktor could tell by the flare of Glen's nostrils that he had struck a nerve. The man was a member of a cult, not a trained intelligence operative. He was not immune to questioning.

That said, Viktor knew it was pointless to try to rehabilitate him in so short a time, so he tried a different angle.

"They'll never let you out of here, Glen. Never. Why do you think they made you come back inside? Why not take you back to Chile?"

Glen looked straight at Viktor, eyes shining with conviction. "Because I have a job to do. When it's done, I'll return."

"You won't. It's over. Didn't they tell you? Of course they didn't, or you wouldn't be helping them. The government shut it down, Glen. The colony dispersed. They sent the children to orphanages and put all the adults in places like this."

"You're lying," Glen said. "Just like he said you would."

"Just like who said?"

"*Him.*"

"The one who let you out yesterday?" Viktor said, then took a stab. "Or the one who replaced Schaefer? Who is he? Tell me and I'll work on your release, you have my word."

Glen pressed his lips together and stilled, his cartoonishly small features lines of stencil on his face.

"Whoever he is," Viktor said calmly, "he's lying. *They shut it down.* You don't have anywhere to go back to, and the people who want me dead don't care about you. If you don't help me, you'll be in here forever. You'll die in here."

Glen slammed his hands on the table, rattling it. "Liar! Filthy heathen liar!"

Maybe, Viktor thought, *he was a little crazy after all.*

Glen rose, and Viktor stepped backwards as the guards rushed forward.

"Your judgment is upon you!" Glen screamed, shrugging off the first guard and wrestling with the second. He looked as strong as a buffalo. "Your judgment," his words began to slur, after one of the guards jammed a syringe in his arm, "isss . . . up . . . onnnn . . . youuu."

41

Early the next morning, Grey listened to a message from Viktor describing his encounter with the mental patient. It disturbed Grey that someone—the General—might be targeting Viktor in Switzerland. Was there something the General didn't want Viktor to piece together? Or was it a warning for Grey to back off? Just in case, Grey called Nya and left a message for her to call him as soon as possible.

He joined Fred in the hotel lounge for a mediocre coffee. If Fred knew Grey had slipped out the previous evening, he gave no indication.

"So how's Colombia these days?" Grey asked.

"Better than it was when you were there. Still rough. Still the world's largest coke refiner. The players are more scattered and under the radar after the break-up of the big cartels, but those motherfuckers don't just take a bow. The new cartels are run more like a business, less flamboyant, making sure they clean up their cookie trails."

"Harder to know who the enemy is."

"You bet," Fred said. "Wondering what the hell we're about to get ourselves into?"

"Something like that."

"If it makes you feel any better, coffee country is as safe as it gets in Colombia. Apparently the drug lords like their coffee and leave the area alone, for the most part."

Grey shook off a yawn and leaned forward with his cup cradled between his hands, elbows resting on his knees. "I give it two days at most before someone figures out we're there."

Fred shook out a toothpick from his case. "In and out, buddy. In and out."

Though Grey and Fred took the same flight to Bogotá, they arrived at the Miami airport at separate times and stayed apart. Lana took a different flight altogether, and assisted with fake passports and boarding cards. Still, Grey knew their pictures were circulating.

Which was why, the morning before their flight, they took a few liberties with their appearance. Grey wore a San Francisco Giants cap pulled low, brushing against rectangular black-rimmed glasses that shielded the middle portion of his face. A week's worth of stubble covered the lower third, and a green North Face pullover and worn jeans completed the outfit.

Fred had shaved his moustache. The exposed skin on his upper lip looked fresher than the rest of his face, as if grafted on from someone younger. Grey thought he looked much less imposing; as if his moustache, like Samson's hair, held the source of his strength. Fred also sported a pair of cosmetic glasses, and was wearing khaki pants and a casual blue button-up. The disguises were far from perfect, but should throw off someone glancing at a photo.

Disguises notwithstanding, there was still the very serious issue of the leak. The trip needed to be a surgical procedure, stitched up before anyone knew they had left.

Hours later, Grey and Fred descended into Bogotá, the Andean ridgeline coiled around the city like the tail of a dragon. With an altitude of eight thousand six hundred feet, the capital was a chilly, gloomy metropolis defined by the mountains hovering at its edges, watching, brooding like a tempestuous artist at odds with its creation.

During the descent, Grey watched a little boy clinging to his father during turbulence. The fear and love comingling in the boy's eyes brought back memories of Grey's first posting with Diplomatic Security. Of a city of warm but guarded Bogotános, their collective psyche a damaged flower struggling to re-open after the horror of the drug wars.

The empty streets at night. Vast swaths of the city under the sway of gangs and street criminals. Teenagers scurrying to school in broad daylight. Younger children playing in the city's parks while their parents clenched coffee cups and jumped at the slightest movement.

The thing was, Grey could relate. His own childhood was a haze of violence. In the eyes of the Bogotános he saw the shame of those endless nights of fear, the rage of the morning after, the crippling memory of not being able to protect oneself or one's family. No one had forgotten, and it was why Bogotá felt so edgy, as if the entire city was expecting violence to erupt at any moment.

Two job-related incidents had defined his posting. The first was an emergency raid on a shack in one of the poorest sections of Bogotá. A U.S. consular officer had used bad judgment in his choice of whorehouse in Chapinero, the rundown student district, and had been kidnapped mid-coitus by a couple of enterprising street criminals. Not used to kidnapping diplomats, the thugs took his cell phone but didn't smash it, unaware that it contained a tracer.

A Special Forces team had led the raid, but Grey was one of the DSOs chosen to ride along and help manage the situation. He would never forget the ride in the middle of the night deep into the slum, a no-man's-land unlike any Grey had ever seen. The abominable scenery seemed to stretch to eternity, a dystopian warren of rotting wood and corrugated metal, the wind off the ridge blowing trash through the streets, bullet-riddled windows and muddy alleys and shacks built on shacks. An eerie lack of ambient light.

Yet it was the omnipresent violence that stunned him, and to which he was acutely attuned: the armed gangs who stood sentry on the corners and slunk through the potholed roads, men whose lightless eyes conveyed an absolute willingness to put a bullet in someone's head without a shred of remorse. Make no mistake, Grey knew— they were driving through a war zone.

The raid had been a joke, a van full of commandos versus a handful of freebasing thugs with rusty handguns. They pulled the diplomat out unharmed, shot everyone else, and the van sped out of Dante's Inferno and back to the embassy. Yet while the rest of the team whooped and high-fived with leftover adrenaline, Grey watched with hooded eyes as the nightmarish scenery rolled by. All he could think about were the voiceless souls living under siege and without hope, of fathers with no jobs trying to keep their families fed and safe, of the neighborhood kids getting shot or conscripted into gangs, at what colonialism had done to the world, at the *injustice* of it all.

The second incident was the one that cost Grey his seniority, and got him transferred from Bogotá to Harare, which was a posting for diplomatic careers on life support.

One fine summer day, which meant the sun showed for almost an hour and the weather neared seventy degrees, Grey was helping oversee the arrival of a minor functionary, a mayor from one of the jungle provinces who was integral to a coca-dusting operation the U.S. was about to launch. Built to withstand a full-on attack by the cartels, the U.S. Embassy in Bogotá was a fortress, a multistory compound near the airport.

Grey was posted on a side street near the embassy, peripheral to the action but guarding against threats from the intersection fifty feet behind him. Just before the mayor entered the embassy, his position relayed by headset, Grey heard a scream from one of the streets approaching the intersection.

He spun towards the sound, gun at the ready, unable to believe his eyes: a carjacking taking place right in front of him.

Scratch that, he could believe it. Though better than in the eighties, Bogotá was still lawless, a Molotov cocktail of government soldiers, local police, ex-cartel assassins, FARC and ELN insurgents, and the new players on the drug scene. All looking for a play, all long ago having abandoned the code of conduct limiting violence against civilians. Robberies and bombings and assassinations by sicarios on motorcycles were commonplace.

Grey's duty was to the consular officer and the visiting mayor. Unless required for the protection of his assets, Grey was not to abandon his post—for *any* reason—until given the okay.

As Grey watched, the bejeweled woman driving the Mercedes locked her doors and reached for her cell phone. Her assailant broke the car window with the butt of his gun. Grey twitched but could only listen, watch out of the corner of his eye to make sure the violence didn't spill over and affect the arrival of the mayor, and seethe in silent rage.

The carjacker pulled the woman out of the car. Stupidly, she struggled, waving her arms and screaming at her assailant.

So he stabbed her.

Grey lurched forward. His partner for the detail screamed at him from five feet away. "Stand your ground, Grey! We don't have clearance!"

Grey's headset blared. *The assets are safely inside. Hold your positions until further notification.*

The carjacker pulled a pistol and aimed it at the woman, who was slumped against the side of the Mercedes, blood pouring over her hands and staining the pavement.

It could have been a decoy. A ploy to divert attention on a side street while someone else fired on the mayor or stormed the embassy. Grey did a split second eval and found it highly, highly unlikely. Any action would have gone down before the assets entered the embassy.

Regardless, Grey knew what he was about to do was against protocol.

He just didn't care.

Grey fired his weapon in the air. The assailant jumped away from the woman and saw Grey advancing, the laser sight from his semiautomatic leveled at the carjacker's chest.

The carjacker fled, the woman survived, and Grey was banished to Southern Africa.

After a *café tinto*, an espresso so thick and black the locals called it ink, Grey hopped on a commuter plane to Armenia, one of the three triangle cities outlining the *Zona Cafetera*, or Coffee District. Fred was seated ten rows ahead of him. The flight took less than an hour.

The Armenia airport was the size of a large retail store. When Grey stepped outside, he saw fields of coffee bushes and a row of banana trees swaying in the warm tropical breeze. A two-lane road led into the verdant countryside.

As discussed, Fred waited five minutes before sidling up to Grey outside the airport. Long enough to throw off any spotters waiting at the gate, and short enough not to raise eyebrows by loitering.

"Not exactly a metropolitan center," Fred said.

"Not exactly."

Most of the twenty or so passengers filed into either the small bus waiting near the exit, or into vehicles filled with family members. A taxi driver parked behind the bus tried without success to coax passengers into his vehicle. In front of the bus, a man in an aging black sedan waited with a sign that bore Fred's alias.

"Our ride," Fred said, taking a step towards the private car.

Grey put a hand on his arm. "How'd you book the car?"

"Rental car agency in Armenia. Gave him the false name, no deposit. I'll have him swing by the address in town Lana gave us to pick up the guns, then take us to Salento."

"What do you know about Lana's contact?"

"About as much as you. Local guy, knows CIA contacts drop in from time to time."

Fred looked down at Grey's soft grip on his arm, then back up. "What's up, partner?"

Grey released his arm. "Let's take that taxi over there. And skip the guns."

Fred gave him a long look, then ran his tongue along the front of his teeth. "I'm not opposed to that. Though I'll feel naked until I find a piece."

"I won't."

———◆———

The taxi driver was more than happy to take them to Salento, about an hour's drive northeast. According to Lana, Medellín had been Julio Ganador's hometown before he moved to Bogotá. Salento was his second home. A passport check showed that Julio had flown all over Latin America for years, presumably on business trips for the General. And those were just the flights he took on the record.

The question was, where was he delivering the payments?

If there was a Palo connection, and if the person they were looking for was Tata Menga's palero, then what could they expect in Salento? Something worse than a fence made of human spines and a sinkhole filled with bodies?

They gave themselves two days to find a link. Anything more was reckless, Grey felt, unless Lana wanted to call for backup.

Steering well clear of Julio's former residence, Grey opted to start the search at La Finca, a combination coffee farm and guesthouse just outside of town, claiming to be one of the oldest coffee farms in Colombia. Though he would have to play it cool, Grey hoped to pump the owners for information.

He also hoped they weren't connected to the General.

———◆———

After passing through the concrete scar that was the town of Armenia, the countryside turned even lusher than before, steep emerald peaks and long sloping valleys drizzled in mist, villas perched on top of knobby hills, a curvaceous silver river running through the valley like the back of a salmon glinting in the sun.

All in all, it looked more like the backdrop to a Colombian *Sound of Music* than a hotbed of Palo Mayombe and drug cartels.

They pulled into Salento, one of the prettiest towns Grey had ever seen, a handsome colonial square cradled by the rippling slopes of coffee country, mist strung like gauze across the tops of the peaks.

Grey spoke to the driver in Spanish. "La Finca. Can you take me there?"

The driver wagged a finger and pointed at a vintage jeep covered in stickers on the far side of the square. "They can," the driver said. "The road is very steep."

"Isn't there another taxi?" Grey asked. Getting into an unlicensed vehicle in Colombia was asking for trouble. "A four-by-four?"

"That *is* the taxi," the driver said.

Grey and Fred exchanged a look. They had already decided Fred would stay in town and dig for information on Palo, while Grey visited the coffee farm.

Fred smirked and spoke to Grey in English. "You're the one who turned down the driver."

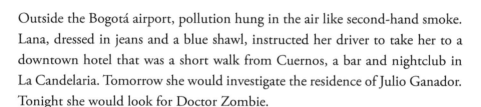

42

Outside the Bogotá airport, pollution hung in the air like second-hand smoke. Lana, dressed in jeans and a blue shawl, instructed her driver to take her to a downtown hotel that was a short walk from Cuernos, a bar and nightclub in La Candelaria. Tomorrow she would investigate the residence of Julio Ganador. Tonight she would look for Doctor Zombie.

Cuernos was where her investigation from a year before had ended—the last breadcrumb on the trail to Señor Guiñol. The rumor on the street was that Guiñol's people frequented the nightclub, but after weeks of mingling with the urban sharks who hung there, she never found a link, and other duties had pulled her away from the case.

As the taxi lurched from red light to red light in the traffic-choked streets, inching through corridors of soot-stained apartment blocks, Lana soaked up the city, getting back into character. Bogotá was not a warm place, tongues and libidos loosened by a tropical breeze. It was cold, stern, and haughty, mimicking the peaks that enclosed the city like some gargantuan stone fence. A city that rewarded competence more than charm, formality more than invention, power more than money.

She ran through the highlights of the previous investigation in her mind, in preparation for the night's charade. Someone in that bar could lead her to Doctor Zombie, she felt it in her bones. And Doctor Zombie could lead her to the General.

Doctor Zombie. Señor Guiñol. No one even knew his real name. The limited knowledge Lana possessed was hearsay, gathered from drug chatter and her previous investigation.

Señor Guiñol was reputed to have been a fixture of the Bogotáno underworld during the drug wars, but dropped off the radar after the death of Pablo Escobar. Whether that meant he had lost his protection and gone to work for the General, or simply that the climate had changed, she didn't know.

But who *was* he? The CIA knew nothing, the DEA less. So a year ago, Lana had gotten on a plane to Bogotá.

Her cover was Mariana Arboleda, a Cuban American playgirl from Miami with a trust fund and a wild streak, known to have a penchant for designer drugs, nightclubs, and men to whom violence came easily. The identity allowed her to lounge with high society types during the day and scour the bars and clubs at night.

After swimming through the incessant traffic, pollution, noise, and crime of the city center, Lana felt as if she had stepped through a portal to another dimension when she found Usaquén, the crème de la crème of Bogotá's neighborhoods, a gem of restored colonial architecture and leafy parks. The calm felt surreal, manufactured. A bubble of order inside the seething chaos of Bogotá, ready to pop at any time and let the barbarians stream through the gates.

After a few weeks of martini lunches, Lana managed to ingratiate herself with a group of society women who were the wives and lovers of drug traffickers. The Bogotános possessed a strange relationship with the violence of the cartels, both loathing and glorifying them in the media, trying to understand how their entire city had been held hostage by animals. Insider stories about the narco life filled the pages of popular magazines, serial dramas about fictional cartels had become some of the most watched shows on television. It reminded Lana of the obsession in the U.S. with shows like *The Sopranos* and *Breaking Bad*, a flirtation with the dark side of the human psyche.

From the cartel mistresses, tittering fake blondes with enough silicone to float Detroit, Lana learned about a name whispered in cartel circles, a frightening figure known as Doctor Zombie who prowled the streets of Bogotá. He was the leader of an urban cult— yes, Lana recalled, the word *cult* had been used—hired by the cartels to strike terror into the hearts of politicians and rival cartels. This made sense: Bogotá had never been home to any one powerful cartel, but instead had become a battleground for their constant internecine and political wars.

Eventually Lana pieced together a rough sketch of Doctor Zombie's background. He had once been a respected pharmacist—since no one knew his real name, it was impossible to verify the story—who often invited his customers for coffee in the back of his shop. Respected, that was, until a jealous husband, suspicious of his wife's lengthy visits to her pharmacist, burst into the back room and found Doctor Zombie straddling her naked body. When the enraged husband barreled forward, the good doctor injected him with a powerful sedative and fled town.

The wife claimed to have no memory of the illicit encounter. The husband didn't believe her story, until the police found bottles full of scopolamine extract in the pharmacist's work room. They also found traces of the drug in the box wine he kept in the fridge, in bottles of Coca-Cola, in a plate of cookies, and even on some of the magazines displayed for his patients' perusal.

As the story went, the next time Guiñol surfaced was in the Bogotáno underworld, a fiendish criminal known as Doctor Zombie who used his pharmaceutical concoctions to paralyze his prey. Lana could find no mention of his crimes in Colombian newspapers or judicial records, but Guiñol might hail from a less developed part of Colombia. Or was his background story an urban myth, a distorted truth?

The taxi passed through Chapinero, blocks and blocks of concrete apartments peppered by old churches and colonial buildings in various stages of decay. She could smell the diesel without having to lower the window. The weather was overcast as always, the dark clouds an ink stain blotching the mountains.

A crawl through the commercial district, a brief respite from the chaos when they passed by the acacias and twisted evergreens fronting the university gardens, and then finally the hotel.

Lana showered and poured herself into a pair of black leather pants and a clingy charcoal gray T-shirt with a plunging neckline. Applied a generous amount of crimson lipstick, teased her hair, vamped it up. Pursed her lips in the mirror and liked what she saw.

Just before she grabbed her cropped suede jacket and left the hotel, Lana checked her email on her cell. She had a new message.

Before leaving Miami, she had renewed her search for MIA agents who might have a Palo Mayombe angle, even widening the search to include the deceased. Nothing had come up. Frustrated, she tried "cult" and got thousands of hits. She had spent the entire night analyzing the data, focusing on agents who had gone MIA in the Southern Cone. A few interested her, and she memorized their pictures and backgrounds just in case.

There was someone in the *Deceased* file who sparked her interest, a man named Devon Taylor. Devon had been sent undercover into Jonestown under the alias of John Wolverton, tasked with keeping tabs on the cult. Tragically, Devon had died at Jonestown, gunned down by one of the Reverend's bodyguards.

Because Devon was deceased, she might not have lingered on his file, except that when she tried to pull up his photo and background info she found it had been archived. It was probably sequestered due to age, but just in case, she had requested retrieval before leaving Miami, and the email she had just received was the response.

She opened the email, expecting Devon Taylor's file to pop up. Instead she got an *access denied* message.

Now *that* was odd. Lana had high clearance, and this man didn't seem to have done anything, at least from what she knew, to warrant a blocked file.

Then she smirked at herself. Wasn't that the point? Anything damning would have been scrubbed or blocked. There was probably something embarrassing about a future president in there.

She could ask the Deputy Director for clearance. She didn't see how this Devon Taylor could have anything to do with the General, but with as little information as they had, it was worth an inquiry.

She typed the request, but froze before she hit "Send," remembering her own words.

There was probably something embarrassing about a future president in there.

She scoffed at her reaction. It was the Deputy Director—who had recently announced his intentions to run for president—who'd sent her after the General in the first place.

But what if, she thought, *he had sent her because the General had something on him personally?* Something that had happened years ago, which the General could hold over the Deputy Director's head if he gained the Oval Office? An unacceptable point of leverage?

Lana didn't think her line of reasoning had any merit. But there was only one way to find out.

Her finger hovered over the "Send" key. What if this file contained something she wasn't supposed to see? Something that could sidetrack her career or . . . worse?

It was clear there was a mole involved. The only people who knew she was in Bogotá were Grey, Fred, and the Deputy Director. Could Grey's insinuation have teeth? Was the Deputy Director dirty?

She clarified that thought. The Deputy Director might be dirty—a relative state in their line of work—but it didn't make sense for him to be the mole. She'd already be dead if that were the case.

She sent the email. If there were indeed higher machinations in place, and she was walking into a hornet's nest, she would rather know now than later.

At least she thought she would.

43

ZONA CAFETERA, COLOMBIA

The World War II–era jeep had a square face and a canvas tarp covering the back. A child was playing with action figures in the passenger seat. Grey negotiated the fare and climbed into the rear compartment.

At the edge of the village, the jeep rolled to a stop at an intersection. The driver didn't move for a few long seconds, though there were no cars visible in any direction. Just as Grey was about to ask what was going on, he saw three men running towards the jeep.

Grey swore. He shouldn't have let the presence of a child overcome his better judgment about sitting in the back. Though he could reach through and choke the driver if needed, the space was too small to crawl through, and he couldn't take control of the jeep in an emergency.

He jumped out of the car, moving on a diagonal away from the jeep. Two of the men had machetes. They were twenty feet away. He focused through the adrenaline and judged their approach, the cadence of their gait, how they held the machetes, their relative positions. One was running ahead of the others. Big mistake. Grey would time his swing and step inside, then use his hold on the weapon to take the man in a circle and complete a hip throw, stripping the machete in the process. The other two might be on him, but they wouldn't swing for fear of hitting their friend. Grey would roll away with the machete in hand, creating space, and then cut down the other two.

"*Hombre! Que haces?!*"

The driver's words, though shouted, were a whisper at the edge of Grey's concentration. *Hey man, what are you doing?*

The men kept running, machetes swinging at their sides. They hadn't raised them.

"*Vete adentro!*" *Get back inside the jeep.*

Machetes still lowered, the men ran past Grey and jumped inside the jeep, slapping hands with the driver and then turning to look at Grey.

His face red, Grey approached the driver side window and spoke in Spanish. "I thought I paid the fare."

"You paid *your* fare."

Grey eyed the men, dressed in work pants and tank tops and sombreros. Field workers returning to their homes. The child was clutching a Batman doll and peering at Grey with curious eyes.

Grey knew he should do the logical thing and pay the driver whatever it took for a private ride to the coffee farm. But then he would be costing these men their ride to their families, all because he had zero faith in humanity.

The driver flung his arm at Grey. "*Vamos!*"

The child scooted into the middle, offering Grey the window seat up front. *At least someone gets it*, he thought.

With a nod at the driver, Grey climbed in next to the kid. The men in back were laughing and talking too fast for Grey to understand, but one of them passed Grey's backpack to him from the rear.

"*Gracias,*" Grey mumbled.

The jeep climbed out of the valley on a rutted dirt road, the air cooler at the higher elevation, smelling of flowers and animal dung. The roar of the river receded as they crossed the first ridge. On the other side he saw a series of hills, knobby and rounded like the toes of dinosaurs, connected by long trails of fog.

Blowing past men on foot and horse-drawn carts, the driver stopped to pick up more passengers along the way, squeezing them inside until the rear compartment was crammed and a group of men stood on the bumper, clinging to the back of the jeep. Each time someone new climbed aboard, Grey's heart skipped a beat, but no one gave him a second look.

They kept picking up passengers and piling them into and onto the jeep until Grey's jaw dropped, twenty-three commuters in all, the last a kid on a bike who held on to the trailer hitch with one hand.

Fifteen minutes later they reached La Finca, perched on top of a hill polka-dotted by green and red rows of coffee bushes. After hopping out of the jeep, Grey stood alone in front of a handsome country manor. A path led to another guesthouse, a barn, and a few small buildings Grey assumed were used in coffee production.

Grey sucked in a breath of fresh air. The sky was huge, shaggy green slopes rising and falling all around, the rush of a river in the distance, birds chirping, as tranquil a place as Grey had ever seen.

From what Grey could tell, Colombia's coffee country was prosperous, at least compared to the rest of the country. It didn't look like the kind of place a cult would take hold and thrive.

But what did Grey know? Viktor could probably rattle off two dozen cults within a five-mile radius. Thinking of Viktor, Grey hoped he was making progress with his personal issues. Grey had faith. If anyone could impose his will on life, it was Viktor Radek.

He missed Viktor's experience and steady mind on this case, felt adrift in unfamiliar seas without him. Grey doubted he would ever feel at home in the world of cults and bizarre religions and mysterious phenomena, but that was okay. He didn't have to be comfortable to make a difference.

Grey booked a room for the night, so as not to raise eyebrows. He asked about the owners and was told that Doña Valencia was away for the week.

Scratch that source of information.

He wandered into the common room, a sprawling lounge with white plaster walls and overhead wooden beams arranged in a sunburst pattern. The room was full of tourists lounging on leather couches in front of a wood-burning stove, most of them gazing out of the glass wall on the far side of the room. Grey took a look for himself and gave a low whistle.

The glass showcased a narrow emerald valley stretching into the mist and covered with two-hundred-foot tall palm trees whose slender trunks thrust upward like giant cornstalks. Leafy diadems topped the majestic trees, and sunlight dappled the far end of the valley.

"Where're you coming from?"

He pulled his gaze away from the stunning vista to regard a tanned blond woman who might have been twenty years old. She was looking at him from a couch to his left. It took Grey a minute to remember there were normal people in the world, tourists admiring the beauty of nature and not chasing down cults and drug lords.

He blinked. "New York."

"So what, you parachuted in?" she said, her smile a camera flash against her tan. "I mean, where'd you come from before here? Bogotá, Medellín, Cali? I just arrived from Santa Marta. It was beautiful, eh? Mountains right down to the sea. Anyway, you don't sound like the New Yorkers I've met in Sydney."

"Sorry."

Her laugh was short, unsure if his deadpan answer was flirtatious or not.

Grey sat on a stone bench next to her, underneath an ornamental textile of woven horsehair. He absorbed the feel of the crowd, gauging if anyone might be useful and wondering what it might have been like to be a carefree tourist exchanging stories from the road.

A role Grey had never played. His father saw to that, under the guise of making sure his son would never be a sissy, or gay, or weak. He made sure of it when he took Grey to a whorehouse when Grey turned fifteen, made sure of it again when later that same year he shoved Grey into the underground fighting ring in Tokyo. In fact, he had made sure of it for as long as Grey had memories.

Grey listened for a while and then stood, mumbling a good-bye to the Australian girl. There was nothing in that room for him. No narcos, no locals. These were kids on vacation.

He bought a Pilsen from the receptionist and took a walk on the property. Night was falling, a purple bruise on the hills. After passing the other guesthouse, he stopped when he heard a grinding noise coming from inside a wooden building with a tin roof. He stepped inside and saw a fiftyish man in a smock and an Adidas cap pouring beans into an industrial-size sifter. The man saw Grey and didn't seem to mind, so Grey watched him work.

Fifteen minutes later, when the batch was finished, the man stepped outside and lit a cigarette. Grey followed.

He looked Grey over, eyes probing but not unfriendly. Almost as tall as Grey, the coffee worker was stout, with large hands and corded forearms, a flat face that looked like it could take a punch, and a ridged jaw line.

"Here for the tour?" the man said, in the rural Colombian Spanish Grey had heard in the jeep. A local, not an imported worker. Good.

"Just watching," Grey said.

The man took short, hard puffs on his cigarette. "You like coffee?"

"Probably too much."

"Could be worse vices."

"I've got some of those, too," Grey said, and the man chuckled.

"You speak good Spanish." He pointed his cigarette at the building. "You know how the process works?"

"Not really."

The man took off his smock and laid it on a tree stump. He then proceeded to give Grey a lecture on coffee production. Grey nodded along as if the man was telling him how to solve world hunger. Halfway through the narrative, Grey told him to hold that thought, then went to reception and returned with two beers. The man shook his hand gravely and said his name was Salvador.

"How long have you lived here?" Grey asked when Salvador was finished.

"All my life. And you? You don't look much like a gringo."

It was the question Grey was waiting for.

"I'm American, but I've lived all over. I was in Mexico recently."

"Ah," he said.

"Beautiful place," Grey said, "but it's got some issues, if you know what I mean."

Salvador's face wrinkled. "We know something about those issues here."

"In Colombia, sure, but in coffee country? It looks pretty insulated."

"Maybe, but the branch of a diseased tree is still infected, is it not?" Salvador flicked his cigarette butt away. "That dirty son of a peasant farmer infected all of Paisa country."

From his research, Grey knew he was talking about Pablo Escobar.

"But you didn't come to Colombia to talk about this," the man said, "or at least I hope you didn't. You came to see the coffee, the wax palms, the beaches. It's beautiful, our country, no? And the food? Have you had *bandeja paisa*?"

"I have," Grey said, remembering the huge plate of peasant food he had once tried in Bogotá. "I ate about a fourth of it."

The man laughed.

"There's something else I came for," Grey said. "Or someone else, a man named Julio Ganador. Do you know him?"

Grey kept his request neutral, so that depending on Salvador's response,

Grey could go either way. Julio could be a friend Grey met in Miami once and whose address he had lost—or he could be someone else entirely.

Salvador's response, a tightening of the mouth and a pause as he extracted another cigarette, told Grey all he needed to know.

"*Sí*," he said, not bothering to hide his disdain. "I know him. And his father."

Grey put his hands up. "You seem like an honest man, so I'll be honest with you. I'm looking for him, and I think you know what it concerns."

Salvador's eyes narrowed even farther, revealing a shrewdness Grey had suspected was lying under the surface. He was surprised when Salvador kept speaking, not expecting him to take the risk.

The coffee worker looked around, lit his cigarette, and said, "So you're that type of gringo, eh? Is it CIA, DEA? Never mind, I don't need to know. That family is friends of no one around here. Julio's father was Pablo's man in Salento, he ran a personal finca that grew coffee just for him. Before he built Hacienda Nápoles, Pablo sometimes came here when it got too dicey in Medellín. When he was killed, Julio's family left Salento. They knew what would happen if they stayed."

Grey gave him his full attention, feeling he was onto something.

"Julio wasn't a bad kid, you know. What do you do when your father has tied himself to a monster? He never had a choice."

"And the father?" Grey asked. He was getting the feeling that the real contact to the General, that old-world club of drug lords and cult leaders, was the father. Julio Ganador was the message boy, the carrier pigeon.

Salvador blew a smoke ring, eyes squinting so tight they were almost shut, lips parted in a soft smile. "Rolando? I know exactly where that devil is."

Without prompting, he gave Grey a street address in Medellín. Grey repeated it twice to make sure he got it right.

"Thank you," Grey murmured.

"With any luck, I'll be the one thanking you. But you watch yourself in that city, señor."

"I'll try. If you don't mind, there's something else I'd like your opinion on." Grey took a swallow of beer as Salvador put a knee up on the log, leaning on an elbow. "Another problem in Mexico that might have found its way here. Ever heard of a religion called Palo Mayombe?"

"Palo what?"

Grey repeated the name.

Salvador shook his head, not even stopping to think. "Never. And around here, I would know."

Grey checked his watch; it was midnight. "Is there any way back to Salento tonight?"

"No."

———————

After another beer with Salvador, Grey threw his bags in his room, then tried Nya again on his burner cell. She had returned his call, which was a huge relief. It was the middle of the night in Harare, but he left another message, this time telling her to watch her back, and to try him again first thing in the morning.

Next he tried Fred. The DEA agent answered on the first ring. "I was about to get worried."

"I'm stuck up here for the night."

"I figured. All okay?"

"I'll catch you up in the morning," Grey said. "Don't get too comfortable, we're taking the first flight to Medellín."

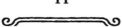

44

Lana left her hotel with a black handbag tucked against her side. In the purse was her cell, her wallet, a makeup kit, a pack of Newports, a tiny canister of mace, and a plastic pistol with a ceramic barrel she had smuggled from Miami. Most gun experts thought the ceramic gun was a myth.

They were wrong.

Eyes on every door and window lining the street, she tightened her shoulders for the short walk. Bogotá was strangely dark and quiet at night, as if it were a tiny village rather than a city of almost seven million. As she passed a line of old brick buildings on either side of a muddy, potholed street, the trapped smog creating an aura of palpable gloom, Lana thought all she needed was a few gas lamps and carriages to bring her back to the end of the nineteenth century.

She skirted Plaza Simon Bolivar, the public square at the edge of La Candelaria. During the day, the plaza was the center of Bogotá's government, a colonial-era pearl ringed by an array of imposing government buildings and ornate lampposts, quite breathtaking except for the panhandlers and cigarette butts and drug addicts and pigeon shit.

A block later and she was there. Hair down, leather pants squeaking against her thighs, Lana saw heads tilt her way through the haze of cigarette smoke when she entered Cuernos. Smoking was banned in most public places in Colombia, and most of those places didn't care.

The music was loud and hip, Latino rap layered over techno. The place was a microcosm of La Candelaria: a series of interconnected small rooms full of hidden alcoves, furtive eyes, danger, and secrets.

The man behind the bar with the pretty face and the wisp of a Fu Manchu goatee didn't make it obvious, but Lana felt his eyes latch on to her as she sauntered through the room.

She eased onto a bar stool and took out the Newports. Lit up as she made eye contact with the bartender. "Got a beer and a shot of whisky for an old friend?"

Without asking, he slid an Aguila draft beer and a double shot of Johnny Walker Black in front of her. The bartender's name was Carlos. He was tall and sinewy in the way of someone who does too much coke, and a year ago they had been lovers.

"Is that what you would call us? Old friends?"

Lana blew a cloud of smoke. "No."

"Good."

Carlos's English was better than before, she thought. He disappeared in the back for a spell and when he returned she switched to Spanish, to make sure nothing got lost in translation. No one else was close enough to hear the conversation. "It's good to see you."

"Are you here for the night, the week, the month?"

She shrugged. "I don't know. We'll see." Her eyes found his. "The night, at least."

He looked away and started drying shot glasses with a towel.

"Or maybe things have changed?" she said. "Perhaps you've got a wife and a new baby? A station wagon and an apartment in Zona Norte?"

That brought a spark to his eyes. "I missed your spirit, Mariana. No one ever gave me hell like you did."

"That's why I came back. In case you might be getting soft."

His grin was wolfish. "I think you know better."

"Do I?"

"We'll see."

She ashed her cigarette. "I'd like to."

As they flirted over the next few hours, she studied the patrons flitting in and out of the rooms and alcoves. Young and edgy, most of them in leather or tatted up, plenty of bikers and narco types, a few young professionals who liked to live on the wild side at night. She saw some of the same faces from before, though if anyone recognized her, no one showed it. The crowd at Cuernos was far too cool for that.

After her spell in the swanky northern suburbs during her previous investigation, she had delved into the party scene, moving from the artist cafés and wine bars of La Macarena to the seedy rave clubs in Chapinero, from bacchanalian parties in Zona G to flitting among the casinos and coke dens swarming Bogotá's tattered excuse for a financial district.

She didn't learn much along the way, except that if she really wanted to meet someone like Doctor Zombie, then she was going to have to immerse herself in La Candelaria, Bogotá's old town, a five-hundred-year-old labyrinth of cobble-stoned streets and crumbling colonial buildings that, except for a few isolated bars and clubs, became a ghost town once the sun went down.

So Lana had entered the world of La Candelaria and did what she was trained to do: infiltrate, deceive, exploit. She befriended DJs, street kids, junkies, dealers. Prowled the old quarter at all hours of the night. Searched, probed, studied, peered behind the curtain of vice.

She learned plenty about the Colombian criminal class, and precious little about her quarry. Doctor Zombie, it was said, was someone whose name was not spoken aloud on the street, and who could do worse than just kill you: he could make you do whatever he wanted. Someone with a reputation of using strange, psychotropic drugs from the jungle. Someone with a network across La Candelaria and in the barrios crawling up the mountainside like worker ants. Someone even the narcos avoided.

All the chatter pointed to Cuernos as the place where, if one was very unlucky, one might run into someone associated with Doctor Zombie. The last time around, she had stayed there for weeks, seducing Carlos, finally asking him outright if he knew anything about Doctor Zombie.

But Carlos had been just as in the dark as everyone else. It was as if the ghost of Señor Guiñol inhabited the place, a phantom everyone talked about but no one had seen. Frustrated and needed on another assignment, Lana had been forced to abandon her search.

Now things were different, she thought.

Now she knew what to look for.

She glanced around the bar. The familiar energy still crackled in the air, something different about this place, darker, more ominous. She wished she had weeks to worm her way back into the scene. Instead she had two or three nights, at best.

After the encounter with the blue lady in Miami, she knew her picture might be circulating. She had vamped up too much to be recognizable at a glance, but if someone noticed her and made a play, then so be it. Sometimes you had to take a risk.

An hour before closing, well after Carlos had started dipping into the whiskey, Lana made her move. "Up for a nightcap?"

Carlos's eyes scanned the crowded bar. "I might be awhile."

"Since when did I go home early? You know," she said, drawing her words out and leaning in, "there's something different going on in Miami these days. Something I think you would like."

His eyes took on a hungry look. Thought she was talking drugs.

"It's a bit of an acquired taste," she said, "like nothing I've done before. Especially if you trip while you're doing it."

"Well? Do I have to guess?"

"It's called Palo Mayombe."

"What?" he said. He looked genuinely confused, and her swallow of beer tasted bitter. While she hadn't expected Carlos to be a player, she expected him to at least be informed.

She backed off, smiling and stroking the back of his hand. "It's a religious ceremony. Trip enough and you'll see spirits, I swear."

He was looking at her strangely, as if she had just confessed to entering rehab. Damn. She had lost ground and would have to rehabilitate. "So where's the after-party these days? The usual?"

"More or less," he said, then brightened. "There's a new place underground. Really cool, great scene."

Underground clubs sprouted up now and then in La Candelaria, places you would never know about without an invitation, makeshift speakeasies in abandoned buildings that were perfect for illicit drug use. This was good; maybe some of his friends were more in the know.

"All the better," she said. "Plenty of snow from the Andes?"

"Oh, yeah."

He scribbled the address on a cocktail napkin. "Go ahead if you want. No sense in watching me close up. Knock twice, four times, then one and two." His eyes moved down her body, lingering on the exposed flesh between her breasts. "They'll let you in."

———————

She finished her drink and left, wanting to spend some time socializing in the club before Carlos arrived and monopolized her attention. Just in case things went south, she texted Fred and Grey the address of the place she was going. They had all bought international burner cells in Miami and exchanged numbers.

The brick and cobblestone streets of La Candelaria were empty, quiet as a monastery at night. She shivered and pulled her jacket tight; it must have been forty degrees.

The underground club was all the way across the old quarter. She hurried through long blocks of shuttered doors and cantilevered windows with iron bars, the occasional hanging lantern lighting the way. Her left hand palmed the canister of mace, her right hand slipped inside her handbag and grasped her gun. The eyes of the eerie blue papier-mâché ghosts dotting the rooftops of La Candelaria seemed to follow her on her journey. Sentinels of Bogotá's violent past, places where someone had been murdered or where someone executed used to live, she couldn't seem to shake their gaze.

The street housing the club was so narrow she thought she could reach out and touch the pastel buildings on either side. The terra cotta rooftops hid the moon, and her heels clacked along the cobblestones, bursts of gunfire in the silence of the night. She had to guess at the address: an iron-studded wooden door in the middle of the block, spaced between two numbered doorways at either end of the street.

After exhaling her tension, she knocked as instructed, her other hand gripping her gun. A few seconds later the door creaked open, revealing a weed-filled courtyard strewn with debris. A burly man in a suit beckoned her inside, lighting the way with a gas torch.

The light from the moon allowed her a glimpse of a cracked archway on the far side of the courtyard. She rolled her eyes, guessing a set of stairs led to the noise and lights of the nightclub she assumed was below. The Bogotá club scene could be so dramatic. Still, she kept a wary eye on the doorman, as well as a few feet of separation.

It was the weirdest thing, and she was sure her subconscious was playing tricks on her, but she had the fleeting impression that she had been there before.

When the doorman closed the door, the shadows came alive. Two men in cowled robes sprang at Lana from behind the door, one of them forcing a rag over her mouth. She tried to yank her gun out of her purse, but the other man grabbed her wrists and held her tight. The doorman jabbed her stomach with the butt end of the torch, releasing the breath she had been holding, speeding up the reaction of whatever odorless chemical was suffocating her from the rag.

Odorless chemical.

Scopolamine.

Doctor Zombie.

In a panic, she tried to snap a front kick, but could no longer feel her legs. Her assailants dragged her through the darkened archway. Just before losing consciousness, her brain sputtering in a chemical fog, she saw more archways and chambers than she would have thought possible, an entire hidden city filled with cowled figures and addicts slumped in corners, eyes burning red in the darkness.

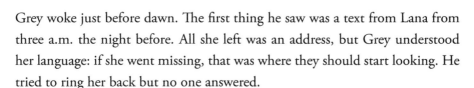

45

Grey woke just before dawn. The first thing he saw was a text from Lana from three a.m. the night before. All she left was an address, but Grey understood her language: if she went missing, that was where they should start looking. He tried to ring her back but no one answered.

It was early. He would try again later.

He caught the first jeep available, pulling into Salento with the morning fog crawling up the ridgeline like the fingers of an advancing wraith. Fred was waiting for him on a café patio in the plaza, eyes bleary and coffee in hand. The smell of frying eggs wafted from inside the café.

"Flight's at eleven," Fred said. "We'll have to use the same passports, unless you've got another idea."

"I don't like it, but if they knew we were here, we'd know by now." Grey sat next to him and ordered a café Americano, rubbing his hands against the chill. "You find anything?"

"Plenty of country bumpkins, some overly fried empanadas, and a few bedbugs. Oh, you mean did I find anything to do with Palo Mayombe? *Nada*. Not even one of those sideways, 'the crazy witch doctor's around the corner' looks we got in Mexico. You're the cult guy, but from what I can tell, there's about as much Palo Mayombe here as there is free Wi-Fi."

Grey nodded and took a sip of coffee. It was dreamy.

"You don't look surprised," Fred said.

"I found the same thing. I don't know what it all means yet, but I don't think Palo's the key. Or not *the* key. I think there's a bigger game being played."

"Really? Such as?"

"Like I said, I'm not sure. I'm going to call my partner and fill him in, see if he has any ideas."

"And the Ganadors?" Fred asked. "You figure Daddy's pulling the strings on Julio? Maybe delivers the money payments himself, after Julio brings them here?"

"That or he forwards them to someone else."

"I've got the feeling the General's about out of layers," Fred said. "You send your money through too many channels, it might get lost. And while Medellín might be a good place for an ex-flunky of Escobar to hole up, I doubt the General's home base is there, after the heat in the nineties. So, my friend, what we need to know is where Rolando delivers the loot." He shook out a toothpick and then spread his hands, his grin cockeyed. "Looks like it's just another follow-the-money-and-the-creepy-cult case."

Grey chuckled. "Welcome to my world."

"Let's talk about Medellín. We've established that the General's the bin Laden type, doesn't do Internet or cell phones. Nor, I'm guessing, banks. Julio picks up millions a year in cash out of Tata Menga's shed alone, for Christ's sake. So we're looking at more transport. The General's far too careful to send the kind of money we're talking any way except private plane."

"I came to the same conclusion."

"Private drug planes are incredibly hard to track. That's a dead end, especially for the resources of our three-person squad. We can't call it in yet because of the leak, and even if we could, I doubt we'd find it that way. So we have to get personal. And at this stage, that means a house call on Señor Ganador."

"Unless he's too well protected," Grey said. "But if we could get a quick look . . ."

"We might find something before this all blows up, if it hasn't already."

Grey pursed his lips and bobbed his head.

Fred stroked his mouth as if his moustache was still there. "What if we're wrong, the father's not involved, and the connection we need is in Bogotá?"

"Then we're wrong."

Fred placed the toothpick between his teeth. "It's gonna be risky as hell," he said, gnawing on the toothpick, "and Medellín ain't Palm Springs." Still chewing, his forearms found the top of the table, and he leaned back in his seat. "It could, in fact, be the lion's den." He met Grey's eyes and held his gaze. "But I *really* don't like drug kingpins."

Grey brought his coffee to his lips. "Me neither."

They landed in Medellín at noon, a thirty-minute flight over the Western Cordillera. From above, the city looked to Grey like a giant concrete river, flowing through a valley surrounded by dimpled green slopes.

Grey didn't like it, but they had to chance a car rental. Instead of a large international company, they went with the seediest local agency they could find, paying cash and hoping the agency's computers weren't linked to the global information network.

On the way to the address the coffee worker had given them, guided by Google Maps, Grey absorbed his surroundings. Medellín had the feel of a low-rent Miami: pleasant weather, ragged palms ruffling in the breeze, empanadas and sugarcane water and fruit in plastic baggies for sale on street corners. Unlike in Bogotá, the surrounding hills and peaks cradled, rather than smothered, the city. To Grey, Medellín's sunny disposition made the dark forces lurking underneath even more ominous, lulling one into a false sense of security.

They skirted downtown, pestered by homeless drunks and street vendors at every light. The city center was a rotten core pimpled with a few examples of stunning public art that looked out of place to Grey. The porcelain spires of Plaza Cisneros and the genius of Plaza Botero didn't begin to compensate for the bombed-out streets of the Prado, beggars bathing in fountains and sleeping on sheets in the middle of pedestrian walkways, the smell of piss and rotting fruit, little girls collecting filthy drinking water off the street.

Rolando Ganador lived in an area of declining colonial homes that looked as if it had once been the talk of the town. Iron gates and high walls shielded the properties, but the guardhouses sat empty, weeds had overtaken the sides of the roads, and most of the brick and plaster villas looked in need of a paint job.

They rolled past their destination, a smaller lot fringed by palms and surrounded by a high wall topped with barbed wire. The address was painted on the wall, but they couldn't see inside. A ¡cuidado con el perro! sign hung from the gate. *Beware of dog.*

Grey and Fred parked outside a bakery two lots down from Rolando Ganador's house. From their table on the far left of the patio, they could just see the gate.

Fred stirred sugar into his coffee. "Nescafé. In Colombia. Can you believe that?"

"I suppose Medellín isn't as interested in coffee as Bogotá." Grey took a sip from his own cup and bit into a pastry filled with guava. The fried dough tasted stale. "Or maybe this bakery just sucks."

"I don't like the look of Ganador's wall. Too risky without knowing what's inside."

Grey focused on the soft parts of the dough, around the edges of the guava filling.

"Don't you think?" Fred asked.

Grey set the pastry down and rubbed at his stubble. "There's an empty guard shack outside, and the streetlight is broken. No electric wire, no signs of a security system. Which either means it's not that secure, or he deals with security himself. I'm guessing the latter."

"You want to case it and go in at night?"

Grey kept his eyes on the Ganador residence, the coils of barbed wire crowning the gate, the thorny bougainvillea snaking atop the wall. He thought about the Walmart-type store he had seen a few blocks away, and the pharmacy next door. A plan started to form.

"Not at night," Grey said. "As soon as we see him leave."

"I don't follow."

"Day breaks are underrated. My guess is some of these guard shacks, probably his, are manned at night. Someone is always home at night. Houses are locked up tighter at night. It's early, so unless he's an invalid, he'll go out sometime today. He doesn't have a nine-to-five. If he's already out for the morning, he'll come back and leave again."

"The dog? The barbed wire? Internal security?"

"My problems."

Two hours and three espressos later, Rolando Ganador's gate slid open and a blue Mercedes from the Reagan era pulled out. The car drove right past where Grey and Fred were sitting. Grey shielded his face with a local paper, but was able to make out a burly driver and an older man in the back seat, his long patrician face punctuated by a nose like an eagle's beak. He had short black hair with gray at the temples, lined skin the color of sandpaper, and one of those thin moustaches that lifted his face into a sneer.

When the car was out of sight, after waiting for the proprietress to finish sweeping the sidewalk in front of the café, Grey grabbed a paper bag from his backpack and pushed away from the table. "Be right back."

He walked down the street, quickening his pace once two commuters on bicycles sped past. When Grey reached the corner of the Ganador residence, he reached into the paper bag and grabbed a ball of raw ground beef wrapped in aluminum foil, then tossed the package over the wall.

The ground beef was stuffed with sleeping pills, which Grey had bought down the street and prepared during the wait. Still in stride, he heard a deep bark at the sound of the package hitting the ground. Paws scrabbled on concrete as a rottweiler rushed to investigate.

Grey returned to the bakery. It was midday and Fred was the only person sitting on the patio.

"Any dogs?" he asked, as Grey reclaimed his coffee.

"Just one. He'll be out soon."

They sat in silence for a few minutes, giving the sleeping pills time to take effect. The air between them was pregnant with the sense of danger. After another fifteen minutes, Grey grabbed his backpack.

Fred grabbed his arm. "I won't bore you with a pep talk. Just remember that if shit goes down, you need to remember who these people are. Escobar ran one of the most ruthless criminal organizations this world has ever seen."

Grey shouldered the backpack, an amused smile on his face. "After what we've been through, you're worried I won't pull the plug?"

"Look, I know you'll pull the plug. I've seen you. But I've also seen the look on your face after it's done. I'm thirsty for more, and you look like you just kicked your dog and feel bad about it. You want to believe there's an ounce of goodness in the human soul, and the people we're dealing with trade in human lives like other people purchase bananas."

"I'm glad you have such a high opinion of me," Grey murmured.

"I know I've seen too much and can't seem to find that balance anymore, or maybe I just stopped caring. But when it comes to this job, there's what's right and what's necessary, and they ain't always the same thing." He pulled out a toothpick and held the two ends between thumb and forefinger. "Anyway, I've got a weird feeling about all this. I just wanted you to remember that these monsters, they swallowed their ounce of goodness in a pint of blood. They'd gun down a Girl Scout troop if the den mother swiped a gram of coke."

Grey appreciated the sentiment, but Fred was wasting his breath, and the knowledge made Grey sad. He had dived into the darkness of the human soul so many times it had become like a warm blanket, one Grey had to constantly shuck off to keep himself shivery and alive. He stepped away from the table. "See you in a bit."

"Be careful, brother."

46

DER HEILIGKEIT DES LUFT SANATORIUM

Viktor paced his room the next morning, waiting for the reply from Interpol. He had been enjoying his long walks in the Alpine woods, but it was no longer prudent to go trekking alone. Whoever had let Glen out could do so again, and this time they might put a gun in his hands.

He made a wry face. He hadn't expected to need a bodyguard in a sanatorium.

After refreshing his email for the umpteenth time, he took a break for lunch. When he returned to the room, he had his reply.

He read the two-page report carefully, summarizing in his mind what Interpol knew about Glen von Reisenberg:

Soon after the death of Paul Schaefer, a splinter group from Colonia Dignidad bought a compound in Barranco, a wealthy seaside neighborhood in Santiago. The founder of the sister cult was unknown, but a few of its members were picked up on drug trafficking charges in 2010. The splinter group distributed Peruvian coca paste to refining factories in the lesser markets of Argentina, Brazil, and Asia.

Glen von Reisenberg had been involved in the 2010 bust, serving as an enforcer during the transaction. He shot one undercover police officer and knifed another. Lucky for him, both had lived.

Shockingly, the original Colonia Dignidad was alive and kicking, though by all accounts the criminal activity was now conducted by the Santiago splinter group. One of the mysteries of the investigation had been that no one could, or would, name the leader of the Colonia Dignidad spinoff. Before the bust, the undercover officers heard talk of someone who "had known Schaefer" and who still "carried out their leader's will." Who that person was, they had no idea.

The undercover officers also heard talk that Glen von Reisenberg was mentally unstable and a liability. He was the only cult member who had been convicted of a felony after the bust. Other cult members had fingered Glen to save themselves; Glen had refused to talk.

Viktor stood and clasped his hands on top of his head. He peered out the window, then paced as he put the pieces together.

The Alianza made payoffs to Tata Menga for spiritual protection. Tata Menga in turn made payoffs to an unknown entity, presumably the General. Why did Tata Menga do this? Perhaps for protection from rival cartels or cult leaders, perhaps for the governmental influence wielded by his shadowy partner, perhaps because the two of them had orchestrated the entire scheme from the beginning.

One thing of which Viktor was relatively certain: he did not think Tata Menga made payoffs to another palero. He thought that when it came to Palo, Tata Menga was the end of the line.

Toss in Colonia Dignidad and Glen von Reisenberg. Two pieces with no ties to Palo Mayombe. Had the General known Paul Schaefer, the original leader of the colony? Had they colluded together from the beginning?

Whoever the General was, the old guard at Colonia Dignidad must have known about him, and after Schaefer's downfall, Viktor assumed the General took control of the colony, probably making an initial visit and leaving the day-to-day to a few trusted lieutenants, leaving no evidence of his own involvement. Yes, that was his method.

Thus, the General used the leaders of both Palo Mayombe and Colonia Dignidad, two completely unrelated organizations, to exert influence over a criminal network.

Viktor stopped pacing, standing as still as fallen snow. *He was using* cults *to control his empire. Not just one cult, but different ones.*

He resumed pacing, this time faster, back and forth in the small room. He had never seen cross-cults utilized before. How many others were in the network?

The more he thought about it, the more respect he had for the General. It was genius, really. Somewhere along the way he had decided to study and employ the power of coercion, and no one manipulated the mind of man better than charismatic politicians and cult leaders—often one and the same.

The genius was that the General didn't even need to start a cult, though Viktor knew the personality type, and was guessing he had tried his hand at one or two of his own. But for his network, he only need utilize existing superstitions and belief systems. Join up with the cult leaders, teach them how to exploit their influence, offer or strong-arm the benefits of partnership, and collect the payoff money.

It was a cult mafia. A meta cult.

With respect, however, came fear. This General, he knew how to manipulate on a scale Viktor had never before seen. This Guiñol character and the blue lady kept the cartels in line, and Viktor had no doubt the General orchestrated cult hits every now and again to show that his juju was stronger.

Viktor felt a chill at the import of his discovery. He had a sudden thought, and returned to the report, skimming until he found what he was looking for: the date of Glen von Reisenberg's transfer from the Chilean jail to Der Heiligkeit Des Luft.

Viktor saw the date, and the chill expanded, running in waves of gooseflesh underneath the sleeves of his dress shirt. Glen von Reisenberg had been transferred to the sanatorium three days after Grey had disrupted the Alianza hit in Miami.

Viktor had been wrong; Glen wasn't from a wealthy family. And while he might have been a liability in Santiago, a use had been found for him.

The General had moved a chess piece.

Viktor reached for his cell. He had to inform Grey, and warn him that Palo Mayombe was a wild goose chase in Colombia. The General would be using a different cult there.

His people could be anywhere, he was a master strategist, and there was no time left to study his moves.

47

Grey approached the Ganador residence again, reaching into the backpack for the two rubber doormats he had purchased, also at the megastore down the block. No one approached from the opposite end of the street, and he had to trust Fred to watch his back.

When he reached the gate, he placed one doormat on top of the other, then slung them atop the razor wire. He tossed the backpack over, then used the bunched doormats to vault the fence. Eying the sleeping rottweiler sprawled near the gate, Grey stuffed the ripped doormats in the backpack and absorbed his surroundings.

A six-foot wall covered in thorny bougainvillea protected the property. Palms and fruit trees sprinkled the garden, and the main house was an L-shaped villa with a trellis-covered courtyard. A stand of bamboo shielded a cottage in the far right corner.

The cottage gave him pause. He didn't want to be surprised by someone waking up from a nap and wandering into the main house.

Slipping into the bamboo, he observed the closed doors and shuttered windows of the detached bungalow. On a small patio there was a motorcycle draped by a canvas sheet, with a covering of twigs and pollen. Grey guessed the cottage was Julio's when he came to town.

Back at the main house, wondering if Señor Ganador had left for the day or for a quick lunch, Grey picked the lock on the rear door and scurried inside. No dogs in the house. No sign of cameras or a security system.

His nerve endings vibrating like plucked guitar strings, Grey cased the house of Rolando Ganador. Took in the aging but fine leather furnishings, the Botero prints and oil paintings of coffee country hanging on the walls, the three out of four bedrooms that looked unoccupied, the bar stocked with brandies and single-malt scotch, the humidor room, the photos of Julio at all ages, the stacks of car magazines. He noticed a couple of multihued textiles used as wall hangings that didn't look Colombian. Other than that, nothing out of the ordinary.

In a bedside drawer in the master suite, he found a Glock and a spare magazine, both of which he took, wiping his prints as he went. Behind an enlarged photo of Rolando and Julio at Machu Picchu in one of the guest bedrooms, he spotted a wall safe. A typical two-foot by two-foot fire safe, not as formidable as either the solid-cast steel behemoths or the expensive modern composites.

Grey could crack almost any safe, especially this one, with the right tools and time.

He had neither.

It would have to be an old-school job. He hustled to the garage, scrounged for a hammer and a chisel and a circular saw, then returned to the bedroom. After kicking through the drywall around the safe, he pried it out of the wall and lugged it to the middle of the room.

He put his hands on the safe and checked the time. Four p.m. This was taking far too long.

He knew he should let it go, fly back to New York and stay in his apartment until things calmed down. But the very thought of that, of watching his back as he accepted the General's reign of terror, wearing those shackles on his freedom, made him lean over the safe and get to work.

It was a simple but time-consuming job. First he cut through the outer layer with the circular saw, then used the hammer and chisel to work through the concrete underneath. When the concrete started to give way, he tore it in half with his hands, exposing an inner compartment shielded by a barrier of thick plastic. He returned to the saw and ripped his way through the final layer.

When the plastic split, Grey exhaled his tension and tossed aside stacks of bills to reach the rest of the contents.

It wasn't much. A diamond wedding ring, a stack of gold ingots, a few papers that looked like real estate deeds, and a square envelope filled with photos. Grey stuffed the deeds and the photos in his backpack.

He had two rooms left to search, but it was time to go. Halfway to the back door, he got the text he was dreading from Fred.

-On their way-

Grey ran outside. The thorny bougainvillea was too high for the mats. The gate was the only option. He sprinted for the bamboo shielding the cottage, planning to hide until Rolando disappeared inside the main house, then dash to the gate and clamber over in the few seconds before Rolando realized his house had been tossed.

Foolish, he berated himself. *Foolish to take so long.*

At least he had the gun, and Fred was waiting outside. Grey crouched inside the thicket of bamboo and watched the gate open. With any luck, Rolando and his driver would enter the house together.

A dog barked, weakly at first and then gaining strength. Grey's breath stopped on the intake.

The rottweiler. He had forgotten all about him. The noise of the gate must have stirred his sensitive ears awake.

The dog would either smell him or see him on the way out, and Grey would never get over the wall in time. He could shoot the dog, though he didn't care for the thought. But a running dog was a tough target, and the noise would draw Rolando and his man. If one or both of them had a gun, and they probably did, Grey could be in trouble.

The gate was a quarter of the way open. Grey's eyes moved from the gate to the covered motorcycle to the gate again, where he could see the signature Mercedes hood ornament entering the grounds.

And behind it, waiting to pull in behind Rolando's car, was a black Hummer.

Grey swore.

He remembered seeing two sets of keys on a hook by the front door, and he sprinted back to the house, dashing inside to grab both sets. The dog was barking furiously.

Grey sprinted back to the cottage as the Mercedes pulled inside the property. The rottweiler was halfway across the lawn and closing fast. Grey yanked the cover off the bike, revealing an older-model red BMW. He tried the first set of keys. Wrong fit. The dog was twenty yards away. Grey jammed the second set into the ignition as he flicked the kickstand with his foot, praying the featureless keys didn't belong to a parked car in Salento.

The motorcycle roared to life. Grey twisted his wrist and the bike shot forward. He veered straight for the dog, which snarled and sprang aside.

On his way to the electric gate, which was closing, Grey saw four Latino men in slacks and dark glasses halfway out of the Hummer and fumbling for their weapons. Rolando was leaning out of the rear window of the Mercedes, neck craned in Grey's direction. As Grey cleared the gate, the first fusillade of bullets sprayed gravel in the street.

After executing a turn that would have thrown most riders, his shoulder two feet from the street, Grey sped towards the bakery. In his rearview he saw the Hummer reversing out of the gate. Fred started the sedan and pulled out from the curb as Grey rushed by. Bullets slammed into the rental car, shattering windows.

The Hummer flipped around to chase them. Grey skidded around the block and stopped to wait for Fred. A second later the sedan cleared the corner, and Grey heard the hiss of a popped tire.

Grey beat his hands in the air. "Get on!"

Fred ditched the car and jumped on behind Grey. His bulk weighed the bike down and would limit Grey's maneuverability, but Grey still liked their chances. If he knew the neighborhood, he could lose the Hummer in seconds. As it was, he could improvise.

He handed the Glock to Fred and accelerated to the next intersection. Turned left, raced to the end of the street, took a right, and ran smack into a pedestrian street market stuffed with stalls and people.

The Hummer was a block behind them. Grey had no choice but to press through. He honked and revved the engine as he worked through the crowd, but the market was noisy and chaotic, filled with speakers blaring *cumbia*.

Fred was waving his gun and screaming at people to move, while Grey revved the engine and popped up on one wheel to intimidate the crowd. By the time the crowd shifted, they were only halfway through the market, and the Hummer had parked and was disgorging narcos.

When Grey finally got the bike through, two of the narcos had almost caught up to them. Fred had his gun leveled but it was too crowded to shoot.

The narcos had no such qualms. One of them fired, a collective scream rose, and everyone dove for cover.

Grey swerved, the bullets missed, and Grey sped away. When he was halfway down the block, accelerating on top of discarded soda cans and fruit rinds, he checked the rearview and saw two narcos shoving riders off their motorcycles near the edge of the market. They whipped the bikes around and raced after Grey and Fred.

"Two on bikes behind us!" Grey shouted.

Fred turned and loosed a volley of bullets. The narcos returned fire. At that distance and speed, with all riders ducking and weaving to avoid getting hit, the gunshots were a lottery ticket.

But the game had changed, and not in Grey's and Fred's favor.

As Grey sped through the neighborhood, he tried to formulate a plan through the madness. His first instinct was to find a highway, but an open road would reward speedier bikes with heavier firepower.

He opted for the city center. Bigger crowds, police, public transport. Tighter roads and the opportunity to use his skill as a rider.

The problem was, he was turned around and had no idea how to get there. "Keep 'em honest," he yelled back to Fred, "but don't waste your bullets."

Fred fired off another round. "This isn't my first rodeo. Just stay on the pavement."

They hit a four-lane highway, and Grey accelerated to eighty, one hundred, one-twenty, one-forty. His pursuers were going even faster, and he started to lose ground. He took the next exit, ripping between a semi and an SUV, almost flipping over the side rail on the curve before righting the bike and cranking his wrist on the straightaway.

In the distance, Grey saw the metro zipping above the street, and he angled towards it. The neighborhood took a turn for the worse, and Grey had to dodge street vendors and homeless drunks teetering through the streets. High-level motorcycle riding was a combination of nerve and skill, but the sicarios pursuing them rode as well as Grey, as if they had been born on a bike and planned to die there.

"I'm low on ammo," Fred said, and Grey grimaced. If Fred couldn't keep them at a distance, they were in trouble. He was going to have to make a move.

They squeezed through a few alleys littered with broken bottles, almost crashed into a garbage man pulling a wooden cart, accelerated through a series of parking lots. Two bullets whizzed by Grey's head, ruffling his hair. Fred fired another round.

Grey tried to work his way to the metro but only seemed to corkscrew deeper into the neighborhood. He slowed to weave through another, less crowded market, and Fred pulled down fruit and clothing stands to slow their pursuers. When they popped out on the other side, Grey found himself staring at a cul-de-sac surrounded by two-story apartment buildings.

Revving his engine as their pursuers appeared in the rearview, he spotted a set of steep stairs climbing the hillside between two of the buildings. A bullet splattered a discarded melon two feet from their bike, and Grey raced for the stairs.

The jolts from the bike bouncing off the stairs felt like a giant was shaking them. Grey flattened on the bike. A frightened walker in yellow spandex jumped out of the way, her exposed stomach jiggling like a bowl full of Jell-O. In the rearview, Grey saw the narcos navigating the stairs behind them.

The staircase spit them out in an overgrown green space. Grey made a sharp right and whipped the bike behind a breadfruit tree, cut the engine, then pointed at the top of the staircase. Fred squeezed his waist in acknowledgment.

Seconds later the first narco cleared the top of the stairs and roared into the park. Fred fired three times. He missed the first rider but hit the second square in the chest, flipping him off the bike and sending the motorcycle crashing into a park bench.

The first narco turned to spray fire at Grey and Fred, the bullets taking chunks out of the breadfruit tree. Fred fired back and then Grey raced in the opposite direction, weaving in and out of trees, the thicket of vegetation saving their lives.

During the exchange, Grey had gotten a glimpse of the mini Uzis the narcos were using. A throwback to another era and the reason Grey and Fred were still alive, since those guns had the range of a slingshot.

"Better odds now," Fred said.

In the rearview, Grey saw Fred raise the pistol to keep the narco at bay, but nothing happened. Fred cursed. "Or not."

Another round of bullets chased them into a neighborhood adjacent to the park. Grey turned down one alley and then another, trying not to give the narco an open shot. "The other mag?"

"Spent."

The neighborhood became a warren of alleys and tight streets, and Grey rode like he had never ridden before, whipping through traffic and onto the sidewalk, kicking up dust and gravel, using every trick in the book. Bullets whizzed overhead and beside them. When Grey entered the next alley he saw in the rearview what he had been waiting for: a raised gun but no sound of a bullet, and a scowl of frustration from their pursuer.

An empty magazine.

The narco slowed to restock his weapon. Grey slid to a stop and pushed Fred off the bike, then whipped the motorcycle around to face his attacker. It was going to end now, one way or the other.

Grey and the narco were fifty yards apart. Grey jammed his wrist forward, shooting the bike towards his quarry. The narco stopped trying to fit the new magazine in, knowing he wouldn't make it in time. He took the challenge, gunning his own bike.

It was a high-speed game of chicken, and as the bikes screamed forward, front wheels aligned, Grey's green eyes locked on to the narco's sunglasses. Grey projected his will outward, letting the narco know in a primal language that Dominic Grey gave no quarter and never, *ever*, thought about backing down.

Thirty yards apart, and neither had swerved. Grey hunched his shoulders and prepared for impact as best he could, knowing one of them wasn't going to survive.

Did the narco have it in him? Grey wondered. Did he have as much battle pride as Grey, was he as driven by childhood rage?

Did he *want it* as bad?

Fifteen yards, and Grey whispered Nya's name.

Ten yards and he released his *chi* with a scream.

Five yards and the narco swerved.

In the bat of an eye, Grey twisted his bike in time to catch the rear wheel of the narco's bike, flipping the helmetless rider over the motorcycle and into the brick wall. The maneuver cost Grey his balance, but he anticipated the crash and slid with his bike down the alley, feeling his flesh shred. Grey let the bike go and crunched into a ball, shielding his vitals as best he could.

The narco was splayed against the wall, head twisted at an unnatural angle. Fred checked him for signs of life, whacked him in the temple with the gun for good measure, then rushed to Grey. Both men looked down at the ripped jeans and exposed pink flesh along the side of Grey's thigh, sheets of blood seeping outward from the pores as if squeezed from a sponge.

Grey struggled to a sitting position, then flexed his limbs and digits. "It's not as bad as it looks."

"It looks like you got kicked by a team of mules."

Grey took a long shuddering breath, his leg quivering in pain as the adrenaline started to fade. "Maybe baby mules."

Fred pulled Grey to his feet, looked at the dead narco, then cupped the back of Grey's head like they were in the locker room after a big game. "That's my *boy.*"

———————

They walked the bike to the other end of the alley and saw the metro bulleting towards a field of skyscrapers in the distance. Behind downtown, evening shadows were starting their slide down a forested slope.

"Once we're in the center," Grey said, "what do you think about our exit options?"

"For the most part, the people here hate narcos. Cops too. I think the airport's safe if we hurry. Let's get you cleaned up and make a run for it. Want me to drive?"

Grey eased onto the back of the battered bike, his injured thigh as stiff as a peg leg, nodding his head in reply.

48

Grey and Fred left the bike in an alley near Plaza Botero, under the stern shadow of a checkered Romanesque cathedral. After walking through the sculptures filling the square, they headed for the main drag, Paseo Peatonal Carabobo.

Sidewalk vendors sprayed machine-gun Spanish into the crowd, hawking pirated DVDs and a dizzying array of cheap goods. Grey and Fred picked up fresh clothes: jeans and a black T-shirt and a green *Atlético Nacional* ball cap for Grey, a light blue guayabera and porkpie hat for Fred.

Grey preferred the safety of the crowd, despite the fact that he was the tallest person around and his Anglo features were a beacon in the sea of black and mestizo faces. A few blocks down they found a pharmacy, and Grey picked up disinfectant, gauze, and a bandage roll for his wounds.

They changed clothes in a public restroom and took a taxi to the airport. The ride was uneventful, the airport modern and calm. Fred dropped the Glock into a trashcan on the way in. After devouring a plateful of empanadas and scouring the crowd for suspicious faces, they downed espressos while Grey tried Lana again, for the third time since the motorcycle chase.

Still no answer.

Grey put the phone away, and Fred eyed him. "So is it Miami or Bogotá? We sure as hell can't wait around here."

"No," Grey murmured.

"We can't call in Lana's absence because of the leak. Could make her a sitting duck. Part of me says screw the CIA, let her fend for herself. The other part says we're all on the same team, Lana's over there without backup, and we're committed to seeing this through." He crushed his espresso cup. "What's she gotten herself into?"

Grey pursed his lips and cracked his knuckles. Lana was probably mid-assignment, tracking a suspect and not in a position to answer her cell.

Then again, maybe she wasn't.

He pondered her motives for the umpteenth time, tried to see all the angles, wondered if he could even trust the man beside him, knew they might be walking into the belly of the beast. But he knew what he had to do.

"I can see it on your face," Fred said, then gave a weary sigh and pushed to his feet. "Bogotá it is."

------•------

Flights to Bogotá left on the hour, and the wait was uneventful. Between cups of coffee, Grey called Viktor, and the two compared notes.

Grey could tell how excited Viktor was by the General's use of multiple cults, and that annoyed him. Viktor got intrigued whenever he thought there were esoteric secrets in play, regardless of the danger involved.

But the professor's insight was invaluable. They were looking for someone highly intelligent, highly organized, and willing to use faith as a weapon. Someone who manipulated entire belief systems to suit his criminal purposes.

Which meant there would be no using the General's religion against him. No appealing to that spark of humanity, however twisted. Grey knew that if they found him, there would be no quarter received from this elusive patriarch of cults—and none given.

------•------

Grey's eyes got heavy as soon as the plane took off, but he pushed away his fatigue and dug in his backpack for the items he had taken from the Ganador place. Fred confirmed the papers were real estate deeds. One for the place in Medellín, another for the coffee estate, and a third for a house in Cartagena.

Grey turned to the envelope of photos. Fred crowded in next to him. All twenty-two images included the same dumpy Latino man with a bushy moustache and curly hair, his face paunchy and dissolute, eyes as hard as a slab of concrete. With him were a variety of men and a few women, alone or in pairs with the principal subject, each photo portraying a different locale. A few of the scenes depicted transactions taking place, exchanges of backpacks or black leather briefcases.

"I recognize Pablo Escobar," Grey said, eying the common denominator to all the photos, the monster of a human being who had bombed a commercial airline, orchestrated the murder of a presidential candidate and an attorney general and more than two hundred judges, and turned Medellín into a carnival of horrors, "and that's about it."

He handed the photos to Fred, who took his time flipping through them, making little grunts of recognition. "Looks like Rolando didn't like the company benefits, kept a little insurance for himself. Most of it useless now, of course."

"So why keep it in the safe?" Grey murmured.

When Fred was finished, he selected one photo from the middle of the pile and placed it on top. He jabbed a finger at a man chatting with Pablo Escobar next to a fountain. "I recognize everyone but this guy. The rest were high-level players in the Escobar Cartel, most either dead or in jail."

The two men in the photo were in a tiled plaza full of people, in front of an imposing two-domed baroque cathedral. Not an unusual sight in Latin America. The other man was the same height as Escobar, swarthy, stern, streaks of silver in his dark hair, the metal from a pair of eyeglasses glinting in the sun. His eyes were just as hard, maybe even shrewder, than those of the infamous cartel leader.

"You recognize the location?" Grey asked.

"No," Fred said slowly.

Even in the photograph, the man standing next to Escobar had a presence, an aura that soaked through the printing paper and made Grey's nerve endings tingle. This was a man who took what he wanted from life and had no qualms about the consequences.

And, judging from Fred's lack of recognition, a major player in the drug world who lived in the shadows.

Fred's voice was quiet. "You think that might be our guy?"

"I think if it's not, then it's someone we'd want to take a stab at anyway."

Fred held the photo up as he stared at it, a touch of hoarseness creeping into his voice. "Yeah."

Grey searched his friend's face for signs of concealed recognition. Finding none, he replaced the items in his backpack and tilted his seat back.

———•———

It was dark when they arrived in Bogotá, but Grey could sense the mountains surrounding them on the descent, their looming bulk straining against the veil of darkness.

Walking through the airport brought back a flood of memories from his posting. Remembrances of the proud and wary eyes of the Bogotános, of how the night settled over the city like a heavy blanket still chilly from the closet, of the diesel fumes and incessant noise and piles of trash and feces on *La Carrera Séptima*, the commercial lifeline of Bogotá and the most intense street Grey had ever seen.

He remembered the graffiti everywhere, not an eyesore but a voice, a soundless urban cry protesting the government and the gringos and the narcos and the sins of colonization that had cracked the spine of Latin America. And he remembered the white beacon of the cathedral of Monserrate floating high above the city, as remote and idealistic as a citadel from heaven, looking down on the fishbowl of humanity swimming beneath it.

The address Lana had texted was in La Candelaria, the historic quarter. They had to risk a taxi, a dicey prospect in Bogotá. The city was notorious for armed assaults on passengers.

When their driver turned off the main road into a blighted neighborhood, Grey tensed in the passenger seat. "*Dónde vamos? Esto no es el camino.*" *Where are we going? This isn't the right way.*

"*Tranquilo,*" the driver said. "*Hay un accidente en la carretera principal. Soy conductor honesto. Tranquilo.*" *Take it easy, there's been an accident on the highway. I'm an honest driver. Take it easy.*

Groups of men congregated on the street corners, rubbing their hands over trash can fires or simply staring at the taxi as it passed. None of the streetlights worked. Potholes loomed like swimming pools, the brick buildings with shattered windows on either side looked like a series of interconnected crack houses.

"This place makes Baghdad look inviting," Fred muttered.

Grey didn't relax until they exited the neighborhood and saw the lights of downtown up ahead. Soon they were cruising along La Carrera Séptima, the scarves of the pedestrians pulled high to combat the pollution adding to the omnipresent sense of danger. A few minutes later the taxi dropped them at a busy Juan Valdez café on the outskirts of La Candelaria.

"The address is a few blocks away," Grey said, stepping towards the café and shielding his face from the drizzle. "I'd prefer to approach on foot."

"If I have any more espresso I'm going to crap coffee beans."

Grey agreed with the sentiment but needed the energy boost. He popped two ibuprofen with a bottle of water and his café tinto, then tried calling Lana one more time, still without success, before leading Fred into the brick and cobblestone streets of La Candelaria.

"What's your plan?" Fred said.

"Let's see what this place is first. Could be a bar, a hotel, a home."

"Think she would have named one of the first two."

"Agreed."

Fred took out a toothpick. "Wish we had some steel."

"Agreed."

———————

La Candelaria looked unchanged to Grey, blocks and blocks of colonial buildings with wrought iron terraces and terra cotta roofs, some of them restored, most with split plaster overlaying the brick. The bottom-floor shops were closed except for a few bars. Lanterns lit the main streets, high-walled side alleys tunneled into darkness.

A pervasive aura of decay overlaid the historic district. Grey had always found the place unsettling at night, filled with figures disappearing around street corners, shuttered windows, and those eerie papier-mâché ghosts looming from the rooftops.

"Should be the next left," Grey said.

They turned onto a quiet cobblestone street that looked like something out of the Middle Ages, absurdly narrow and punctuated by iron-studded wooden doors.

They found a door halfway down the block that had to be the address, unmarked but placed between adjoining numbers. Fred blew into his hands to warm them. "So much for a bar or a hotel."

Grey gently tried the door handle. Locked. No windows, no evidence of what might be inside.

Waving for Fred to follow, Grey walked to the end of the block, past another locked door. He tried Lana one more time; straight to voicemail.

"We can break cover and call the embassy, or the local cops," Fred said, "though we both know that'll be as helpful as a hot air balloon in a tornado. Or we can wait until daylight, find some hardware in the meantime. None of those options are good for Lana. Waiting has a tendency to make a missing-persons trail ice over."

"In that case," Grey said, his eyes searching the darkness and finding nothing but questions, "we'll have to see what's behind Door Number One."

SOUTH AMERICA
1985

John Wolverton was dead.

The General—his new moniker had taken off in the criminal world—moved quickly after Colonia Dignidad, from the Santa Muerte cult in Mexico to Voodoo in the Caribbean to LUS in Brazil, even utilizing the Catholic Church and the Apostolics when the opportunity arose. Using a structure already in place—there were thousands of cults in the Americas—he sought out the criminal organizations whose constituents possessed the requisite faith and superstitions, then simply harnessed the awesome power of mankind's fear of the unknown.

He became an expert in dozens of religions, studying the doctrines and practices that inspired the most fear and loyalty. Utilizing talented demagogues as his lieutenants, he wormed his way into the highest levels of religious societies, existing cartels, and, when possible, governments.

The drug boom of the eighties provided him with almost limitless opportunity. Colombia became so important to the cause he decided to establish a presence in the capital. At the CIA, John Wolverton had been heavily involved with the use of mind-control drugs. Combining this expertise with the powerful psychotropics available in South America, his urban drug cult thrived in the shadows of Colombia's cities, led by the sinister Señor Guiñol.

Through a series of kidnappings of politicians and cartel bigwigs, and a propaganda campaign that fanned the flames, the General proved that his new cult could hit anyone at any time, could put scopolamine in a drink or a cigar or the back seat of a limo. The horror stories of people dragged into decaying fortresses in the abandoned bowels of cities were enough to spur payouts from most of the cartels. And for those organizations outside the cities, well, there were plenty of black magic cults in the wilds of Colombia.

Yet as important as Colombia was, and Mexico would become, neither was where the General chose to base his empire. He wanted someplace isolated and secure, out of the limelight, with no local business ties that could trace back to him.

He found a place high in the sierra, he avoided technology like a cancer, he did what it took to terrify the locals and secure their loyalty, he paid off and then killed the right people in government so no one would know he was there.

He indulged his every passion and prospered beyond anyone's wildest dreams. Yet from the very beginning of his empire, when he set up another cult of his own twisted design, an homage to his past, he was self-aware enough to know that his mind was not a normal mind, and that he was sinking slowly into madness.

49

LA CANDELARIA, BOGOTÁ
PRESENT DAY

Grey peered down the cobblestone street, then up at the eaves of the terra cotta roofing hanging over the ten-foot wall. Odd that there were only three doors on the entire street, and no windows.

He circumnavigated the block, with Fred trailing behind. All four sides were the same: long narrow alleys, ten-foot-high stone walls, three doors per side, contiguous roofing, no windows.

Grey tried the door in the middle of the street behind the one they had first tried, assuming it was the rear entrance. Locked. He took out his filings and went to work on the deadbolt. It was a tough one and took him a few minutes, opening to reveal a concrete wall behind the door. He tried two more doors and found the same thing.

"It's been walled up," Grey murmured. "This place is a fortress."

"Maybe it's a false address."

"My guess is the front door opens, but it's not the way we want to go in." Grey looked up at the roof, then placed his hands on the wall and raised his uninjured leg. "Give me a lift."

Fred interlaced his fingers under Grey's heel. Grey swung onto the roof, grimacing as pain shot through his injured leg, then helped Fred climb up behind him. The spires of La Candelaria's cathedrals pierced the darkness around them, backlit by the city lights.

The aging terra cotta roof spanned an entire block, with one exception: an aperture twenty feet out from the front door. Grey curled a finger, and they slunk towards the opening.

Peering over the edge on their bellies, the moonlight revealed a weed-filled courtyard strewn with debris and rubble. Grey could just make out a broken archway on the opposite side from the door. He kept his position until, a few minutes later, two cowled figures with torches walked across the courtyard and disappeared into the archway.

After exchanging a glance, Grey and Fred backed away. Grey checked the street for observers and bent to grasp a loose tile he had stepped on earlier. He pulled it up, then with Fred's help pried off the tiles around it, until they had a hole big enough to fit through. Below them was the wooden framework of the roof, below that an empty room. If there had once been drywall or some other type of ceiling, it had long ago been stripped.

Grey's eyes found Fred's, and he shrugged. "It's weird enough, but those guys didn't look armed. Let's take a look."

Grey used the support beam to drop to the floor without a sound. Fred followed with less grace. The only egress was an old wooden door half off its hinges. Grey peered around it and saw a stone hallway leading in three directions. They kicked up dust when they walked and the place smelled like old socks.

In the next room over, they saw two people slumped in a corner underneath a wall torch, one of them holding a needle. Grey tensed, but they were staring glassy-eyed at the wall, unmoving, lips parted in pleasure.

Grey and Fred backed away and tried the other direction, seeing more of the same. Bare stone rooms, either empty or populated by addicts, sometimes alone, sometimes in twos or threes.

They worked their way outward from the room into which they had dropped. The place was a maze of ruined stone corridors and archways, often with entire walls or sections of passages missing. Rats and cockroaches scurried underfoot. They crept along by the light of their cell phones and the glow from the torches emanating from some of the rooms. His senses on high alert, Grey focused on remembering the route.

Fred pulled Grey inside an empty room. "I don't know what that stuff is, but crack addicts don't slump in corners. They bounce off walls. This is a heroin den, maybe. Or something else."

"Scopolamine?"

Fred pursed his lips, grim. "Or some type of cocktail. Let's finish the sweep, make sure Lana's not here, then get the hell out."

Grey couldn't have been more in agreement. It was hard to tell exactly where they had been, but they explored the place as best they could. Just as Grey was wondering where the men in cowls had gone, Fred curled a finger, and Grey crept to where he was standing. Through an archway at the end of the hall, they saw the courtyard they had spotted from above, strewn with rubble and lit by moonlight streaming through the open ceiling.

"The grand foyer," Grey muttered.

They decided to wait and see what transpired. Grey was glad they did. Seconds later, two robed men passed through, disappearing into the darkened archway. Ten minutes later, two more men did the same thing.

"What do you think?" Fred said.

"I think we need to see what's through that archway."

"My guess is it's the same pair of guards, watching the front door and circling back through. Let's give it a look. We can take those two kooks out, if it comes to it."

Grey nodded and checked his watch. Ten minutes later, two more cowled figures passed, and another two swept through ten minutes after that. Grey and Fred waited five minutes before darting into the courtyard, noticing two other exit passages before they slipped through the archway.

The opening led to a short corridor, which ended at a wooden door reinforced with iron bands. Before they could decide what to do, the door swung open and two of the robed figures stepped out, carrying torches. For a brief moment everyone froze. Then Grey rushed forward, Fred a step behind, as the two other men reached into their robes and pulled out six-inch-long needles, rushing into the fight with a silence that unnerved Grey.

The passage was wide enough for two abreast, and Grey engaged the first man as Fred fought beside him with the second. The cowled man lunged for Grey with the needle, holding the torch back with his other hand, ready to shove it into Grey's face after the needle thrust. By reading his body mechanics, Grey saw both moves coming. Grey caught the wrist holding the needle, yanked the arm forward to disrupt his attacker's balance, and then snapped a kick at the man's kneecap to distract him while he inverted the trapped wrist and stabbed him in the chest with his own needle. After that, he dropped him with an elbow to the temple.

Fred was holding both of his assailant's wrists and trying to force him to the ground. Grey came up behind the robed man and struck him across the back of the neck with a stiff forearm, jumping forward with both feet and whipping his entire body into the blow. The man fell like a comet.

"Thanks," Fred said.

"Don't mention it. You up for a change of clothing?"

Fred stripped off one of the robes. Underneath was a solidly built Latino man with thick lips and a sloping forehead, wearing work boots, jeans, and a cheap vinyl jacket.

"Freak," Fred muttered.

Grey didn't respond. He was relieved it had been a normal thug, and not something . . . else.

"Odd they didn't speak," Fred said.

"They must have been trained for silence and thought they could take us. Gunshots would tip off the neighborhood to their creep show."

They stripped the other guard and donned the robes. Fred picked up one of the needles, Grey didn't. He could do more damage with his hands. They also took the torches and pocketed two plastic cards with magnetic strips.

Fred injected both men with a good dose from the needle, and Grey helped drag them into one of the empty rooms. They returned to the wooden door and stepped through. On the other side, a set of wide stone steps descended into darkness.

Grey looked at Fred with raised eyebrows. The place wasn't as simple as it appeared.

Faces hidden within the cowls, torches in hand, they took the stairs side by side.

50

The next level down contained a landing room similar to the first. Down a short hallway, Grey and Fred found a small stone room with corridors leading in four directions. Again, the walls and archways were cracked, and loose stones littered the ground, as if the place had suffered an earthquake at one time.

"Looks like more of the same," Fred said.

Grey gripped his torch as he peered into the shadows. "Let's see where the stairs go. If someone's keeping Lana here, it's probably somewhere more secure."

The third level looked similar to the first two, but on the fourth level the mystery increased: the stone on the floor of the landing was lighter and polished, years rather than centuries old. A steel door barred their way to the rest of the level.

"We go through that," Fred said in a low voice, "we might not come back."

Grey lifted his eyebrows above and to the left, leading Fred's gaze to the camera at the top of the far wall. Fred acknowledged the camera with a grimace.

When they reached the fifth and final landing, Grey had to resist the urge to dash back up the staircase. In front of them, a thick glass door shielded a hallway lit by fluorescent light. On the other side of the door, a guard with a square face and close-cropped hair sat behind a metal table, feet propped up and watching a television mounted on the wall. A set of keys was splayed on the table, and he had a semiautomatic in a hip holster. Three monitors faced the guard.

Set into the wall to the left of the glass door, Grey spied a three-inch box with a slit. He swiped the plastic card he had taken through the slit, and the glass door slid open. Then he walked right through, turtling his face inside the cowl. Fred followed.

The guard barely glanced their way, giving a brief nod and then returning to the soccer game. Grey kept walking down the hallway, every muscle tense, holding his torch at chest level. Metal doors, spaced twenty feet apart, lined both sides of the corridor. Set into each of the doors at head height was a square glass window.

A pair of robed men appeared at the far end of the hallway, carrying torches and chatting with their cowls raised. There was nothing to do except keep walking. The oncoming guards passed them without a word.

Grey's breath seeped out of his mouth. He knew their luck wouldn't hold forever. The corridor ended at a T-junction, and Grey chose the hallway on the right. More doors.

Grey stepped to the first window and looked inside. He saw a room with a bulky, middle-aged Latino man sitting on a couch against the far wall. The man was looking right at Grey but gave no sign of recognition. Drool seeped out of the side of his mouth.

"Mother of Christ," Fred whispered.

"Check the other side," Grey said.

Fred scooted to the other side of the hallway, and Grey hustled forward, peering through each window to find a person inside, in various stages of stupor. At the end of the hallway, just before another intersection, he found Lana.

The door was locked, and there was a slot box beside it. Grey swiped his card, and the door unlocked with a click. Grey pushed it open and saw Lana lying on the couch in jeans and a blue sweater, staring at the ceiling. Beside the couch, a half-open door led to another room.

"Watch the door," Grey said, then ran to Lana and shook her. "Lana!"

Her head moved slowly to face him. "Yes?"

"It's Grey and Fred. You know who we are?"

"Yes," she said, without changing her expression.

"Then get the hell up!" Fred barked.

Lana stood, then looked from Fred to the door and back again, as if confused.

"Sit down again, Lana," Grey said softly.

She complied, and Fred and Grey exchanged a look. "Scopolamine," Fred muttered. "She'll do whatever we tell her and not remember a thing."

There was another slot box on the inside of the door, and Grey had Fred stand in the hallway while Grey tried the key card from the inside. It worked. Grey ushered Fred inside and then closed the door behind them.

"In here, away from the window," Grey said, moving Lana through the door into the other room, which contained two chairs and a twin bed with a woolen blanket. Beside the bed was an alcove with a toilet, a showerhead, and a drain in the concrete floor.

Fred was muttering to himself and stalking the room. Grey's voice was tight. "I'll go first and take care of the guard. Wait thirty seconds and come right behind me. If Lana doesn't cooperate—"

He cut off at the sound of a click. Fred was closer, and by the time he moved into the first room, a man in a lab coat and jeans was coming through the hallway door, holding a needle in one hand and a tape recorder in the other. A notebook was tucked under his arm. He saw Fred, dropped the notebook, and tried to run back into the hallway. Fred caught him and dragged him inside, knocking him out with a few blows to the head. "Sick bastard," he muttered, then injected him with his own needle.

While Fred pulled the doctor into the sleeping area, Grey picked up the tape recorder and the notebook and gave them to Lana. "Hold these and don't drop them," he said, his voice husky. "You're going to have to help us get out of here."

She didn't answer.

Fred's eyes looked a bit wild, and Grey could see the barely controlled rage swimming in the pupils. "Same plan?" Fred asked.

"Make it ten seconds."

Grey rushed down the hallway and slowed when he reached the intersection, approaching the guard from behind and not bothering to disguise his footsteps. The guard had no reason to think he was a threat.

Just before Grey reached the desk, he reversed his grip on the torch, holding it right below the hot tip and swinging it like a baseball bat. He struck the guard in the temple, and the man slumped in his chair. Grey whisked the guard's gun off the desk.

Fred and Lana came down the hallway moments later. Though Lana's eyes were glassy, her movements didn't appear affected.

Grey handed the gun to Fred, to maximize their resources. "I say we walk right out the front door."

They headed back up the stairs. When they reached the fourth-floor landing, the steel door popped open to reveal a group of robed men clustered in a white-walled hallway, all with guns and waiting to rush out. Behind them, Grey got a brief glimpse of more men in lab coats, another guard's desk with cameras Grey assumed had betrayed their position, and a stainless steel laboratory at the far end of the hallway.

Fred fired twice into the doorway, dropping two men in front and causing the rest to scramble backward. "Go!" Fred roared, and Grey pulled Lana up the stairs. Fred covered their back as the crowd of men poured through the doorway.

They dashed up the stairs. Down hallways on the third and second levels, they saw more men rushing towards them, some holding guns and some carrying needles.

By the time they reached the top floor, the stairwell below was thick with men. They reached the main courtyard just as four robed attackers raced through the opposite archway.

Fred fired to back them up, and Grey led the rush down the hallway to their right. Grey's stomach clenched with fear. With the front door covered, their only choice was to try to reach the hole in the roof, and this direction was new territory.

Footsteps pounded behind them. Again, there was no shouting and no gun blasts, though Grey was sure they'd shoot if needed.

They ran for minutes that felt like hours, darting in and out of corridors, jumping over rubble, trying to weave their way back to the section where they had entered, afraid at every turn they would run into a swarm of robed men.

At last they reached a section Grey recognized. If he remembered correctly, they were only a few corridors from their exit. They reached a familiar courtyard, turned left, and ran straight into two robed men.

Fred shot one of them before they could react, but the other hit Fred with two rounds, one in the leg and one in the gut. Fred managed to return fire and drop the second attacker, then hobbled on one leg to the corner and fell against the wall.

His left knee was shattered, and purple lifeblood was pumping out of a hole in his stomach. Grey started towards him, ready to put his wounded friend on his back and carry him the rest of the way, but Fred gasped and pointed the gun at him. "Don't even think about it. Get her out of here."

They both looked down at the crater in Fred's gut. Grey knew a mortal wound when he saw one.

"I can't leave a man down," Grey said.

Fred tried to raise himself up, but his face bunched in pain and he slumped, his fingers trying and failing to keep his intestines from slipping out of his abdomen. Grey looked away.

"You can and you will," Fred said. "I'm not going anywhere. Do your job or we all die." He choked on his next breath and a gob of blood poured out of his mouth.

Grey took another step towards him. Fred switched the gun from pointing at Grey to pointing at his own temple. "*Now.*"

More footsteps from the corridor behind them, this time lots of them. Fred cocked the trigger. Grey clutched at his hair and turned away. Forcing back a surge of bile, he picked up one of the dropped guns. He hated leaving Fred more than he had ever hated anything, but Fred wasn't giving him a choice, and he was right. Fred was dying and Grey had to get Lana out of there.

The corridor he needed was on the other side of the DEA agent. As he passed his fallen companion, Grey bent to clasp his shoulder. "Thank you," he whispered. "I'm sorry."

"Get the General, Grey. Put a bullet between his eyes."

With a numbed feeling, Grey let his hand slide away and ordered Lana, who was standing with her arms hanging at her sides, to follow him out. She obeyed without a word.

The footsteps were right around the corner. Just before Grey left the room, Fred said, "If you make it home, tell my son I love him."

"You have my word," Grey said, and then dashed down the hallway, Lana trailing behind. Seconds later he heard an exchange of gunfire, followed by a prolonged scream from Fred. Grey gritted his teeth and ran faster. Fred had given them a sliver of hope, and he had to make it count.

They rushed through a few intersections where Grey was sure he would run into another party of robed men, but the shadows remained still. He could hear footsteps pounding in the distance, and a few of the drug addicts stumbled into his path, but he pushed them aside and kept retracing his steps. When they reached the room with the hole in the roof, he picked Lana up and thrust her towards the wooden beam.

"Climb out of that hole," he ordered.

She did as asked, agile as a gymnast. It was one of the eeriest things he had ever seen, watching someone whose mind was enthralled but whose body worked as normal.

He followed her up and then raced across the roof, looking over his shoulder every few steps. No one appeared, and after making sure no one was waiting in the street, he dropped off the roof and helped Lana do the same.

They sprinted down the murky streets of La Candelaria, Grey's heart skipping a beat at every blind corner, Fred's last scream ringing in his ears, a cold wind from the mountains pressing against their backs.

51

ANDES MOUNTAINS
PRESENT DAY

The General strolled the perimeter of his vast coca fields, idly checking the health of his shrubs. An army of mercenaries accompanied him, peasants labored beside them in the fields, and a black helicopter squatted on a landing pad.

The General had come to think and reflect. Hours ago, one of his lieutenants had informed him that Lana Valenciano had escaped.

The General had lasted as long as he had not just by outmaneuvering the authorities and rival cartels, but by valuing power over wealth, and not overreaching. His true secret to success, however, was his intimate knowledge of his best customer, his progenitor, the most powerful and well-connected organization in Latin America, instiller of cult leaders and dictatorships and pseudo-Christian organizations, mover of drugs and arms and governments, chess master on a global scale, cult of all cults.

The CIA.

He laughed every time he pulled the strings on his former puppet master, using their informants against them, always the first to profit as they fomented terror and chaos around the continent. Beating them at their own game.

For a long time, he had considered the note he'd left beside the empty cassette recorder at Jonestown the biggest mistake of his career. Still reeling from Tashmeni's death, he thought the note would keep them off his back while he disappeared. Instead, it had left a loose end, and the General had long suspected that someone at the CIA had tied together the empty cassette recorder, the alleged death of Devon Taylor, and the gringo crime lord in Guyana.

In the end, it didn't matter. His true identity was now irrelevant, and the Jonestown tape gave him a powerful trump card. No one wanted that recording exposed, allowing the world to see how the CIA had all but pulled the trigger in Guyana and then wiped away the evidence. Most people knew the CIA was dirty, but the confessions of the Reverend and the taped conversations with his contact were something else altogether. Revelations of the CIA's machinations not just below the border, but in the heartland of America, in the hearts and minds of its children.

Just last year, as the General had suspected, he first received confirmation that someone knew who he was. Not everyone: the agent who he had now captured twice in Colombia, Lana Valenciano, had not even known his true identity.

But someone special did.

Someone who had sent Lana after the General on a covert mission. Someone who didn't want him to know about the manhunt, someone who knew the truth.

Someone who knew that the General could—and would—ruin him.

No, it was not Lana Valenciano who had caused the General to reflect, but her superior: Jeffrey Lasgetone, the current Deputy Director of the CIA and old acquaintance of the General's.

Very old.

The loss of the Bogotá operation was a minor inconvenience. He had already issued the order to strip and destroy the facility.

The General knew he held all the cards. No one could find him. He possessed no ties to the past. There was no leverage.

And he had the tape.

The CIA had taught him to be self-aware and analyze his own limitations. His only weakness, as far as he could tell, was that somewhere along the way he had become fixated on Tashmeni, the only girl he had ever loved.

He had already found a way to keep her spirit alive and honor her memory, and now, after all these years and by a stroke of fate, he had found a way to exact his revenge.

Perhaps those dark gods in which he himself did not believe had smiled on him, rewarding him for his service. Revenge, as they say, was a dish best served cold, and the revenge of the man once known as John Wolverton would be one of the chilliest, most savory entrées ever served to a fellow man.

———•———

Later that evening, when the General was ensconced in the study of his mountain fortress, there was an expected knock at his door.

Ah, yes. He has arrived. "Come in," the General called out in Spanish, in a voice laced with insipid menace. The voice of another man.

A handsome young sicario entered the room, violence in his step, his brow dark and troubled. Lucho, a man the General had decided was going to work directly for him.

"The man who comes back from the watery grave," the General said in Spanish. "Welcome."

Lucho gave a curt nod. "Revenge keeps the heart beating, Señor Guiñol."

"I trust the details of our offer have been explained?"

"*Sí.*"

"And?"

"There is one thing more I desire," Lucho said.

The General clinked the ice in his Scotch. "I know what you want," he said softly, in that same oily voice. "Your sister's murderer will be delivered."

Lucho's face twitched, a movement that looked involuntary, as if he couldn't contain his excitement. "Then we have nothing more to discuss, and it is my pleasure to serve you. And forgive me, it matters not, but the guards outside told me I was meeting with the boss."

The General took a long drink as he afforded Lucho an intense stare, relishing the assassin's confusion. Then the master strategist reached underneath his jaw line, gripped the bottom of the flesh-colored mask that gave him an extra chin and thinning hair, and stripped away the face of Señor Guiñol to reveal the virile silver hair and heavy but dignified features of the General.

"Guiñol," Lucho whispered, comprehension dawning in his eyes. "It means a theatre of marionettes, a puppet show."

"Sometimes," the General said in his powerful voice, breaking into a slow grin, "God lives in the machine."

52

BOGOTÁ, COLOMBIA

The first thing Grey did after paying cash at the anonymous *pensión* in Usaquén, a neighborhood as far from La Candelaria as he could get, was to kneel and meditate on the bathroom rug, using it as a makeshift tatami mat until the shaking subsided.

The violence of the night, the shock of Fred's death, the underground laboratory where human beings were stripped of their will and kept like cattle—it all swelled up within him, robbing him of his senses, infusing him with rage.

He meditated not to destroy the demons inside him—he doubted their mortality—but to diffuse and control his anger, focus it with rational, white-hot purpose.

When he calmed enough to think, he researched scopolamine on his smartphone. The dark history of the drug known as "devil's breath" ran from Colombian Indian tribes who used the drug to bury alive the wives and mistresses of fallen chieftains, to Nazi experiments using the drug as an interrogation aid. *And of course*, Grey thought, *the CIA had a history with the drug.*

Native to the forests around Bogotá, in recent years the use of scopolamine in Colombian street crime had escalated, not just in robberies but also with women targeted as objects of gang rapes or by-the-day "zombie" prostitution rings. There were even reports of women waking up on the side of the road with no memory and missing an organ or their infant children, with authorities claiming the women were victims of an unimaginable but growing black market. The thought of that factoid spiked Grey's blood pressure to dangerous levels.

He also learned that any immediate antidote involved access to chemicals that were out of his reach. The good news was that a night of rest should cleanse the system of the drug, which was why the doctor had continued to dose Lana.

He looked at her sleeping in the twin bed beside him, the peaceful rise and fall of her chest. Would she wake as Lana, or as the robot he had freed from the compound?

The next thing he did was listen to the tape he had taken from Lana's doctor, and then flip through the notebook he had tucked under his arm. What Grey learned gave him chills.

At the beginning of the tape, the doctor's voice had announced the sixth interrogation session of Lana Valenciano. Grey rewound the tape and listened to the sessions, which contained detailed analyses by Lana of the CIA's movements in Latin America, particularly pertaining to the criminal activities of the drug cartels.

The contents of the notebook were simpler, but even more chill-inducing. The second page contained the dates and times of Lana's interrogations over the last two days. On the first page, Grey found the same types of notations, except the date at the top of the page was nearly twelve months old.

A year ago.

They had taken her before.

Grey put his hand to his temple and let out a long breath. He had just found the leak, and it was far more insidious than they could have imagined.

Lingering adrenaline kept him awake, and he started thinking about the photos he had found in Rolando Ganador's house, particularly the one with the unidentified man.

He pulled out the photo. The plaza in the background showcased an enormous baroque cathedral in the background, backed by a line of brown peaks. In the foreground, next to the two men, the gold statue of an indigenous warrior or chieftain loomed atop the fountain. Grey sensed it himself, the connection between the photo and the case. He thought of everything that had happened over the wild course of the investigation, of the appearances of the blue lady, of the contents of the Ganador place, of what he knew of the General's methods.

He did a Google search for the plaza depicted in the photo. Within thirty minutes he was surprised to find a match, and when he dropped off to sleep just before dawn, the effects of physical exhaustion finally eclipsing his mental agitation, a smile of grim satisfaction lifted his face.

Grey woke to the feeling of something cold pressed against his cheek. He opened his eyes to find Lana standing over him, both hands gripping the gun he had taken from the guard at the compound in La Candelaria.

"Where the hell are we?" she said. "Why don't I remember a thing? Who are you, really? What did you *do*?"

"Put the gun down, Lana, and I'll explain."

"Like hell."

Grey shifted his face to the side, out of line with the muzzle. At the same time, he grabbed and twisted her wrists. She kept her hold on the weapon, and he continued the movement, stripping the gun and flipping her on her back onto the bed.

"Damn you," she said.

Grey walked across the room and laid the gun beside the television. He moved to sit beside her. She flinched but didn't get up.

He told her everything that had happened in Salento and Medellín, and then told her about the night before, leaving out the tape and the notebook. Her eyes grew wider and wider, then flashed so brightly with anger that Grey leaned away from her.

"What's the last thing you remember?" he asked.

"At the bar with Carlos . . ." Her voice became very still and quiet. "I'll kill him."

"Who's Carlos?"

"A bartender at a place I was . . ."

"Looking for Guiñol? The same place you were looking a year ago?" Grey asked.

"How do you know about that?"

"Why didn't you tell us?"

Lana turned to look out the window, at a morning sky the color of wet newspaper. When she turned back, her lips were pressed together and her shoulders had sagged.

"There's something you should see," he said.

He took the doctor's notebook out of a drawer and handed it to her. As she looked at the notations on the first two pages, her fingers shook. When she listened to the tape, she looked as if she had just seen the Devil.

"Let me guess," Grey said, "you thought you were getting close to him and the trail disappeared. Were you missing a day or two in there? Really bad hangover from Carlos's bar?"

"Nearly a day," she said dully. "The memory was so fuzzy . . . we were out all night partying . . . he said someone must have slipped me something, and that he took me home." She gave a bitter laugh. "I guess someone slipped me something, all right."

Her hands moved to her face, and she looked past him on the bed. "I can barely believe what you're telling me about last night, but if I was really in that . . . place . . . last night and a year ago, then I have to assume they got it all. Details of the investigation, my user ID and password . . . my God, Grey. They had access to *everything*. So why did they let me—"

She swallowed and cut herself off. "Of course they let me go. My access ID was a gold mine. They sent the blue lady when I threatened them with exposure, and then I came here and walked back into their web. I went right back to Carlos."

"My guess is this time they weren't going to let you leave. Pump you dry and then kill you."

She stood and slowly paced the room, shivering, face pale and hands crossed against her chest. "They could have done anything to me. Anything. I'll kill them all or die trying, I swear. Every last one of them." She stopped and turned to him. "I'm sorry about Fred. He was a good man."

Grey didn't answer. He was dealing with his own dark thoughts of revenge, flapping in his head like the beating wings of bats.

"We have a small advantage," Lana said, "since we know where the leak was—or at least the major one—but the trail's cold. Whatever was in that compound has already been moved or destroyed."

Grey knew she was right. He had reported the incident, but he knew how slow the Colombian police moved, especially on an anonymous tip.

Lana lowered her head and pressed her fingers to her temples. "So I don't know. I don't know. If I tell the Director about the leak I'll be crucified. All we've done is spook the General and driven him deeper underground." She walked to the window and placed her hands on the sill. "I just don't know what to do."

"I might."

She turned.

"I don't think the General's in Colombia—it's too obvious. I think his base is somewhere remote. He'll have protection, sure, but I think his main safeguard is his anonymity, his cults, his layers." Grey eased to his feet and showed her the pictures they had found at the Ganador house. When he showed her the picture of the man Fred couldn't identify, she grabbed it and stared at it.

"Do you know him?"

"No."

"What about that plaza?" Grey asked.

She squinted. "It looks familiar, but I can't place it."

"It's the Plaza de Armas in Cuzco, Peru. In Rolando's house I found a picture of him and his son at Machu Picchu. I also found a tapestry that didn't look Colombian. I Googled that, too, and it looks just like the type produced by the Quechuans around Cuzco."

She looked up at him, her eyes intense.

"There's something else. The one constant over the years has been the General's use of the blue assassin. Our best guess is she's some sort of Incan warrior priestess, though who knows why he chose that. I did a little research on Cuzco, and guess what? Coca country is nearby, it's the gateway to Machu Picchu—and it was once the center of the Incan empire."

Lana's face was glowing, flushed as if heated in a forge. Grey was thinking of Fred trying to keep his insides from spilling out with a bloodied hand, and of Nya weeping in silence over the death of Sekai. His smile turned as cold as the tops of the peaks towering outside their window. "Want to take a trip to Peru?" he asked.

53

Before they left Usaquén, Grey and Lana found a Wi-Fi café so Lana could log into her work account via remote server. She sent an email stating she was returning to Miami to debrief, then changed her password.

Grey realized a day had passed—a very long twenty-four hours— since he had last heard from Nya. Perhaps not cause for panic, but he left another message and an email, then called one of his old colleagues at the American Embassy in Harare and asked him to check up on her.

Neither Grey nor Lana trusted the airport, but neither of them saw a choice. Lana knew a guy outside of Bogotá who flew for the CIA, but they didn't want to place their lives in the hands of someone this deep in enemy territory, who might be on the General's payroll.

They took a taxi to Chapinero to procure two fake passports each from a black market vendor Lana knew from her previous assignment. Making the trip downtown made Grey feel as if they were targets at a shooting range, but no one approached them.

So it was more fake IDs, thin disguises, and fear-laced waits in airports. Grey shaved his ten-day stubble into a goatee, swapped his Atlético Nacional hat for a Millonarios Fútbol Club cap, and picked up some sunglasses. Lana pulled her hair into a bun and tucked it into a head scarf, then applied heavy makeup and her own pair of oversize shades. Grey wished they had time to come up with something better, but speed was their principal ally.

At the airport, they bought round-trip flights to Lima to avoid a random check. They passed the wait before departure hunched in a secluded corner of an airport café, eyes searching every face that passed. Grey called Viktor again to update him.

When he relayed his suspicions about Cuzco and the reasoning behind it, Viktor murmured, "Very good, Grey. Very good."

"The problem is, we're still winging it," Grey said. "I have no idea where to look when we get to Peru."

Viktor was quiet for a moment, and Grey could almost see the hunch in the professor's dark brow and the tension in his blacksmith's shoulders. "I've thought for some time that the blue lady is the key, the link," Viktor said.

"She's dead."

"Irrelevant. I suspect he was using her not just as an assassin, but as a way to terrify a local indigenous population into silence, perhaps even complicity."

Grey's eyes slipped to Lana. She was listening.

"You think he's in the Andes somewhere outside of Cuzco?" Grey asked.

"Given what you've told me," Viktor said, "I think it's likely. I would focus my search on nearby villages where there is talk about the old ways, especially rumors of a sighting similar to our blue lady."

"Will do."

"I also believe this blue lady might represent something personal to the General."

"Why?"

"She's a random addition to his milieu," Viktor said. "Too random, in my opinion. Something about her . . . invokes the familiar."

"You think it might be a weak spot?"

"Perhaps she is something to exploit. Perhaps not. The General does not appear to have many weaknesses."

"Thanks for pointing that out."

After a pause, Viktor said, "Do you think it might be time to step aside, Grey? Leave the endgame to the government?"

"You mean leave Lana by herself? Look, if we don't find this guy in the next few days, he'll be gone forever."

"Never underestimate the ego of a cult leader. He'll trust in his carefully constructed defenses, and won't believe the game is up until the bitter end."

"You yourself said he's different," Grey said.

"In most respects, yes. When it comes to ego, I have my doubts. And I have to ask," Viktor said softly, "whether this is about justice, or revenge?"

Grey gave a harsh laugh to cover up the images of Nya and Fred floating in his head. "Both. If this case involved buried secrets you'd be shoving me on the plane. Your weak spot is solving the mysteries of the universe, Viktor. Putting bastards like this in the ground is mine."

Grey had barely slept an hour in two days. After they cleared Colombian airspace, Lana noticed his red eyes and drawn face and told him she needed him alert when they landed.

His leg was throbbing, so he took a few Tylenol and let his eyelids droop. Before he knew it, Lana's face receded with the realm of the conscious, replaced by someone underneath him with mocha skin and dark knowing eyes, her athletic body pressed into his, hair spread in a halo of willful curls on the sheet.

Nya made little sounds of pleasure as they rocked together, her voice throaty and intelligent, sensuous and sure. Her thighs clamped against his waist and she pulled Grey's head close, fingers pressing into his hair, caressing his stubbled face, tracing the tattoos and scars covering his back.

At the moment of release, he pressed his hands into her breasts and she arched, moaning his name and shuddering as the waves of pleasure ran their course. His grip on her softened, and they rolled to the side and faced one another. She ran her nails back and forth across the ridges in his abdomen.

"I have something for you," Nya said, pushing away and then climbing out of bed. Grey was curious; she had never given him anything.

She returned holding something behind her back, an eager but nervous look on her face, as if unsure how he would react. Sliding in next to him, she handed him an impressionist soapstone carving of two intertwined lovers.

Stone carving was the predominant art form of the Shona culture, practiced to honor the otherworldly balancing rocks that defined the Zimbabwean landscape. Grey could tell that this piece, though only a few inches high, had been crafted with care.

He took it in his hands, staring at it for a long time without moving. He never thought he would find a woman who would want to give him a gift like this—and from whom he would want to accept. "Thank you," he said softly.

She held him from behind in the hazy semi-darkness that came just before the dawn. "You're welcome, my love."

Even in the dream, he knew he was operating on hope for the future and knew what a perilous thing that was. Especially for him, who had no right to hope, to dream.

The scene shifted, to the time they had climbed Domboshowa at dusk with a bottle of wine, sitting cross-legged together on that moonscape perch just outside Harare, the grunts of the baboons keeping them company as they gazed on a red and gold sunset searing the peaks of the lower Rift Valley, the beginning of mankind at their feet, all red earth and stone and *life*.

Just as the sun went down and Grey leaned in to kiss her, the dream shifted again, to a torchlit cave through which Grey was walking, approaching an altar of skulls and candles.

No, Grey whispered, squirming inside the dream. *Not there.*

Past the altar and down more tunnels and up to the line of blood on the cavern floor, the embodiment of the sorcery of the N'anga, fear rippling through Grey like a hypothermic chill.

Wake me up, he told his subconscious, knowing he was stuck in a nightmare. *I told you I never want to see that, not ever again.*

Padding through the cavern towards the light at the end of the tunnel where Nya was tied to the slab of stone, torso wet with blood, the N'anga standing beside her with his knife. Grey arriving far too late, the damage done, he was going to lose her and she would never love him again, the N'anga watching as Grey ran forward in a rage and fell into the pit—

"Grey!" Someone was shaking him awake, calling his name in a low but urgent voice. "People are staring. Wake up."

He opened his eyes, his breath coming in shallow gasps. Lana was beside him, eyes cloudy with worry. "You okay?"

He sat up and rubbed his eyes, jittery, still half-inside the dream. "Yeah. Sure."

"Good, because we're there."

———•———

To throw off anyone watching the flight manifests, they switched airlines in Lima and bought two more round-trip tickets, this time to Cuzco using the other set of passports. After grabbing a bite to eat, Grey stepped outside the airport to stretch his legs.

He had passed through Lima once before, and the view of the city outskirts was just as he remembered: half-finished buildings that looked like a broken jigsaw puzzle beneath dusty slopes pockmarked by the remains of adobe ruins. Lima's weird milky sky, caused by layers of fog and pollution, made Grey feel as if he were in a waking dream, visiting a dystopian city hovering on the edge of reality.

As Grey rolled his neck to work out a crick, his thoughts turned to Nya, memories of his dream infusing his mind like a teabag spreading through hot water.

He had to hear her voice. It shouldn't be too late in Zimbabwe, so he found a pay phone and tried a collect call, avoiding his cell just to be safe.

Still no answer.

He called his DSO colleague, who said he couldn't reach her either. He had driven by her house and while no one had answered, nothing seemed amiss.

"What about the dogs?" Grey had asked. "Did you hear barking?"

His contact had not.

Grey held his cell in his hand, staring at it, pushing away the idea that had scuttled into his head like a hungry beetle. Surely Nya had gone to the Eastern Highlands, somewhere out of cell range, and taken her dogs with her? Heeding the advice in Grey's message?

Perhaps, but wouldn't she have called him first? Let him know she was disappearing?

Or was she thinking a step ahead, in case someone was tapping her phone? Leaving no trace of her whereabouts?

Please, he whispered to himself. *Please let that be the case.*

Lana signaled with a raised finger from the terminal. He went inside, and they boarded the plane to Cuzco.

54

CUZCO, PERU

Do you suffer from altitude sickness?" Lana asked as they walked onto the tarmac in Cuzco. The dry, windswept peaks surrounding them gave Grey the impression of stepping into an unfinished bowl of pottery.

"Never have," Grey said.

"Good, because we're over eleven thousand feet."

Grey whistled and stuffed his hands in his pockets. It was even chillier than Bogotá, though the sun peeking in and out of the clouds made the weather seem capricious.

The taxi ride in was an easy journey. First through patchwork construction as crumbly as stale bread on the outskirts of town, into the congested modern center rife with the earthy smells of the street markets, and then bumping along the cobblestone streets of the old town.

They had the taxi drop them at the Plaza de Armas, and Grey felt a tingle as they stood in the same spot depicted in Rolando Ganador's photo. Graceful lampposts and wooden balconies surrounded the plaza, and the two hulking baroque cathedrals looked more like citadels than churches. Behind the plaza, the ruins of Sacsayhuamán fortress loomed high on the sierra, underneath chunks of cloud drifting through the endless Andean sky. Truly a regal setting for the Incan emperors, the conquistadores who followed—and for the two criminal masterminds caught by the flash of a lens.

"It'll be risky asking around," Lana said.

"We'll play it as low-key as possible. Two tourists looking for lost Incan legends."

Lana had bought an alpaca shawl off a street vendor, and she wrapped herself tightly in the cool mountain air. "Yes," she murmured.

Grey had the idea to start with the numerous tour operators lining the Plaza de Armas. One by one, they inquired about tours to the surrounding area, Lana explaining that they were visiting scholars researching Quechuan mythology and the present-day remnants of belief, keen on visiting villages with legends of blue spirits of vengeance haunting the cordillera.

They were told there were plenty of villagers who still worshipped in the old ways, and that religion in the highlands was a syncretism of ancient beliefs and Catholicism. But no one, they were told with a smirk, had heard of anyone claiming to see an incarnation of Mama Huaco.

After the fifteenth tour guide muttered *locos gringos* under his breath, Grey decided to expand their witness pool. They started talking to the community of Quechuans in the old city, most of them selling indigenous wares on blankets spread out on the street. They even talked to the little old ladies in brightly colored shawls, their faces wrinkled and brown as crushed paper bags, who led baby llamas through the streets on a rope leash and posed for pictures without changing their expressions.

Up and down the precipitous stone steps of Cuzco they walked, through cobblestone corridors with twenty-foot-high walls, a city of stone and dust, stopping for a cup of coca leaf tea when they got light-headed from the altitude. The Quechuan vendors took them much more seriously than the tour guides, listening to their scholarly inquiries about ancient Incan spirits with humble nods of recognition. Still, no one claimed to have heard of a blue-painted in-digenous woman terrorizing the countryside.

They stopped for dinner, grouper ceviche with toasted corn kernels and sweet potato. "Maybe this isn't the place," Lana said.

Grey washed down a bite of ceviche with a swig of Sol beer. "I suppose the General could have flown in from Bolivia or Chile for the meeting, but something feels right here. The remoteness of the setting, the belief system, the photo . . . let's give it another day before we head to the villages."

"We've talked to everyone in town."

"Not everyone. There's a great source of information we haven't tapped yet." Lana raised her eyebrows, and Grey raised his beer. "Bartenders."

———•———

They found a hotel for the night in San Blas, the artist quarter that climbed the hill a few streets away from the Plaza de Armas. After cleaning up, Lana wanted to stop at an Internet café before they hit the bars.

While Lana checked her email, Grey stepped outside on the street and tried Nya again.

Still no answer.

A female backpacker trudged up the steep street, breathing like an asthma sufferer, followed by an old woman in a black sombrero trying to show her a folder full of watercolors. Grey leaned a hand against the wall and let out a shuddering breath, his other hand balled into a fist.

"Grey."

Lana was standing in the doorway of the café. Her face was pale. "Come inside. You need to see this."

She led him to a computer monitor displaying a photo and a dossier underneath. It was stamped *CIA Classified* on the sides. The dossier was a few pages long, but everything after the first page was blacked out.

Grey honed in on the photo. Though he looked twenty years younger, it was without a doubt the same man from the photo Grey had taken from the Ganador house.

His fingers tightened on the mouse. "That's him. Is it safe to do this here?"

"Not really. Just take a look. It's a response to an inquiry I sent in Bogotá, retrieval of an archived file."

"Why is half of it classified?"

"Read and we'll talk."

The first part was a character profile. It described a young man named Devon Taylor, an American born in Wisconsin to a military father and a Puerto Rican mother. Intelligence tests off the charts, educated at Dartmouth and then Yale Law in the early 1970s, recruited into the CIA after graduation.

Grey read through the detailed personality analysis, the gist of which was that Devon Taylor had high levels of intelligence and charisma but was a borderline sociopath, a person able to justify and implement difficult moral decisions. Someone who had no problem with the ends justifying the means.

Such a lovely turn of phrase, Grey thought, *the ends justifying the means. So nice and sterile.*

He read on. Devon Taylor had been given an interesting task at the CIA. They had planted him within the organization of Reverend Jim Jones, both to keep tabs on the cult and to study the mind-control methods of Jones himself.

Study the methods. The phrase set off alarm bells.

They created him, Grey thought. They put this young genius in the hands of a master manipulator, and he learned from him and improved.

He read about Tashmeni, the village girl who had borne Devon Taylor a child and with whom the CIA concluded he had fallen in love. He read about the growing unrest concerning the cult, the public outcry from Congressman Ryan, and then the tragedy in Guyana. According to the file, Devon Taylor had been gunned down by one of the Reverend's bodyguards the night of the mass suicide, and had been found lying next to his lover and their infant child.

The rest was classified.

Grey read the profile two more times, absorbing the details, reading between the lines. "They tried to kill him," he said softly. "Maybe they didn't orchestrate the mass suicide—or maybe they did—but either way, if the CIA was that deep into Jonestown they would have sent a cleanup crew to destroy the evidence. And Devon had become part of the problem. He knew too much, his emotions were compromised by Tashmeni and her child. They couldn't risk a spectacle."

He looked up. Lana didn't respond, but he saw the agreement in her eyes.

"But he escaped somehow," Grey said, "and became the General." He tapped a finger on the screen. "Someone like that, Lana, with that personality profile and that level of PTSD, he could have gone one of two ways. Either embraced his sociopathy or gone off the deep end. Maybe both. What else do you know about Jonestown?"

"I did some research when I couldn't access his file. Except for what you just read, the public knows what I know. Jim Jones was a twisted cult leader, the CIA and the FBI and everyone else was keeping tabs on him, he had a congressman killed, and he orchestrated a mass suicide."

"We both know there's more to the story. The CIA had its hands all over Latin America."

She bit her lip and gave a slow nod. "You know there's a death tape available to the public, right? Jonestown Tape Q 042. The FBI released it under a FOIA request. It's a live recording of the massacre."

"I didn't know that, but why does the FBI have it? They wouldn't have been on the scene."

"Exactly," she murmured. "As shocking as it is, everyone on the inside knows that tape is sanitized."

"You mean fake?"

"Oh, it's not fake. In fact it's rather chilling. But it's *harmless*. At least to the CIA. Jones was a prolific recorder, but you know what's missing on the hundreds of tapes we released of his worship services? Mention of his government ties. If Jones knew he was going to die and had any dirt on the CIA, and we know he did, then he would have recorded and tried to release it. Fortunately for the CIA, he was stuck in the Guyanese jungle and there was no Internet. But if he did record something, Q 042 isn't that tape."

"So why're we talking about this?"

"Ever heard of Michael Prokes?" she asked.

"No."

"He was one of the few Jonestown survivors, a former journalist who was a key player in the Reverend's organization. Four months after Prokes returned from Guyana, he held a press conference and told a room full of people that the FBI and the CIA were withholding an audiotape of the massacre. Just after the press conference he committed suicide in a bathroom."

She steepled her fingers and pressed them against her lips. "Most people think Stokes was referring to Q 042. But what if the release of Q 042 to the public was a smokescreen?"

"Designed to calm the conspiracy rumors and draw attention away from something damaging," Grey said. "You think there's a missing tape out there, don't you? If there is, then the General has a copy, probably even the original."

Lana's eyes were fixated on the screen. The intensity of her stare was answer enough for Grey.

They closed out of the file and stepped outside. Lana was squatting with her back to the wall, Grey standing beside her. The street smelled like flowers wrapped in wet wool.

"Did the Deputy Director know all along?" she said rhetorically. "Who the General was? If he did, why not tell me?"

"Because it doesn't matter," Grey said. "Whoever the General used to be, he's been someone else for a very long time. And revealing his ID could only," he tapped the folder, "bring whatever else is in here to someone's attention."

"So why approve my request?" she said, then answered her own question. "To let me know I'm on the right track. And that there're other things I don't need to know about. Granting me access to this file was his seal of approval."

"What a guy."

"The General's still the bogeyman, Grey. One of the world's worst criminals and, after the file we've just seen, someone who probably has an unacceptable amount of leverage."

"So why the rush now? If the General has sensitive information, he could have released it at any time. Obviously some sort of détente has been reached over the years."

"Maybe something's changed," Lana said. "Maybe the stakes are higher, maybe the General *has* threatened to release sensitive information. I don't know, and it's not my job to ask."

"That's what the SS officers said. What if it's something to do with your boss?"

"And if it is? Even more reason to go forward. He could be our *President*. Whose side are you on, anyway?"

He started to walk away, and she grabbed his arm from behind. "I'm sorry. You came for me in Bogotá and I'll never forget that." She stepped around to face him. "Look, I don't expect you to stick around. The General's going to throw everything he has at us. If he finds us before we find him, we're worse than dead. I can keep asking around about the cult by myself. You should go home. You deserve a medal for what you've done."

Grey shook his arm free and started walking down the hill, towards San Blas Square. He didn't want a medal. He wanted Fred Hernandez and Sekai to still be alive, he wanted a reckoning for every child who had accepted a crack rock or a gun from someone in the General's organization.

And most of all, he wanted to know that Nya Mashumba was safe and sound in Zimbabwe.

Lana started walking behind him. "Where're you going?"

"To that pub on the corner."

55

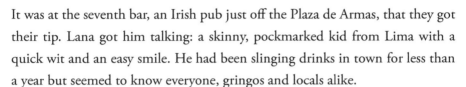

It was at the seventh bar, an Irish pub just off the Plaza de Armas, that they got their tip. Lana got him talking: a skinny, pockmarked kid from Lima with a quick wit and an easy smile. He had been slinging drinks in town for less than a year but seemed to know everyone, gringos and locals alike.

Lana had already given him the researcher spiel. Grey was at a cocktail table behind her, scanning for trouble. Out of the corner of his eye, he saw Lana lean forward.

"And if I were looking for someone who knew the sierra like no one else," she said, her hair spilling over the bar and wearing an intoxicated smile she didn't have to fake, "who would be my guy?"

The bartender put his hands on the counter, ignoring the raised beer mugs of a pair of Western Europeans in mountaineer gear. "I know just the man," he said, "but it'll cost you."

"Is that right?"

"Only a fool gives a pretty girl something for free. You have to promise me I'll see you in here again, when it's less crowded, so we can have a proper conversation."

Lana stirred her cocktail, the corners of her lips upturned. "Deal."

The bartender winked at her, went into a flurry of action for his other customers, then returned a few minutes later with a piece of paper.

"The street's a few blocks behind the Temple of the Sun. Ask around if you can't find it. The guy you want is Pepe, he trades all over the sierra. Our version of a gypsy. You're in luck, he's in town for the week."

———————

Grey and Lana tried a few more places, staying out until the last bar closed. As they slunk back through the long and claustrophobic streets of the old town, Grey kept expecting a group of narcos to emerge from the darkness. Both he and Lana had their hands on Smith & Wesson revolvers that Lana had procured from one of the stalls in the central market. The woman seemed to know every black market vendor west of the Atlantic.

The gun gave Grey little confidence, but the only trouble they encountered on the walk back was a group of local teens who shouted a few machismo taunts at Lana, insouciance oozing out of their cheap leather jackets.

Grey's and Lana's hotel was a former colonial mansion divided into smaller rooms, with balconies that overlooked Plaza San Blas. Before turning in, Grey had a glass of water on the balcony, staring down at the pretty square lit by globe lanterns.

Lana joined him. "Not drunk after twelve beers?"

"I had about half of each."

"Ah."

Her body language was tense beside him, as if she had something to say. He waited her out, guessing the subject before she voiced it, knowing it was why she had let herself get hammered in the middle of a mission.

"It happened again," she said. "Someone took my freedom from me."

"They used scopolamine, Lana. It could have happened to anyone. You can't blame yourself."

She was staring straight ahead. "I can and I will. I thought I had put all of that behind me . . . but who knows what happened to me when I was in there. *Both* times. Did they gang rape me, put me on video, place bets on how long each of them would last?"

He placed a hand on her forearm. "Don't, Lana. They can't take anything from you, not unless you let them."

"Thanks for the pop psychology."

"It's true."

Grey looked down and noticed her knuckles were white from squeezing the railing. "I don't really care if I live through this," she said. "I stopped caring about that a long time ago." Her eyes found his, twin pools of sadness and rage. "And I know you know what I mean."

He knew what she meant, and she was not wrong to think that of him. But as he thought of Nya for the hundredth time that day, his insides churning with worry, he wondered if he still felt the same.

After lingering over coffee and breakfast at the hotel, giving the trader time to set up, Grey and Lana headed out just after nine.

They found the street without having to ask, a snake's belly of stone a few blocks past the tourist section, populated by a line of children sleeping on blankets beside their parents. Near the middle of the street, a doorway set into the stone wall led to a courtyard lit by a pocket of weak sunlight. It was rife with the grassy, bittersweet smell of brewed coca leaves.

A greasy long-haired Quechuan was sitting cross-legged on a blanket, surrounded by a dozen other blankets piled high with natural-dye alpaca clothing, jewelry, wooden pipes, and children's trinkets. Three women in colorful shawls lingered on the edges of the courtyard, watching a handful of stout Quechuan children who looked like walking thimbles.

The trader noticed Grey and Lana, saluting them with a clear plastic cup of what was probably homemade *chicha* beer. Grey scanned the courtyard for danger, in case someone had gotten to the bartender. Satisfied it wasn't a setup, he moved to where he could watch the entrance, and let Lana conduct the conversation.

Before engaging, she selected a few items to purchase, textiles and silver jewelry, to make the trader more amenable to conversation. Dressed in jeans and scuffed sandals and a moth-eaten sport coat, a wooden necklace splayed over a faded black-and-white-striped dress shirt, the Quechuan man watched her like a cat eying a songbird as she sifted through the goods. When she approached and sat beside him to pay, she complimented him on his wares and told him that she and Grey were in Peru on a research assignment.

Unlike the bartender, the trader didn't seem captivated by Lana. He was smiling and waving his hands as he talked, but his smile was predatory. When she told him about the blue Indian lady, he made a noise somewhere between a grunt and a laugh, and fingered an embroidered cloth bag hanging from his belt.

"You want to do some coca tourism, I see," he said, his Spanish accent surprisingly neutral. Grey couldn't even tell if he was Peruvian.

"Sorry?" Lana said. "I'm not sure what you mean."

He leered at her. "Aren't you? Your friend over there doesn't look like much of a scholar. And neither of you are dressed to be traipsing through the sierra. It's okay," he held up the embroidered bag and grinned, "I know what you're looking for."

As if to prove his point, he pulled out a wad of coca leaves from the bag and stuffed them into the side of his mouth. "Yes, I know where you want to go. Would you like a few bags for the journey?"

Grey was watching the entrance as he kept an eye on Lana and the trader, but he had heard the man loud and clear. *I know where you want to go.*

Lana gave a nonchalant shrug. "Why not?"

He called out an order, and a woman stood with a roll of her hips and moved towards a blanket in the corner.

The trader gave Lana a sly grin and ran a hand through his hair, strands of which fell across his chest. "I know you're looking for the other thing, the thing you gringos like. I like that too. You won't find it in that place, but of course you know that. You're making friends, looking for connections. You're smart to look here and not Colombia, the Colombians are devils in human skin. And it's no good in Bolivia anymore, the *cocaleros* there have unions, if you can believe such a thing. But here in Peru, we're wild and free and lawless. You can make little connections here and there in the sierra, find your own heart of darkness."

"I don't suppose you can point us to anyone in particular?" Lana said. "Someone who might give you a kickback?"

He spat. "I choose this life because I want it. I answer to no narco, no government, no son of a bitch communist guerrilla."

Lana put her hands up. "I'm sorry, I didn't meant to insult you. But you said you know where we're trying to go?"

One of the women approached Lana and shoved two of the patterned cloth bags in her hands, stuffed with coca leaves. As she waddled away, the trader said, "I don't know where you heard the rumor about Mama Huaco, no one outside the sierra talks about such things." He shook his head, his leer replaced by a grim smirk. "People who know of the old ways avoid that village. You should choose another. That's my advice, free of charge for your purchases."

Lana slid three hundred-dollar bills out of her wallet and placed them on the table. "This should more than cover it, I should think? And if we did want to go? What would you advise?"

He snatched the bills with a flick of his fingers, but his smirk only deepened. "You don't get it, do you? It's not about the coca. You gringos come here with stars in your eyes, you think the Incas were this mystical race of people who read coca leaves and planted quinoa and made love under the stars. Children of the earth, innocents slaughtered by the Spanish." He again ran a hand through his greasy hair. "No no no, my friend. Ask the Chancas and the Huancas how peaceful the Incas were. Ask the dead enemies whose flayed skin was used to make war drums. Ask those who were sacrificed to the *apus*, their livers and brains and kidneys consumed by the Inca priests."

Lana let him finish his rant, and his smirk softened a fraction. "Of course you don't care about myths and legends, the reality of pesos and dollars is far too strong. But it's not what you believe that matters. It's what the villagers believe. Watch yourself, gringa. There are bad rumors about this place. It's not even Peru. It's somewhere else, lost in the sierra. Lost in time. And in this place the descendants of the Incas are alive, really alive, and they don't like visitors."

56

DER HEILIGKEIT DES LUFT SANATORIUM

The icy trees shone in the darkness, both pressing in and allowing glimpses into the forest. Glimpses into the danger Viktor knew lurked within.

Glen was out there, Viktor could feel it. His hands were inside his coat, one grasping his knife and the other a handgun.

The footpath wound down the hill, through virgin pine bowed with the weight of snow. Viktor had left the road twenty minutes earlier to tramp down the forest path, the silence broken only by the crunch of his footsteps.

This was the third night in a row he had walked this same route, at the same time of night. Hoping to give his assailant a routine. Hoping to draw him out.

As he rounded a corner that squeezed between two boulders, the perfect place for an ambush, Viktor's nerve endings lit up like flares. He had to keep walking as if nothing was wrong, because if he spooked Glen, the plan would be ruined.

And that was unacceptable.

Eyes straining to see past the boulders, some of the tension eased out of his shoulders when he rounded the corner and saw the path straightening. Still, he kept his fingers wrapped around the trigger.

He heard the squeak of a shoe scuffing on snow, and turned in time to see a huge body flying through the air off the top of one of the boulders. Viktor might have had time to pull a weapon, but he couldn't take the risk. Instead he caught Glen in mid-flight.

Though Viktor was larger, he was crushed by the heavy body plummeting off the boulder. The fall knocked the wind out of Viktor, and Glen sprang off him and drew a long syringe out of his coat. He grabbed Viktor's throat with his other hand, and Viktor felt as if a python had seized him.

Viktor fumbled for his knife, but knew he'd never reach it in time. With a crazed light in his eyes, Glen raised the syringe above his head and started to plunge it downward.

A gunshot rang through the night, followed by a voice in Swiss-German calling for Glen to freeze.

Glen didn't freeze, but the gunshot distracted him, allowing Viktor to roll out from underneath him. The needle in the syringe stabbed through the tail of Viktor's coat. More shouting followed, someone shot Glen in the arm, and then the woods were full of security guards sprinting to the scene.

Viktor scrambled away from the madman, who was holding his bloody arm in silence in the middle of the path, his thin lips contorted in pain, his entire body dusted in white. Viktor had scanned the tops of the boulders earlier, and hadn't seen him. He must have been hiding in the snow, Viktor realized with a chill.

One of the guards ran to Viktor. "Are you injured?"

"Just," Viktor worked to catch his breath, "a little winded."

"You were right," the guard said. "None of us believed you, but you were right. Are you sure you don't need the clinic?"

Viktor eased to his feet and brushed the snow off of his hair and clothing. "His accomplice?"

The guard grinned. "We've already radioed it in. There're only two night watchmen in the criminal ward, and we detained them both. We'll have the bastard before midnight."

Viktor started walking towards the sanatorium. "When you find the one responsible, place him in a room by himself, and call me immediately. And don't notify the police."

57

PERUVIAN ANDES

"How much farther?" Lana called out to the driver, a tour guide they had hired in Cuzco.

"Not much, Señora."

The guide was the only one they could find who knew the way to Kukuka-tari, the village where, according to the Quechuan trader in Cuzco, there were rumors of a blue Indian woman appearing on the sierra. The guide also had a vehicle up to the task: a twenty-year-old beige Land Cruiser that took the bumps like an old pro. Twice Grey had to help lay boards on the road to free the vehicle from a mud pit.

They hadn't asked if their guide shared the trader's superstitions, but he hadn't balked at the journey, especially when Lana offered him five hundred dollars a day. By his expression, Grey thought he might have carried them to the village on his back for that much money.

The journey had been a long one. Riding along while the driver listened to some type of Peruvian highland techno, an annoying mix of synthesized flute and pipes, they lurched through the chaos and poverty on the outskirts of Cuzco, then cruised through the lush meadows of the Sacred Valley, laden with cultivations of corn and grain. After Urabamba, the valley narrowed and the scenery became much more intense, an unending succession of jagged peaks with bowl-shaped impressions in between, a layer of mist covering everything like a Styrofoam lid. It was a towering, otherworldly place.

If the spirits of Palo Mayombe haunted the forests, Grey thought, *then the ghosts of fallen gods lived in the Andes.*

The Quechuan trader had laughed when Lana asked if they could go by car, and Grey could see why. After Ollantaytambo— the last stop in the Sacred Valley before Machu Picchu, and the last town accessible by road—they had taken a dirt road through the valley for a few miles, and then the road had turned into a track of mud and rubble, inaccessible except by the hardiest of off-road vehicles. That was two hours ago, and it seemed to grow worse by the minute.

After winding slowly higher for another hour, the crisp air punctuated by the smell of animal dung, they approached a village surrounded by mountains so steep they looked like slides, almost violent in their proximity. A river gushed along the west edge of town.

The guide announced their arrival at their destination, and Grey gripped his gun as they pulled into Kukukatari. He knew this was a fool's mission, that he and Lana had pushed too far. He just didn't know what to do about it. The stakes were too high now. If he had just listened to Nya and dropped the case after Miami . . . he didn't want to think about the potential consequences of his decision.

He hadn't told Lana, but even if they were successful, Grey's mission wasn't going to end with a call to CIA headquarters. He had tried Nya again before they left Cuzco, and this time her phone had gone straight to voicemail.

Which made no sense. She would have called him back.

His contact at the embassy had tried again to reach her, and said the house looked abandoned. Grey had let the phone slide out of his grasp. The General had found his pressure point.

Even if they managed to locate the General, Grey couldn't risk an onslaught of random drone fire, or a sky full of parachuting Navy Seals, or the General deciding Nya was no longer needed.

So he was going in after her. He just had to stay alive long enough to get there.

And if his instincts were wrong, and Nya's phone had been lost or stolen, or she had disappeared into the countryside without telling him?

It was a risk he had to take.

The town was a maze of stone walls and cobblestone streets, with sluice-like canals running down the sides of each road. Everyone short and squat and wary, faces disappearing into doorways, the whole village giving Grey the feeling that someone was watching them, perhaps the mountains themselves.

Their guide pointed at a wall as they eased along the main road into the village, the smell of roasting corn wafting through the cracked windows of the SUV. "Not a trace of mortar," he said. "And see those doorways made out of slabs that narrow at the top? The canals on the streets, the cobblestone houses? This town is Incan, not Spanish. It's a living relic."

Groups of old women with thick black braids and leathery calves, wearing brightly colored shawls and even more colorful sacks tied to their backs, waddled down the street like a muster of peacocks, eying the Land Cruiser as it passed. The guide parked in the center of the village, a small square with a single gnarled, leafless tree on display. It was near dusk, and long shadows were rolling down the mountains, smothering the village.

"End of the line," the guide said. He patted the Land Cruiser. "The other streets are too narrow for this beast."

The trader had given them the name of a woman who might put them up for the night. After their guide inquired at the general store, they were pointed down one of the streets and told to look for the last doorway on the left.

There was something missing in the town, and Grey tried to put a finger on what it was. When he finally figured it out, he wished he hadn't.

He realized he had not seen a single cathedral. What city, town, or village in Latin America didn't have a church commandeering the town square?

He remembered the words the trader had uttered. *But it's not what you believe that matters. It's what the villagers believe.*

Words that could have come from Viktor's mouth, and a warning Grey had learned to heed.

Grey noticed Lana doing the same thing he was, eying everyone and everything. He did not relish the thought of asking questions in this town, and decided to brief the guide in the morning and use him as a proxy. These people would never talk to Grey or Lana.

The General was close, he could feel it. They had come to the end of the earth and he was there.

As promised, they found the pensión at the end of a long street at the edge of the village, on the banks of the river. A middle-aged Quechuan woman in a black sombrero and knee-high, multicolored socks opened the door. She agreed to put them up and led them into an interior courtyard full of potted herbs, hanging laundry, and a few hardy fruit trees. An eight-foot stone wall surrounded the property.

She led them up a rickety flight of steps to a banistered outdoor hallway lined with doors. "Three rooms?" she asked in Spanish.

"*Sí*," Lana said. Their guide had agreed to stay with them as needed.

The Quechuan woman left them with keys and disappeared.

"These buildings were used as communal living quarters for families," the guide explained. "They shared the courtyard and divided the living space."

"And those?" Lana asked through tight lips, pointing at a line of skulls displayed in an open cabinet at the end of the hallway.

The guide grinned. "Ancestor shrine. Common practice among the Quechua."

After they had dropped their bags and washed up, the guide went into town to look for a cantina. Grey and Lana sat on a stone bench in the courtyard, eating apples and trail mix bars they had brought from Cuzco. The string of serrated peaks looming above them reminded Grey of the ridged back of an alligator.

"We'll start in the morning," Lana said. "We'll talk to every last villager if we have to."

"The General didn't let them see the blue lady at random," Grey said. "There's a good chance these people are in his thrall."

"Cash loosens lips. So does pain. Someone will talk, and we'll move fast once they do."

"We should use the guide, brief him on the research angle."

"Good idea," she said. "Remember, we just have to figure out where he's holed up. Then it's all over. One call and the commandoes take it from there."

He rose. "I'm going to find some water."

"Try to get some sleep. With any luck, this will end tomorrow."

———•———

When Grey knocked on the owner's door and inquired about water, she gave him a plastic cup and pointed towards the river.

He took his gun, unlatched the heavy courtyard door, and peered down the street. The rest of the wooden doors and iron-grilled windows were shut as tight as a puzzle box.

There were no streetlights, no ambient light. Just a panoply of stars in a night that had settled like a bottle of spilled ink. The exotic celestial patterns of the Southern Hemisphere made him think of Nya, and his heart pumped faster. He tried her yet again, and got the same dead signal.

He hopped the wooden railing and stepped down to the bank of the river. The smell of pine drifted on the breeze, and the roar of water drowned out the insect chatter.

As he knelt to fill his cup, he noticed a flicker of movement across the river. He jumped back and felt a prick on his neck as he reached for his gun. Looking up, he saw a young indigenous woman lowering a blowgun. She was painted blue and looked from a distance like the same woman who had fired a slingshot at him in Miami.

By the time Grey raised his gun, she had melted behind a tree. He groped at his neck and felt the feathered end of a dart. The barbed tip stung as he pulled it out.

He didn't bother chasing her, knowing she would evade him in the unfamiliar, darkened terrain. He also didn't bother pondering the impossibility of her appearance. Instead he sprinted back to the street and through the door to the villa, bursting into the courtyard and calling out for Lana.

The courtyard was filled with men wearing bandanas pulled above their mouths like bandits, pointing automatic weapons at him. Lana was slumped on the bench, unconscious. The owner of the villa was watching from the balcony with folded arms and an impassive face.

Grey lowered his weapon. Part of him wasn't even unhappy with the outcome. He had little faith that they would find the General on their own, and if this was the only way he could get to Nya, then so be it.

The drug from the dart was already making him fuzzy. He stayed awake long enough to watch the men drag him and Lana to a clearing at the edge of town, where a group of pack animals had been tethered. Grey stumbled to his knees as his brain shut down.

He wondered if he would ever wake up.

58

DER HEILIGKEIT DES LUFT SANATORIUM

Viktor stalked into the interrogation room to confront the true object of the night's maneuver: the guard who had let Glen out of his cell. Interrogating Glen further was a lost cause, but his accomplice was another story.

The night watchman, a sullen German with uneven teeth and too much gel in his hair, sat in handcuffs behind a metal desk. Two of the sanatorium's private guards, armed with rifles, watched from a corner of the room.

Viktor sat and folded his hands on the table. "I assume you know who I am?" he said in Swiss-German.

No response.

"His name's Andreas," one of the guards called out. "He's only been here a few days."

"Andreas," Viktor said, "what was in the syringe? Poison? Scopolamine?"

CCTV had caught a black SUV waiting at the bottom of the mountain. When security had approached the car, the two men inside had claimed ignorance. Their records and the car's plates were clean, and security had no basis to hold them.

"Was the order to kidnap or kill me?" Viktor pressed. "Who were the men in the black car?" Viktor stood and leaned over the desk, looming over the smaller man. "Whether or not you're charged as an accomplice for attempted murder, or for a lesser charge, depends on what you tell me before the authorities arrive."

Andreas stared at the desk.

"Who paid you to let Glen out?" Viktor said. "Where can I find them? Do you know who the General is?"

Andreas paled ever so slightly at the question, but refused to say a word.

Viktor placed his cell phone on the table. "Once the authorities are involved, there will be no going back. You'd much rather talk to me than to the police."

Andreas whispered a response under downcast eyes, so low Viktor had to lean in to hear him. "That's where you're wrong."

A few hours later, Viktor gave up. Andreas wasn't talking, and they couldn't hold him any longer without calling the authorities. Private security laws allowed only so much leeway.

While they had him confined, Viktor used his Interpol resources to look into Andreas's background. Then things got interesting. Andreas Bohm was a Swiss citizen with a spotty work history and no criminal record—but this man wasn't Andreas Bohm, if such a person even existed.

From the cell photo Viktor had snapped, Interpol's database had identified the face as belonging to an Austrian national named Klaus Hitzig, a member of a fascist pseudo-church connected to the drug community. An organization whose leaders, Viktor had no doubt, had ties to the General.

Klaus was also a freelance mercenary who had spent years working hotspots in Central and South America. Under the guise of a tourist named Heinrich Zieler, Klaus had recently boarded a plane from Cuzco to Zurich.

Cuzco.

Whether because the General considered Viktor a high-priority target, or was simply too careful to trust the communication network, Viktor knew the General had sent one of his own men to release Glen.

Which got Viktor nowhere.

In a rare loss of control, he slammed his fists on the desk before leaving the interrogation room. Despite repeated attempts to reach him, it had been almost forty-eight hours since he had spoken to Grey. He even tried calling Nya, but couldn't reach her either.

Just like in the woods, Viktor's instincts told him that something was terribly, terribly wrong.

He spent the rest of the day on the phone or on the computer, trying to reach Grey and looking into every angle he could think of.

Despite his efforts, his attempts were futile. Peru was a huge country, and the General could be anywhere in the Andes.

As the sun descended, he put his head in his hands, nauseous at his inability to help his friend, knowing it was quite possible he would never again see Dominic Grey alive.

59

Grey's eyes fluttered open. He was lying on his back, his head on a pillow, staring at a finished concrete ceiling. After a moment of disorientation, he remembered what had happened and sprang out of the cot.

His prison had concrete walls in the front and the rear, and glass walls on either side. To his left, Lana was sleeping on a cot in a similar cell.

To his right was Nya.

She was lying on her side on the cot, facing him, dressed in cotton pants and a fitted white sweater. When he saw the rise and fall of her chest, he almost swooned with relief.

She looked unharmed, but it was hard to tell. He beat against the thick glass and called her name. She didn't stir.

Lana was facing away from him, also unmoving. After making sure she was breathing, he turned back to Nya. The relief faded; the nightmare had come true. The General had reached into Africa and plucked her away, the second time she had been abducted on Grey's watch.

Hands pressed against the glass, he slumped against the wall facing her cell, willing her to wake up. Seeing her there felt like a pit to the abyss had opened inside him, and his soul was teetering on the edge, counterweighted only by the knowledge that he still had a chance to help her, slim though it might be.

The only woman he had loved, and he had brought her nothing but misery and pain.

When she didn't stir, his eyes found her bare feet tucked into the cot, the narrow brown toes and the curve of her arch. Roamed the length of her long athletic legs, past the narrow waist and the torso that he knew bore the scars of the N'anga's knife, then up the firm but graceful sweep of her neckline to the face he longed to cup in his hands. There he lingered, remembering past nights by candlelight, her sculpted features cast in amber.

His hands slid down the glass and he watched her for a very long time, lost in the sight of her, trembling with love and rage, unwilling to accept that he could not sweep her into his arms and carry her from this place.

————— ◆ —————

Someone was unlocking Grey's door. Nya stirred, and he assumed she had heard a similar noise. As his door opened, he evaluated the situation. The first guard came inside dangling handcuffs. He had no weapon for Grey to swipe. The weapons, M-16 rifles, were in the hands of two guards behind him. Smart.

A guard shook Nya awake. She sat and looked at Grey. A sad smile appeared on her lips. She didn't look surprised, which meant she already knew he was there. He wondered how long he had been a mindless sheep.

On the other side, a guard shook Lana awake. She stumbled to her feet and looked at Grey, then past him to Nya. Lana's eyes widened and then narrowed. She hadn't known.

After handcuffing Grey in the front, his captors waited until Nya and Lana were led out of their rooms, then prodded Grey into a beige hallway. They walked him past a bathroom and down a long corridor, through a door at the other end and up a set of stairs, then down two more hallways and through another closed door, into the rear of a banquet hall filled with people.

Grey blinked. The sudden commotion took him by surprise. There must have been two hundred men and women inside, sitting at circular tables with blue tablecloths, talking and laughing and drinking out of beer mugs. Firearms hung at their sides or rested on the table beside them, and they had the straight-backed bearing of soldiers. Most looked Latino, but Grey saw white, black, and Asian faces sprinkled among the crowd.

At the far end of the room, Nya and Lana sat behind a semicircular wooden table facing the crowd. There were six chairs. Both women watched him with expressionless faces, though he didn't think either was still drugged. He thought they were keeping their cool.

The people at the tables gave him sidelong glances as the guards led him to the front. A few smirked and toasted him. His captors placed him between Lana and Nya on the left side of the table, leaving him in handcuffs.

"Grey," Nya whispered, placing a hand on his knee.

"I'm sorry," he whispered back.

He forced his gaze away from her and absorbed his surroundings. The ceiling and walls were glass, showcasing a stunning vista. They were perched on the side of a mountain, facing another mountain covered with the grey smudge of ruins, so close it seemed he could throw a baseball and hit it. Mist swirled around the latticework of old stone.

Tall peaks rose out of the cloud forest in every direction, and in the distance, the tops of snowcapped volcanoes loomed like swaths of white paint. Far below, he saw a river winding through a gorge.

Plush rugs covered the room, dyed in natural colors. Peruvian tapestries and cured animal skins hung on the walls. Track lighting provided illumination.

"Any idea where we are?" he asked Nya.

"I woke up in that cell two days ago. I've been to the toilet and nowhere else. They drop food off and leave."

"No one's touched you?"

"No."

Grey's fists unclenched, then tightened again. *Stay in control, Grey. Going berserk helps no one.* "Do you know how long I've been here?"

"A full day. A man came in three times with a needle. I could see them interrogating you." Nya nodded towards Lana. "Her too."

"Jesus," Grey said. "Lana, meet Nya."

Lana spoke without turning her head. Grey knew she was canvassing the room, looking for a way out of the impossible scenario. "What's she doing here?" Lana said. "Insurance?"

Nya lifted her chin as she responded, her gaze every bit as confident and commanding as Lana's. "As I *said*, I've spoken to no one."

"I think we got close enough that he needed to know what we knew," Grey said. "He knew you would keep plowing forward, but wasn't so sure about me, unless she was here. And," he said softly, "he was right."

"So what's this?" Lana said. "The Last Supper?"

Grey inclined his head towards the door through which they had just entered. "We're about to find out."

The commotion ceased as three people entered the room. The first was a tall and thin indigenous woman wearing a sleeveless embroidered dress and a garland of white flowers. An assortment of tribal jewelry adorned her neck and wrists. Though her hair was graying, she was still quite striking.

The man in the white sport coat and open-collared shirt next to her was the man from Rolando Ganador's photo, and from the CIA file. He was about Grey's height and much thicker in person, with the chest and shoulders of a bull. He had short gray hair and metal-rimmed glasses, and everything about him, from the size of his hands to the weathered lines of his face to the spring in his step, suggested vigor.

The third person was Lucho, wearing green camouflage pants and a black sweater, his right pinky in a splint. His flat eyes met Grey's, and Grey could feel the hate pouring outward like heat from an open stove.

Behind the first three were two female guards who made Grey grip the edge of the table. The two women, dressed in black khaki pants and long-sleeved shirts color-splashed with indigenous dyes, looked like twins and could have been the older woman's daughters. They carried spears, knives, and blowguns, and the exposed parts of their bodies were covered in blue body paint. From a distance they looked identical to the assassins who had come after Grey.

"My God," Lana said. "That's . . . that can't be."

Grey kept looking back and forth between the older woman and the two younger ones. "He's breeding them," he said in awe. "Different generations to keep the myth alive. Ready replacements if one dies."

"What is this, some sort of incestuous harem in honor of that girl who died at Jonestown?" Lana said. "Twisted bastard."

The General waved a hand, and the commotion resumed. A man carrying a guitar followed the blue women inside and began strumming a ballad.

Like an emperor taking the throne, the General strode to the other side of Grey's table, sitting between the older woman and Lucho. The two women in blue paint walked behind Grey's section of the table. Out of the corner of his eye, Grey saw them standing a few feet back, hands poised on their weapons.

As soon as everyone was in place, servants scurried forth from the wings with wine bottles and glasses. They poured glasses of Chilean Malbec and then retreated.

"Welcome to my humble abode," the General boomed. "What do you think of the view?"

Grey held up his handcuffs. "I don't like any view with chains."

The General shrugged and waved a hand. "So try it without them."

Another of the servants ran to uncuff the three of them. Grey rubbed and flexed his wrists below the table.

"Better?" the General asked.

Grey didn't answer. He knew he was being toyed with, and that he wasn't going anywhere. Not with a room full of mercenaries and two assassins, trained by an ex-CIA agent, standing at his back. The General also had the ultimate trump card, and she was sitting right beside Grey. He had been outmaneuvered, and there was nothing he could do about it.

"Why bother letting us wake up?" Lana asked. "So we can fawn over your empire?"

The General swirled his wine. "I'm a civilized man, and prefer civilized endings. I also wanted to congratulate the adversaries who have come closest to besting me. Like any man of action, I prize a well-fought battle above all else. Of course," he said calmly, but with an edge to his voice that was like a laser cutting into glass, "I prefer to win."

Grey tilted his head towards Nya. "Let her leave. She doesn't even know where she is. Drug her and send her home."

"Ah," the General said, "there's no one as selfless as a man in love. Trust me," he said, spreading his arms to the room and winking at the woman beside him, "I should know. Or," he mused, barking a laugh and slapping the table, "is it no one's as *self-centered* as a man in love?" The General took the chin of the woman beside him in his hands, and they exchanged a loving glance. He looked back to Grey. "Your request is reasonable from your perspective, but she's seen too much. I do apologize, but none of you will see the dawn."

It took all of Grey's willpower not to throw himself across the table to try to reach the General, to try to inflict some measure of pain before he died. He swallowed his rage. In addition to the women at his back, Lucho was watching every twitch Grey made, his hand on his gun, begging him to move.

Instead, Grey smiled at the General and tried to inflict another sort of pain.

"I understand your agony in Jonestown all those years ago, your fury, but that jungle full of dead children is yours now. How many people have you killed? How many drug babies have you fostered?"

Grey didn't get the flash of anger he was hoping for. Instead he got, behind the squinty blue eyes, a glimpse of a man who had seen and done everything in life, who knew he had sunk into his own dark fantasy and didn't even care. A man to whom life had become an experiment and nothing more.

A man Grey didn't know how to reach, except with violence.

"My people will be here any second," Lana said. "There's still time to make a deal."

The General sounded bored. "The portable tracking devices in your phone and your purse were destroyed before you left the village. Which is hours from here and quite useless as a reference point. Do you have any idea how inaccessible this part of the world is?" He waited as the waiter refilled his wine glass, and he raised it to Grey. "You were right to come for her. Had you not, I would have killed her and taken you another day, and you wouldn't have had your good-bye."

The appetizers arrived, wontons stuffed with goat cheese and a platter of olives and prosciutto. The woman beside the General placed an olive into her mouth with dainty fingers. Before the servants retreated, the General snapped his fingers. "Bring the folders."

A servant disappeared and returned with two thin manila folders, which he placed in front of Grey and Lana.

"A little dinner entertainment," the General said. "I think you, Lana, will find it particularly enlightening."

Grey opened the manila folder. Inside was a printout of the same CIA file he had seen on Lana's computer screen, except that nothing was blacked out.

Lana seized her copy. "The name in small print in the top right wasn't there in the other version. That's the author." She looked up at the General. "My God, he was your handler."

Grey's eyes moved upward to read the name printed in the corner. *Jeffrey Lasgetone.*

The current Deputy Director of the CIA.

The General gestured as if shooing away her words. "Please, keep reading."

Grey read the classified portion of the report. The gist of it was that the CIA had predicted exactly what would happen at Jonestown when Congressman Ryan arrived. The socialist cult was considered a propaganda nightmare and there were even contingencies in place to trigger a mass suicide—of American men, women, and children— should events not take their own course. Also in the report was the directive to send in a cleanup crew to whitewash the evidence. Near the bottom of the page, Jeffrey Lasgetone gave his analysis that Devon Taylor had been compromised and would be a liability after witnessing the death of Tashmeni and their child, and recommended he be terminated if he survived.

Grey closed the folder and found Lana staring at the General. "This was never about insecure borders," she said. "This was about revenge. He knew you'd ruin his bid for election."

"Oh no, I'll wait until after the election. He's doing well in the polls. I'll ruin his *presidency*." He nodded towards the paper in Lana's hands. "Turn it over."

Grey flipped over his own copy and saw a few more paragraphs detailing the cleanup at Jonestown. Marked with an asterisk was the description of an empty cassette tape found next to the body of Jim Jones, along with an unsigned note.

I think you know what this means.
From now on, Devon Taylor is dead.

"The tape is a full confessional," the General said almost sadly, as if sparring with children, "including recordings of Reverend Jones's conversations with Jeffrey, who was his contact at the CIA. The CIA allowed the cult to survive long enough to study it, knowing how it would end. Even the American public will be horrified. I'll ruin Jeffrey, I'll ruin the CIA, I'll ruin the credibility of your government. I'll finish the game he started so very long ago."

Lana looked as if she had seen a ghost, and turned the paper over to read the report again. A few minutes later the main course arrived, medallions of beef ladled with a garlic cream sauce. The General and the woman cut into the meat with relish, but Lucho sat with folded arms, his eyes never leaving Grey.

Grey had left his food and wine untouched, as had Nya and Lana. During the meal his eyes roamed the room, searching for an angle. When he scooted back in his chair to cross his legs, testing response times, one of the women behind him placed the tip of a blowgun on his back.

Nya reached for Grey's hand and intertwined their fingers. "I'm sorry I left you," she said, low enough for Grey alone to hear. "It was myself I hated, not you."

"It's okay," Grey said. "I always understood."

"It's not okay. It never was. I want you to know I see the beauty inside you, your soul. I know who you are." She squeezed his hand and met his eyes. "I love you, Dominic Grey."

Her words washed over him, a purification before the burial chamber. He couldn't even speak, could only hold her hand in silence as shivers of emotion rippled through him, while the madman across from them finished forking bites of filet mignon into his mouth.

After the General drained the last of his wine, the servants brought chocolate mousse and a bottle of Argentinian port. The crowd was still boisterous, Lana was still gripping the report, Lucho was still staring at Grey.

The General dipped his spoon into the mousse, then offered it to his partner. She gazed at him with longing as the spoon neared her mouth. When it touched her lips, a projectile crashed through the glass and an explosion rocked the room, shattering the windows and caving in the ceiling.

60

Men in black masks and combat gear stormed inside, spraying the mercenaries with bullets and tear gas. Screams and shouts filled the air. Half of the General's people had been knocked out of their chairs, and the dining hall was in shambles.

Grey didn't hesitate. He dove to the floor behind him, ignoring the shattered glass, reaching for the knee and ankle of the blue woman at his back. Knowing she was distracted by the commotion and not expecting such a low maneuver, Grey yanked her off her feet with an ankle grab, then hit her so hard in the face with his open palm that she was out cold before her head hit the floor.

The other blue assassin raised her blowgun, the weapon Grey feared most. Grey flipped to his feet, knowing he was too late, but before the blowgun fired, Nya smashed her in the face with a wine glass, then kicked her into the wall. Grey sprang on the blue woman like a leopard and finished the job with a blow to the head.

Taking Nya by the hand, Grey picked up one of the spears and dashed for the nearest hole in the glass. Lana followed. Bullets flew through the room, filling the air with the smell of sulfur. Though the tear gas was concentrated on the other side of the room, Grey covered his mouth and nose as they crossed the fifteen feet to the shattered glass wall.

When they reached the outside, a ray of late afternoon sun blinded him. He shielded his eyes and saw people in combat gear storming the hill. Three choppers hovered overhead, whipping dust into a frenzy.

"Are they yours?" he asked Lana.

"No," she said, confusion lacing her voice.

One of the assailants noticed Grey and the two women. He pointed his gun at them but didn't fire. Before anyone could speak, Grey heard a spray of gunfire and their confronter pitched forward. Behind him, Grey saw a contingent of the General's men, led by another of the blue-painted women.

To his left, the chaos had left a gap in the swarm of assailants, and Grey took the opening. He nodded at Lana, grabbed Nya's hand again and sprinted for the line of gnarled trees twenty yards away. They reached it without incident, then stopped to survey their surroundings.

They were behind the compound, on the opposite side of the slope. A cloud forest covered the mountain below them, a tangle of trees and vines and mist.

It was an easy choice. Neither the combat gear nor the helicopter bore any insignia, and the commandoes had been shouting in Spanish. None of them had any idea who had just stormed the General's compound, and Grey wasn't about to stick around to find out if they were friend or foe.

As he started down the hill, Lana grabbed his shoulder. "I'm staying," she said.

Grey turned. "Don't be a fool."

"I'm finishing this."

"Even if it means your life?"

"We talked about that already."

Grey gripped her forearm. "Come with us, Lana."

She glanced at Nya, then at the war zone beside them, then back at Grey. "Get to the bottom of the mountain. I'll find you later."

Lana crouched and snaked her way along the tree line, back towards the compound.

Grey and Nya fled.

Hand in hand, they moved through the forest as fast as the terrain allowed, stepping over rocks and giant roots, squishing through layers of moss and mud, pawing through spider webs, careening down a vertical hillside.

At first the sound of gunfire and shouting accompanied their every step, but it gradually faded, until the forest around them returned to life. The chitter of birds and insects seemed surreal after the maelstrom out of which they had just stepped.

The mist was omnipresent, encasing them in a hoary cocoon. The forest looked like an alien planet, trees and flowers and leeching bromeliads contorted in their search for sunlight, vines as tall as skyscrapers disappearing into the canopy. They scrambled down over loose rocks, waist-high brambles, and jagged stones that cut into their legs.

Grey had no doubt the General had sentries posted on the hill. The only question was whether they had all reported to the compound, or were still waiting in the forest.

They also were in desperate need of a path. Plodding through the heart of the cloud forest was taking far too long. He knew a path might lead them into more danger, but he could deal with that when it arose.

Nya spotted it long before he did. She had been a tracker in Zimbabwe in her youth, and could work wonders in the forest. "Over there," she said, pointing to their right, through a copse of pink and yellow flowers that hung from their vines like upside-down bells. "There's a gap in the foliage."

She was right. A hundred feet away they emerged onto a tiny footpath that curved down the hill. After following it for a few minutes, the trail led them near the edge of the mountain, and they were able to get a look at their surroundings.

The drop at their feet was precipitous. Opposite the valley below them, in the distance, was a cliff face that looked sheared by scissors. And in the narrow valley, stretching as far as they could see under a metallic blue sky untouched by mist, were rows and rows of leafy shrubs with white flowers.

"Coca," Grey said. "No wonder he's holed up here."

Nya tugged at his hand. "Come."

The path wound through the forest, next to a creek dribbling down the slope. Cool damp air clung to their skin.

As the throaty cry of a primate echoed through the woods, Nya grabbed Grey and pulled him off the path. She put a finger to his lips and pointed. Thirty yards below, just visible through the trees, a man in jeans and a windbreaker was walking up the path towards them, scanning the forest with his handgun raised to eye level.

Grey handed Nya the spear he had taken from the blue assassin, and Nya got the idea. She stepped out of the brush and moved twenty feet up the path from where Grey was crouched. Half-hidden in the mist, she waited until the man approached, then raised her spear in a salute. He looked relieved and lowered his weapon, and Grey pounced from behind, covering his mouth with one hand and pointing a stick into the small of the man's back. "Drop the gun," he said.

The man complied. Grey kicked the weapon away, relieved he hadn't fired, then kicked out the back of the man's knees and applied a two-handed rear choke. The man bucked and jerked, which only tightened the hold. Seconds later he was out.

Grey picked up the gun, dragged the unconscious body off the path, and they set off again. The faint sound of gushing water drifted through the air, increasing as they descended.

A carpet of dark green appeared on either side of the path. The air grew even moister, a world of lichen and vines and soggy earth. Pieces of broken ruins squatted in the jungle like untold secrets. The roar of water increased as the terrain shifted and the path turned upward, merging into a set of moss-covered stone steps.

The steps led to the top of a knoll that overlooked a waterfall dropping into the mist. Beside the overlook, arms folded and grinning, was the General. His hands were in front of his body, holding something oblong and black.

Lucho and the General's consort were beside him. Lucho's gun was pointed at Grey.

Before Grey could think about making a move, four of the blue-painted assassins emerged out of the forest on either side of him and Nya, silent as death, spears poised to throw.

———◆———

At the edge of the forest, Lana found a Glock next to one of the General's dead mercenaries. She picked it up and stalked towards the compound, eyes straining through the mist. The gunshots had faded to sporadic bursts.

She spotted a guard shack along the perimeter and ran behind it, peering around the edge. Scores of the General's men were strewn in and around the compound, either dead or dying. One of the helicopters drifted above a stone outcropping just beside the main house. Two more hovered a hundred yards away. Dozens of men in black gear stalked the grounds with raised weapons, looking for survivors and shooting any they found.

Voices shouting a name, over and over.

Her name.

She thought she must have gone insane, or slipped back into a scopolamine-induced fever dream.

"Lana! Lana Valenciano!"

The men were sweeping the perimeter, calling her name and peering into the forest. Soon they would reach her hiding place. They weren't CIA, she was sure of that. Perhaps a private defense contractor had been sent, but how in the world had they found them?

One of the men closest to her had white stripes on his sleeve and was wearing a blue beret. He was giving orders, guiding his men around the perimeter. "Lana Valenciano!" he called, and then in English, "Are you out there? We're here to bring you home!"

The man's voice bore no trace of disguised malice. She took a deep breath and stepped into view with her gun raised. She could still sprint into the jungle if needed.

"I'm right here," she said. "Who the hell are you?"

The man in the blue beret saw her, lowered his weapon, and wiped his brow. "Thank God," he said, again in English but with a heavy Spanish accent. An accent, she thought, that sounded Bolivian. "We thought we'd lost you."

Behind his relief was a tinge of unrealized fear. Lana kept her gun pointed at him. "And you are?"

"Colonel Ganso sent us. He sends his regards."

Lana took a step back and felt her head spin. *Colonel Ganso?*

"Come with me, please. The chopper's waiting. We're not far from the Bolivian border."

She recovered in a flash. Though dying to know how they had found the compound, that could wait for later. "Is everything secure? Where's the General?"

The soldier shook his head, face grim. "We took out his helicopters and his communications, but we haven't found him. There's no one left alive up here, I can tell you that."

Lana gripped her gun and turned towards the forest, where a path near the edge of the guard shack led down the mountain. "Then bring some men and come with me. *Now.*"

Spears at their backs, the water from the falls a deafening roar, Grey and Nya were led to the General at the edge of the rocky promontory. A curtain of mist was behind him. As they drew closer, Grey realized what the General was holding.

A black-wrapped bilongo.

Lucho was bouncing on the balls of his feet, eying Grey with the desperate hunger of a starving animal. The older Indian woman was gazing into the forest as if unaware of the gravity of the situation.

The General raised the bilongo to chest level and held it out towards Grey and Nya. His voice thundered above the waterfall. "Tata Menga says the spirits never lie. I must admit, I've never known him to be wrong. What do you think, Dominic Grey? Do you believe in fate, in the power of the dead? Will the spirits claim the owner of this bilongo as well?"

Lucho strode forward to meet Grey, taking his gun and then striking him in the face, spitting on him when he dropped to a knee. As the assassins leveled their spears at Nya, Lucho pulled Grey up, spun him around, and walked him to the edge of the cliff.

"You take from me," Lucho rasped in his ear, "I take from you."

At the edge of the cliff, through a gap in the mist, Grey could see a frothy brown river at the bottom of a sheer drop, at least a thousand feet below.

The General lowered the bilongo and took Nya by the arm. "Him first," he said to Lucho.

Grey felt the gun press into the back of his head. Nya screamed. Before Lucho could fire, Grey heard shouts and gunfire in the clearing behind him.

He used the distraction. Without turning, Grey grabbed the arm that was gripping his shoulder, then dropped to one knee too fast for Lucho to fire his weapon. As Lucho's body weight tilted forward, Grey yanked down on the limb with both hands and gave a violent twist of his torso, letting go of Lucho's arm as he brought his own shoulder almost to the ground. Lucho flipped forward, tumbling over the edge of the cliff. His gun went off as he fell, a harmless shot that echoed in the gorge, drowning his scream.

Grey turned. All four of the blue-painted women were slumped in pools of blood. Lana was racing towards him with a contingent of men in black combat gear, weapons raised. Then he looked to his right and saw the General backed against the edge of the cliff, holding Nya in a bear hug. The General's consort was at his feet, blood pouring from a head wound.

"Stop!" Grey screamed at Lana. "Don't shoot!"

Lana held out a hand, and the men stopped advancing. She took a step forward, her weapon pointed at Nya and the General. She had no shot and Grey knew it.

Grey's heart was thumping wildly against his chest. He had to force the words through his mouth. "Take me," he said to the General.

The General smiled. Nya tried to squirm, but her arms were pinned. When she tried to rear back with her head, he raised her off the ground as if she were a toy.

"Anything," Grey said. "Amnesty. Anything. I can make it happen."

The General looked from Grey to Lana to the phalanx of men behind her. Grey saw it in his eyes, not just the madness but the terrible ego and pride, the willingness to die rather than admit defeat, give society its due.

"No," Grey moaned, as the General stepped backwards off the cliff, Nya tucked into his arms.

Grey lunged for them, but he was too late. The last thing he saw was Nya looking back at him as she fell, her eyes full of love.

Grey's lunge had taken him to the edge of the cliff, off balance. He hung suspended for a moment, teetering on the precipice, not bothering to right himself, and then Lana was pulling him backwards. He bellowed and threw her off him, unable to think, unable to breathe. His moral compass spinning wildly, he looked around for someone to kill, some of the General's people who might still be alive, their blood a balm for the jagged tear in his soul.

Finding no one, he sank to his knees and then the ground, crawling towards the edge of the cliff, calling for Nya with a soundless scream.

61

CORAL GABLES, MIAMI

The dominoes slipped through Colonel Ganso's fingers, stacking and falling in neat little rows. Lana saw him look up as she approached from across the garden.

"Lana, what a pleasant surprise."

"As if you didn't know I was coming."

Lana sat. The maid brought tea for the Colonel and coffee for Lana. As soon as the maid retreated, Lana said, "How'd you do it?"

The dominoes stacked and fell, stacked and fell.

"I finish debriefing today, with the Deputy Director," Lana said. "He's going to want answers."

Colonel Ganso looked at her calmly. "He already has them."

"Excuse me?"

The Colonel brought his cup to his lips. "It was an easy choice for him. The General was disposed of, and the life of his most promising agent was spared."

It was a hot morning, clear and bright. Lana wiped a bead of sweat from her lip as a blue and gold macaw swooped into a palm. "What? Why am I hearing this from you? You need to tell me right now what the hell happened back there, and why you were involved."

Click click click click click went the dominoes. When the Colonel finally met her eyes, she saw the too-familiar concern that had always unnerved her.

"Are you sure you want to know, Lana? Some things are better left buried. But I won't deny your request, not this time, if that is your wish. It was agreed that I should be the one to tell you."

"Talk."

The sun glinted off his slicked-back hair. He crossed his legs at the knee. "Did you never wonder why I stayed in Miami?"

"Political asylum, of course. Though criminal asylum is a better term."

"In the beginning, perhaps. But regimes change, the old guard has been replaced. No, Lana, I could have returned. As you discovered in Peru, I still have many friends in the Andes, many allies."

He looked her in the eye, a long and lingering gaze. Lana looked down at her hands and back up, swallowing hard. "Don't tell me you stayed for me."

Stacked and fell, stacked and fell, stacked and fell. Then, for the first time she could remember, Colonel Ganso picked up the dominoes and placed them carefully in their case. He folded his hands on the table and met her eyes.

"Lana, it wasn't just you I've been looking at all these years. And when I look at you, it is not for the reason you think."

A bead of sweat dropped from Lana's forehead to the back of her arm. Her voice was a shimmer of sound above the waves of heat in the garden. "What are you saying?"

"Think about it," he said softly. "I think you know."

Not for the reason she thought it was . . . the Colonel staring at her in the pool as a teenager, and at her mother as well . . . his resemblance to her father, her mother's type of man . . . the men who found her during the rape, just the type of thug the Colonel would employ . . . her father leaving and her mother choosing to stay in that huge house by herself, even after Lana left . . . Lana's green eyes that no one else in her family had . . . no one but the monster sitting across from her . . .

Lana put a hand to her temple, feeling as if the ground had just slipped out from under her feet.

"It was a brief affair in the beginning," the Colonel said, his voice quiet. "Physically, at least. We have always loved each other. We love each other still. But after you were born and she realized who your father was, your mother swore me to secrecy. And I agreed."

"Why would she care?" Lana said bitterly. "She hated my father."

The Colonel leveled his gaze. "She didn't do it for him."

Lana hesitated, then murmured, "You wanted to protect me." She pressed her fingers harder into her temples and took a deep breath. "I . . . this is all too much. Too much. But even if it's true, how'd you find me in Peru?"

"I knew your mission. My men were on standby as soon as you left Cuzco.

We lost you in the Andes, but thanks to an Interpol request from an associate of Dominic Grey's, the Deputy Director and I tracked you to a village named Kukukatari. When you went deeper into the mountains and . . . stopped moving . . . we knew we had the right place."

"You're not answering my questions. How did you—" She cut herself off. "The Deputy Director? You were working with him? But that still doesn't explain the raid."

The General uncrossed his legs and crossed them over the other knee, his back straight throughout the shift in posture. Lana didn't think he was going to respond, until he folded his hands in his lap and looked pained, as if embarrassed by what he was about to say.

"Secrecy wasn't the only step your mother and I took to protect you," he said. "After what happened to my family in Bolivia, the enemies I knew were out there, your mother and I . . . did something else."

"Something else? Like *what?*"

"What would you have done, Lana? If you were me? If your entire family had just been murdered by your rival, and your new family, your precious little girl, would suffer the same fate if your enemies discovered a hint of the truth?"

"I would have moved."

"The risk would have remained. I preferred to stand guard against it."

Lana thought about what had happened at the General's hideout, at the improbability of the rescue team finding their location. She thought about it some more, and then it all came together like the crash of a thousand marbles. Feeling dizzy, she put a hand on the table to steady herself.

"You gave me a tracking implant," she said, her voice barely above a whisper. "When I was a child." She looked away, and when she looked back, she saw the truth in his eyes. "My God," she said, her mind spinning at the knowledge, "that's how you found me during the rape."

"No, my dear, the rape was the *catalyst*. After that point, we realized constant surveillance was impractical, and the implant technology—at least on the black market—had improved. The procedure was administered during the exam for your school physical, under the guise of a vaccine."

"If you had me under surveillance before that," she said bitterly, "then what the hell happened in that house?"

The Colonel covered one of her hands with his own, his face drawn. "To this day, I regret that your mother and I waited so long to look for you. You must understand, you were house-sitting and the rapist must have already been inside, attempting a robbery. We did not start searching until you failed to return our calls. I am truly sorry, Lana. My heart was broken. And I am pleased to say I did not make the same mistake twice."

62

PRAGUE OLD TOWN, CZECH REPUBLIC

Viktor unlocked the door to his study, then sat in a leather chair and basked in the familiar gaslit glow of the street outside his bay window.

He eyed the bottles of vintage absinthe filling the shelves along one of the walls. While desirous of a drink, he was pleased that he did not feel the same itch inside his skull, that all-consuming urge to imbibe. The thought of his emerald muse felt more like the remembrance of an old friend than a lover.

At least for now.

Speaking of old friends, Viktor was worried about his. He had not heard from Grey in a week, except for a one-line email sent two days after the rescue from the General's stronghold.

Case closed. Nya's dead.

Viktor had tried to call Grey dozens of times, with no response, and had to piece the story together. Jacques, Viktor's Interpol contact, informed him that Viktor's Interpol report and request on Klaus Hitzig had been flagged by the CIA, since Viktor was working with Grey and Lana. Running with the tip, CIA agents on the ground in Peru discovered that Klaus had taken a five a.m. flight out of Cuzco, and traced his movements backwards, all the way to a remote village named Kukukatari. It was a good thing, because the signal on Lana's tracking device had moved out of range in the mountains, until helicopters flying above Kukukatari had picked it up again.

What happened after that was whitewashed, but Viktor gathered that a rescue mission had taken place, either led or financed by the CIA. The General had been killed, his hideout destroyed, and Grey and Lana Valenciano had survived.

Agent Federico Hernandez and Nya Mashumba had not.

Nya's body had not been found, but her blood had spattered on the same rocks where the General's crushed body had landed, one of his legs trapped by a log. The cliff off which they had fallen was a twelve-hundred-foot drop into a swift and shallow jungle river filled with boulders. That river flowed into another river, which merged into a tributary of the Amazon. Her body could be anywhere, and most likely had been eaten by crocodiles or piranhas. The search party, accompanied by a distraught American named Dominic Grey, had scoured the river for days.

The chance of her survival, he was told, was nil.

An uncomfortable thought emerged. Grey had told him about seeing Tata Menga in the jungle preparing two bilongos, one with the soapstone carving and one with Fred's baseball. Viktor knew Nya had given Grey the carving; was *she* the true owner? Had the sea of dead souls allegedly commanded by Tata Menga claimed their second victim in the end?

Viktor, of course, thought not. But like so many of his cases, there was no way to be certain, and it riled him.

Restless, Viktor entered the adjoining library. The room was the size of a small apartment, stacked floor to ceiling with bookshelves. It was one of the largest collections of religious and occult literature in the world. Viktor had traveled far and wide to gather his material, from the homes of wealthy collectors to the archives of churches and secret societies around the world.

Viktor wondered what his next case would be. He knew he had another addiction, one that the absinthe helped soothe but could never tame. One that tugged at his every thought, lurked around every corner, lounged on the gravestones of every cemetery he passed.

That which Viktor craved was the inexplicable, the divine, the pieces of the cosmic puzzle. More than ever, he had grown weary of the evil that men do, and wished only to sink into the mysteries of the world.

Yet he knew the two went hand in hand. As he thought of Dominic Grey and of the unbearable pain with which he must be dealing, Viktor thought that without good and evil, without love and loss and the awareness of one's desires, without humanity, then there was no great enigma. There was only a universe of dying stars and empty space.

The phone in the study rang. Viktor hurried back into the room. With mixed emotion he saw that the caller was Jacques Bertrand, his Interpol contact.

"Good evening, Jacques," Viktor said.

"To you as well. I'm glad you answered. Something's come up, and I need your help. We've never seen anything quite like this before. Are you available?"

Viktor glanced at the bookshelves in his study, then outside the window at a pair of tourists strolling through the fog. "I am."

63

LIVE OAKS METHAMPHETAMINE CLINIC,
CAMILLA, GEORGIA
ONE MONTH LATER

Danny Hernandez walked into the room with his head bowed, fiddling with the cuff of his sleeve. Though skinnier, and without the same spark in his eye, he was a snapshot of his father in his youth.

He walked through the visitors' lounge and sat across from the man with the gaunt cheekbones and haunted eyes, the stranger who had requested to see him. "Who are you?" Danny asked, without making eye contact.

"Someone who made a promise to your father," Grey said.

"Well he's dead, so I guess you don't need to keep it."

"I know he's dead. I was there."

Danny blinked and raised his head a little higher.

"I was there, and I don't have a son, and I wished it had been me that had died that day, instead of your dad. But it wasn't. So here I am."

Danny looked at Grey as if he was the one who needed to check himself into the clinic.

"The irony of your father's life wasn't lost on him, you know," Grey said softly. He had already decided to take off the kid gloves with Danny. In his mind, his promise to Fred meant more than just saying the words.

"He spent his entire career fighting drug trafficking," Grey continued, "and he had to watch his own family, his *son*, destroyed by the thing he hated most."

"Yeah, well, he wasn't around very much—"

"Shut up, kid," Grey said. "He wasn't around because he was putting food on the table and dodging bullets from the kind of people who sell meth to kids too young to know any better and who end up wasting their lives in rehab."

Danny looked as if he were about to retort, then looked away and rose from the chair. Grey took him by the elbow and exerted pressure on his funny bone, too subtle for anyone else in the room to notice but enough to force Danny back to his seat.

"What the hell?" Danny said, jerking his arm away. "That hurts."

"So you *are* alive. You're your father's son, you know. I can see it in your eyes, behind all the anger and hurt and self-righteousness. And if there's one thing your father was, it was tough."

"Is that what he wanted you to tell me? To man up and beat this? Thanks for the advice."

"No, that's what *I* wanted to tell you. So stop feeling sorry for yourself and get out of this dump. Take care of your mom and sisters. Don't let your father's life be in vain. He'd have traded every bust he ever made to see his son clean."

"Seriously, man? You have *no idea* what it's like. You don't just wave a magic wand and make this go away."

"Then don't rely on magic."

"Whatever."

Grey stood. "Good luck, kid."

"Where're you going?"

"Does it matter?"

After Grey took a few steps, Danny called out, "So what'd he want you to tell me? Get back in school? Stay away from drugs? I inherited our broken-down camper van?"

Grey stopped, turned, and looked Danny in the eye. "When he died, we were helping a woman kidnapped by drug dealers. Your father was shot twice with hollow point bullets by some very bad men. Once in the leg and once in the stomach. You ever seen anyone shot in the stomach? If the wound's bad enough, and your father's was, you have to hold your intestines inside so they don't spill out. I wanted to stay with your dad, even though I knew he was dying, but the next to last thing your father did was point his gun at my head and tell me that if I didn't get the woman with us out of there, he'd shoot me himself. Then he covered us while we ran away. It was the bravest thing I've ever seen. I can still hear his final scream, and only hope he died quickly when they tortured him."

Danny stopped fiddling with his sleeve. His face had paled.

Grey walked back to Danny and stood over him. "And do you want to know the *last* thing your father did before I left him in that room alone, with his life-blood pumping between his fingers and a group of cold-blooded killers rushing through the door?"

Danny's voice was just above a whisper. "Sure."

"He made me promise to tell his son he loves him."

———————

Grey found a diner a few streets from the clinic. Steam rose off the pavement from a morning rain. Houses with vinyl siding lined the streets, but he didn't bother lifting his head to observe the crowd. People without faces, streets without names.

He slid into a booth in the rear, facing the wall. A waitress with bright red hair and a gap in her front teeth laid a menu in front of him.

"Just coffee," he said.

"You sure, hon? You look like you ain't eaten in weeks. Some grits, pancakes?"

"I'm sure."

When she left, Grey reached into the pocket of his cargo pants and took out the soapstone carving of two intertwined lovers, the only thing he had found after weeks of searching the river. He had spotted it stuck in a pile of driftwood a mile from the bottom of the cliff. A piece of black wax paper had been flapping in the current, still attached to the statuette. Grey had made a fire and burned it.

As he placed the little carving on the table, he caught a glimpse of himself in the grime-streaked window. Dirty and unshaven, but otherwise intact. The minor knife wound and the road burns from the motorcycle crash had already healed.

All of that horror, all of that suffering, and he wasn't even injured. He stared at his reflection and barked a laugh. Dominic Grey: martial arts expert, taker of lives, warrior supreme.

Murderer of friends and lovers.

The General's words pounded in his head, as they had since the day of her death. *No one's as self-centered as a man in love.*

"Hon?" the waitress said, returning with his coffee. "You okay?"

One of the best things about Nya was that she had rarely asked him questions, and never about the future or the past. They had lived fully in the present, two souls in a canoe working in tandem against the rapids, drifting in silence when the river grew calm.

A river churned brown and creamy like peanut butter, hidden deep in the jungle, a highway of memories disappearing into the mist.

"No," Grey murmured, his eyes never leaving the statuette. "I don't think I am."

ACKNOWLEDGMENTS

As always, there are too many to list, but here are the highlights: to the team at Thomas & Mercer, Kjersti and Jacque and Tiffany and Gracie and Diane and all the rest—I can't praise your energy and brilliance enough. And especially to Alan, for taking a chance, sharing a vision, and placing your faith in my work. Andrea, thanks for a great edit. Ayesha, your high standards are always in the back of my mind as I write, improving my work. Rusty, what can I say, I owe you a debt that can probably never be repaid, so all I can say is thank you. C-Money, I can't imagine a better travel companion, and I'm glad that man with the scars let you out of the back of his SKV in Bogotá, as that might have ruined our Colombia trip. Mom and John, thanks a million for the early reads and fantastic comments. Dear Suzanne and Aidan, thanks for housing a hand-wringing author during the completion of this work. Mike Burke, physician to Dominic Grey, thanks for interesting conversations over good beer. Miami peeps, especially Jimmy and Stephanie but also Frank, Sal, Curtis, Jair and their families: I love your city, thanks for your amazing hospitality, and I miss too many things to list. Special thanks to Frank Mena for his help with translations. Jamie and Jennifer, thanks for the sage legal counsel—and everything else. And as always, to my wife, for your enthusiasm, incisive comments, and for picking up my slack during the research trips that brought this book to life. That debt will be repaid.

LAYTON GREEN is a bestselling author who writes across a number of genres, including mystery & thriller, suspense, horror, and fantasy. He is the author of the Dominic Grey series, the Genesis Trilogy, the Blackwood Saga, and other works of fiction. His novels have been optioned for film, translated into multiple languages, and nominated for many awards (including a rare three-time finalist for an International Thriller Writers award).

Word of mouth is crucial to the success of any author. If you enjoyed the book, please consider leaving an honest review on Amazon, Goodreads, or another book site, even if it's only a line or two.

Finally, if you are new to the world of Layton Green, please visit him on Goodreads, Facebook, and at www.laytongreen.com. for additional information on the author, his works, and more.

Lightning Source UK Ltd.
Milton Keynes UK
UKHW022320231222
414383UK00018B/976